A *BOOM* RUMBLED OUT OF the monitor speakers, fuzzing them out briefly.

Everyone at the table jumped.

The crowd on the other side of the television erupted in gasps and cries.

The two newscasters gasped with the crowd, staring at the images on the monitor.

The camera phone tilted up, flashing white in the sun, then showing an image of blue sky, broken by large, white clouds.

The reporter on the ground, presumably Rudy Nguyen, gasped like he'd been running, or maybe like he was in the beginnings of a panic attack. He spoke into a microphone that fuzzed in and out, distorted by the yells, pushing, and other panicked sounds and chaos around him.

Meanwhile, the camera on his phone continued to jerk and lose focus.

I struggled to see what he pointed the damned thing at.

I wanted to yell at the television to tell him to keep still.

Then a shadow covered the light.

I saw a glimpse of a massive, gray-colored wing, covering the sun.

Everyone at the table cried out, flinching back for real.

The French President and the German Chancellor rose to their feet.

They backed away from the table.

Somewhere in that, I'd gotten to my feet as well.

Now over half the table stood around the wall monitor, staring at the flickering images. Shadows cut into the sunlight. I felt my heart pound, my breath start to hitch.

Then I heard it.

That tell-tale, echoing scream into the sky.

BLACK OF WING

Quentin Black Mystery #14

JC ANDRIJESKI

BLACK OF WING: A Quentin Black Paranormal
Mystery Romance (Book #14)

Copyright 2021 by JC Andrijeski

Published by White Sun Press

First Edition

ISBN: 9798461361242

Cover Art & Design by Damonza http://damonza.com

2021

Link with me at: jcandrijeski.com

Or at: www.facebook.com/JCAndrijeski/

Mailing List: http://hyperurl.co/JCA-Newsletter

White Sun Press

For more information

about any book published by White Sun Press, please go to
www.whitesunpress.com

Printed in the United States of America 2018

To my friend SKQ
Who never, ever stops trying to make this a better world.

PROLOGUE
PARADISE LOST

Love's breath ignites in pools of gold, but it is not the first...
...Nor the last, nor even the beginning.
A people swim the surface of Muuld, in a world marked garden for the
chosen.
- The Myth of Three

It is said The Demon would live in paradise for a month and a day...
...And they would writhe in pain
As though a thousand knives punctured every inch of their skin.
So much would the One Light wound them.
- Anonymous

Charles... Faustus... raised his head from a soft surface, squinting into the sharp sunlight shining through a tall doorway made of thick, green and black trunks.

He remembered.

He remembered where he was.

He remembered who put him here.

That she would leave him here, of all places. That she would dump him *here,* knowing he would hate it here with every fiber of his being. There was no possible way she wouldn't *know* how much he would detest the base existence such a world offered.

All of it was so primitive.

It reeked of early life, of the vapid idiocy and superstition of primitive minds. The hut was like something his one and only human wife's people would have made, beginning a thousand years earlier, back on the version of Earth he'd left behind.

Of course, that had been a different history.

It had been a different people... a different Earth.

Sadly, this new version of Earth had apparently never evolved past that stage of existence at all. They'd never climbed out of the mud and base simplicity of a subsistence culture, or learned to command the vagaries of their environment.

They remained at the mercy of the elements.

They remained at the mercy of the indigenous animals and plants.

Hell, they remained at the mercy of the *weather.*

From what Faustus could tell from the months and months he'd spent here... easily over a year by now, and likely more than one, although he loathed to think about it... no one had advanced any form of *real* civilization at all.

Nor would they, likely until long after he was dead.

She'd done it to him on purpose.

She'd sent him here, a final stab of the knife into his heart.

Faustus stared at the carvings in the dark wood, and fought to make them mean something to him. He fought to make sense of where he was, in a way that didn't anger him beyond reason.

He couldn't do it.

His mind simply returned to the same thing, the same face.

Miriam.

His own goddamned niece.

Little Miri.

That race-traitor *cunt* had destroyed everything.

Literally *everything* he had worked for, she'd blown to ash and dust.

Remembering her, remembering how she'd looked at him, in the seconds after they landed here, those few seconds she bothered to regard him at all before she jumped away, his rage turned to something blinding, something murderous. She'd looked at him pityingly, maybe even with some maudlin sense of nostalgia.

Then she'd simply vanished... leaving the air to rush back into the space she'd occupied with a shocking *POP*.

Remembering that look on her face, the bullshit, performative *regret* in her eyes, he felt a cold hatred that made it difficult not to scream into the rising sun.

She had betrayed him.

Not just him... she had betrayed her entire race.

She had betrayed all of them.

Like every morning here, the thought got him out of bed.

Anger powered most of what he'd done here, in the years since he'd arrived.

He knew that wouldn't sustain him forever, but for now, he wouldn't think about that.

The locals were easy to push into feeding him, and into giving him the largest of their primitive shelters. He'd slept with a different female every night, more out of rage and feelings of impotence over his situation than out of any true desire.

He'd become their king in less than a day, and it meant nothing to him.

He punished the primitives because he had no one else.

He had nothing else.

Walking out of the fifteen-foot tall, narrow doorway, he gazed down a grass-covered hill towards a swampy lake. He'd more or less pinpointed where he was on the planet that roughly approximated the other Earths he'd known, in geography at least.

This version was relatively unspoiled, for all the same reasons he despised it.

The waters teemed with fish.

The trees they cultivated were mostly the same as those he'd known before, with versions of fruits and nuts he'd known from those other Earths. Between them, the venison, the fish, even the occasional bear, the land provided more food than he would ever need, in a temperate climate with few meaningful predators.

An idiot would love it here.

Someone who required no real intellectual stimulation, who could sit around eating berries and nuts, watching the sunrise and going for a naked swim before spending their day doing needlepoint and rug-weaving, sewing their own clothing, making pots from mud and clay, whatever... they would probably find this wooded existence some sort of spiritual paradise.

Kneelers would love it, too.

They could pray and chant and commune with the Ancestors.

They could spend all of their days congratulating themselves for their incorruptible magnificence... build constructs full of fluffy animals and rainbows and perfect peoples living together in harmony without any sense of reality or self-preservation.

If an alien race ever landed here, this settlement would be wiped out in nanoseconds.

More to the point, as far as Faustus was concerned... this type of living was what ruined the seer race on Old Earth.

It practically ensured their enslavement, when humans finally stumbled upon them. The ancients sat in their sanctimonious caves, chanting their sanctimonious, superstitious nonsense, and allowed themselves to culturally atrophy to the point of learned helplessness.

They'd destroyed themselves.

Seers on Old Earth conquered themselves.

They made themselves into sheep.

They created slaves out of warriors, through sheer force of will.

Faustus raised a hand against the bright sunlight, squinting over what had been called the Potomac River in the two worlds he'd occupied before this one. Old Earth, he now realized, had been far more similar to the version he'd just left than he'd ever known.

The location also told him just how much thought and care Miri put into bringing him here. She'd left him on this version of Earth more or less in the *exact same* geographical location from which she'd taken him.

Clearly, she hadn't much cared... as long as he was out of the way.

His stomach growled.

Realizing he was famished, remembering he'd barely eaten the night before, he turned away from the view of the river and the verdant valley below.

He was about to walk to the center of the village, get one of the squaws there to cook him some breakfast, then maybe suck his cock while he ate it—

When something trembled his seer's light.

Power.

So much power, he came to a dead stop.

It brushed him again, and he sucked in a breath.

It barely touched him, both times, but every hair on his arms and the back of his neck rose. He felt it in his gut, his groin, his tongue, the ends of his fingers, his lips.

He stood there, feeling the vibration and reverberations for seconds after the presence had left his light. Holding his breath, he remained totally still.

He waited to see if it would return.

Then he was breathing hard, his heart pounding in his chest.

Gaos.

Holy fucking gaos, gaos, gaos...

He hadn't felt anything remotely like that since—

His head and eyes jerked around, looking behind him, then up the hill.

His body followed, a half-second later.

He walked in the direction of his best guess, then stopped again.

He never stopped looking around.

He scanned his environment frantically, with his eyes and light, searching for the source of that intense flood of presence that scarcely passed through his *aleimi,* or living light. He searched the hill above him, the trees, the grass, the bushes, the various wooden houses and tents that dotted the settlement of humans.

He felt a yearning so intense, he cried out in frustration.

Then... out of nowhere.

"Do I know you?"

Faustus turned, so violently, he hurt his neck.

A male seer stood in front of him, stark naked.

Seer in cock, in height, in the eyes, the strange symmetry of his body.

The male stood there, eyes glowing the palest of golds, nearly white with a faint reflection of gold sunlight. The being's expression remained blank as he stared, utterly lacking in emotion. Despite his words, the question they formed, he didn't even sound curious.

He didn't sound anything.

He sounded blank.

Faustus turned around, looking for where he might have come from.

There was nothing nearby.

Not a tree close enough to have hidden behind, not a bush.

The doorway to the house where Charles had slept stood maybe twelve feet away. It was the closest thing, but surely, Charles would have seen him? He had been staring up the hill, right in the direction of that door. The door stood just to the right of his focus, the carved wooden trunks of the doorway directly within the main arc of his view.

Behind the man himself, Faustus saw only the sloping field of grass.

"I felt you," the male said. "I felt you come."

There was another silence.

In it, Faustus only stared at the other seer.

"It took some time. I was... away. I was in another world."

Faustus blinked.

The strange, blank seer now stood so close, Faustus felt his heart pounding in his chest. His skin flushed from the contact with this brother's *aleimi*. He had never felt so much power in a single being before. The closest he had ever felt, was—

"You were not alone," the being said. "You did not come here alone."

Faustus stared up at him.

He fought to think, to make sense of this new development before he spoke.

If there were other seers here, if he wasn't alone, as he'd believed—

"I have been looking for her," the being said. "I cannot find her now."

Faustus stared at those pale, glowing eyes.

He remembered the old stories... the ones from the First Earth.

He remembered what they said about beings whose eyes glowed.

First Race.

Intermediary.

The Old Gods.

"Where is she?" The gold-eyed seer took a step closer. "Where did she go?"

Faustus blinked.

"Can you take me to her?" he said.

For the first time, Faustus truly noticed the being was naked.

He'd *noticed* of course, almost in rote. He'd noticed well enough to identify him as a seer, without thinking about the nakedness itself.

But now, that information penetrated his forward mind.

It impacted him in a way that was meaningful.

The male seer's skin steamed in the morning sun.

He emitted so much *aleimic* light, it blended with that steam, making the creature's skin appear to be smoke and shadows. The combination gave his whole outline a strangely blurry quality, like he only half-existed here, like he only had one foot in this world, and the rest of him remained elsewhere.

Staring at that nakedness, at the glowing eyes, the steaming skin, Faustus found he understood.

He understood how the being had come to be here.

He understood how he, Faustus, hadn't seen or felt him approach.

He understood how he'd felt the being's presence, a bare second before he appeared.

He understood.

When Charles' vision clicked back into focus, he found the naked seer looking at him, head cocked, that inhumanly calm expression on his face.

Faustus remembered Black inside that bunker under the Pentagon.

He remembered talking to the thing inside Black, right before his nephew-in-law ripped his entire research facility apart.

Looking at the naked being in front of him, Faustus felt the first faint flicker of hope.

Redemption.

Resurrection.

Revenge.

The being in front of him seemed to understand.

Relief flickered across that empty face, even as those pale eyes glowed brighter.

"Can you take me to her?" the being asked. His voice

remained calm, polite, but now the faintest edge of eagerness tinged his words. "Can you show me where she is?"

Faustus stood there, paralyzed.

Then, slowly, as the being's words sank in...

He smiled.

I

THE BIGGER DRAGON

My love, my brother, my God...
It is time to come home.
We whisper together.
Love together.
Always one, always bound...
I drown with you in the ether.
Leathery wings beat clouds in night skies.
Stars rotate in the darkness.
Into the blackest night...
Our love will never die.

M y dreams had been waking me for weeks... two, three, four, five in the morning.

The voice.

That heartbreaking, love-filled voice.

There didn't seem to be any pattern, any rhyme or reason to when it came.

It started seemingly that first morning back on this version of Earth, back in our bed at the building on California Street, inside the penthouse that finally felt like home again, even after all the horrible things that happened there.

Black and I hadn't really talked about Nick yet.

To be fair, we hadn't really had time, and other things took precedence.

After Black gave that press conference, after his announcement about vampires being real... that yes, he could transform into an enormous dragon... and yes, he'd been fighting the United States military at the border wall with Mexico... and yes, he'd been involved in the disappearance of dozens of people who'd worked inside the U.S. government... and yes, he'd been behind that crazy thing in Hawaii... and yes, he was one of those so-called "seers" from another dimension... oh, and he'd been fighting with *other, anti-human* seers who'd been in the process of overthrowing the human governments across the globe...

After all *that,* we'd been a little busy.

A lot of decisions had to be made, and damned fast.

Some of those decisions, Black and I already discussed, even before he gave that crazy speech to the press. We'd discussed a lot of the "what next" while on that other version of Earth, in that other-dimensional version of Hawaii.

A lot of things we'd discussed sounded crazy now.

Things that struck us as clear and self-evident in that other place—that place without humans, or vampires, or messy governments, or hundreds possibly thousands of traumatized, angry seers who hated human beings—now sounded a little naïve and a lot nuts.

At best, they sounded pretty damned reckless.

At worst, they sounded like the "I have this cool idea" phase that occurs right before an apocalypse where millions of people die.

Of course, that hadn't stopped us from starting to implement some of those ideas.

Like me going to London.

Like Black approaching the military leaders here in the United States.

Like me trying to find us a potential Plan B via another dimension, in the event we needed to move all seers off this version of Earth, to somewhere we wouldn't be risking a massive race-war, whether with humans or vampires or both.

Like us talking about forming some kind of non-human bureau that dealt with seer and vampire affairs.

Most of it, maybe all of it, sounded a bit nuts to us now.

Not only because Brick the Vampire King was a malignant narcissist.

Not only because Brick seemed to thrive in chaos.

Not even because Brick remained completely untrustworthy, open to massive corruption if we gave him any kind of *real* power, and fundamentally wired to hunt, eat, and mentally enslave seers and human beings.

Even apart from all the vampire complications, the idea that these institutions and "world rules" could be created or implemented cleanly, that they wouldn't evolve in directions Black already experienced on the human and seer world he'd left behind... a world that didn't have the added complication of vampires, or vampire venom, or the problems both things presented for humans and seers...

Well. It all just struck us as a pipe dream.

We were building a new world.

It was impossible not to fear we might be putting the building blocks in place for a new world order that resulted in suffering on a scale I couldn't really imagine.

So maybe that's all the dreams were.

Maybe it was all of that rolling around in my head.

Maybe the pressure was getting to me.

Maybe those thoughts, those worries, those impossibilities are what brought them on, creating vague anxieties that overcame my mental space.

That's what I told myself.

That's what I told Black, when I inadvertently woke him up.

I didn't tell Black about the dreams themselves.

I told myself he didn't need to know the content of my stress-induced anxiety dreams, much less the details of how my mind translated my worries into images.

I didn't really believe it, though.

I didn't really believe any of it.

Truthfully, I wasn't entirely sure those places and beings I saw were "dreams" at all, or even that they originated from something inside my own mind.

I heard them calling for me through the ether.

I heard them calling for both of us.

I even recognized a few of them.

I remembered them from trips I'd taken, back in the early days of my other-dimensional traveling. I remembered seeing them in those worlds... feeling their resonance with Black... knowing what they were, even before I'd admitted to myself that Black was the same.

Massive, leathery wings beat hard against solar winds.

They were free now, untethered from their worlds.

Not just one, but many came to me.

Many, but they morphed into one at the end of every dream.

That, or the largest of them—the most powerful, the most demanding—pushed its way to the forefront, past the rest, looming in the darkness of my mind.

It stared at me with brightly-colored, fire-filled eyes.

Pale, gold eyes, like a burning sunset.

Like a burning world.

There is always a bigger dragon, my mind whispered.

As big as Black was, as seemingly invincible in that form...

...he wasn't alone in that interconnected labyrinth of threads connecting all of our worlds.

He wasn't alone, and I could feel them now, vibrating those strings that tied them to us, resonating at a frequency that shocked my heart, making it beat painfully hard inside my chest.

That solid, stone-filled heartbeat vibrated my body at a molecular level, turning my bones to liquid, my skin to air, my limbs to fire.

It burned me alive, from the inside out.

The changes woke me up.

The changes terrified me, right before they reached their culmination.

I never got to see how things came out.

I could feel them coming though.

I felt *it* coming.

The bigger dragon.

I was certain he was out there. I was certain he'd been waiting.

Now, that time was slowly ticking down to its end.

Because, as my mind whispered.

...There is always a bigger dragon.

2

REAL TALK

I frowned, coming back from wherever my mind had gone.

Luckily, my mental wandering had been short.

A silence fell after I finished speaking.

Somehow, I managed to bring my mind back before it ended.

The one guy at the table I hadn't yet been able to identify, at least not to my satisfaction, gave me serious side-eye through most of my longest speech yet.

I felt his cold stare, the entire time I was talking, but I didn't react.

Well... I *mostly* didn't react.

Hopefully, I didn't react where the humans could see it.

I was exhausted though, and still not sleeping well, so I couldn't be sure.

Even in my half-delirious state, I had theories about who the mystery guy was, sitting at the table full of world leaders, giving me a forty-year-old's version of stink eye.

I strongly suspected he came from the same world I had, back before I knew what I was. I strongly suspected he was military intelligence. Possibly military intelligence with a strong psychology background, from the little bit I'd picked up off his heavily-shielded mind.

Given where we were, I assumed he worked for the United Kingdom.

That meant probably Mi6.

Well... it meant that for now, anyway.

Black already warned me it was a damned good bet the human governments would band together and quickly start to build branches of government—not to mention courts, law enforcement, military and intelligence services—solely dedicated to dealing with races other than the human one.

In that sense, Mi6 constituted more of a temporary relic of a past world... a world that still mostly existed a few months ago, until Black blew it up.

For now, however, the humans were stuck with the institutions they had.

I knew the UK's Prime Minister wanted him here, and the other leaders must have okay'd it, as well. We'd already positively ID'd at least one member of the French security services. That one sat at the table even now, masquerading as an advisor to the German Chancellor, likely to throw us off.

I suspected we hadn't found even half of them yet.

Most probably didn't sit at the table for meetings like this, but I had zero doubt other intelligence agents worked here in the building, likely at least one from every world power.

To say the humans were nervous was a laughable understatement at this point.

I knew behind the scenes they had to be losing their collective minds.

We're only in the early stages of this, I reminded myself. *Breathe, Miri. Don't freak out. Don't give up on them when we've barely started. Don't let Black and Charles psyche you out. Most of all, don't let their paranoia about humans from Old Earth get to you... or influence how cynical you let yourself become...*

I knew it wasn't all Black and Charles.

Every single one of the seers I'd met from that version of Earth maintained a deep paranoia and suspicion around human beings.

Understandable really, since seers had been slaves there.

But that was then.

This was now.

Circumstances were so different in that other world, in terms of how First Contact occurred, the two worlds were unable to be compared at this point. As Black told me, time and again, this current generation of seers, the generation that came to this world, weren't a bunch of monks singing *kumbaya* in the mountains, the way their forebears had been.

Most were vets of multiple wars, and had a significantly less mystical view of their role in the multiverse, particularly *vis a vis* the human race.

Still, things were tense.

Things were tense on both sides right now.

For the same reason, we'd only pulled in a relatively small group for this.

We weren't ready to start giving speeches in front of the United Nations.

We weren't even close to that.

These early discussions were supposed to lay the groundwork for something more official, but even at this stage, we had leaders refuse our invitation.

China wouldn't respond to our attempts to contact them.

The Russian president gave us a hard no at first, then attempted to negotiate a private meeting that all the seers vetoed on our end.

The United States refused as well, and denounced the meetings aggressively, claimed we were terrorists, and *blah-blah-blah...* which made sense, whether or not we'd managed to root all of the seers out of the current administration. Of course, after it came out that the U.K., Canada, Mexico, India, Japan, and the European Union were sending people, President Bradford "Buck" Regent changed his mind and wanted to come after all.

We told him no.

It was a LONG discussion, but in the end, we all agreed.

From his speeches and rhetoric, it was pretty clear Regent only wanted to go so he could derail the talks.

In some ways, I wished we'd just told him yes.

I mean, I knew we needed him.

We needed the United States.

We talked about letting him come and maybe pushing him... psychically, that is... to keep him from blowing up the talks.

We decided against that, too.

For one thing, it would have been a hell of a way to start negotiations. For another, there was a chance other countries would have noticed. It definitely would've raised eyebrows if Regent suddenly started acting calm and reasonable.

Or remotely intelligent.

Sadly, Uncle Charles, despite being wrong about humans in so many respects, was a thousand percent right about our country's current Commander in Chief.

Regent was an absolute moron.

Unlike the leaders of the E.U. and the United Kingdom, he also didn't seem to have even a basic understanding of what was currently at stake.

I knew a handful of the human governments already had preliminary cooperation agreements in place, specifically to deal with the threat of "intelligent non-human species," which is how they termed seers and vampires in most of their official documents. Those same human governments had already begun the process of joining forces to deal with the non-human threat.

I mean, come on.

They were still in full-blown panic mode.

They were sitting here, looking grim and serious and official, but I knew they were mostly shitting their pants.

Which is why I got paranoid whenever I saw new faces at the table.

We're working on it, Mika murmured in my mind. *That guy, doc. We're working on identifying who he is. Don't sweat the small stuff, okay? We're on it. Whoever he is, there's nothing there* you *need to worry about. We need that big doc brain of yours focused on the bigwigs, okay? On the geo-political threat. We need you to figure out how to reassure them we aren't about to enslave them all with our psychic powers... or eat them...*

Quirking an eyebrow over her faint smile, Mika added more seriously,

Let us handle security, doc. We won't let anyone fuck with you. Promise.

I knew she was right.

I knew she was right that I was distracting myself.

I also knew what she was telling me about that man at the table.

She was telling me he wasn't a seer.

He wasn't one of Charles' plants.

Still, there was *something* there.

He might not be a seer, but his living light didn't feel quite right.

His mind was too silent.

We don't think he's a vampire, either, doc, Mika sent, sighing a little at me. *Really, you don't need to worry about this. We're going over his living light with a fine-toothed—*

Is he wearing something? I sent. *Some kind of blocking mechanism?*

There was a slight pause.

It was small, but I heard it.

Then Mika sighed, at least on the inside.

Yes, the infiltrator said, clearly reluctant to answer me, but likely thinking it would be faster if she did. *We think a number of people in here are using various forms of sight-blocking tech. Apparently Charles had a few things at the prototype stage. We're not pushing back on those devices too hard just yet, in part because we want to see if we can get around them on our own. They aren't overly sophisticated at this point...*

She must have felt me about to say something.

She quickly cut me off.

...I've already sent a number of things back to the labs, doc. Implants,

a few organic wristbands that emit fields, even a type of human "collar"
meant to block seer sight. But we need to trace them back to the source.
That's the bigger issue right now. We need to figure out who's creating all
of these things...

I nodded to myself, thinking about this, even as I refocused on the Prime Minister sitting in front of me. Next to him, the side-eye guy from Mi6 watched me a little too closely, a faint frown hardening his mouth.

He was handsome.

Maybe forty-five years old.

Brown hair, green eyes, a ruggedly handsome face, one that looked like its wearer had spent a lot of time outdoors, in pretty heavy sun.

The Middle East? Somewhere in Asia?

Doc... Mika warned.

Refocusing on the actual words the Prime Minister was saying, I found myself shaking my head, interrupting him without thought.

"No," I said. "We can't do that. Not yet."

Pausing at his silence, I glanced around the table a second time, modifying my voice to make it more polite, if not exactly full-blown friendly.

"I'm sorry," I said, letting my eyes return to Prime Minister Garrity. "But we're going to have to insist on being treated more or less as a sovereign nation. Or at the very least... as a private company with proprietary information we are legally entitled to protect. That includes what relates to whatever security measures we might have in place... to maintain safety and privacy for ourselves and our employees."

There was a silence.

I let my eyes flicker around the long table, taking in faces.

"Black Securities and Investigations is the primary employer of most of the seers we have pulled into our orbit," I added. "Through that organization, we have strong contractual alliances with the largest organized segment of the vampire population as well."

I gestured vaguely with a hand, not fully realizing it was a seer gesture until I'd done it.

"...But really it's Black Industries as a whole that's providing the organizational focal point for the seer race at this time. Even in terms of housing, which we are currently supplying out of our own resources."

Prime Minister Garrity frowned.

"But that's only the seers who've joined *your* side, correct?" he said, his voice sharper. "It doesn't include the *other* side... the ones you claim pose the far greater risk to humans."

I leaned back in my seat, keeping my posture and facial expression calm.

"That is correct," I said, holding his gaze. "We are willing, however, to claim responsibility for the maintenance of peaceful relations with the seer race as a whole. We are attempting to 'police' our own people, as it were... at least within our some-what limited means."

I was understating that.

By a fair amount, really.

Our means were pretty significant, even for a lot of mid-sized countries.

But I was there to downplay the scary factor with us, not give them more reasons to be paranoid. Black and I talked about how truthful I would be, and decided it would fall into the range of "mostly truthful"—meaning firmly in the "hoping to be allies" camp, while recognizing they had very different goals and concerns in some areas.

And also recognizing that yes... they were likely to be pretty twitchy when it came to us.

Right now, the older man sitting across from me, his previ-ously black hair now mostly gone to gray, watched me warily, obviously suspecting me of withholding information.

Of course, we knew they weren't telling us everything, either.

"Look." I changed tacks slightly, leaning over the table, resting my arms on the polished wood. "I get that you have no reason to trust us right now. I really do. We're more than willing to do our best to reassure you on that front... including entertaining any good-faith gestures you'd like to see from our camp. The truth is, our people are just as afraid of you as you are of them. We'd like to keep things calm... and non-reactionary... on both sides."

I saw Garrity flinch perceptibly, as if my words surprised him.

He didn't change expression apart from that.

I had to give him credit.

Guy was pretty danged cool, even for someone in his position.

I shuddered to think what President Regent would be doing, if he were here.

There was a reason the other human leaders chose Garrity to lead the initial discussions.

As I watched, he glanced at his colleagues on both sides of the table, most of whom represented countries in the E.U., along with the Indian Prime Minister, and the leader of Japan. From his unspoken question to them, I definitely got the sense he'd expected me to say something like this, that the human leaders discussed it.

Even as I thought it, Garrity looked back at me.

"But you're reading our minds right now," he said. "Aren't you, Dr. Fox?"

Pausing meaningfully, he added in a harder voice.

"Not only that, you've told us that your kind can... what is the word you used? *Push* human minds to do your bidding? Manipulate our thoughts, our belief systems, our loyalties... our entire view of the world?"

He paused again.

I watched him gauge my eyes openly.

"How can we possibly trust you," he said. "If what you say is true? Do you expect us to just take your word that you won't enslave us, when clearly, that would be the easiest path forward for you and your kind?"

I held his gaze.

When he finished speaking, I held up my hands in a shrug, letting them fall back to the table.

"I'm sorry to say this to you, sir..." I kept my eyes on his, my voice firmly polite. "...but I'm not sure you have much choice."

Pausing, I added,

"My people were enslaved in their previous world... by human beings. They won't allow that again. They just won't. The reality is, the seer race has learned a lot since that time. Moreover, their culture has evolved as a result of that experience. It's a longer story, in terms of seer history, but suffice it to say, these seers are not the same as those who allowed that enslavement to happen. That means, in part, that they won't do the things you would likely ask for, in order to feel totally 'out of danger' from any rogue seers who might abuse their powers..."

Seeing the alarm verging on anger in Garrity's eyes, I held up a hand.

"Nor would you, if you were them," I added, warning. "Both races have to compromise. It's not fair in any way to put the entire burden of this on the seer race. You can't expect them to willingly succumb to restraints on their powers, their freedom of movement, their free will... any more than you would agree to this for humans."

Pausing to let my words sink in, I leaned back in my chair.

I dialed back some of the warning in my voice.

"That being said, most seers have absolutely no desire to impinge on the freedom or free will of human beings either, Prime Minister... in part for those same reasons. My people love freedom as much as yours do. Are there seers who lust for power over others? Yes. Of course. Just as there are humans who do the same."

I let that sink in, too.

I added, "We've already told you about one of our kind with that kind of... instability. My uncle, Charles Vasiliev, was damaged from his time on that previous world. His fear of humans got the better of him, and he decided the best way to deal with it was to do to them what was done to him."

My voice shifted back to a near warning.

"He won't be the last to try this. But the truth is, that's the very reason you *need* us. You *need* seers of integrity, and you need strong allies among my people. You *need* a functioning government of seers with which to negotiate, one that desires the same kind of world that you do... one you can build strong alliances, treaties, and peace agreements with. You need us to police those seers who are more dangerous... like my uncle."

"And where is he now?"

My head turned.

I found myself looking at the man from Mi6, who was now staring me straight in the face. His voice was deep, and surprised me by sounding American.

"This uncle of yours," he said, gesturing to the side, his eyes remaining coldly on mine. "No one seems to know where he is. No one seems to know where a good *number* of people are... including appointees to the United States' presidential cabinet... and a number of high-ranking officials in other parts of your government..."

His eyes grew a few shades colder.

"...notably, quite a number of people who used to work in your Pentagon. And in the C.I.A. Not to mention the F.B.I."

I held his gaze, feeling his attempt to intimidate me.

Truthfully, humans couldn't really get away with that, not when it came to seers.

They just didn't have the mental *oomph* to push us around.

Which, of course, tended to really piss them off, if they were used to being able to do this with other humans.

I didn't shove that aggression back at him, I only nodded, my voice calm.

"Yes," I said. "Quite a few people were removed. Charles' people. We were transparent about this."

I felt humans stiffen around me, and I folded my arms, staring around at them pointedly.

"What race do you suppose they were?" I said then, gesturing expansively. "Why do you suppose we felt the need to remove them, when... like you said... if they were human, we could have merely taken over their minds? Pushed them to do our bidding?"

The silence after that felt more weighted.

I saw them exchanging looks.

I knew I was taking a risk, saying such a thing.

There was a lot we couldn't tell them, at least not yet.

Black and I both agreed we'd need to ease people into certain facts, as we began to educate them more about seers... while still telling them the important things they needed to know.

One of the big things we needed them to understand... hopefully without scaring the *bejesus* out of them... was the severity of the dangers and security risks posed by Charles' seers, and how they needed us to lead the teams addressing that.

"So this... 'policing' of your people you mentioned," Garrity said, exchanging looks with the President of France, and the representative from Germany. "That would include these so-called 'disappearances'? Is that what you are telling us?"

He glanced sideways, that time looking at the man I'd pegged as Mi6.

I now questioned whether he was C.I.A., thinking maybe the other leaders allowed the United States into the meeting, after all, if indirectly.

Bingo, doc, Mika murmured grimly in my mind. *Which explains where he got the sight-blocking tech. We're working on getting more out of him now—*

I absorbed her words, still focused on Garrity in front of me.

"...all of those government appointees and career officials, not to mention military leaders, scientists, members of the Defense Department and the military contractors. You want us to believe that all of those individuals within your own country..."

The Prime Minister paused, as if second-guessing that, given what I'd just said about Black running a quasi-sovereign, independent nation-state of seers.

"...err, I mean the *United States* government... they were, literally *dozens* of them, extra-judicially *removed* by your people as part of this 'self-policing' of seers?"

When I glanced across the table, I saw the C.I.A. agent glaring at me.

I saw him about to open his mouth.

I turned to Garrity before he could.

"Yes," I said, blunt. "That's exactly what I'm telling you."

3

DIVERSION

"You pulled me out of a meeting for this?" I stared at him through the monitor of my laptop. "A meeting with heads of state. Representing a good chunk of the civilized world? Really?"

Not waiting for his answer, I exhaled in exasperation.

"I thought you were going to wait on this," I said. "I thought you were waiting until I got back... that you'd told Steele *no*. As in absolutely no. As in not until we could do the interview *together*, Black."

He clicked at me, smiling one of those killer smiles of his.

"I'm running cover for you, baby," he informed me, without an ounce of shame in his voice. "You're creating too much of a hullabaloo, with your whole fancy-schmancy end of things. I need to draw eyes a bit, at least until you've done some of the heavy lifting. Get down and dirty with the unruly masses..."

He folded his muscular arms, his flecked gold eyes catching sunlight as he leaned back in what looked like a director's cloth and wooden chair.

"This way," he added expansively, adjusting his weight in the chair. "I pull some of those eyeballs off you, sweetheart. I get the press to focus on me instead, and my 'buffoonish antics' as you so flatteringly call them."

He winked at me, flashing another of those smiles.

"Trust me... people would *much* rather watch me act like an ass than watch a bunch of boring meetings about anything of real consequence—"

"This doesn't help me," I cut in, blunt. "This doesn't help anything, Black."

My mouth turned down in a frown.

Hearing him click at me reproachfully, I gave him a bewildered look.

"Why would you think this would help me, Black? The interview is pre-taped, right? It won't even show until tonight. You're not pulling any headlines from me, doing this now. You could have waited for me to come back, and then the two of us..."

I trailed, watching him grin at me from the other side of the video screen.

Glimpsing the narrow dressing area where he sat, thinking about his words, I tried to read between the lines to what he wasn't actually telling me.

"You're not doing it live?" I said, blunt. "Is this interview live?"

The killer grin widened, right before he winked.

"No." I shook my head, adamant. "Absolutely not, Black. No. Does Yarli know where you are? There's no possible way she and Manny approved this... much less Dex!"

Thinking about my own words, I looked around the narrow space where his chair appeared to be located. A mirror took up most of the background. Since it was a mirror, I could see a lot more of the area around his dressing table than I would be able to normally, especially the area on the other side of the laptop he was using to speak to me.

Where was Cowboy? Where was his security detail?

Where was Dex?

I had a handful of the seers with me, but he should have Luce, Kiessa, Holo, Larisse, not to mention whoever they'd moved into security from the team of seers they'd been training at the Raptor's Nest over the past few months.

I had no idea who he'd brought from San Francisco to Los Angeles with him, but it would at least have included a few seers.

Black's make-up table definitely appeared to be outside, sandwiched between two cast trailers, instead of inside the studio where they normally got their guests ready for an inter-view of this kind. I didn't see any of the studio staff around him, or even regular studio security, which made me wonder what the hell was going on.

If it was a live show, where was everyone?

"Why are you outside?" I asked him, frowning. "Can anyone else see you out there?"

He rolled his eyes, grinning wider.

"You worried about me, doc?" Refolding his arms, he leered at me openly. "Come on. Don't tempt me. You know our little agreement isn't just about actual, in-person fucking, right? No phone sex. No oral. No *nothing* until after the wedding. That was the deal. *You* agreed to it, doc. I want us to go full animal crazy on one another during the honeymoon..."

I ignored that.

Knowing it was one hundred percent distraction, I didn't bother to roll my eyes.

Then he rearranged his arms, so that his left forearm faced his laptop's webcam.

Seeing the new tattoo he'd gotten there, I scowled a little, mostly because some part of me was tempted to soften. When we'd gotten back from Hawaii, he'd asked Jax for new ink. That's when I found out that Jax apparently studied under one of the best seer tattoo artists on Old Earth, and specialized in elabo-rate, detailed designs.

Black gave Jax a drawing for this one... a drawing he'd appar-

ently done himself... and requested seer ink. I had no idea what
seer ink was made of, but Black and Holo joked it lasted a lot
longer than "that weak-ass shit" humans used on their skin. Holo
also informed me it was "made of acid and stuff," which didn't
really elucidate much.

The more relevant information I got from both of them was
that seer ink designs remained for decades, even centuries, in
nearly pristine condition, contained sharper, more vibrant colors,
and hurt like hell to get applied.

Seeing the tattoo now, brightly colored and twisting around
his forearm and up to his bicep before it disappeared under his
shirt sleeve, I fought not to react.

It really was beautiful.

I'm pretty sure it was the most beautiful tattoo I'd ever seen.

I was strongly considering getting one like it on my back, but
I hadn't told Black that yet, and I hadn't talked to Jax about it
yet, either.

Black's new tattoo was of a dragon coiled around a blackfish,
what most Americans called an orca, or a killer whale.

It more or less combined the two designs of our wedding rings.

Black had drawn the designs for those, too.

Knowing Black might have even shown me the tattoo to
distract me, or to at least nudge me into being a little less mad at
him, I bit my lip, frowning.

Unfortunately, Black wasn't above those kinds of psychological maneuvers.

He was damned good at them, truthfully.

"Black," I began, exhaling. "Can we just talk about this?
Without all of the mental and verbal musical chairs? What are
you up to right now? And are you really safe there?"

My husband had been stalked pretty much twenty-four-seven
by reporters and camera people for the past four months, ever
since he single-handedly caused the entire human civilization on
Earth to lose its collective mind.

"No one can see me here, doc," he said, his voice more serious. "No one even knows I'm here. We had a small crowd at the gate..."

Seeing my expression, even as I opened my mouth, he held up a hand.

"...it was a *small* crowd, doc. Less than a sixty people. Our people handled it."

I snorted at his definition of "small," but otherwise blew past it, folding my arms.

"Seers?" I clarified. "Seers handled it?"

"Of course."

I considered asking him who he'd brought with him, then brushed that aside.

Instead I asked, "Have you had any problems inside? Since you got there?"

There was a silence.

A beat too late, he shrugged, his gold eyes shifting into that difficult-to-read mask of his, making it clear he didn't want to get into details, not with me, at least not right then.

Of course, that only struck me as an oblique way for him to answer the question in the affirmative.

"No," he said, a touch sharper. "It's *not* that, doc. The truth is, I don't know for sure. But if there's been anything in here, it wasn't big enough for Cowboy or Dex to bother me with it."

Pausing, and now studying my face more cautiously, he added,

"Really, doc... everything's fine. Just finish your gig there and come the fuck home. I mean it. I know what I'm doing. Get your ass back here. Then neither of us has to worry."

I exhaled at that, not answering.

A big part of me agreed with him.

Neither of us would sleep easy this far away from one another, not for long.

Especially not now, with everything going on.

Even apart from the impending wedding... and the lack of sex we'd both agreed to until after the ceremony.

Separations just sucked for us, period.

That was the way of seer bonds.

I knew it would be worse for Black than for me right now, given what he was dealing with, in terms of the dragon thing. He'd told me more than once before I left that he needed to hear from me *every day* while I was gone... *at least once* every day... since he still wasn't entirely confident in terms of controlling his living light.

Remembering that now made my teeth grind.

Given all that, given everything, what the hell business did he have going to Los Angeles for a major interview without me?

What if something happened?

And it wasn't just him, not anymore.

Imagining a cadre of our seers pushing a crowd of people in front of a major movie studio right now, given the amount of scrutiny on us, given how high tensions were in the human community already, especially in relation to this exact topic—

"Relax, doc." Black held up a hand, giving me his most sincere voice. "Really. I've got this. And everyone knows to be careful. Everyone. I gave them a long lecture and everything."

"I have no idea what that means, Quentin."

My voice came out short.

I was tempted to say more, but bit my lip.

I got the gist what he was saying.

He likely told all the seers to use restraint, and to make sure there were no witnesses if they did have to push someone for some reason. I also knew our people wouldn't have done it the way Charles and his seers did even without being told. They wouldn't screw with humans at all, not like that, and certainly not the way Charles had—with his attempts to brainwash humans into extreme ideologies and volatile emotions so he could manipulate them into playing the part of pawns and foot soldiers.

I knew our people would never mess with humans in terms of how they saw the world.

They would only do the bare minimum to keep an unruly crowd from attacking one of us, or going full-blown violent.

It made me damned nervous, anyway.

Given how hard we'd been trying to convince them that we were the "good guys," not the evil puppet-masters and conquering aliens they feared, I didn't want any videos to pop up on social media of seers screwing around with human beings, warranted or not.

For the same reason, Black's understatements and omissions around whatever the hell it was he was doing made my teeth grind.

Black must have heard some of that.

Knowing him, he heard all of it.

His grin slid wider.

"Miriam. Light of my Life. My darling pookie-wookie snookie-cookie baby-cakes—"

"Where's Cowboy?" I cut in.

As I waited, thinking, watching him grin at me, something else occurred to me, and I frowned.

"Why are you outside, Black? You're not doing the full interview outside, are you?"

"Well. We are, actually—"

"Why?"

My voice was openly wary now.

He must have heard that, too.

He shrugged, his gold, tiger-like eyes sliding back to that inscrutable emptiness, back to flashing nearly blank in the afternoon sun.

But my mind was already working to fill in those blanks.

"Well," he said, shrugging. "I got here, and Grant and I talked, and that's what made the most sense. So they moved a few things around..."

He trailed, gesturing gracefully in seer with one hand.

My jaw hardened more.

Black promised them a live show.

Black agreed to do the show outside... in the Los Angeles sun... instead of inside the air-conditioned studio.

A show that normally aired at night.

That was *after* Black found a crowd waiting for them at the studio gates.

The show's *star* wanted that... a man normally based in New York City.

I could only think of one real reason for any of that.

"Absolutely not," I snapped, once full understanding sank in. "Have you lost your mind? Seriously, Black... what the fuck?"

He shrugged. His shark-like smile only grew wider.

"Come on, doc. Live a little."

"Live a little? Really?" I fought somewhere between wanting to smack him, long distance, and wanting to laugh. "You one hundred percent cannot turn into a damned *dragon* on national television. All right? Is that clear enough?"

"International," he corrected, winking at me through the screen. "And why not? I already told everyone what I am. The whole damned world watched hours of news footage during that shit-show at the border. Might as well put my cards all out on the table... so to speak."

"No."

"Come on, doc. It'll demystify me. Make me harmless. Like a big, scaly kitten."

"No!"

"Just one little wing?"

"NO!"

"It's called deterrence, my super-hot, bossy, extra-dangerous wife."

"It's called 'attention whore'," I shot back, again inexplicably fighting not to laugh. "And I think you've had quite enough of that recently. I also think you've got quite enough targets painted on your chest already, husband."

He grinned. "Husband. I just got a little hard from that—"

"Coreq won't do it anyway," I cut in, before he could wander too far down that tangent. "He'll never go for it, and you know it."

Coreq was Black's dragon's alter-ego.

Coreq called the shots when it came to Black's dragon transformations, not Black himself. As to what "Coreq" himself was, we still hadn't quite figured that out yet, although the seer infiltration team was working on it.

Regardless of the exact breakdown of physiological traits, psychological components, non-physical seer light, or whatever composition of "Coreq" vs. "Black" might exist, the logistics of the thing worked the same.

Black only turned into a dragon when Coreq decided Black should turn into a dragon. Black only came *back* from being a dragon when Coreq let him... which, up until now, for whatever reason, only happened when I was there.

When I came to Black, in person, and asked Black to return to his regular, seer form, then Coreq morphed my husband back into his human-like shape.

So far, at least.

Let's just say, Coreq's mind wasn't exactly the most predictable... or stable... part of Black's consciousness as a whole.

Which, come to think of it, was saying a lot.

"He won't do it," I repeated, a little triumphantly that time. "Not to show off to a bunch of humans. You know he's weirdly racist. And sociopathic. And lacking in any discernible sense of humor—"

"He absolutely *will* do it," Black said, his voice supremely confident. "We've already had that discussion, sweetheart. Coreq agrees it might be helpful to remind 'the humans'..."

Black unfolded his arms to create air quotes with his fingers.

"...that he's around. Coreq thinks the occasional 'demonstration' of his 'true form' might be the 'most efficient' means of ensuring that humankind remains 'properly respectful' towards one of our kind…"

Black's grin widened more after each of the air quotes.

He knew I hated air quotes.

"He *also* thought it might help you with your negotiations, doc. Nothing like a little shock and awe to remind them why it's not a good idea to piss us off…"

I exhaled at that, shaking my head.

"No," I said.

"You don't approve?" he said innocently.

"I ONE HUNDRED PERCENT *do not* approve," I said, throwing up my hands. "Which I just said. Like a dozen times. I DO NOT APPROVE, Black. At all—"

"What're you wearing there, doc?" he cut in.

He motioned with a hand, seer-fashion, indicating my clothes.

A pulse of heat left his seer's light as he continued to stare.

"Are those new?" he said. "If not, why the *hell* haven't you worn them around me?"

I looked down at the designer pant suit I wore, sans jacket, the pants in particular, where his eyes clearly rested.

When I looked up at him, that heat in his eyes grew more prominent.

"Are you *kidding* me right now?" I said.

"How's about doing me a little spin?" he coaxed, giving me a wider shark grin. "Letting me see how well those form-fitting little beauties hug your ass? Just for… you know… fashion's sake. We just established we're both deprived…"

"No!" I snapped, fighting not to laugh. "Absolutely not!"

When he grinned wider, lifting his eyebrows suggestively, I rolled my eyes.

"What the hell is up with him…?" a voice muttered behind me. "Is he on drugs?"

I turned, giving the seer who said it, who happened to be Jax, a hard stare, even as Mika was throwing up her hands, letting

Holo know in no uncertain terms that she saw the same thing Holo did.

Kiko sat at the same side of the table, arms folded, smirking.

When I returned my eyes to the monitor, and Black, he quirked an eyebrow.

"Really?" he said. "You're letting the kids hang out in the room while we have grown-up talk? That's not very nice, wifey-poo."

I snorted. "At least one of those 'kids' is probably a hundred years older than me, Quentin. Two of them, more likely."

"You know what I mean."

"Not really, no."

The tone went off overhead, signaling the end of our break.

I looked up in rote, frowning, knowing I was out of time.

"That the five-minute bell, doc?" Black said.

I didn't bother to answer.

We both knew it was.

Sighing, I walked over to where I'd left my suit jacket slung over a leather office chair. I retrieved the tablet on the table as well, and stuck it temporarily under my arm. Looking back at Black, I felt a kind of frustration wash over me, not sure what I could say to him that would make any difference at this point.

He was going to do what he was going to do, just like always.

It hit me then... I was worried about him.

Not just a little, either.

A lot.

Strangely, he looked vulnerable to me, sitting in a make-up chair on the grounds of a major movie studio, waiting to go on national television.

"International television," he said, breaking into my thoughts.

I looked up, ready to scowl at him, but when I saw his expression, the more nuanced smile he now wore on his face, my annoyance and frustration faded.

"For the love of the gods, be careful," I said, losing the edge in my voice. "Please, Black. Don't do anything crazy. Not while I'm here and you're there."

He shrugged, that more subtle smile still toying at his lips, visible in his flecked gold irises.

"One advantage of having a wife who teleports," he told me, letting that smile grow a few millimeters wider. "If I get too far in the shit, I know you'll come for me."

I did scowl a bit at that.

If he saw it, he ignored it, eyeing me instead in the fitted red suit pants.

"Gaos," he said, sending another pulse of heat. "I can't believe that's what you're wearing with those stiffs. Not to mention the top," he added, indicating the cream-colored blouse I wore. "Tell Kiks and Jax to grab every single article of your clothing and bring it back with them on the plane, if you *do* have to jump... that, or write down the brand and measurements, so I can have a new pair waiting for you when you get back here."

I felt a harder whisper of his pain and took another step back.

"Focus. Okay?" Exhaling, I folded my arms. "We still have two weeks until the wedding. And I have to go. Don't do the dragon thing, okay? Please don't."

"I told you," he said, waving me off. "Coreq's cool with it. He said he'd change me back. You won't have to jump back to save me, doc. Not this time. Promise."

"Coreq agreeing with you on this particular subject doesn't exactly reassure me," I muttered, setting down the tablet long enough to shoulder on the matching, dark red suit jacket. "...Not at all, in fact."

"My point is, I know you have the *real* job right now, sweetheart." His eyes and voice grew almost serious, or the closest they'd been since we'd started this conversation. "I'm the distraction, love. I'm the diversion. I can dance a bit, take some of the pressure off. I'm good at this part, and you know it."

I nodded, but my time was really up now.

Biting my lip, keeping my expression still with an effort, I just nodded once.

Then I clicked the connection off.

It was game time.

For both of us, as it turned out.

4

MOVIE STUDIO

"Really?" Grant Steele, the number one late night talk show host in the United States, barely could contain his glee. "She approves? That's *fantastic,* Quentin! Just *fantastic!* I thought you said she wouldn't be in favor of any demonstration of this kind?"

Black grunted, barely looking over from where a make-up artist bent over him, touching up his face now that they were seated in the studio set chairs under the sun.

"She absolutely one hundred percent is *not* in favor of it," the gold-eyed seer said, giving the late-night talk show host another sideways look with his strange, tiger-like eyes. "She told me I was out of my damned mind."

Angel grunted, exchanging looks with Cowboy, who stood at the other side of the set area, wearing an earpiece.

Cowboy quirked an eyebrow in return, a faint humor ghosting his lips.

Angel didn't bother to voice through the earpiece what she thought about Black's words.

At the same time, a slightly more evil part of her wished she'd been a fly on the wall for *that* conversation.

Miri probably ripped Black a new one.

Then again, Miri was in London. There wasn't a lot she could do from there to control her crazy-ass husband's more reckless impulses.

Cowboy, almost like he heard her, grunted a laugh.

Angel touched her headset that time, switching to sub-vocals so the camera and production people around her wouldn't hear.

"You think Miri's going to have to jump back here?" Angel murmured.

There was a brief silence, then Cowboy grunted.

"If you're lookin' for a wager, I'm not sure I'd take those odds, darlin'," he returned easily. "Not even if we were the gambling sorts... which neither of us is."

Pausing, he added, "Not like it means much, but Captain Black assures me he can turn back on his own this time."

Angel snorted. "Of course he does."

Cowboy chuckled, shaking his head as he continued to scope out the area, his gray eyes taking in every detail and every face.

"Did they finally manage to take care of that protest out front?" Angel said next still using the sub-vocals. "I heard from Frank that some of them came back. Dog said the same. Waving their we're all the devil signs..."

"Holo's got it. Luce's out there with him now."

"What?" Angel frowned. She looked around for the Filipino vet, seeking out the boxer's short, spiky, bleached-blond hair. "Who do we have on the inside? Did they all go out there? Besides us?"

"Dex is here," Cowboy said patiently. "Kiessa. Easton. Devin."

"That's a lot of humans," Angel muttered.

"Ayuh."

"That means *not* a lot of seers," Angel emphasized more sourly.

"Well. Yeah." Cowboy exhaled, hands on his hips on the other side of the camera crew. "Luce is a human, an' that's what started this whole discussion, darlin'."

At Angel's flat look, Cowboy added,

"The bosses seem to think we best keep a low-profile with the seers for now. Most of 'em, at least. Especially those as tend to *look* and act more seer-ish. That's why Black told a lot of 'em to stay home. 'Least the ones who weren't already in D.C., scouring for more of Charles' people. Or backing up the doc in London."

Pausing, Cowboy added, his voice more reassuring.

"Yarli's team's keepin' an eye out. We're good, babe."

Angel grunted, refolding her arms.

She refocused back on the two chairs that had been put out, with the perfectly manicured lawns behind them. The section they were in formed part of the studio's backlot. Grant Steele's team set up the interview at the edge of a fake town square complete with white-painted bandstand under a large elm, scattered park benches, fire hydrants, rose bushes, tulips, red, white and blue bunting, a clock on the Town Hall.

Black was still talking to Steele.

"My wife is definitely the wiser of the two of us," the billionaire-dragon-seer was saying now, as the make-up person continued to fuss with his hair. "I'd love to say it's made me smarter, being with her, but I doubt she'd agree..."

Grant Steele laughed, shaking his head.

The blond, handsome, thirty-something host, who'd previously been based out of New York but recently changed networks and now worked out of his home town of Los Angeles, looked positively delighted at this news.

Steele had to be positively tickled to have gotten the first exclusive interview with Black since he'd "come out." Steele managed to scoop all of his friends in the media on the Quentin Black Story, Straight from the Dragon's Mouth... (Angel just knew *that* was coming) ...even though more prestigious venues had called, as well.

Black told her that he'd do the "serious" interviews with Miri.

Grant Steele, on the other hand, was all his.

Clearly, Steele thought the fact that Miri might skin Black alive for this stunt—not to mention that Black and Miri possibly fought about "the dragon thing" at all—only added to the drama and conflict of the interview.

Angel found it deeply weird, honestly, that Steele didn't seem at all unnerved by Black, now that he knew what he was.

In fact, Grant Steele's whole demeanor towards Black struck Angel as *exactly the same* as she remembered from New York, back during that original interview Black gave him.

Back then, Black was Wall Street's wonder boy and Steele hosted a fast-rising, hip new show in the late-night slot.

Back then, Black was still pretending to be the notorious womanizer he had been before he met Miri.

He'd also been singularly focused on finding and killing the vampire king, Brick.

...Brick, who now more or less had become Black's ally, if only in the thinnest, least-trusting, most expedient and sheer-act-of-desperation sense.

"So how is married life treating you?" Steele reached over to clap Black on the shoulder, a wide grin on his face. "Wait," he said, eyes widening suddenly. "She's like you, isn't she? She's one of those 'seer'-things you came out about?"

Black opened his mouth, a faint puzzlement on his lips.

Before he could quite think his way out of that one, Steele burst out in a laugh.

"Damn. How did THAT just *whoosh* on by over my head?"

Steele made a corresponding hand gesture over his near-pompadour of blond hair.

Answering his own question, he added,

"I admit, I was pretty blown away by that press conference you gave... and the fact that we were still on for this interview, given that..."

Black gave him an indulgent smile, clicking his fingers for Cowboy.

Angel watched, a faint frown on her lips as her boyfriend—

Fiancé, her mind whispered.

—walked up to the lit area in front of the cameras, lowering his head and ear to Black's lips while the seer spoke to him.

Black spoke in a lower-than-usual voice, too low for Grant Steele to hear. The seer's hand wrapped over the top of his chest microphone anyway, cutting the sound more.

Angel saw an odd look come to Cowboy's face as Black spoke.

When Black gave him a warning look, the lean Louisianan nodded, once, his expression clearing as he straightened. He gave Angel a fleeting sideways look, right before he backed away from the staging area and the two comfortable chairs where Black and Steele sat across from one another on a paved, decorative walkway between sections of lawn.

Walking back down to the other side of the cameras, Cowboy touched his ear, clicking on the microphone on his headset.

"Darlin'?" he said, speaking through the sub-vocals.

"What was that about?" Angel murmured back. "Do I even want to know?"

"He says he's thinking about turning into dragon... or part of a dragon... at some point in the interview. He wants us to keep the studio people from, like... lighting him on fire... or something."

Angel didn't answer at first.

Honestly, she was kind of waiting on the punchline.

"What?" she said, forgetting the sub-vocals and speaking out loud.

A production assistant and a camera man looked over at her.

Angel switched to sub-vocals.

"What?" she repeated.

Cowboy let out a long, audible sigh.

"You heard me correct, darlin'. Apparently Miri tried to talk him out of it, but he thinks it might be a good idea still."

Before Angel could answer, a third voice joined their conversation.

"You two remember I'm a seer, right?" Black rumbled in their ears. "You know I can *hear* you... right? Even when I have my headset turned off?"

Angel turned towards the makeshift stage, only to see Black had pulled his headset out, presumably from one of his pockets, and now held it to his ear.

Angel let him see her roll her eyes.

"You're not turning into a dragon, Quentin," she informed him.

"Why... in the dragon levels of hell... am I not?"

"Are you ever going to learn to listen to your wife?" Angel said, not hiding her exasperation as she folded her arms. "And why is that wedding taking so damned long to happen, anyway? How long does it take you to fix up a venue that *you* own for what amount to twenty-four hours of drunken debauchery and a bunch of fingerfoods?"

"Don't talk to me about weddings," Black grumbled. "I would have had it weeks ago. WEEKS AGO. If it were only up to me, Miri and I would be basking in the Tahitian sun right now. As I recall, I'm arranging this for everyone... and paying for everyone, too."

"Only because you've insisted about a million times," Cowboy butted in, annoyed. "Even when I've spent half the night arguing with you about it. Even when I gave up arguing and just put money in your damned bank. You *still* took it out and put it back in mine... which goes to show what a penny-pinching dragon you are in the first place, by the way, that you'd even notice that little amount from me in all your pile of gold..."

"Ain't that the truth," Angel muttered.

"And you don't care about the money anyway," Yarli added over the line, clearly listening in. "You just like needling your friends. I swear I've never met *anyone* who likes to hold things over people's heads that he couldn't give two shits about..."

Angel laughed again. "You tell 'em, Yarli!"

"Hush, sister Yarli... this doesn't concern you," Black growled. "Anyway, money or not, I don't have all the weird, alligator-wrestling relatives flying in from Louisiana. We're mostly waiting for humans to make the *arduous, unbelievably scary* trip to New Mexico... a whopping five states away, or whatever. Their tiny human brains have to schedule everything like six months in advance or they overheat and explode..."

Angel burst into an involuntary laugh, hiding it behind a hand when the production assistant and the cameraman stared at her again.

She waved them off, smiling.

"Now you're just desperate," Cowboy informed him. "That's just a sad, desperate act to blame my old Aunt Nelly and her kids and my cousin Georgie. Not to mention Angel's working nephews and nieces. You're a snob, Quentin. A classist."

"No shit," Black said. "Is this news?"

Angel laughed again.

"Well, just button that nonsense down," Cowboy said. "You're an ex-felon. And the last thing you need is another reason for the common man to be wary of you. Should be enough they all think you might eat them... or light them on fire..."

Black let out a half-annoyed laugh.

Then his voice grew more serious.

"Look. I really think the dragon thing... here, I mean... today... is a good idea. Miri could use it. As leverage. I know she's afraid of blowback, and she's stuck trying to calm all of them down... but I honestly think a little reminder that they can't take us in a straight fight wouldn't go amiss right now, either. Frightened people tend to do aggressive things. If we push back on that aggression from the get-go—"

"You'll just make them more frightened," Angel cut in, exhaling another excess of frustration. "Do you actually listen to yourself speak, Quentin?"

"If you'd let me finish—" he began.

"You said it yourself," Angel said, motioning with a hand, forgetting she wasn't supposed to make it obvious they were arguing. "Miri's trying to calm them down. To make them NOT afraid of us. Or at least LESS afraid—"

"And I'm saying that's never going to happen," Black growled, throwing a touch of heat into his voice. "She's never going to calm them down, Ang. She's NEVER going to make them not afraid of us. You have to stop thinking of these people as rational... as able to deal with what I've thrown at them. They aren't rational. They *can't* deal with it. You think just because you and Cowboy, Alice and Frank, Dog and Easton, Dex, Kiko, Ace, and whoever else can deal with this, that you-all can face reality, and accept it as real, everyone can?"

Black paused, waiting for Angel to think about this.

"...Because I'm here to tell you they can't," he went on, his voice a heavier growl. "They *can't* deal with it, Angel. They can't. They'll deny reality, and they'll tell themselves they can take us, they can outsmart us, or out-weapon us, or outnumber us. They'll cause all kinds of problems attacking us... and in the end, we'll have to use violence to keep them from hurting us, anyway, because that'll be the only thing to stop them from destroying the whole damned planet, Ang. Including themselves."

Angel frowned.

Thinking about his words, she felt her jaw slowly clench.

She hated that he was right.

She hated it.

But his words felt true.

"So?" She motioned sharply with a hand yet again. "So why did you tell them at all, then? If you knew they wouldn't be able to handle it—"

"I told them because Miri was right," Black said, his voice now verging on a warning. "They were going to find out... no matter what we did. It was just a matter of time. A fair-few in the government already knew. And we had to stop Charles. We needed to bring as many reasonable humans over as we possibly could... not to mention the scientific community... and the only way to do that was to control *how* they learned about us. We needed to be the ones to tell them. And now, we have to do what we can to make it real to them. The rational, reasonable humans will see that, and they'll realize they need to compromise."

His voice grew a touch deeper, more rough.

"The less-rational ones will be more like kids touching a hot stove. They'll hate us. They'll be afraid. They'll blame us for every problem. They'll want us all dead..."

Feeling Angel about to interrupt, he raised his voice, still using the sub-vocals.

"...but they'll respect our raw strength enough to back down. The more frightened ones can only be controlled through strength. Unfortunately, there's no 'peaceful' way to win them over. The rational ones, sure... we can work with them. But we need them to acknowledge what we are, and what we're capable of."

There was a silence on the line.

Angel glanced to the side, watching security guards lead a crowd of tourist-civilian types through the studio lot towards the bleachers they'd set up behind her while Black had still been in the make-up and trailer area.

Looking back at Black, Angel grunted, shaking her head.

"You're sounding pretty Old Testament, Black," she muttered. "What if you're wrong? What if you're just alienating anyone who might have been our allies? What if fear is what makes them desperate enough to drop a nuclear bomb on the building on California Street?"

Black didn't answer at first.

Then he exhaled, sounding suddenly tired, even through the headset.

"Ang... I can pretty much guarantee some of them will want to do that anyway."

Giving her a level stare across the space between them, over the camera operators' heads and to where she still stood to the left of the bleachers, he added dourly,

"...Anyway, non-humans caused this problem, not humans. If Charles could've just gone to a damned psychiatrist for his trauma, dealt with his issues, and lived here quietly, at peace with human beings like a normal fucking person, they never would have needed to know about us at all. And if vampires could have just left seers the hell alone... and vice-versa... we probably could have dealt with our issues with them without involving humans, either."

"Well, that's the damned truth," Manny muttered over the line.

Before Angel could finish thinking about any of this, the crowd reached the end of the studio backlot street.

She watched their faces as they went from talking and laughing to hushing one another as they rounded the edge of the bleachers and saw Black sitting in the interview chair across from Grant Steele. They stared at him, mouths ajar in cartoonish surprise, their expressions openly incredulous when they saw him sitting at one of the two gold comfy chairs set up on the walkway between the lawns.

Angel found herself thinking they hadn't known.

They really hadn't known Black was the guest.

They'd probably been told they could come participate in a special live broadcast of the Grant Steel show and that had been enough of a draw to get them back here.

Looking at the utter shock bleeding over those painfully normal-looking human faces... shock that was rapidly turning into full-blown fear on some of them... Angel felt a shiver of misgiving, like someone just walked over her grave.

Black might be right about everything he'd said.

But this was still a huge mistake.

It made the time Black went on camera to goad a psycho-pathic, murderous, vampire king on live television seem like a harmless prank.

She glanced at Cowboy, who frowned, his gray eyes flickering up to watch the staring, gaping, and unnervingly quiet humans fill the bleachers behind the line of cameras.

Some of their faces were white as chalk now.

They watched Black like he was a unicorn, or a leprechaun, or a full-blown demon... stumbling on the stairs as they found their seats when they couldn't tear their eyes off him long enough to pay attention to where they were walking.

Remembering most of them... realistically, *all* of them... had seen footage of Black-as-dragon ripping through the United States military on the border of Mexico, and possibly at the Pentagon, Angel felt her misgivings exponentially worsen.

"This is going to be bad," she muttered into her headset, barely conscious she'd spoken out loud. "This is going to be real bad."

That time, it wasn't Black who answered.

"Ayuh," Cowboy said grimly, gazing up at the now-filling bleachers. "I'm afraid you're probably right about that, sweetheart."

Black, uncharacteristically, remained silent.

5

INTERVIEW

"Sooo..." Grant beamed at Black, looking him over with a look verging on lust in his eyes. "...How's your summer been so far, Quentin? Anything interesting going on?"

The outdoor audience laughed.

They'd all found seats on the tiered bleachers by then, and seemed to perch on the edge of their metal seats, staring unblinkingly down at Black.

Some of the faces Angel saw still looked tense, but the laughter came out surprisingly natural-sounding now—mostly because Steele spent roughly nine or ten minutes warming up the crowd and calming them down. He even drew Black into a few minutes of back and forth banter, obviously attempting to take some of the supernatural stench off him, and remind the audience who Black had been to them before all this.

Black rose to the occasion surprisingly well.

He slipped into his "charming asshole" persona, which the media had always adored. The same persona earned him a rabid fanbase back when he'd just been an eccentric billionaire, and not a shape-shifting alien from another dimensional version of Earth.

Of course, none of this felt remotely normal.

Then again, the interviews of Black before—meaning prior to Black's press conference confirming the existence of seers and vampires—never felt all that normal either. Back then, the big worry and preoccupation for Black's staff generally concerned Black doing or saying something that would out him as not-human.

Now, obviously, that was less of a concern.

Now they were all more afraid he'd do something to scare the shit out of any human beings who might be watching this.

The fact that they were outside also made the interview a bit strange.

The laughter sounded different outside, under a big elm tree in a studio back-lot, versus being shot inside a sound studio... but Angel, who stood to the right of the metal bleachers, found herself thinking it was a smart move on Steele's part, to have a live audience.

Now that they'd relaxed a bit more, the laughter normalized things.

It normalized things in a way she wouldn't have thought possible, frankly.

It struck her that the interview, and Black himself, would have felt much more distant and alien without any audience at all.

It didn't hurt that Grant Steele still gushed over Black like he was a movie star. If anything, Steele had gotten even weirder about being in Black's immediate presence.

The way he stared at Black's face and his flecked, gold irises, the way he looked Black over in the matching gold chair... including staring a beat too long at Black's crotch... all of it made Angel wonder if the guy was bisexual, or, at the very least, if he had a huge, platonic man-crush on the seer.

Steele was married to a woman, wasn't he?

Angel honestly couldn't remember.

If she wasn't working right then, she might have been tempted to look it up on her phone.

"Could you think about something else?" Black muttered through her earpiece. "Or at least think it less loudly? It's damned distracting. Because I'm a *seer...*" the seer added tersely. "Like you've only known for a few *years* now, Ange. Like I've only reminded you *a few hundred times* since we met, whenever you're thinking so loudly I can't block you out..."

Without missing a beat, he aimed one of his killer smiles at Grant Steele.

"Well, I've got a wedding coming," he smiled, folding his muscular arms and leaning back in the velvet-upholstered chair. "You should definitely try to make that, by the way, now that you're living out here in the Golden State. I sent you an invite..."

Steele's eyes widened.

"A wedding?" he said. "I thought you were already—"

"We are." Black shrugged with a sideways smile. "But I deprived her of a good party... or, really, I deprived myself of one... not to mention the ceremony itself. She got stuck with the equivalent of a gas station Elvis chapel in Vegas, I'm afraid. I didn't want to torture her with all that crap back then, and risk her divorcing me before we even got our honeymoon."

Steele broke out in a delighted laugh. "A gas station? Really?"

"There might have been a few ruffled shirts," Black said, deadpan. "And some 'Love Me Tender' playing in the background..."

He propped his ankle on the opposite knee.

For the first time, Angel really noticed his clothes.

Unlike the last time he'd been interviewed by Steele, Black ditched the power suit, and went more Hollywood-casual.

Despite the warm morning sun, which had heated up even more in the last two or so hours since they'd arrived, he wore a black, gold, red, and white ribbed motorcycle jacket over a black T-shirt, black armored pants, and black motorcycle boots.

So... more or less what he wore every day when he *wasn't* conducting a live interview with the most popular host on late-night t.v.

"A wedding's great," Steele grinned, leaning back in his own chair and resting his arms on the chair's arms. Slapping his hands easily on those same chair arms, he let his smile grow more shrewd. "And you know *I'll* be there, even if it means a scuba suit and clog dancing. I'll have to yell at my assistant for not telling me about that."

"I *did* tell you about that," a woman's voice half-yelled from the area of the cameras.

The audience laughed.

Grant Steele bantered back and forth with her for a few beats more, and Angel realized this was a bit, one he and Black likely planned in advance.

When they were done and the audience was still laughing, Steele turned to Black.

He kept smiling, but his eyes turned shrewd as he studied Black's face.

"...but come on, man... you have to know...weddings are great, but that's not what people really want to hear about. Not right now. Not after what you announced the other day. I mean, you had to know that would grab a few headlines, my friend..."

Black gave him an equally subtle, significantly more wicked grin.

"Whatever could you mean, Grant?"

Something about the way he said it brought another explosion of laughter through the crowd on the bleachers.

Steele shook his head, still with that sideways smile.

"You're going to make me work for it, Quentin."

"Not at all, Grant," Black said, winking at the audience. "Don't be coy. You know how I just *love* coy on you, brother, but if you've got a question for me... ask it."

Angel could almost feel the mood in the crowd shift.

It was as if every person in the stadium seats behind her leaned forward, holding their collective breaths as they waited for Steele to speak.

"Do I really need to?" the host said, winking at the crowd himself. "Ask it?"

"You know you want to."

Again, laughter from the stadium, but it came through as considerably tenser that time.

"All right, then."

Grant Steele paused, leaning forward over his thighs and lacing his fingers together. He looked Black right in the eye, his expression serious.

That time, funnily enough, Angel suspected it was at least ninety percent theater, despite the seriousness of the crowd behind her.

"Is it true?" Steele's words carried, his voice sounding louder in the utter silence of everyone else. "What you said that day, in the lobby of your building... is it true?"

Black's smile lingered at his lips.

He stared at Steele, his oddly flecked, gold eyes looking maybe more animal than Angel had ever seen them.

He leaned back in his chair, and Angel realized only then that he'd leaned forward, mirroring part of Grant's pose.

Black cleared his throat then, smiling wider.

"You mean the dragon thing?" he said loudly. "Is that what all this fuss is about?"

The two of them might have timed it out as another bit.

That whole back and forth might have been planned.

Either way, it worked.

Either way, his words somehow fell into place like puzzle pieces on a board.

The crowd behind Angel erupted.

Not in screams, not in hysteria, or even shock.

They laughed.

She knew a good chunk of that laugher was likely still nerves, but somehow, Black managed to work with Steele to make the revelation more exciting than scary... more superhero than aliens from some other world, about to destroy this version of Earth.

It went from being about dangerous outsiders conquering humanity, to the elevation of one of their own, a man who'd had an insane fan following for almost as long as Angel had known him. It had become about Black suddenly becoming an angelic protector of the human race, and of this country, the United States, in particular.

Realizing again the utter brilliance behind Black's seeming chaos, Angel didn't know if she should roll her eyes, sigh in relief, or throw something at him where he sat.

She honestly didn't know if this would help things with human beings in the long run, or simply make them worse when they decided they couldn't trust him, or he did something too out-there, or it hit them that, in order for humans to retain supremacy, seers were too powerful to be allowed to exist without some kind of insanely restrictive "protections" put into place.

She didn't know.

That was always the nightmare with Black.

Everything about him evoked a metaphorical wandering in the wilderness, starting fires at random even as it put out others.

Now, listening to the audience laugh and clap and stomp their feet behind her, Angel glanced across the way at Cowboy and lifted an eyebrow.

He returned her pointed look with a wry smile of his own.

He opened his mouth, like he was about to say something—

—when a sound jerked her head back towards the street running through the middle of the studio backlot.

Unfortunately, it was a sound she'd grown disturbingly familiar with over the past few years.

Automatic gunfire.

6

ECLIPSE

All of them looked towards the sound, including the camera people, every person on those metal bleachers, not to mention Grant Steele and Black himself.

Black rose to his feet.

His voice rose in Angel's ear, and Cowboy's... and every other seer and human ear hooked into the main channel.

"Who's shooting?" he asked. "Ours?"

Dex's voice rose, sounding grim.

"No, boss," he said. "Not yet."

"Is it more of those Purity Movement assholes?"

Angel felt her jaw clench.

Most of Charles' creepy cult was still walking around, since the majority of them were human. Getting rid of the construct hadn't solved that particular problem. The only way to solve *that* would be to create a construct of their own, which posed all kinds of logistical issues... not to mention ethical ones, given that it was tantamount to brainwashing large numbers of humans to change their ideology artificially.

Black wasn't in favor of that.

Miri was adamantly opposed.

Truthfully? Angel wasn't so sure it was right to dismiss that option wholesale.

These Purity types weren't exactly stable.

They'd also been recruiting heavily since Black came out. Now, instead of obsessing solely on vampires and immoral humans, they were obsessing on seers, as well.

Black, in particular.

Most of them ranted non-stop about fire and brimstone and the need for "blood purity" even *before* Black outed himself as a damned dragon.

They'd already left a handful of creepy and ominous messages on the street in front of Black's flagship building in San Francisco, using poured gasoline to spell out things like "DEMONS BEWARE" and "HUMANITY FIRST" and "THE BLOOD WILL TELL." Angel saw one written on the windows across the street in viscous, stringy liquid that turned out to be actual blood.

That one said, "GOD IS WATCHING."

Angel about puked when she found out it had been dog and cat blood.

It turned out the guy broke into an animal shelter and slaughtered a bunch of the animals being held there.

Jax and some of the other seers managed to hunt that guy down, sharing the information they dug up with the F.B.I., but he was part of a whole pod of these Purity assholes, so getting rid of one didn't exactly solve the problem.

Now, similar movements had sprung up all over the globe.

They were starting to organize across countries.

Some increasingly had government support.

Angel focused on Dex and Black, realizing she'd missed a few things, standing there, worrying about human fanatics.

"Are they inside?" Black was saying. "Did they make it past the gates?"

"They're still outside," Dex assured him. "At least the lot out here is. We've got some reason to think this is a distraction, though. Zairei's got a lock on others coming around the other side of the studio lot. I sent him and a handful of our people over there to check it out... and Yarli's backing him up from the Raptor's Nest."

Angel saw Black frown.

From his expression, she wondered if he was using his seer abilities to look at whatever Zairei and the other seers had seen.

That, or he was talking to them, seer-to-seer.

Angel noticed the seers doing more of that in the field lately, now that Charles and his people were less of a direct threat.

She briefly had a flashback to the desert where they'd been pinned down by Charles' seers. They'd been stuck there for weeks: low on water and food, dirty, some of them injured before they'd been trapped underground with a few hundred vampires, everyone claustrophobic and verging on anxiety attacks.

Frowning at the thought, she watched as security guards from the studio ran up to Black. The guy in front, a Latino weight-lifter-looking type guy who struck Angel as an ex-cop, or possibly ex-military, began talking in Black's ear, his expressions tense.

The guy was maybe six feet tall, and looked like he spent serious time in the gym.

He still looked weirdly small next to Black.

The guard was motioning towards the audience then, speaking louder, and Black was frowning.

Black turned to Grant when the guard finished, saying something to him, but Angel didn't catch any of it.

Eerily loud, the sound of gunfire echoed down the backlot streets, drowning out their words. Angel knew it was at least partly acoustics, but it unnerved her how close it sounded.

She clicked her headset to speak.

"We need to get them out of here," she said to Black. "The audience."

"I know." Black gave her a bare glance. "We're talking about that now. Grant wants to try moving the interview back into the

studio, if we can get the go-ahead from the security team here...
but we might have to postpone."

"Ya think?" Angel said, faintly outraged.

Black gave her another sideways look, lifting an eyebrow, but
didn't respond.

The screaming outside the gates grew louder, and now the
sounds of the crowd echoed down the fake streets of the backlot, making Angel distinctly nervous.

"I'd prefer we get you out of here, brother," Cowboy said,
putting in his vote. "Do this another day... maybe start it off
indoors... or on one of your properties, where we can control the
environment more. I'm not so sure we've got this place as
secured as I'd like..." he added, watching a few studio types roll
by in a golf-cart, staring at all of them.

Angel knew what he meant.

So many people came and went in here, it was difficult to
know if they might have missed someone at the gates.

Black still hadn't answered when a new voice rose in their
headsets.

"Zairei here," the seer said, his voice hard. "We've got eyes on
the second group, on the north side of the studio. They went
through the cemetery..."

He sounded out of breath, like he'd been running.

"You need to get out of there, boss. We have reason to
believe they might have one of those robot things."

Angel heard Black rattle off a string of words in the seer
language.

A lot of it sounded like cursing.

Most of it sounded like cursing.

Glaring briefly in the direction of the audience, he motioned
towards the security guards, who were waiting by the aisles.

"Bring them in!" he shouted over the echoing sound of the
crowd surging outside the gate. "Inside! We need to move them!
Now!"

Angel felt her jaw harden.

She knew Black was right, but that also likely meant this area would be another damned war zone.

Not a lot of things took those robots out easily.

A rocket launcher could do it, with a direct hit.

The only other effective method they'd found for killing the damned things was dragon.

Meaning Black.

Black, in dragon form, dealt with them handily.

He also made an unbelievable mess.

The robot-cyborg things first showed up in Hawaii, more or less ruining Miri and Black's wedding plans, not to mention their semi-vacation at a ritzy resort on Oahu. Black managed to destroy all of the ones that showed up there, but whoever sent that first batch had sent more in the time since, starting just a few weeks ago.

Two showed up in San Francisco, wading out of the Bay to attack the building on California Street.

Two more showed up at a Black property in London.

Now they'd apparently followed Black here.

They always seemed to come in pairs.

At each new wave of attacks, the models seemed to work better, too.

Other new toys had been showing up recently, as well: strange, disturbing drones with animal-like components. Odd viruses in their computer systems. At least one cybernetic animal, a half-robot dog that behaved almost like the cybernetic humans.

One of the seers came across something that looked like a rat but that also had cybernetic components. It showed up in one of the computer labs inside the Raptor's Nest. Manny and the others "killed" it, and Luric immediately dissected it inside his California Street lab, trying to determine exactly what it was. Angel never got the full scoop on that, but Cowboy said Luric struck him as "unsettled" by what he'd found when he cut the thing open.

Because of oddities like that, everyone at the Raptor's Nest more or less assumed they were being surveilled... likely by things they hadn't found yet.

They didn't even know who was behind it, exactly.

Charles was gone.

Every member of Charles' leadership team was either dead or in custody.

Black put out a priority order to find (and hopefully destroy) the facility designing and building the damned things, but so far, they hadn't had any luck tracing them back to the source.

Angel was still turning all of that over in her when it happened.

BOOM.

A deafening sound exploded over the sky, like a sonic charge.

Windows shattered, car alarms went off, the ground trembled.

Angel ducked in reflex, panting.

It wasn't gunfire.

It wasn't even a bomb.

It sounded more like a volcanic eruption, like the chunks of lava might start raining down, setting the city on fire.

Every pair of eyes turned up towards the sky.

The sound continued to expand, rolling outwards like a descending boom of thunder. Even that softer sound managed to vibrate the brick and asphalt.

A blinding light flashed.

Then all hell broke loose for real.

7

THE BAD SOUND

"You can't seriously expect us to trust you, under these circumstances..."

The French translator spoke clipped English, even as the President of France stared at me, as if trying to transmit the emotion behind his words with his eyes alone.

He went on speaking in rapid French, his eyes hard, his hands moving in a series of chopping-like gestures.

"...Garrity is being too polite," the translator informed me, looking across the table and quirking his own dark eyebrow as he folded his hands primly. "Or he is playing some game, buying time by telling you what he thinks you need to hear... perhaps out of fear, or perhaps until he can get the rest of us alone. But I know the futility of this..."

The French President glared at her.

"...You are mind-readers, are you not?" the translator continued, keeping up with the other's rapid French. "You know what we are thinking? What we believe? So there is no point in being anything but honest with you. We cannot possibly trust you. The power imbalance is too great. The danger is too great for us... how is this not obvious to you..."

I waited through the pauses and weirdly distracting hand-gestures.

When he finished a few seconds later, I leaned back in my chair, my expression unmoving.

"We *do* know that, Mr. President, sir," I assured him then, pausing to let his translator repeat the phrase in French.

Down the table, I heard a few other languages being murmured as well.

"...We're extremely aware of the difficulty of what we're asking," I went on carefully. "But *both* sides will need to compromise on this point. I've been extremely clear on our willingness to meet you halfway, to provide you with various safeguards, to do whatever we can to even the playing field..."

My voice grew warning.

"I've made it *equally* clear we are entirely unwilling to enslave ourselves to reassure your people that you are in control of the situation. I understand the impulse... I do. But that's not on the table." I gave him a more explicitly warning look. "There will be no compromise in regard to our bodily or mental autonomy. Not a single seer will give up their basic rights simply to reassure humans that we are harmless. There will be no rules around assembly, around how and when we are able to use our abilities, or around some kind of 'racial registry'..."

I glared at the Belgian Prime Minister, who'd already raised that as a suggestion.

"Not a single seer will agree to that," I said, my voice flat as I hammered the words. "If any of you try to enforce something like that on your seer populations, even at a local level, not a single seer will comply. The fastest way to provoke a war with my people is to attempt to institute a system that renders them second-class citizens or attempts to constrain them in ways no human would ever agree to for themselves."

I spoke louder, hoping like hell they were hearing me on this.

"Please understand me," I said. "To even *attempt* to walk that road is dangerous with some of my kind. They have long lives... and even longer memories. You will trigger a reaction in some of them akin to what you saw in Charles Vasiliev and his followers. Potentially a much *worse* reaction. After all, Charles and his people were reacting to the mere *fear* of such a thing."

I leaned over the table, folding my hands.

"If you give them concrete reason to believe that is the desired outcome of most humans in a position of power... much less if you make a concerted effort to put such a system in place... it will be extremely difficult for our races to live together peacefully."

I fell silent for a few seconds.

Watching Garrity exchange looks with a few others at the table, including the American I now knew to be C.I.A., I didn't have to read them to know some version of that conversation had already taken place.

They were afraid.

So were we.

The sooner they recognized that, the better.

I pinged Mika with my light.

Instantly, I felt her and Jax focus on me.

Any news on who that guy is? I murmured in my mind. *C.I.A. dude. The one Garrity brought in.*

Jax's mental voice rose at once.

We've confirmed the I.D., he thought at me. *He's definitely C.I.A. Apparently he's done a lot of work with Mi6, and they let him in after Regent threw a fit about the United States being left out of the talks. We got audio on a call where Regent was ranting about being "excluded" and "vilified" by us... even though they were originally invited. We're still doing background on the agent himself, but his name's Weston Banks. "Westie" to his friends. He has a long history in military and private sec work.*

Jax hesitated, then his thoughts grew a touch colder.

He worked with your vampire pal, back in his military days, he sent, blunt. *Banks actually served under Nick for about a year. They did what the Pentagon categorized as "specialized jobs." In Panama, the Congo, Guatemala.*

There was a silence where I chewed over that.

My eyes never left Garrity and the C.I.A. agent as they continued to talk.

Anyway, we're still looking into him, Jax added, his voice subdued and now somewhat cautious. *I don't suppose the name rings any bells with you?*

No, I told him. *It doesn't. But that doesn't mean much. Nick took his security clearances seriously. He's never told me anything about any of those missions, or the kind of work they were doing there.*

I watched Garrity lean back in his chair.

The tall human cleared his throat, aiming his eyes back at me, his handsome face now holding a harder, somehow more real look.

I was about to try and calm things down again, to reassure Garrity and the rest that we all wanted essentially the same things... but before I could, my headset let off a low, discordant, highly-distinctive series of tones.

I knew that sound.

I recognized it.

We'd picked out that exact tonal sequence so we wouldn't have to transmit sensitive information over a potentially open line in the event of a security breach.

This particular sequence of tones, Black picked out himself.

We joked about it, standing around the massive table in the main conference room at the Raptor's Nest. Black called it his "Oh Shit!" alarm.

It meant something bad was happening.

It meant something really, really bad was happening.

It meant EMERGENCY.

It meant 911.

Before I could click over my headset to find out what it was, Black's voice rose in my head.

Turn on the television, doc, he sent, his thoughts tense. *I'm not even going to try and describe this one...*

❦

I swallowed, but only nodded—to no one, since Black was already gone.

Even his presence had vanished.

Whatever was happening, he couldn't stick around long enough to explain it to me.

When my eyes slid back into focus, I found Garrity looking at me, frowning.

From his expression, he thought I was reading his mind again.

His mind, and likely the minds of every human in the room.

Without bothering to reassure him on that point, I motioned towards the giant monitor on the wall just past the head of the table.

"Can you turn on the television?" I said, keeping my voice as level as I could.

It didn't even occur to me to try and view whatever this was privately.

If it was on t.v., they were going to know about it soon enough.

"...I just heard from my people," I added before anyone could react. "Something is happening. I'm assuming in Los Angeles. That's where my husband is right now. He didn't have time to explain, so I'm as in the dark as the rest of you."

Confusion flickered across Garrity's eyes, right before he glanced at C.I.A. asshole, who lifted an eyebrow, his poker face admittedly decent.

C.I.A. guy looked at me then, his expression still impressively difficult to read.

"Your husband?" he clarified. "That's who contacted you?"

I nodded. Motioning a touch more impatiently at the monitor, I added as evenly as I could, "He seemed to think it was pretty urgent. He knows where I am right now... he wouldn't have interrupted this meeting, if it wasn't an immediate concern."

Garrity was already motioning to one of his aids.

The woman in the dark blue power suit walked to a nearby credenza, found a remote in a top drawer and aimed it at the monitor on the wall.

She clicked it on.

The television there must have been set to one of the twenty-four-hour cable news stations already. The sound blared, making everyone around the table jump until the aid turned it down to a more reasonable volume.

Images appeared—first a glimpse of blue sky and some kind of light, then the camera swung down, showing sharper, more immediate images of Los Angeles.

Everyone around the table fell silent.

I fell silent along with them.

We'd all barely glimpsed that thing in the sky, but now the person holding the camera had that camera focused on the ground.

I realized they'd been talking the whole time, but I grew aware of the female newscaster's voice when the person holding the smart phone with the relatively decent camera panned that camera around at their immediate surroundings.

"The phenomenon began just a few minutes ago," the woman said, sounding breathless, but definitely speaking from the studio. "We have a full camera crew on the way down there, but right now, Rudy Nguyen is the only person we have on the scene, and he's using his phone..."

In the jumping, jostled video, I noted a twenty-foot, cement outer wall I recognized in the background of a glass-fronted building. I knew the purpose of that wall; it hid the backlot of a movie studio I recognized as well, mostly from the photos Black had been texting me all morning, maybe figuring I'd be more calm about his insane interview if I felt more involved, or could at least picture where he was.

It only occurred to me later that he might also have done it as a form of "emergency backup." Meaning, if something *really* bad went down, I'd know exactly where and how to find him, in the event I needed to pop in with some form of damage control.

I could tell from the angle that whoever was shooting the video, they remained outside the wall, on the street near one of the studio access gates.

A crowd of people jostled and knocked into the person recording on their phone.

Half of the people making up that crowd held phones up, aiming them at the sky.

I wasn't all that interested in the crowd though, to be honest.

I wanted him to point the camera up again... at that odd light.

As it was, it was reflecting strangely on the faces of the crowd, washing out and polarizing the color and shadows, washing out and distorting the faces and skin tone of the people who obviously stood directly belong it.

"What the bloody hell..." Garrity muttered.

He and his aid exchanged grim looks.

I pinged Mika and Jax with my light.

My eyes never left the wall monitor.

They were still showing the crowd.

Without waiting for Jax or Mika to speak, I sent words in their direction.

If you're not watching television, turn it on. Make sure Yarli and the others back in San Francisco are monitoring this, too.

I felt them acknowledge my words.

My eyes refocused on the monitor.

The newscasters' voices rose.

"...That phenomenon in the sky hasn't repeated," the male of the pair was saying. "We're waiting on some footage from when it initially occurred. But how to describe it, Lani?"

"A really bright light," the woman commentator said, obviously still watching the monitor herself. "We're told it flashed around a dark space, almost like an eclipse. Witnesses on the ground described it as a 'big hole' in the sky... like some kind of projection, or optical illusion. It was reported that something came through it..."

A surge of... something... hit at me, right in the chest.

Foreboding. Misgiving.

Plain old fear.

Maybe it came from some kind of supernatural, built-in alarm system.

Whatever it was, a flash of knowing came with it.

I knew what caused this.

I knew what had come through that "hole" in the sky.

Not exactly, but I knew in terms of ballpark.

But it couldn't be.

I couldn't possibly be right.

Nothing could do that.

Nothing.

Except me.

The thought brought another wave of panic through my living light. I was about to reach out to Yarli, to Mika, to Jax, maybe even Dalejem—

A *BOOM* rumbled out of the monitor speakers, fuzzing them out briefly.

Everyone at the table jumped.

The crowd on the other side of the television erupted in gasps and cries.

The two newscasters gasped with the crowd, staring at the images on the monitor.

The camera phone tilted up, flashing white in the sun, then showing an image of blue sky, broken by large, white clouds.

The reporter on the ground, presumably Rudy Nguyen, gasped like he'd been running, or maybe like he was in the beginnings of a panic attack. He spoke into a microphone that fuzzed in and out, distorted by the yells, pushing, and other panicked sounds and chaos around him.

Meanwhile, the camera on his phone continued to jerk and lose focus.

I struggled to see what he pointed the damned thing at.

I wanted to yell at the television to tell him to keep still.

Then a shadow covered the light.

I saw a glimpse of a massive, gray-colored wing, covering the sun.

Everyone at the table cried out, flinching back for real.

The French President and the German Chancellor rose to their feet.

They backed away from the table.

Somewhere in that, I'd gotten to my feet as well.

Now over half the table stood around the wall monitor, staring at the flickering images. Shadows cut into the sunlight. I felt my heart pound, my breath start to hitch.

Then I heard it.

That tell-tale, echoing scream into the sky.

8

A NEW PROBLEM

B *LACK.* I threw my light and mind at him, my thoughts hard as glass. *BLACK WE TALKED ABOUT THIS... I THOUGHT YOU WEREN'T GOING TO DO THIS.*

Silence.

I remembered he'd never *actually agreed* to not do this.

I'd told him not to do it, and he'd more or less blown me off.

I fought not to think about the gray-white, mottled, boulder-like skin I'd seen in those flashing images, or the darker gray leather of those wings... neither of which was anything remotely like the shimmering, iridescent black I associated with my husband's dragon form.

I bit my lip at the thought... then shook it off.

It had to be a trick of the light.

Something wrong with the camera.

BLACK! I yelled into the space. *ANSWER ME DAMN IT!*

Then something else occurred to me.

I wasn't totally sure he could answer me in this form.

It hadn't really hit me until that exact second, but I couldn't remember actually *talking* to him when he'd been a dragon before.

I don't think I'd ever even tried.

Really, seeing Black as a dragon had been an almost mystical experience for me.

Both times I'd encountered his dragon before, I'd watched him until it seemed time to bring him back. Then it hadn't required speaking to bring him back to me. He'd come back more or less on his own, as soon as he'd seen me, and I opened my light to his.

I watched now as shadows flitted across the screen, trying to get another glimpse of the creature itself. The camera jumped and jolted too much. Screams rent the air, and I tried to decide if I should leave the room, look for a quieter place... a closet maybe... to open a damned dimensional portal and go get my husband.

I looked around at the pale faces at the table.

The only one who met my gaze was Weston "Westie" Banks, of the C.I.A.

Shadows and light flickered across his pale blue eyes from the monitor, and I looked away. My jaw hardened. I turned towards the door to the conference room—

Miri?

I froze, my eyes swiveling back to the wall monitor.

Black?

I felt the preoccupation on him, the half-attention he gave me.

I refocused on the monitor.

The phone's camera pointed up once more, but couldn't find the dragon at first.

Then a glimpse of a rough white... something... passed over-head. The gray-white skin reminded me of rock, or possibly a rhino's hide, or an elephant's. Again, it looked nothing like what I remembered of Black, the two times I'd seen him as a dragon.

That mottled, bulging, lumpy flesh rippled across and filled the monitor. Despite its size, the animal moved so quickly, I could barely glimpse it before it was gone.

Still, everything about it felt off.

It felt even more off when I realized how clear Black's voice sounded.

Shouldn't he sound a *little* different, at least?

Black, what are you doing? Why didn't you answer me?

I felt amusement on him.

I'm a little busy right now, love—

But I couldn't deal with amused, snarky Black right then.

I thought we talked about this! I snapped. *I know you said you wanted to do it, but what the hell are you up to right now? This isn't some bland demonstration! You're terrorizing people... in the middle of damned Hollywood!*

I forced myself to stop.

It took biting my lip hard enough to taste blood, but I forced myself to stop.

I wanted to yell the damned words out loud.

I really had to fight not to use my outdoor voice.

Hearing another keening scream echo through the other-wise-silent conference room, I forced myself to calm my mind.

Honey— Black began.

Black, don't. Just don't. I fought to calm my mind, couldn't. *I don't want to hear it. Not now. Just tell me how to stop this. Do you need me to come there? Are you able to change back on your own, or do you need me to—*

Miri. He felt bewildered now. *I don't think you—*

Just tell me what the hell you need! I snapped.

I felt a kind of stunned silence settle over him.

BLACK! I snapped.

But he seemed to come out of his shock.

Darlin', he sent, his mind a touch sharp. *That ain't me.*

Black— I began angrily.

MIRIAM.

His mind slammed into mine, a hot gust of wind.

It stunned me briefly into silence.

WIFE... THAT IS NOT ME. IT IS NOT ME! HOW COULD

YOU POSSIBLY THINK THAT IS ME? I'M WITH GRANT STEELE IN A STUDIO BUILDING RIGHT NOW!

Silence fell over both of our minds.

I felt him take a breath, like he had to fight to dial it back.

Then his words came out almost normal.

Gaos, Miriam. Have I messed you up that badly with my erratic, idiosyncratic shit over the years? What you're saying doesn't even make any sense.

Not bothering to wait for a reply, Black added,

Seriously, I don't know how the hell you think I could just casually chat with you while dive-bombing a movie studio and breathing fire. He sounded like some part of him found the idea darkly funny as he said it, despite the near-incredulity still in his voice. *Or how I'd just be like, "ho-hum, wife... just calling to say 'howdy' while I terrorize Los Angeles and scare humans into thinking they probably need to nuke me—"*

Black— I began angrily.

No, Miri. No. His thought grew overtly warning. *Stop. Just stop, honey. Okay? Think about what you're saying. Take a breath, doc, and think. Think. Does what you just accused me of make any kind of sense, whatsoever?*

He paused, like he meant his words literally.

Like he wanted me to really think about it.

For some reason, I did.

I realized why I was screaming at him.

My heart pounded in my chest. My breathing was tight, labored. I'd already sweated through the blouse and jacket I wore. Worse than any of that, I felt sick, like I might throw up. I felt sick to my stomach, on the verge of tears.

I was terrified.

Some part of me had known all along that it wasn't Black.

How? I sent finally.

My thoughts came out deadened that time.

Black seemed to feel the change in me. He completely

dropped his more sarcastic, cocky, drive-me-crazy-for-fun demeanor.

I don't know, he sent frankly.

Is it after you? Is it attacking you?

We probably need to assume it's here because of me, right? he sent. *That's not just my famous narcissism talking, is it? I mean, it's not like a dragon showing up here, of all places, could possibly be a coincidence.*

His thoughts grew a touch more amused.

I'm a little offended you didn't recognize me, doc. I would have thought I would be more memorable to my own wife, even in that form. I didn't realize I was just another dragon to you—

Don't joke about this, I warned. *I think I might throw up if you do. I might throw up anyway, but if you start joking about this—*

His mind stripped itself of humor.

Did you see the whole thing?

Briefly, I forgot he wasn't there, with me, in the flesh.

I shook my head.

No.

Looking down, I saw my hand gripping the back of a leather chair, white-knuckled. It was the same chair where I'd been sitting. I glanced around the room, taking in human faces. They still stared up at the monitor—all but Weston Banks, who now studied my expression with wariness mixed with caution, mixed with a denser understanding, like he knew exactly who I was talking to, and exactly what I was doing.

I can't do this in here, I told Black.

Thinking about his question then, I added,

I didn't see it. I didn't see the beginning of this. How did it start? They haven't shown us, not that I've seen. The footage has all been live. We probably need to change the channel—

Don't worry about that, Black cut in, his thoughts soothing. *It's not important right now. Don't worry about any of that, Miri.*

He sounded worried, though.

He felt worried, I should say—and not about the new dragon.

He felt worried about me.

Miri, honey. His thoughts grew soft, even as I thought it. *I think you should get out of there. Make some excuse. Tell them we'll reschedule the talks. Tell them this complicates things too much. You said none of the human leaders seemed to come all that prepared. Tell them we'll give them a few weeks to think through everything you said... maybe even come back with some concrete policy proposals, now that they know more about where we stand...*

He sounded like he was soothing a wild animal.

He sounded like he was trying to keep me from freaking out.

Maybe he was even right to sound like that.

I felt lost, like I'd been shaken roughly, or even punched in the face.

I couldn't remember the last time I'd felt so unmoored.

You want me to come there? I heard that confusion reach my voice. *To Los Angeles? Right now? Even with all of this—*

No. Black cut me off, unambiguous. *Absolutely not, Miriam. I want you to go to the Raptor's Nest. Now. I'll come up there to be with you, as soon as I can.*

He trailed.

Feeling his seer's light, reading it through our connection, I frowned.

I could feel how distracted he was.

Moreover, I could feel something else.

Someone else was there.

Something was happening.

What? I sent, alarmed. *What is it, Black? What's wrong?*

I have to go.

Black's mind came through hard, crisp.

I knew that part of him, too.

It was his military mind. It was his strategy-war-fight mind.

He must have felt my alarm.

I felt him make an effort to hide his state of mind from me. I felt him do his best to subdue his thoughts, to infuse some warmth, something other than that cold-as-ice calculation.

Please, honey, he sent. *Go back to the Raptor's Nest. Tell Mika, Jax and the others to get on a plane and follow you. But I have to go. I have to go right now, doc. Please do as I ask... I'll tell you everything as soon as I can.*

Black—

I was too late.

My mind met nothing.

Black had disappeared.

9

LIGHT BOND

"Where the hell did it go?"

Angel half-shouted the words. She stood just inside the main door to a sound studio, the door gripped in one hand. Her eyes never left the sky, not even to look at Cowboy, who stood slightly in front of her, gazing up and down the main road through this part of the studio backlot.

The dragon had disappeared.

She shouted anyway.

Gunfire still echoed down the fake city streets.

Angel thought she'd heard the softer *whump* of grenade launchers too, probably from gas cannisters being lobbed at the protesters who were still outside the gates.

Those idiot Purity assholes were still coming after Black, trying to break into the studio even with everything else going on.

On the plus side, Zairei told them the robot-cyborg things left.

Maybe it was the sight of a dragon in the sky, given they hadn't the best track record with dragons in the past, or maybe it was something else, but Zairei said they'd tracked them going in the opposite direction, pretty much the instant the dragon appeared.

They were still tracking them.

Zairei's team had traced them to a boat so far, and would continue to track their movements as long as they could. Even with everything else, with all of *this* going on, Black wanted the team to use the retreating units to find out who'd sent them.

The sound studio where the rest of them had ended up—the same one where studio security brought Grant Steele and his audience—stood only about a hundred yards from the gate.

When Angel leaned out far enough, she could see the real street.

"Where's Black?" she muttered.

It hadn't been a question she expected an answer to.

Cowboy gave her one anyway.

"Over there," he said easily.

When she glanced at him, Cowboy used his chin and jaw to motion to his left, down the opposite row of storefronts.

Angel tore her eyes off him, then off the side security gate, then off the sky when she glanced up nervously in reflex, like a rabbit under a circling hawk...

...and aimed her stare down the fake city street in the opposite direction.

It took her a second to realize what she was seeing.

"Christ," she muttered. "Now what?"

Cowboy didn't answer.

Probably because he didn't have an answer for her.

Both of them stared out over the street.

They had a vantage point where they were, being a good half-story off the ground, since the door to the sound studio was built at the top of a short flight of stairs. It gave them an unusually good view of what was happening about fifty yards to their left.

Black stood there.

So did an entirely naked man.

A naked man whose entire body steamed in the Los Angeles sun.

He looked like he'd just climbed out of a jacuzzi on a snowy, wintery morning in the Swiss Alps, or maybe in the wilds of Canada.

It wasn't snowing here, though.

It had to be at least seventy-six, seventy-seven degrees Fahrenheit.

Angel watched the man walk, barefoot, buck-naked, emitting wisps and curls of steam, down the center of the street towards Black. She took her eyes off the naked guy's muscular back and arms, away from his lean, muscled legs, long enough to look at Black's face. She gauged the stillness of Black's expression, and couldn't read a damned thing.

Just looking at him, she had absolutely no idea how he was reacting to this, much less what he was thinking.

"That has to be him," she whispered.

She wasn't even sure why she was whispering.

They were too far away for anyone to hear them, even without the automatic weapon fire she could hear, or the concussive sounds of the smoke grenade launchers.

"That has to be him," she whispered to Cowboy. "Right?"

"Ayuh," Cowboy said only.

The two of them watched, silent, as the steaming, naked man with the raw-red skin came to a stop, his legs slightly apart as he stared at Black.

Angel half-expected a tumbleweed to roll down the street between them.

But this wasn't an Old West area of the backlot. Instead, it served as an approximation of a modern financial district, a downtown area of New York, San Francisco, Chicago, maybe even Sydney, London, Cincinnati.

Angel figured Black would talk first.

Black could be a talker.

Of course, a lot of time, that was misdirection.

Black had a tendency to snow people with a lot of bullshit in tense situations.

He didn't do that now, though.

He looked the naked man over unapologetically, his gold eyes flashing where they caught the sun, his perfectly-shaped mouth frozen in a hard, if subtle frown.

In the end, it was the naked man who spoke.

When he did, Angel jumped.

That may have been partly because the naked, possibly-dragon man spoke perfect English, if with an odd impossible-to-identify accent. That accent caused him to clip his words strangely, even as he trilled a bit on the "r" sound.

He only said three words.

"Where is she?" the dragon hissed, staring at Black.

B lack blinked.
       The man's words seemed to surprise him, too.

Then he scowled.

That time, the hostility on his face wasn't remotely subtle.

"Who?" he growled.

Angel had a feeling Black knew exactly who the new guy meant.

From the look on his face, and the aggression seething off him, she had a feeling she knew exactly what name popped into Black's head.

"You know who," the other said. "She is the mate. The other half."

Again, his voice remained eerily calm.

Angel really looked at his face, realizing she hadn't before now.

Not just his face—she looked at all of him.

She looked at his face, hair, arms, height, eyes... and the expression she saw in all of it, including in his exact stance as he faced Black. For the first time, she looked at him as a person, not simply an unknown, freakishly-steaming collection of skin, bones, and machine-like muscles.

He was tall... definitely over six feet.

In fact, watching them face off, she realized he stood just under Black's six-five or six-six, or whatever he was these days.

Black's height was still a moving target, according to Miri, in that Black was apparently still gaining in that area. Angel had no idea how, but something to do with seer physiology had him growing still... at whatever age Black was, since that was yet another enigma when it came to seer versus human biology.

The new guy being so tall definitely hinted at his race.

Then again, if he'd just been a freaking *dragon* a few seconds ago, the whole seer versus human question was pretty much moot.

Angel noticed a tattoo along his arm.

It wasn't the colorful, peacock green and blue winged dragon tattoo Black wore on his back, or the new one he'd just gotten on his arm. The new guy's tat was obsidian black with white and purple highlights, a winding snake that coiled up his forearm and around his elbow to thicken around his bicep.

It could have been a king cobra, but Angel wasn't ready to label it that.

She wasn't ready to label anything about this guy yet.

His brown hair contained streaks of silvery-white.

It didn't look gray, or like anything to do with ageing.

His eyes were a pale gold, or white and gold-*ish*, depending on how you looked at it, so roughly in the same rough color category as Black's.

Unlike Black's irises, the new guy's didn't contain the same depth, or the same flecks of light and dark. The pale, white-gold eyes of the new seer-dragon-whoever-whatever appeared to be basically empty. His eyes glowed faintly, as if lit from within, but Angel got nothing off him, no sense of personality or even emotion.

His eyes shone blindly from a tanned face, contrasting his brown and silver hair.

He seemed to be waiting as he stared at Black.

Was he really going to stand there, naked, and wait for Miri to show up?

Even as Angel thought it, the new male spoke again.

"Where is she?" he said again.

Black folded his arms.

He answered the guy's question with a death stare.

Uncharacteristically, he was also doing it silently.

"Where is she?" the male asked again.

Angel was beginning to wonder if it was another robot, like what they encountered on Hawaii. Of course, that left a HELL of a lot of unanswered questions. Like, for example, how a robot could turn into a dragon, then back into a robot—

"Not a robot, Ang." The voice was soft, and obviously sub-vocals. "Nice theory, though... positively genius."

Angel frowned, but didn't answer.

Black didn't sound particularly welcoming of her specula-tions, or overly impressed with the non-insights her brain had come up with so far.

"Anyone looking into this?" Black growled next. "Or are you all going to just stand there, holding your dicks? Wait and see if this fucking thing kills me or not?"

Angel felt her face grow hot.

That's more or less exactly what she'd been doing.

Well... minus the dick part.

Cowboy spoke up before she could.

"Yarli's on it, boss. She's called in some help." Cowboy paused, his voice edging on apologetic. "She figured this was an all-hands-on-deck type situation, boss."

Angel flinched a tiny bit.

Even before her boyfriend said that last part, she'd had a pretty good idea who Cowboy meant, when he'd talked about "calling for help."

There were really only two options.

Black clearly got the not-so-subtle message there, too.

His scowl deepened.

He refocused on the male in front of him.

The mystery male chose that moment to try again.

"Bring her to me," he said.

As before, his voice came through flat, unemotional.

It also contained not so much as the tiniest *hint* of a request.

He spoke the words as an order, like he was unused to being questioned, second-guessed, or disobeyed by anyone, in any way.

Black didn't answer him.

The male, undaunted, tried again.

"You must bring her to me—" he began.

"Never going to happen," Black growled.

There was a silence.

Again, the other male didn't appear angry, or frustrated. He looked just as immobile, unfazed, and totally single-minded as he had since he appeared.

The two of them stared at one another, and now Angel really did feel nervous. What if Black wasn't just being melodramatic? What if this thing really could kill him? What if he knew something she and Cowboy didn't, and he really did think this... guy... might be able to overpower him in a fight?

"You mean besides the fact that his dragon form weighed probably fifteen tons more than mine?" Black murmured in her ear.

"Yeah," Angel sent back through the sub-vocals. "Besides that."

The silence was brief.

That time, Angel practically felt him thinking through it.

When he next spoke, his voice was dry.

"Let's just say, it doesn't strike me as outside the realm of possibility," Black remarked. "Speaking of which, it would be really damned nice if someone would get back to me with something I can actually fucking use. Today, if possible—"

"Sir."

A deep voice broke through Black's sub-vocal growl, coming through clearly on the line.

Crystal-clear. Melodic.

Cultured to the point of sounding scholarly.

That male voice contained a vibrating kind of charge Angel had learned to associate with certain seers, especially those trained to a high level, and especially those who might have been older, or maybe just more steeped in "seer-ness" from that other version of Earth.

It was almost a spiritual quality, like something you'd see on someone who'd been meditating in caves for a few dozen years.

Or maybe a few hundred, in the case of seers.

Unlike the voice belonging to the naked male on the street below where she stood, Angel knew the voice on the headset immediately.

She knew every inflection in that strangely-accented English.

"Sir," the male seer repeated. "We're working on an ID. All we can tell you so far is what you've likely guessed... he contains the same tell-tale light markers for the 'dragon' entity you had us map in your own living light. There are nuances of difference, but in terms of composition of the primary, high-functioning structures—"

"Jem!" Not Black that time—Zairei, who must have been listening on the line. Joy infused his voice, a kind of disbelief mixed with pure happiness. "Brother! I did not know you were back! *Gaos d'lalente*, I did not know you were even *alive*, brother—"

"None of us knew he was alive," Dex growled, his voice openly hostile. "Well, except Black, apparently. And Cowboy, apparently. And Yarli, apparently. And presumably the doc. And presumably Angel. And presumably Manny... and all the seers still at the Raptor's Nest. Which is suddenly sounding like a hell of a lot of people who aren't me, despite me *supposedly* being one-half in charge of ops—"

Black was having none of it.

"Clear the line," Black growled. "All of you. You can have your fucking reunion and bitch at me for not knowing things later."

Angel exchanged looks with Cowboy.

Then her fiancé shrugged. He went back to looking at the naked man standing in the middle of the studio street.

Steam still coiled off the male's dense arms and muscular thighs.

"Yeah," Cowboy muttered. "This ain't the time, brother Dexter... as shitty as that is, and regardless of the fairness and truth of your words."

Angel felt a stab of guilt.

It hadn't been her place to tell Dex about Jem and Nick, but she still felt guilty. Hell, they'd been living at her house.

She knew Cowboy felt guilty, too.

Part of the reason they'd split up the team the way they had was to break it to different members of Black's inner circle that Nick and Dalejem were still alive, and back in town.

Clearly, Black hadn't done his side of things yet.

He hadn't yet told his half of the team that Nick was alive, that Dalejem was alive, and that the two of them were back in San Francisco.

Angel hadn't been privy to the real-time conversation between Black and Miri on that whole plan, to divide the team up the way they did, but she had to assume it was Black's job to tell this portion of the team, meaning the half he'd brought with him to Los Angeles.

That should have included the seers Kiessa and Zairei, the human Black Securities and Investigations employees, Luce, A.J., and Miguel, along with Dog and Easton, and the other ex-cons Black had working out of New Mexico...

...and yeah, Dex.

Dexter should have been at the top of that list.

Yarli had the easiest group, in terms of breaking the news.

The only one who really mattered was Holo.

Holo—who'd fought in a war alongside Dalejem on that other version of Earth, and who, along with Jax, had known Dalejem longer than any of them, even Yarli—was definitely one person who would want to know that Jem was still alive.

Holo hadn't been able to leave San Francisco at all, since he still suffered from medical complications after the attack he barely survived by a cyborg in Oahu. The damned thing nearly killed him, and injured every major organ in his body.

It was bad enough, Miri said he likely would have gotten a heart, liver, and kidney transplant if he'd been human.

Unfortunately, he wasn't human... and there simply weren't enough seers on the entire planet, even now, for them to have spare organs lying around for transplants.

Holo had to tough out the healing process on his own.

In any case, the whole team should know about Jem and Nick by now, and clearly they didn't.

Dex clearly hadn't known.

Black should have told him.

After what Nick did to Kiko, Dex was going to lose his ever-loving mind when he found out Nick the vampire was still alive. Dex might actually have a stroke when he found out Nick was living at Angel's place in San Francisco, feeding off Solonik when he got the munchies, going surfing in Santa Cruz every other night with his new boyfriend, Dalejem.

Hell, Dex would freak out just about *Solonik* being alive.

Solonik, who previously kidnapped and nearly killed Miri, and who'd been a damned dangerous seer in his own right, was currently chained up in Angel's garage, sulking because Nick didn't love him.

Really, after all this, Dex might need medication.

Therapy, anyway.

Wincing as she turned all this over in her mind, Angel found herself thinking she didn't blame Black for putting off "The Talk."

Then again, Miri had still gotten the hardest job.

Miri had to be the one to tell Kiko.

It was probably better that both of them waited until their respective teams were well outside of San Francisco, and in Kiko's case, a few thousand miles away, on a whole other continent, before they dumped *that* news on them.

Angel wondered if Dex was on the line even now, listening to this, wondering how the hell Dalejem was back, given how they'd all been so sure Nick murdered him. Dex was likely biting his tongue nearly in half with wanting to ask Jem if he'd "taken care of" *that fucking vampire* for the rest of them.

Dex wasn't stupid. He would put it together.

It was just a matter of time.

Again, Angel was damned glad she wasn't tasked with telling him the truth.

"What else?" Black growled. "Jem? Do you have anything I can actually use?"

On the line, Dalejem hesitated.

When that deep voice rose a third time, it remained melodious, calm—business-like verging on blunt.

Even so, Angel heard the reluctance there.

"He's tied to you," Jem said. "This new seer. He's connected to you, specifically, brother."

"What the fuck does that mean?" Black stared at the naked, tattooed seer, his gold eyes hard as glass. "Explain, Jem. Now. What the hell does that mean?"

"Exactly what I said," Jem said, sighing. "He's tied to you, brother. To your *aleimi*. I can see the cord... and it's not insubstantial. It's the kind of cord one would normally see with a family-member, or a military unit from the Pamir. There's a multi-layered energetic cord between the two of you. I see it well within your own *aleimic* shield, connected to those dragon structures in your light. I also see it tied to another part of you."

Again, Jem hesitated, as if unsure he should elaborate.

"Where?" Black said. "Where else is it tied to me?"

Before Jem could answer, Holo cursed over the line.

"Shit. He's right, boss. I see it, too. I don't know how I missed that—"

"Because you're not Jem," Black growled. His voice hardened, focusing back on the older seer. "Where?" Black growled, louder. "Where else is it tied to me?"

Dalejem sighed, clicking under his breath.

"Your light bond," he admitted. "It's connected to the structure you share with your mate... with Miriam."

Angel, who'd been focused on Black's face when Dalejem spoke, saw the seer flinch.

To his credit, he didn't change expression beyond that.

His darker gold eyes remained warily on the face of the seer in front of him.

"Is he connected to Miri, too?" Black asked.

Another faint pause quieted the line.

Angel heard Dalejem sigh, like he was getting ready to answer...

...then there was a strange *whoosh* sound.

Unlike the boom in the sky earlier, this noise, Angel almost recognized.

It was the sound of all the air in a particular spot being abruptly shunted out of the way.

It might not have been audible at all, but the gunfire at the outer gate had finally quieted, leaving a strange sort of silence over the studio's backlot. The strange seer hadn't spoken since Black's last words. The two of them just stood there, staring at one another.

Then there was that sound.

The *whoosh*.

A body-shaped hole punched into space and time, and—

A new person stood there.

Miri.

Miri, stark-naked, panting, with a faint sheen of sweat.

Something about seeing her there, looking so strangely small next to the two males, caused Angel's heart to just... stop.

☙❦☙

S eemingly as one, both of the dragon seers turned to stare at her.

Angel's heart jerked back into motion, now beating too fast, and seemingly all over her body. That heart beat throbbed in her hands and fingers. It beat at her ribs.

It stuck painfully in her throat, rendering her silent.

It must have similarly affected Cowboy, although he didn't lose his voice.

Not only that, but he understood Miri's appearance here, next to Black and that seer, in a different light than Angel.

Well, he understood it faster, anyway.

He let out a low whistle, and she looked at him.

"Well, damn," he muttered.

Cowboy's hands rested on his lean hips. His gray eyes never left the three seers standing in the studio street, but he spoke to Angel alone.

"...I hope these studio folks have good insurance."

It took a handful of seconds for Cowboy's meaning to penetrate.

Then Angel looked back at Miri.

The doc just stood there, panting, seemingly trying to regain her equilibrium. She held out her arms on either side, as if afraid she might lose her balance and fall... or maybe like she thought she might have to run out of there as fast as her legs would carry her.

She stared up at the strange male seer, an odd look on her high-cheekboned face. Her delicate jaw jutted slightly upward as she stared up to meet his light-gold eyes.

She looked at him almost like she knew him.

She looked at him almost like she recognized him.

Something about that struck Angel as ominous as hell.

"Shit," she muttered.

That was before she saw Black's face.

Black looked between Miri and the new dragon like he was trying to decide which of them he wanted to murder first.

Then, and only then, did Angel understand what Cowboy had meant.

If Miri didn't have a way to stop it, this was going to be a damned bloodbath.

10

TOO MANY OURS

I wasn't there.

Then I was.

I'd gotten a lot better at the interdimensional jumps.

I still got out of breath.

It still felt like I'd gotten a good, solid, hard punch to the solar plexus, maybe a half-second before I landed. I generally had to fight my body's rhythms back to normal after I got to the new place, more or less for the same reason.

I also showed up covered in a thin sheen of sweat.

Before I left, I talked to Jax, Mika, Kiko, Larisse, and then to Yarli and Dalejem.

Jem was at the Raptor's Nest with Yarli and the other seers.

Yarli finally cracked that nut, and 'fessed up to the seers and humans we'd left behind to hold down the fort in San Francisco. Unlike me—or Black, who I was ninety-nine percent positive hadn't yet said a word to Dex—Yarli actually *did* the thing we'd all agreed to do and talked to her portion of the team about Nick and Dalejem.

After I'd spoken to everyone in London about my plan, and gave them Black's instructions, I didn't stick around when they started arguing with me about how Black might be right about me going to the Raptor's Nest instead of Los Angeles.

I knew where I needed to be.

To me, it wasn't even a question.

I climbed into a closet at the building in Kensington...

...and *poof,* I was gone.

It took me less than five seconds to gear into the right structures, and resonate with Black.

Then, out of nowhere, I stood in the middle of a fake city street, surrounded by fake buildings on both sides, only about half of them containing anything approximating an interior.

Sucking in breaths to ground myself, I looked to my right, and saw Black.

I looked to my left, and saw...

Someone else.

I didn't know him, but something about the stare he leveled on my face ran a shiver up my spine that made me wrap my arms around my chest.

I remembered I was naked.

Usually I didn't care about that these days, but right then, I fervently wished I wasn't.

I never took my eyes off his face.

His skin shone with a strange, near-gold sheen. It let off faint breaths of what looked like steam, barely perceptible, but enough to make his outline oddly blurry.

I knew how crazy and impossible this was, and how crazy it would sound if I spoke it out loud... but I knew him.

Somehow, I knew him.

The thought made my jaw clench, even as I continued to study those pale, gold-white eyes.

"Who are you?" I said.

My voice came out sharp, uncompromising.

The strange male didn't blink.

He looked me over.

As he did, a tension I'd seen in his eyes when I first looked up at him slowly began to ease. It was almost like seeing me there, in the flesh, relieved him of some intense, possibly even semi-conscious fear he'd held in his light.

The longer he looked at me, the longer his light skirted around mine, the more I saw his expression lose its hardness.

"Who are you?" I repeated. "Answer me."

He adjusted his feet, never taking his eyes off me.

The sheer relief in his expression as he looked me over unnerved me more than any amount of hostility he might have aimed in my direction.

"Who are—" I began angrily.

"You know who I am."

He cut me off without stopping his appraisal of my naked body.

He spoke calmly, almost dismissively.

For the first time, I looked at Black.

I barely glanced at him, though.

I was afraid to look at him for long. I was afraid to turn my back on the other seer, to take my eyes off him for even a second.

I saw Black's gold eyes, staring at me.

I felt his blinding fury that I was there, that I'd come *here,* after he specifically told me not to.

Even knowing how intensely Black felt, I couldn't look away from that other seer. Fear coursed through me; I felt unnerved by how badly I didn't want to turn my back on him, or on the stare of those pale, blank eyes.

I felt an irrational certainty he might attack me—or maybe just grab me, open a portal and drop both of us through to some other world.

That had to be how I knew him.

I didn't know his face.

I didn't know his body, or that strange tattoo on his arm.

It had to be his light.

I'd felt his light before—somewhere.

The only explanation that struck me as remotely possible had to do with the unintentional jumps I'd made when my powers to portal-jump first began to manifest. In those early weeks, I got whisked to numerous worlds, worlds I still scarcely remembered because of the state I'd been in at the time.

All I'd managed to figure out in the time since, was that they were all worlds where the Dragon manifested.

I'd felt some aspect of Dragon on every one of those versions of Earth I'd been drawn to.

I must have felt this one too, on one of the many places housing some form of the Dragon God... the same Dragon God that lived inside my husband.

"How did you get here?" My voice came out harsher each time. "Where did you come from? What are you doing here? Why would you come to this world?"

The questions fired out of me.

Hostile, tinged with aggression.

I pointed away from us, back towards the studio gate, but I didn't mean the gesture to indicate anywhere on this world.

"You need to go," I told him. "Now. You can't be here."

The tall man with the broad chest and muscular arms met my gaze, a smile toying at the edges of his lips. I felt that Dragon-light all over him. It made my skin vibrate, like it did when that light grew prominent in Black.

It felt different on this being, though.

It felt like insanity on him.

It felt like the vibration keened off in strange, chaotic directions.

"Miri." Black's voice was soft, dangerous, deeper than hell. "Miri. I need you to go. Now."

I didn't look at him.

My eyes remained on the male seer who stared at me.

He stared at me like I belonged to him.

"Goddamn it, Miri—"

"No," I cut in. "You need to come with me, Black. Now."

I didn't dare take my eyes off the other dragon.

"...I'm not leaving without you," I added. "So bare your fucking arm. Grab my hand. Whatever. We both go... or neither of us do."

I needed contact with his skin to take him with me.

Just holding his hand made me nervous, although I suppose I could have managed it fine.

I preferred to be able to touch a lot more of his skin.

"We can't just leave him here," Black growled. "He could kill half of Los Angeles. Just fucking *leave*, Miriam. Let me handle this."

I shook my head, frowning up at that oddly familiar face.

My eyes took in the brown hair streaked with silvery-white, the high cheekbones, the tawny skin. He was still smiling at me, seemingly oblivious to everything I'd said, and everything Black had said.

He didn't seem to care about Black at all.

He ignored him entirely, looking at me with a pleased smile toying at his lips.

"I came for you," the male said. "Are you happy? I am so happy."

"No," I snapped. "I'm *not* fucking happy! I want you to go."

"I came for you," he repeated. "I cannot wait much longer to claim you. My body and light have ached for you. For so long—"

Another voice cut him off.

"Back away from her. Now. Or I will kill you."

It wasn't Black.

It used Black's voice, Black's body, Black's vocal chords to speak, but the instant I heard it, I *knew* it wasn't Black. I heard his deep voice. I felt that distinct vibration in the center of my chest. I could almost see the being through that voice, as his words hung in the air.

That, finally, got me to turn.

I stared at Black's face, but he was no longer inside it.

I was looking at Coreq.

Coreq—who somehow embodied the dragon part of Black.

I still didn't know how any of that worked.

Black didn't know, either.

Regardless of the cause, or even the *when* of it—if it was something Black had been born with, or something he picked up at some point in his life—Black was, in a sense, two people.

He was the Quentin Black I knew.

He was also Coreq, who I knew and understood a lot less.

I couldn't say I didn't know Coreq at all, though.

The truth was, Coreq felt even more eerily familiar to me than the naked seer currently standing to my left.

"If you don't back away from her, I'm going to have to kill you," Coreq repeated, eerily calm. "My mate already told you. You are not welcome here."

His light churned through the sunlight, blurring Black's outline when I glanced his way.

"This isn't acceptable," Coreq added. "You are bothering my mate. If you attempt to make some kind of claim, or even just disrespect mine—"

"She is our mate," the naked one said. "I will claim her. My body and light desire it."

I felt the hairs on my arms and the back of my neck go up.

At the same time, I felt some part of me getting angry.

We didn't need this shit right now.

We were already on the cusp of a damned race war.

We still had to find whoever the hell was building those robots and creepy cybernetic animal-machines. The human race was totally freaked out and probably trying to figure out ways to either nuke us or enslave us or boot us all out into space... if not some combination of those things.

Worse, I could feel Black/Coreq gearing up behind me.

His light had already started to spark hotter, crackling the air around me, creating a resonance in the male seer who stood in front of me.

I remembered what I'd done with Uncle Charles.

I didn't think.

I sure as hell didn't tell Black what I intended to do... or Coreq... assuming I could make meaningful contact with either of them.

I leapt forward, and grabbed hold of the naked seer in both of my hands.

I geared into those structures in my light...

...there was a crunching, telescoping sensation.

Then everything went dark.

II

GO TO BLACK

L ight spiraled in a dense vortex, blinding me.

I'd set a trajectory.

Sort of.

I mean, it was *enough* of a trajectory.

It might have been more wishful thinking than a full-blown, locked and loaded, precisely targeted destination.

I didn't even resonate with an exact *place* to create that trajectory, but I made a rough calculation. I just happened to base that calculation more on altitude, atmosphere, and a kind of "vibe," versus precise coordinates in terms of latitude and longitude.

Still, I *did* aim for a place I'd been before.

I just combined the feeling of that dimension with coordinates of a more transitional nature, meaning the one and only time I'd made an effort to collect light impressions while I traveled on a non-dimensional plane.

Which meant, if I did everything *exactly right,* and resonated *exactly the way* I'd intended, then I was likely going to bring us out—

—Light flashed, sucking in my breath.

Again, I felt like someone punched me.

I felt like I'd been punched in the center of my chest.

I broke out in a sweat.

I couldn't breathe—

Abruptly, my stomach dropped.

I plummeted through cold, wet clouds.

Light and shadow flashed around me, making me panic.

Vertigo hit without warning.

I was still holding onto him.

Wind whipped my face, throwing my hair violently against my neck, back, cheeks, lips, forehead. Gasping, I looked up at the light.

I was falling.

I couldn't see him, but I gripped his arms tightly in mine.

I grew conscious of the feel of my last air flight, remembering how I'd consciously tried to feel the air outside the plane as we flew through it, hoping I could get enough of an imprint into my light that I could do exactly this.

During my brief few months of training in interdimensional travel, I'd been advised to gather such impressions whenever I could. The idea was to give myself, and Black, as many options as possible for potential jumps.

For the same reason, I'd made an exercise out of it, whenever I got to a new or interesting location. I'd gathered such impressions all over London, San Francisco, at the airports on both ends, not to mention the Raptor's Nest, Angel's apartment, Golden Gate Park, the beach, the house in Santa Cruz, the Presidio, Chinatown, the Albuquerque airport, the resort hotel and spa in Santa Fe, New Mexico, where our wedding was supposed to take place...

The airplane one had been pure experimentation on my part.

I had my doubts I could jump accurately enough to make it *inside* a plane—not without killing myself, or possibly Black, or likely both of us—but it was an interesting exercise.

I wasn't in a plane now.

I *was* roughly thirty-five thousand feet above the ground, though.

That elevation was dropping fast.

I'd popped us out on a different version of Earth, only at the same height I'd been when I played around with my light on my last transatlantic flight on *our* Earth, which happened to be somewhere along the journey between San Francisco and London.

This dimension's Pacific Ocean should be below, and growing closer.

All of that went through my mind in a flash.

It couldn't be considered "thoughts" really.

Rather, the packed timeline smashed into my consciousness, and abruptly, remembering the point of all this...

...I let the other seer go.

I geared back into those structures in my *aleimi,* or living light.

I changed my resonance from memory.

That time, I attuned my living flame to the easiest, fastest, most natural resonance there was, at least for me. Basically, I told my light where it always wanted to go anyway, no matter where else I might be.

I even spoke the words out loud, maybe in the hopes of giving it a little extra punch.

As I did, my heart felt nothing but relief.

"Black," I murmured into the wind. "Go to Black."

I yanked those structures into the precise order I needed—

—and again, everything around me disappeared.

12

NOTHING IS EVER EASY

I must have been in a strange position when I reemerged.

Then again, I'd never jumped from a free-fall through space, in an attempt to land back on solid ground.

Really, I was damned lucky I didn't land with my foot embedded in the asphalt road of the studio's backlot... or broken in half from smashing too hard into the curb.

As it was, I popped back into existence maybe a half-inch above the pavement, and still in the position I'd been in while falling.

I landed hard, my body's weight and the odd position of my limbs throwing me from the bottom of one bare foot and the top of another, so that I sprawled face-down onto the pavement, letting out a cry when I landed on my palms, then forearms, and knees.

"Goddamn it."

A voice exploded in relief and fury over me.

He was down on the ground with me then, crouched next to me.

Then, wrapping an arm around my waist, he picked me up, doing it with surprising gentleness and care, despite the rage expanding off him.

He tried setting me equally carefully on my feet, but when he started to let go of me, I sucked in a breath, grabbing onto his arm when my full weight landed on my foot, putting pressure on my ankle.

I was still leaning on him, gasping, when I heard footsteps pounding in our direction, a yelp and a gasp from a voice I knew as well as my own.

"MIRI!" Angel cried out. "Miri, are you okay?"

Black's light practically smothered me by then.

I fell into it with a gratitude that briefly brought tears to my eyes.

Realizing at least part of that was from having been separated from him for the past few weeks, I gripped him more tightly, letting go of his arm to wrap myself around his waist.

He opened his arms to accommodate me.

Then he just held me.

I felt his relief expand over me, too.

Cowboy and Angel must have just stood there.

Then Black nodded to one of them—probably Cowboy—and muttered something that had the word "clothes" in it somewhere.

I heard Cowboy say, "Ayuh," right before he ran off.

He was likely relieved.

I knew Cowboy still wasn't overly comfortable with the boss's wife being stark naked, even if he knew the reason for it, and the fact that it couldn't be helped.

"Where?" Angel said then, breathless. "Where did you take him, doc?"

Still holding on to Black, I turned slightly so I could look at her, my cheek and the side of my head still leaning against the thin, black T-shirt he wore.

"I don't know what it's called," I told her, shaking my head. "One of the other places I've been. One of the more primitive ones... although..." I frowned, thinking. "I seem to remember they had some pretty nasty, dinosaur-like creatures. Including in the ocean. So if he survived the fall, he could end up eaten by something with a lot of teeth."

Realizing I might have actually murdered him, I felt my jaw harden.

I looked up at Black, then back over my shoulder at Angel.

"I dropped him," I explained. "I aimed for the sky... and when we got there, we were falling. I let him go. Then I jumped back here."

I fell silent when Cowboy ran back up to us, panting now, and holding out a robe.

I noticed he didn't look at me at all as he handed it over vaguely, in a way that made it difficult to know if he was trying to hand it to me, or to Black, or to both of us at the same time. Either way, I wasn't willing to let go of Black just yet, so Black ended up being the one to take it from Cowboy's outstretched hand.

He wrapped the terrycloth covering around my back, and I let go of him with each arm, one by one, but only long enough to shove my hands and arms through the sleeves, and then tie the belt around the front to keep it closed.

Sighing in relief, I sank into Black again.

I knew it probably looked weird.

I didn't care.

For Black's part, he wrapped a hand into my hair, and his other arm around my back, gripping my shoulder. He pulled me into him even more tightly, then turned to Angel and Cowboy.

"Get every piece of footage you can," Black growled. "Anything. Any angle. Anyone who got eyes on that fucker... and most of all, how he got here. Tell the seers they need to start dealing with witnesses. Anyone who got a good view of what happened. Read them for any details, then erase whatever they can... especially in relation to there being a *second* dragon down here, one who came through a fucking portal."

Pausing, still thinking, he added,

"Actually, come to think of it, have at least one of them come in here. Zairei would be best, but I don't really care who... it's probably more realistic to have them erase any memories they find of people who saw me on the ground at the same time that other dragon *fuck* was in the air. We'll tell everyone the other dragon was me. It'll still make the press lose their minds, but we can at least do damage control on the worst of it."

I felt him shaking as he spoke, and not wholly from anger.

It wasn't wholly *not*-anger, either.

Anger. Adrenaline. Anxiety.

Fear.

Shock.

Relief mixed with terror around how close we'd come to a true disaster.

Just sheer reaction around the reality of it all.

It hit me a second later that he was Black again.

Not Coreq... Black.

I didn't hear an ounce of Coreq in his voice. I didn't feel the smallest whisper of the alien, not-Black presence in Black's light.

I gripped him tighter when the thought reached me, snuggling into his body.

I wanted to get him out of there.

I still didn't feel safe, and the irrational, animal-instinct part of me just wanted to wrap my arms around him under the shirt and take him... away. Somewhere better.

Somewhere that wasn't here.

I was about to tell him as much, when a booming sound echoed across the sky.

All of us looked up.

For the first time, I stepped out of Black's arms. Moving a few feet backwards, away from Black, I stared up at the sky with the rest of them.

A hole had ripped through the sky.

What I'd scarcely glimpsed in that monitor in London, I now saw in technicolor detail, almost directly overhead. I saw the ring of light I'd heard the commentators describe. I glimpsed a black sky through the opening, a patterning of stars I only halfway recognized.

Then, the biggest damned dragon I'd ever seen in my life flew through that opening.

The creature beat massive, vein-covered wings, larger than any airplane's—its body an ugly, corpse-like gray-white, with bumpy, rock-like skin, a lumpy, scarred nose, muzzle, and throat, bulging, pale gold eyes.

This new dragon couldn't have been more different than Black's if it had been designed that way purposefully.

Like before, I didn't think.

I took one look at that bulging, diseased-looking monstrosity with the massive jaws and teeth and turned to Angel and Cowboy, clicking my fingers at them, even as I grabbed hold of Black's bare wrist below the end of his leather jacket.

When Angel and Cowboy got close enough I held out my bare arm.

"Grab hold!" I snapped. "Right now!"

"Miri!" Black said. "We can't! We can't just leave everyone here!"

"He's after us," I shot back. "He's after *us*, Black. We need to get out of here—"

"I can slow him down," Black growled.

"No. FUCK no. We're going. Now. We need the construct."

I wasn't asking him.

I wasn't even really warning him.

I definitely wasn't opening things up for some kind of discussion.

I was already gearing into the jump structures in my *aleimi*.

Angel and Cowboy both reached for my free arm, which I'd tilted upright so the robe sleeve fell down to my elbow. The instant I could feel Angel and Cowboy gripping hold of me, the instant I was *sure* both held me tightly enough, I reinforced my grip on Black...

"Miriam! Doc!"

...and winked all four of us out of Los Angeles.

13

EMOTIONALLY TWELVE

Nick scowled, staring at his boyfriend through the laptop
monitor.

"Why are you calling me from there? Do you have a death
wish?"

Grunting, thinking about his own words, he muttered,

"Or are you just sick of me? Maybe you're hoping for a nice,
traditional, vampire-killing mob armed with torches to set
Angel's place on fire?"

"You're such a drama queen," Dalajem remarked affec-
tionately.

Nick barely heard him.

He scanned the entirety of the view through the rectangular
screen, unable to help himself. He'd already identified the area of
Black's offices where Dalejem sat, inside the bullpen just outside
the main conference room. Realizing anyone else in the room
could likely hear his voice, or see him if they ambled by, he felt
another whisper of nerves.

Dalejem had his back to the main doors into the front office,
for fuck's sake.

Anyone could walk through there.

Anyone.

The front lobby area of Black's company offices had always reminded Nick of the prow of a ship. The space had a triangular, prow-like shape, tall metal doors, and two burnished copper pipes as handles on those doors leading to reception.

The private elevator, which still served as the only way onto the penthouse floor, had been beefed up quite a bit in security since the first time Nick came up here, back when he'd been investigating Black as a possible murder suspect.

Despite that, the front offices remained open, and more or less accessible if you had an appointment, or made it through the elevator protocols some other way.

The only time that wasn't true was during some kind of security lockdown.

Then again, in the last few years, security lockdowns weren't exactly an uncommon occurrence.

"Just come home," Nick said, gruff. "Unless they still need you there. Yarli's got plenty of other seers who can do Barrier jumps, for fuck's sake—"

Jem was already shaking his head, his voice incredulous.

"Have you not been watching the news at all, Nick?"

Nick frowned.

Watching the news?

Why the fuck would he be watching the news?

What was Jem talking about?

"No," he said, blunt. "And I don't want to know." Pausing, he added, "We're supposed to do dinner at my parents' house tonight. Did you forget?"

"Nick, for fuck's sake... look at the news. Then tell me if you still think tonight is really the best night for me to meet your father and mother for the first time, and inform them that you're no longer human..."

Nick scowled.

He hadn't just said it; he really didn't want to know.

"Is it vampire-related?" he said, gruff. Thinking about that, he frowned. "Is it Brick related? Or something to do with what happened to Dorian?"

"What 'happened' to Dorian?" Dalejem grunted an unamused laugh. "Interesting euphemism, Nick. Do you mean when I shot three explosive arrows into your vampire lover's chest and blew him up all over your friend Angel's foyer?"

Nick scowled again, but didn't respond to that, not directly.

"Fine." He exhaled in frustration. "What is it? Is it the London thing? Because I thought Miri's whole meeting with the EU bigwigs was supposed to be super hush-hush. Did Regent get pissed off at being uninvited and leak it?"

Dalejem stared at him.

He blinked, once, then shook his head again.

"No," he said, that incredulity sharpening. "Nick, look at the news. Look at the breaking news in *Los Angeles*. Trust me, you're not going to be able to guess what this is. And frankly, I have no idea where I'd even begin in *explaining* what's occurred today. Look at the news. Drink some blood. Then get back to me when—"

Behind him, there was an odd whoosh sound.

Dalejem turned his head.

Nick followed his boyfriend's stare.

Four, totally nude people appeared in the middle of the bullpen.

They just *appeared...* with little or no fanfare, standing in the open area of the lobby not far from the massive reception desk made of black marble.

Nick somehow missed seeing Lizbeth, Black's executive assistant, sitting behind that same desk.

When the four people appeared, however, she let out an ear-piercing shriek.

The shriek, more than the four nude people, made Nick just about jump out of his vampire skin.

The fifty-something woman—or possibly sixty-something,

Nick had never really gotten a handle on Lizbeth's exact age—with her fluffy blond-white hair and a gold cross around her neck, let out a second terrified shriek after the first, standing up too fast from her seat and half-falling into the back counter behind the desk.

The stack of papers she'd been doing something with all ended up on the floor.

Honestly, it might have been darkly funny, in different circumstances.

As it was, seeing Black, Miri, Cowboy, and Angel all standing there, looking shell-shocked, sweaty, panting... and very, very nude... Nick felt a thrill of panic of his own.

Seeing Black suddenly staring at him, seeing his face on Dale-jem's monitor, Nick didn't think. He didn't even wait to see what look would come to the seer's face.

Reaching over to the top of the laptop screen, he brought it down with a sharp snap.

Fuck.

It looked like dinner was probably out.

B lack's words exploded out of him.
       I leapt back in pure reflex, totally broadsided when my husband's voice rose to a near shout. I was still panting, fighting back the panic that brought us here.

I was still fighting against that feeling of having been punched, wincing as I rubbed my chest, fighting to slow my heart rate. It took me another second to take in a terrified-looking Lizbeth staring at the four of us. It took me a few more to look at Black, to see the direction of his furious stare, to follow that stare back to where Dalejem sat at one of the bullpen desks, an open laptop on the etched glass in front of him.

Then Black was moving away from me.

He moved so fast, I let go of his wrist in reflex, remembering only then I still held it.

Cowboy and Angel let go of my arm in the same instant.

"Was that him?" Black shouted the words a second time. "Really, Jem? That's the first damned thing I have to see? Right now? What the fuck are you doing here, anyway?"

Aleimic light infused his voice.

The sheer power behind it made the glass walls tremble; it felt strong enough I wondered fleetingly if he'd caused a mild earthquake.

Black's voice boomed out again.

"SPEAK!" he bellowed. "What are you doing here, Jem? Why are you here?"

His words caused another semi-instinctive fear reaction in the rest of us.

I winced, putting my hands over my ears as Cowboy and Angel took a step back, retreating towards where Lizbeth huddled by the cabinet behind reception.

The glass walls seemed to shake again when Black stalked directly up to where Jem rose gracefully to his feet.

"Calm down," Dalejem said.

He held up a hand, as though calming a horse.

"FUCK YOU."

"*Di'lanlente a' guete...* Black. You are clearly in shock." Dalejem's voice came out more accented than usual. Clearly, the seer was upset, but he also sounded frustrated. "This is not the time to discuss—"

"Then maybe don't talk to him on MY FUCKING EQUIP-MENT," Black snarled.

"Black!" Something about Jem's words snapped me out of my own slack-jawed staring. "Black, he's right! For fuck's sake... why are you *screaming* at him? You know damned well why he's here, and now isn't the time to hash out your issues around Nick. All of us are WAY too wound up to have that conversation..."

Black didn't even look at me.

I might as well not have spoken.

By the time I finished, Black had reached Jem.

He stood in front of him, stark naked, his black hair still strangely perfect-looking. I knew they'd coiffed it and sprayed it and hell, maybe shellacked it, for his interview with Grant Steele, but it looked totally bizarre to me now, especially with the rest of us panting, and me with my twisted ankle, windblown hair, and sweaty neck, chest, back, and face.

Everything else Black had worn at the studio was gone, of course.

His semi-organic head set, expensive work shirt, armored pants, his favorite leather jacket... his wallet, keys, hotel key-card, boots...

All of it was gone.

Dalejem—who was maybe the only seer in the place who had some height on Black, even if it was only an inch or so— straightened to that full height. He stood in front of my naked husband, staring down at him from that added inch, and folded his arms, maybe to force some space between the two of them.

I bit my lip, watching them look at one another.

The air between them vibrated.

Even without using my seer's sight, I could almost see it with my eyes.

It hit me... really *hit* me... that Black hadn't seen Jem since Jem and Nick got back to the United States. Black had thought Jem was dead for months.

Like the rest of us, he'd assumed Nick killed him.

Or that Solonik killed both of them.

Whatever exact story he told himself about the *how* of it, Black one hundred percent believed Jem to be dead.

I knew that, because he tried to convince me of the same. He told me there was no way Jem wouldn't have contacted them in all of that time, not unless he was dead. Black said Jem would have called... at least *once*... if only to let them know he was okay.

Jem hadn't called.

Ergo, Jem was dead.

Black told me I had to accept that Nick most likely killed him.

Now, looking at my husband's face, I realized he was dealing with the shock of seeing Dalejem alive at all, even apart from everything that happened that day.

Now Black stood in front of his friend, chest heaving, staring at him like he was a ghost.

I looked at Jem, and saw emotion in his face, as well.

Jem's emotion was maybe more honest... or possibly more self-aware. Dalejem looked at Black like he was genuinely happy to see him. His eyes brightened as I watched, and I realized he was crying when I saw him wipe his face with the side of one hand.

"Brother—" Dalejem began, his voice thick.

But just then, Black moved.

He moved so fast, I couldn't even yell at him not to do it.

He wound up his right arm and punched Jem right in the face.

☙❧

"What the fuck is wrong with you?" I scowled up at Black, dabbing the swollen part of Jem's cheek with a cold rag.

Angel had walked out the agency's front door to find us clothes.

Cowboy went with her to help, muttering about getting ice to keep Dalejem's face from swelling out a few more inches.

I suspect both of them left *mostly* just to get away from the three of us.

At the very least, they did it to get away from me and Black.

Black hit Dalejem pretty much at full strength.

"Seriously." My scowl deepened. I fought between rage and a kind of semi-amused disbelief. "Do you have no self-control at all? I swear, emotionally I think you're about twelve years old sometimes, Quentin..."

Dalejem erupted in a low laugh.

The laugh didn't contain a lot of humor. Instead the sound came out in a short burst, like he couldn't help himself.

He was still staring warily at Black, like he half-expected Black to hit him again.

Thinking about all of it, remembering seeing Black punch Jem in the face, knowing it was coming by then but being powerless to stop it, I glared back over my shoulder at my husband's handsome face.

"I mean it. What the hell is wrong with you?"

Black frowned, his arms folded.

He didn't really look at either of us.

I could feel on him that he was embarrassed at what he'd done, but he clearly wasn't ready to admit that, much less to apologize.

Instead, he addressed his words to Jem.

"Are you still working on it?" he growled. "Or are you too pissed at me?"

Jem gave him a look. "I am working on it, brother."

"Are you making progress?"

Again, that cold stare. "Yes."

Black touched his ear, barking into his headset as he turned away.

He didn't quite pace the floor of the bullpen, but he walked away a few steps, still naked apart from the headset, which Lizbeth handed over to him, all while covering her eyes with a hand and scolding him for nearly giving her a heart attack.

"Well?" Black growled into the headset. "Sister? How does it look? Can he track us here? Should we be thinking about leaving? Because I need to make some calls. Normal, business, human calls. That thing in L.A. is blowing up, and we have to tell the media *something*. I can't do that until I know if we're going to have to leave here in a hurry first..."

He trailed, obviously listening to whatever Yarli was saying.

I hadn't bothered to find a headset for myself yet.

More than anything, I wanted a shower.

"Yeah," Jem said, his voice quiet as he looked at my hair with a frown. "What happened to you? You look like you were fighting sixteen angry cats in a wind tunnel..."

I laughed at that for real, earning a cold glare from Black.

He was still walking the row of desks, naked, growling at Yarli over the headset.

"Don't worry about that," he was saying now. "I'll put Farraday on that. If you want to help on that front, get someone to look in on Mika, Jax, Kiko. Find out what they're doing to stabilize the situation over there."

Hearing his words, I was forced to think about them.

My jaw gradually clenched as I did.

Black was right. This was going to be a damned mess.

We needed to deal with this dragon asshole, and fast.

If we didn't, literally everything we'd been trying to do to calm down the humans and set up some basis for species-to-species harmony and compromise would get flushed down the toilet in a hurry.

We couldn't just hide out behind a construct indefinitely.

This had to be a serious regrouping time, but a brief one.

Then we needed to go out and deal with that jackass, whoever he was.

When I looked up that time, Black was staring at me.

I saw agreement in his eyes, and for the first time, what might have been an apology.

"Ah," Jem retorted. "I see. Your *wife* gets an apology. I didn't realize how you punching *me* in the face necessitated an apology to your wife, or implied that in some way *she* is the true victim here."

He winked at me, even as he aimed his scowl at Black.

"Clearly, it is your *wife* who was harmed in this exchange... from sheer embarrassment at her spouse's inability to behave like a civilized, adult person, one presumes..."

I grunted a laugh of my own, earning another glare from Black.

I heard the tension in my laugh, though, nerves mixed with genuine humor.

I couldn't help but be grateful Jem was being such a good sport.

"Only because he doesn't want me to kill his boyfriend..." Black muttered darkly, glaring at the two of us again. "And could you not hang over him like that?" he growled in more of a regular voice. "I know you two are friends, and he prefers blood-sucking rapists in his bed, but you're starting to try my toler-ance, wife."

Dalejem rolled his eyes, folding his arms, even as I straightened.

"You're a child," Jem informed him.

"Yeah? You think so?" Black glowered at him. "Maybe when she does that to Nick, stark naked, and you just look on with that condescending smile on your goddamned face... then you can tell me what a *child* I am, brother."

Jem's eyes flashed with genuine coldness at that.

Black grunted a laugh that contained zero humor.

"My point exactly."

Dalejem opened his mouth, but before he could speak, Cowboy pushed through the front doors by reception, gripping a heavy-looking duffle bag by the handles.

Behind him, Angel carried what looked like bathrobes, along with about a pound of ice in a Ziploc bag.

Cowboy nodded at Lizbeth as he passed, now that he was wearing clothes, and brought the duffle over to plunk down on a nearby desk.

I heard metal hit the glass tabletop, and realized they hadn't brought clothes.

Cowboy gave me a look.

"Ayuh," he said, shrugging a little, apologetic. "We brought guns, not a lot of clothes. Ange's got some robes for you and the boss... none of my clothes're gonna fit 'em, anyway. Ange thought you might want a shower or something, anyway."

Angel handed Jem the bag of ice, which he promptly put to his face.

She handed me a robe next.

I shouldered it on, chuckling a little as I saw her hold out a second robe to Black, her face turned deliberately away.

She shook it when he didn't notice at first.

"Quentin? Are you going to cover that thing of yours? Or not?"

Black grunted, but walked back to take the robe, quirking an eyebrow at me as he stuck his arm into the first sleeve, then the second, tying it in front.

Like Cowboy, Angel also came back clothed, wearing a pair of jeans and a white T-shirt.

Her braids were also wet, I realized; she looked like she'd taken a shower.

"Just a quick rinse-off with soap," she informed me, obviously seeing me looking at her hair. "Cowboy and me both. I couldn't bear to put clean clothes on without rinsing off."

"I get it," I said, holding up my hands. "Not judging, believe me."

She motioned towards the back-end of the offices, where there were men's and women's locker rooms and showers for Black's employees.

"You should do the same, doc."

I followed her pointing fingers with my eyes.

Thinking about her words, I realized she was right.

I did want a shower.

But it made a lot more sense to just go to the penthouse.

Jem, who clearly hadn't finished with Black, looked up past the bag of ice to the now robed dragon-seer.

"You know, I was supposed to go to a dinner tonight," he grumbled in accented English. "Now I suppose I'll be going with a black eye."

"...Black eye suddenly striking me as a sort of ironical term," Cowboy muttered, even as he unzipped the duffle bag, pulling out a holster and his two, pearl-handled guns.

I looked at Cowboy, blinked.

Then I looked at Angel.

Both of us burst out in uncontrolled laughter.

14

A SHOWER AND PIE

"Y ou didn't tell Dex." I frowned at him, my hands on my hips. "How the hell did you *not* tell Dex? Isn't he one of your best friends? What were you thinking, leaving that so long?"

He glared up at me, his gold irises flashing from the overhead lights.

"Did you tell Kiko?" he growled.

I opened my mouth.

Then I closed it.

Frowning at him, I sat down heavily on the white leather couch of our living room, combing a hand through my wet hair, which had already created a huge wet spot on the back and shoulders of the light-blue T-shirt I'd thrown on, over a lace bra and dark-blue jean leggings.

Between the shower and the clothes, I felt almost like myself again.

I also couldn't help but feel an enormous relief at being home.

"I told Jax," I mumbled.

"You what?"

"You heard me," I said, folding my arms and blowing my

bangs out of my face. "I told Jax. Well... Jax heard me thinking, and then I told him."

"So you're letting *Jax* tell Kiko?" Black frowned. "Really, doc? I thought you were supposed to be trained in this shit?"

"I was planning to tell her. Tonight, if you must know. We were going to go out for dinner and drinks at a place she likes in London, just the two of us."

Realizing he was right, that I'd chickened out as much as he had, I sighed again, frowning as I stared out through the enormous bay windows.

"God, I'm starving." I exhaled in a sigh. "I could really use a beer, too."

There was a silence.

Then Black sighed with me.

He'd showered and dressed right after I did, and wore more or less what he'd worn in Los Angeles, but somehow looked a lot more "normal" wearing it here, inside his own home.

Maybe it was the fact of us both being back in San Francisco, or both being together... or just the fact that he'd washed all of the product out of his hair and looked less "on" than he had in Hollywood... but he looked more like quintessential Black to me again.

Which meant I really wanted to order a ton of food, lock the penthouse door, and more or less curl up on his lap.

When I glanced up at him next, his expression had softened.

"Should we try to tell them en route?" he said, gruff. "Kiko and Dex. We shouldn't broadside them... and we can't keep it from them for long once they get back here."

I nodded, not so much in a yes, but more because I was thinking about his words.

He was right.

We couldn't keep it from them any longer.

If we waited until they got here, we risked a number of bigger problems.

I hated the idea of doing it over a video call, though.

"We're okay now," Black said, before I'd finished thinking it through. "There're still mapping the cords between me and you and that asshole in Los Angeles... but he doesn't seem able to locate us here behind the construct."

He paused, as if waiting for my reaction.

When I said nothing, he added,

"They lost him. He flew off, over the ocean... then disappeared, if you can believe that. They don't know if he went into the water, like I did, or transformed back into a regular seer, got on a boat... or flew to Guam under the radar... or left this dimension altogether."

"What about the robot?" I said, still staring out the window. "There was a robot. Right? Wasn't Zairei tracking that?"

"There was," he affirmed. "And he was."

"What happened to it? Are we still following it?"

"It disappeared." Pausing, maybe waiting for a reaction from me, he went on when I didn't give him one. "We have to assume whoever is controlling those things has a way to shut them down so we can't track their signals. I've got people looking on the docks, where it was last spotted, in case they just shut it down and hid it somewhere."

I thought about that, frowning.

Then I turned, still frowning, to study his gold eyes.

"Why send it after you at all? If they're afraid of dragons, I mean. Why not just send it after me? Or hell, send it here... have it take out our home base?"

Black studied my eyes.

I saw his gaze flicker over the rest of me, right before he cleared his throat.

"I don't know," he said frankly.

He shrugged, seer-fashion, gesturing fluidly with one hand.

"Maybe to provoke me into turning into a dragon? Or maybe in the hopes I *wouldn't* turn, not while surrounded by media and a studio audience. Maybe it was always meant to be a distraction... to be pulled back as soon as we noticed it there. Dunno."

Black shrugged again, his eyes and voice flat.

"Until we know who's sending the damned things, there's no way to know for sure what they're trying to do."

I nodded, turning to stare out the window again.

Again, he paused.

Again, he seemed to be waiting for me to speak.

When I didn't, he cleared his throat.

"Either way, the good news is, the shield seems to be holding," he said. "Yarli, Mika, Jem, and Jax all agree nothing's getting through... and they've tested it from various places, including from the air. They said we shouldn't even need to stay in the construct all the time. Yarli's getting better with the mobile constructs, and says if we don't wander too far, or for too long, we should be okay. She's currently got a field around you, me, Angel, Cowboy, Dex, Kiko. Pretty much everyone who was on our two teams in London and Los Angeles."

Pausing, he added,

"She'd let all of that shit go dormant after Charles' people were neutralized... mostly to give us all privacy, since the construct means all the seers are more or less connected. Which means our minds are connected, too."

He added, his voice darker,

"...Needless to say, she's fixed that problem. So you might want to keep that in mind when you're chewing me out for being a bastard. We're likely to be overheard. Including when we're *not* arguing. Including just when we're just thinking impure thoughts..."

I nodded, but only half-heard him.

I heard the faint innuendo there too, but didn't react.

We still had over a week before the wedding, so part of that was me not wanting to go there, even as a joke. I was in enough separation pain as it was.

I was still thinking about Kiko.

I was still kicking myself for not talking to Kiko.

Exhaling, I looked up at him.

"Should we ask Jax to do it, really?" When Black frowned, I clarified. "Kiko. Should we ask Jax to talk to Kiko. At least he's there. He'll be gentle with her."

Black grunted.

He probably grunted at me saying Jax would be gentle with Kiko. It was one of the team's biggest non-secrets that Jax was in love with Black's second.

"Or we could all do it," I said, still thinking out loud. "We could ask him to sit in on the conversation, so she'd have someone there... with her, I mean."

That time, Black was the one who fell silent.

I watched him stare out the same window I had.

Pain flickered across his expression, right before he raised a hand, rubbing his face and jaw.

"I don't know."

"Neither of us know," I pointed out. "No one knows. But what do you *think* we should do, Black? You know her better than anyone. What will be the least horrible for her?"

"Me killing him. Me giving her Nick's head... gift wrapped."

My jaw tightened. "Besides that."

"Me giving her his head *not* gift-wrapped."

"Black. Can we be serious for one second—"

He turned, his voice a denser growl. "What makes you think I'm not being fucking serious right now, Miriam?"

I stared at him.

Then I frowned.

That time, the silence between us felt hostile.

"So that's it?" I said. "We're back to this?"

The silence between us deepened more.

Then Black leaned back, exhaling in frustration.

Throwing an arm over the back of the couch, he stared out the window at the San Francisco Bay, and the Bay Bridge in the distance. I watched as different emotions skated over the surface of his eyes, there and gone too quickly for me to pin most of it down.

After what must have been a few minutes of that, he exhaled again.

Reaching up, he rubbed his face, using the hand not thrown over the back of the couch. I felt a sharper, harder ripple of frustration and grief go through his light.

"*Gaos.* I hate this." Still with his face covered with his hand, he asked, "Can't I just kill him? It would be so much easier."

I might have frowned, but for the first time, I could tell he didn't mean it.

Maybe for the same reason, I smiled.

"No," I said, shoving at his arm. "Would you really do that to my dog? You'd traumatize Panther for life. He thinks Nick is his mommy."

"What if he's eaten your dog by now?" Black muttered. "Can I kill him then?"

I leaned my head on the back cushion of his couch.

After a beat of staring up at his ceiling, I closed my eyes. I adjusted my back.

When he nudged me with a hand, I exhaled again.

"Sure, Black," I said, my eyes still closed. "If Nick eats my dog, you can kill him."

"Is he really the same?"

I opened my eyes.

Warily, I raised my head, and met his gaze.

His gold irises studied mine.

"As before," he prodded. "Is Nick really the same as he was before he got turned?"

"You mean besides the weird eyes? And the blood drinking?"

"Besides those things."

I heard a faint warning in his voice.

Reaching out, I caught hold of his arm.

I tugged on it, but more as a means of bringing myself closer to him, not the reverse. Pulling myself across the leather couch, using his arm as a rope, I ended up curled up against him. I leaned my head on his chest, and sighed, my hand on his thigh.

"He's the same," I told him, listening to his heart through the thin shirt he wore. "It was the weirdest thing, Black. I walked up to him and hugged him in Russia... after everything. After all that he did to me, to Kiko. He looked positively *terrified* of me. He looked at me like he fully expected me to kill him, and he'd come to peace with it."

Thinking about that, remembering my shock when I realized it was Nick, I grunted.

"I was so happy he was alive. It was like he'd risen from the dead."

Still thinking, I added,

"I could feel it. He's a vampire, so I couldn't read it off him or anything, but I could still *feel* he was Nick again... somehow. I think he might have passed out if he'd been human, when I walked up and hugged him like that. He wouldn't even meet my eyes at first. Dalejem told me he was suicidal, that he probably still needed vampire therapy or whatever. I know it's a cliché, Black, but he hates himself. He really *hates* himself for what he did. I think if Dalejem hadn't been there, watching him like a hawk, he definitely would have killed himself."

My mouth firmed as I added,

"I know you're probably not ready. I know Dex and Kiko definitely aren't ready. But he's really gone, Black. That other... Nick... Brick's 'Naoko'... the vampire who did those things to me and Kiko... that *thing* he'd been. It's gone. It's just not there anymore."

There was a silence.

Black raised his hand to my hair, and began stroking through it, combing the long, damp strands with his fingers.

I could feel him thinking.

Even so, he shielded the actual contents of his thoughts from me.

"You know while you were in the shower, that fucker had the audacity to invite us to dinner?"

I raised my head, staring at him.

Then I realized what he meant.

"*Dalejem?*" I said, incredulous.

Black just held my gaze, but I could see the answer all over him.

Even so, some part of me just couldn't believe it.

"*Dalejem* invited us to dinner?" I asked again. "With him and Nick?"

"And Cowboy and Angel." Black held my gaze, voice flat. "And Nick's parents. At the house on Potrero Hill."

I blinked.

Then I stared at him again, still sure he must be joking.

As I held his gaze, I realized he wasn't.

◈

We decided to talk to Kiko and Dex right after the dinner.

Yes, as crazy as it was, we'd decided to accept Jem's invitation.

Black wanted to see Nick for himself.

He claimed he'd have a better idea what to say to Kiko and Dex if he'd witnessed Nick firsthand, and could see for himself what I'd described.

Black argued, significantly more sourly, that he could hardly be convincing, in regards to describing Nick's "miraculous transformation" (his air quotes, not mine) if he didn't really believe it himself.

Luckily, we had a slight breather with Dex.

Dex had been the bigger worry initially, since Los Angeles was only an hour away by plane.

But Dex wasn't coming straight to San Francisco; he'd decided to go to New Mexico, instead. Frank Blackfoot called from the White Eagle Resort, asking for back-up to deal with security arrangements, and Dex volunteered.

We knew it was at least partly because he was pissed off at all of us. Even so, it was a relief, honestly.

It definitely didn't get us off the hook, but it bought us some time.

As for the dinner, Black wasn't exactly inspiring confidence that everything would go smoothly. He already seemed to be gearing up for a fight. For starters, he openly accused Nick of choosing the time and place for calculated, manipulative reasons.

And sure, he likely wasn't *entirely* wrong, although I suspected Dalejem had more to do with those calculations than Nick himself did.

The dinner was obviously meant to be neutral ground.

According to Black, that was the exact and *only* reason we got the invite.

Nick knew damned well Black wouldn't kill him in front of Yumi and Hiroto Tanaka.

Black wouldn't threaten him, either, or beat the shit out of him, not in front of two people who'd been so kind to both of us, and who'd more or less acted as my adopted parents after my own parents and sister died.

Which meant Black would be more likely to hear whatever it was Nick had to say, whether it was "a shitload of excuses and bullshit" (again, his words, not mine), or some kind of half-assed apology (also his words).

Despite his editorializing, and his assumptions about Nick's motives, which I wasn't altogether convinced of myself, I believed Black that he intended to accept the temporary truce, and view the dinner as a peace offering.

Black, to me at least, seemed willing to accept the neutral ground, if only as an opportunity to observe Nick for himself.

Of course, he told me bluntly that if he got any hint Nick wasn't who I thought he was, that he posed any kind of danger to me at all, or to Kiko, or to anyone else he loved, Black would kill him without a second's thought.

I knew he meant it.

Black one hundred percent believed he was telling me the unvarnished truth.

I honestly had my doubts he could do it as easily as he said, however, even now.

Still, it was like the fourth time he'd threatened it.

The repeated threats made me nervous.

Some part of me wanted to call ahead, warn Nick to be especially careful not to do or say anything—even as a joke—that might make Black want to murder him.

I figured that wouldn't exactly help things stay friendly, though.

Instead, I climbed out of Black's car.

I walked up to the gate leading into the Tanakas' garden, and the path that went up to the front door. As I did, I found myself thinking about Nick's parents. I wondered how they'd taken it, when Nick told them what he was now.

I wondered how they'd taken it, even just *seeing* Nick.

In a more gossipy, me, Nick, and Angel from the old days way, I also wondered how they'd taken it when he told them about Dalejem.

Thinking about all that, about how *much* it all was, I realized I shouldn't assume Nick *had* told them about Jem. Given the other revelations he'd been forced to lay on them, it struck me as likely Nick would have skipped the Jem thing... for now, at least.

Of all the things that could wait, the Jem thing struck me as the most obvious.

Nick could only disguise his appearance so much.

He could only disguise his race so much.

It wasn't even just that he'd reverse-aged by at least twenty years.

Or that his eyes were a different color.

Or that he was deathly pale, and more beautiful than he'd ever been as a human man.

Nick *moved* differently now.

He interacted with his body, with his environment, in entirely different ways.

On the plus side, his bum knee no longer bothered him.

Neither did the shoulder he'd screwed up from a surfing accident in his twenties.

I glanced at Black, who must have given himself an extra few seconds in the car.

I watched him climb out of the black and white McLaren now, straightening to his full height after pushing the button to lower the gull-style door back to the car's frame.

I wondered why he'd brought this particular car, then dismissed that, too.

I was stalling.

Both of us were stalling.

Standing by the gate leading up to the Tanaka residence, holding a bakery-bought pie in one hand—rhubarb, Nick's mother's favorite—with an expensive bottle of red wine under my arm, I felt totally bizarre suddenly.

Were we really going to do this?

Were we really going to play normal with Nick the Vampire and his four-hundred-year-old seer boyfriend in front of Yumi and Hiroto Tanaka?

"Yes," Black murmured, reaching my side. "We are."

Leaning down, he kissed my temple as he lightly touched my back. His eyes never left the Tanakas' front door, and suddenly, it struck me as too quiet. Not just here, outside their house, but the whole neighborhood.

Black was opening the gate then, the hinges squeaking in the early evening air.

I followed him without a word.

My heart hammered in my chest, loud enough, I realized Nick would probably hear it once we got inside.

I was terrified.

I didn't even know why exactly, but I was terrified to see Yumi Tanaka open that door.

15

ANOTHER WORLD

"Miriam!"

I nearly had forgotten how angry Yumi Tanaka had been with me, the last time I'd seen her. It hadn't even crossed my mind until I found myself face to face with her, the two of us less than a yard apart, and I felt a faint flicker of guilt off her light.

She tried to keep it off her face, beaming at me as soon as she opened the door.

Before I could make sense of either thing, she was already leaving the doorway, meeting us halfway between the door and the porch steps. She moved before I could wrap my mind around anything I could see in her smiling face, or the brightness of her eyes... and then her arms were around me as she enveloped me in a smothering, mom-like hug.

I couldn't help it.

I started crying.

Then, still gripping the wine bottle under one arm, balancing the pie box on my palm in the same hand, I hugged her back as strongly as I could with my free arm.

When we both let go, she laughed, and hugged me again.

A rush of love rose in me, overwhelming me briefly.

They'd been my second family.

Not just Nick, but the whole Tanaka family had taken me in after I left the military, becoming the only family I knew after my sister died.

They insisted I come to every holiday, every big family dinner, every silly birthday and anniversary party, every unveiling of a new family pet. I'd missed them too much to even let myself think about missing them, but now it all came rushing back, making it impossible for me to keep up my act of polite distance in coming here.

By the time I'd gotten past that first, overwhelming wave of emotion, Yumi was still hugging me around the shoulders, and already scolding Black.

"You make her carry everything? You are a worthless husband, just like I thought."

"Why would you even bother to sound surprised, Mrs. Tanaka?" Black retorted, rescuing the bottle of wine from under my arm, even as he muttered his answer. "If I wasn't useless, you'd only be disappointed anyway..."

"Yumi," she snapped. "Yumi, Yumi, Yumi. How many times do I have to tell you my name? Do you have Alzheimer's? Are you a drug addict, that you can't remember a simple thing like an old lady's name?"

Black burst out in a surprised laugh, like he couldn't help himself.

I saw Yumi give him a wry smile, and again, I felt a whisper of guilt on her.

I found myself wondering about that guilt.

I also wondered at how relieved she seemed to see not only me, but Black, too, who she'd always seemed to like in spite of herself, and despite her best efforts to dislike him as much as possible... probably out of some sense of loyalty to her son.

Not that Nick hated Black, per se—they'd been real friends over the past few years before he got turned into a vampire—but there'd been a time when the two of them disliked each other intensely, and Yumi probably got an earful about Black during that period.

Nick and his mother had always been close.

Knowing Nick, he told her a lot.

Maybe Yumi hadn't been able to forget all of those things, even after Nick grudgingly grew used to having Black in his life... and even grew to like him.

Then there was me.

For quite a few years, there was a not-subtle hope in Yumi Tanaka that I might become a member of the family on a more permanent, legal basis, and... probably more to the point... that I might give her little versions of her son as grandchildren.

Pushing all of that out of my mind, even as I fielded a harder look from Black, I followed Yumi into their house, glancing around for who else was there as we entered the foyer, then the living room.

It was an odd scene, to say the least.

Nick's father sat in his usual recliner, but the chair wasn't reclined.

He sat bolt upright, holding a whisky in one hand.

Cowboy and Angel sat on the long couch across from him, with a lot of space on one side, likely making room for me and Black.

On my left, and Angel's right, Nick and Dalejem sat on the matching love seat.

I flinched a little when I saw them.

Really, I flinched when I saw Nick.

Nick had never looked so utterly alien to me before, so wholly and completely different from how he'd been as a human, as he did on Hiroto and Yumi's flower-patterned love seat next to his seer boyfriend. A darker part of me might have found it funny, but when I saw Nick's face, it was impossible to laugh.

The first thing I noticed was the direction of his eyes.

He stared past me, at Black.

Like his father, he also sat too stiffly, too straight.

Unfortunately, both things—the staring and the weird sitting —made him appear even less like human Nick, and more like a vampire.

Trying to diffuse at least some of that, I instinctively turned to Nick's father.

Hiroto had already regained his feet, and gave me a hug.

"It is so lovely to see you, Miriam."

He smiled, and I was shocked to see his eyes bright, too. I hugged him back squeezing his arms. I opened my mouth, about to say something to him, when Dalejem's voice rose in my head.

They just found out. About two hours ago. Yumi's taking it better than Hiroto.

I turned, staring at Dalejem.

Which part? About the two of you?

Any of it. Dalejem's green eyes met mine, still as a windless pond. *He didn't tell them anything, Miriam. Not until about three hours before I got here... around one o'clock today. Nick told me Yumi about fainted when she saw him. He was afraid his father might have a stroke—*

Holy shit.

I didn't have any better words really.

I was still staring at Jem.

Gaping at him, really.

Why? I sent finally. *Why didn't he do it with you, at least?*

Dalejem lifted his hands subtly from where they rested on his thighs, a barely perceptible version of a seer's shrug.

But I thought he told them weeks ago... months...

No, Dalejem said only.

From the way his mind sounded, this news was relatively new to him, too.

Does he know about you? I asked next. *About us? Me and Black?*

We haven't talked about it yet. We haven't gotten that far.

Dalejem's mental voice turned grim.

Nick had to tell them most of what happened that led up to him becoming a vampire. The island. The fire in the forest. Brick taking him to Paris and the rest of us believing him to be dead. He omitted a lot of details, of course... but he gave them a high-level explanation of the newborn thing... a VERY high-level explanation, Dalejem added warningly. *He told them the newborn thing is why he's only telling them the truth about what happened to him now.*

Pausing, Dalejem added,

But they've been watching the news. They saw Black's press confer-ence. They know you're both claiming to be seers. They've likely guessed the same about me. They've been asking Nick about all of this for weeks, from what he's told me. They've especially been asking about you. I think that was the thing that finally convinced Nick to tell them the truth—

"Unbelievable," Black muttered from next to me.

I glanced at him.

I hadn't fully realized he was listening in until he spoke.

Now Black was looking at Dalejem, too.

His eyes returned to Nick a second later.

"You really are a dumbass," Black told Nick.

Only then did I realize I was still holding Nick's dad's arms. I released him, and Nick's father retreated to the kitchen, muttering about helping his wife.

"He's damned lucky he didn't kill both of them," Black muttered, much lower, glancing at Hiroto's back. "Fucking *idiot.*"

That time it was too low for Nick's dad to hear.

Nick was a vampire.

He one hundred percent heard that.

Even if I hadn't known vampires had insanely good hearing, I would have known it by the look that came to Nick's face.

That look was so utterly Nick, and so much like a look that would have come to his face before the change, I snorted a laugh.

When I looked at Black, though, he wasn't laughing.

He didn't look angry, either.

Instead, he stared at Nick, his eyes faintly wide.

For the first time, he looked like he'd seen a ghost.

Even as I thought it, Black removed his hand from the inside of his jacket.

I hadn't even noticed where it had been.

I'd been so busy taking in the weirdness that was this room, I hadn't noticed anything about Black at all. Now it hit me that he'd had his hand on his gun, probably from the second we walked through that door, probably the instant he handed off the pie and wine to Yumi.

Staring up at him incredulously, I was about to say something, when Yumi pushed through the swinging doors to the kitchen and beamed at all of us.

"Dinner's ready!" she announced cheerfully.

That time, however, I heard the full-blown strain behind her voice.

That's when I realized our true purpose here, at the Tanaka house.

We were here to keep Nick's parents from flipping the fuck out.

16

HOME

Mr. Tanaka had always been the relatively quiet one. Nick used to joke he was "too Japanese" to get mad at him like an American dad would.

Angel only rolled her eyes when Nick said it.

She told me she'd heard Mr. Tanaka yell *plenty* back when they'd been neighbors out on Hunter's Point, and Nick had been in high school.

She told me Nick and him used to butt heads all the time.

Angel's family had a running joke about hearing Nick's name yelled from next door in accented Japanese-English. She could still imitate Hiroto saying Nick's name, which cracked all of us up when she did it a few times at the North Precinct of the SFPD, back when they were both still homicide detectives.

Tonight, however, Hiroto Tanaka was quiet.

I noticed he didn't take his eyes off Nick.

He also didn't really stop frowning.

"Nick told us you thought he was dead," Yumi said, her voice still containing that false cheery note. "He said when you came to the house that day, you were really shocked to find out I'd been talking to you... that Naoko had been calling us."

I looked away from Mr. Tanaka, smiling at Yumi.

"Yes. That's true." I hesitated, not sure if I should apologize for that whole thing again, or if that would only make her feel worse.

Yumi looked embarrassed, and that guilt again made her wince.

"Mrs. Tanaka—" I began.

"Yumi," she insisted.

"There's no possible way you could have known what was happening."

She nodded, but her expression remained pinched.

She forced a smile as she handed the platter of roast beef to the right, sending it down the table. She continued to talk to me for some reason, maybe just because she'd already talked to Angel, since they'd gotten here earlier, or maybe because she saw me as familiar with this in a way Angel wasn't... which was kind of funny, since Nick had been living with Angel for a few months now.

Either way, Yumi smiled at me when she spoke next.

"He won't eat," she told me, her voice holding another thread of tension. "He says he's not hungry, but it's weird to have a son sit at my table... and not eat."

She glanced at Nick, and seemed to wince at how his face looked.

"He was like a bottomless pit before. He'd eat enough for three people."

Hiroto grunted.

I glanced at him, then back at Yumi.

I had no idea what to say. I felt like I was watching a group mental breakdown happen in real time, and it was my family, so my training felt useless.

A worried frown touched Nick's lips as he looked at Yumi. Seeing such a "Nick" expression on that perfect, inhumanly white face again made me wince.

When I looked at Dalejem, I saw him scowl at me.

It hit me that he may have misunderstood the wince.

I didn't, Jem growled in my mind. *I didn't misunderstand, Miri. But I wish you'd get used to this. You're making things harder on his parents, not easier.*

You're going to lay that on me? I sent back, incredulous. *How is this suddenly my responsibility? They're not my parents—*

It is your responsibility, Jem shot back. *And they are your fucking parents, from what Nick tells me... at least in part. Not to mention what happened in Koh Mangaan. You and Black were in charge. You're the ones who let Brick near him in the first place. Are you going to tell me... yet again... how this is all Nick's fault? You could at least try and make things a little more fucking normal for them, Miri—*

"Oh, for fuck's sake," Black broke in, glaring between both of us. "Do you honestly think you're making things *normal,* talking to one another in each other's heads? Making weird faces and glaring across the table at one another, so it's obvious something is going on that's leaving them out?"

There was a dead silence.

In it, Yumi gripped her fork in one hand.

Hiroto sat perfectly still at the end of the table, looking down at his plate.

Black exhaled in exasperation.

He looked at Yumi first.

"Your son is a vampire," he said, blunt. "He's not going to eat your cooking anymore, Yumi. It sucks, but it's the least of his problems, frankly."

Nick glared at him, his eyes showing disbelief.

Black scowled right back at him, leaning back in his chair.

Folding his muscular arms across his chest in the suit he wore, he glared at Nick.

"Miri says you're yourself again," he said, his gold eyes glowing faintly.

His words came out like an accusation.

"Miri says you're *you* again, Nick," he said, still glowering at him. "Post-newborn. How about you start fucking *acting* like it? In the whole time I've known you, I've *never* known you to be this damned weird and quiet. Is this supposed to convince any of us we can have a normal fucking relationship with you again? With you sitting there all goth and glowery... like some Bela Lugosi wannabe? You're supposed to be the social one. Right?"

Black planted his feet under the table.

He continued to gauge Nick's face.

Nick stared at him right back.

Then he looked at his parents—at his mother, staring at his face, her eyes round and worried, and his father, who still focused on his plate.

Nick looked back at Black, scowling.

"You can't swear like that around my parents," he growled. "What is the matter with you? Can't you control yourself at all?"

There was a silence.

Then Angel snorted an uncontrolled laugh.

She clapped her hand over her mouth, waving an apology.

Black blinked at Nick. "You're kidding, right?"

"Do I look like I'm kidding, dickhead? Show a little respect..."

"Naoko!" His mother's mouth pursed in a frown, probably more in reflex than conscious thought. "Watch your mouth! He's a guest!"

She turned then, looking at Black.

I saw a faint relief begin to grow in her eyes, even as one of those dry, sideways smiles curved her lips.

"...Even if he is a dickhead," she added mischievously. "You don't say it. It's rude."

The silence deepened.

Then, unable to help myself, I burst out in a laugh.

Everyone else at the table except Angel stared at me like I'd lost my mind.

Well, and Dalejem, who I caught smiling, too.

Then Angel leaned forward, looking Yumi in the eye.

"Has Nick dumped it on you that he's gay now, Yumi?"

"Angel!" Nick growled.

"Yes," Black said, scowling. "Your son's a gay vampire. Can we move on? I'm starving. And the roast beef hasn't moved in like... forever..."

I smacked his arm, but I was still giggling.

Hiroto was staring at Nick now, though.

"Is this true?" He looked at Dalejem, then back at Nick. "Is this your... romantic partner?" Hiroto frowned at Dalejem's face. "Did you give him the black eye?"

Nick leaned back in his dining room chair, as if unsure how to answer.

Hiroto prodded him again. "You didn't hit him? Did you?"

"No," Black retorted. "I did that. Because this asshole was gone for like eight months and we all thought he was dead. He couldn't bother with one damned phone call."

Yumi looked between Dalejem and Black, frowning.

"Is this true?" she said, hesitant.

"Of course it's true." Black jerked his chin towards Dalejem. "He was with your son in Siberia somewhere. Waiting for him to return to normal from the vampire thing—"

"I meant, is it true you hit my son's boyfriend?"

She sounded more indignant that time.

Black looked stumped. He opened his mouth, then shut it, looking at Nick.

"I guess it is true. Yeah."

Yumi gave Black an openly disapproving look.

Nick looked furious.

"No wonder he wouldn't tell me who did it," he muttered.

Folding his arms, he scowled around at all of us. Despite the anger I could see in his eyes, I got the impression he was at a total loss.

He also looked so intensely "Nick," I burst out in another giggle.

Hiroto glanced at me, then frowned at Nick.

"Are you really not going to answer?" he said, now sounding a little hurt. "Is this your boyfriend? Because I would rather if you told us. Not Miriam's husband."

Nick exhaled in a frustrated sigh.

He looked at his dad briefly.

"Yeah," he grumbled, shifting his gaze to glare at me. He turned then, aiming a death stare at Angel. "Thanks a lot for that, by the way. Isn't that a huge no-no? Outing someone without their permission?"

"Oh, for crying out loud!" Angel snapped. "You're a *vampire,* Nick. I think who you're sleeping with is kind of a detail at this point, isn't it?"

"Wait," I said, unable to help it. "You're *sleeping* together?"

There was another silence.

That time, Dalejem broke out in an uncontrollable giggle.

Nick glared at him next.

"Laugh it up," he said, scowling. "Why don't we all get it out of our system?"

As for Yumi, she only rolled her eyes, looking directly at Angel and leaning over the table.

"He thinks he's so sneaky," she said, shaking her head. "But I guessed about the boyfriend. I guessed even on the phone... and they've been making googly eyes at each other since they got here. Subtly is not my son's strong point when it comes to romance—"

"Mom!" Nick complained. "Do you have to? Seriously?"

Mr. Tanaka looked at her, too, frowning. "Why didn't you tell me?"

"I thought *he* wanted to tell us," Yumi said, motioning at their son. She smiled that mischievous smile of hers. "Anyway, I admit, I kind of wanted to watch him squirm, thinking I had no idea... thinking he was going to blow my mind..."

Nick stared at her incredulously. "You're a sadist."

She laughed, patting his arm. "I'm old, honey. I need my entertainment. And I know these things are more... fluid... these days. As long as you and your friend are happy—"

Nick cringed. "My friend? Jesus. Stop. Please stop."

I snorted another loud laugh, and Nick stared at me.

"Shut. Up." When I only laughed harder, he glared around at all of us. "Why in God's name did I think any of you were going to help make *any* of this go more smoothly? Jesus fucking Christ... I'm surrounded by infants." He glared at Black. "And dickheads."

"NAOKO!" his mother scolded.

I laughed harder, half-choking on the water I'd just sipped.

When I glanced up at Black, he was staring at Nick again, but now I saw the look in his eyes had changed.

When he reached up a hand, wiping his eyes, I curled my arm around him, pulsing warmth at his chest.

Nick seemed to notice Black's expression then, and stared.

Everyone else around the table stared at Black, too.

There was a weighted-feeling silence while Black wiped his eyes.

Then Yumi got up and walked around the table.

I honestly had no idea what she was going to do... yell at us for not telling her, apologize for yelling at us before, when she thought we were lying to her about Nick being dead, tell us she wasn't coming to our wedding, which we'd invited her and Hiroto to, along with all of Nick's sisters, and which just hit the newspapers that week.

For all I knew, she'd tell me and Black to get out of her house.

Before I could make sense of her expression well enough to guess, Yumi threw her arms around Black, kissing him on the cheek before she hugged him, tight to her chest.

Black hugged her back, one-armed, his other hand still gripping mine.

The rest of us just stared, silent.

When I glanced at Nick, I saw him wiping his eyes, even as Dalejem moved closer to him, wrapping his arm around Nick's back.

Yumi patted Black on the back a few times, then released him, tears in her eyes.

"You thought he was dead," she said. "You really thought he was dead."

Black nodded, pausing to glare at Nick. "Yes."

There was another silence.

Black continued to stare at Nick, but Nick avoided his gaze.

After another few seconds, Black scowled, aiming his words back at Yumi.

"Yes. I thought he was dead," he said. "In more ways than one."

Black's anger and pain shimmered around me briefly, coloring his light.

He couldn't really maintain his anger, though... not as he stared at Nick's face.

"...I thought he was gone forever," Black repeated. "But he's not. He's not gone. Are you, Nick?"

There was another silence.

Then Yumi straightened, her expression stern.

"No," she said, absolute authority in her voice. "No, he's not gone. My son isn't going anywhere... ever again. Not while I'm alive."

There was another silence.

Yet somehow, Yumi's words settled it.

I couldn't have said how exactly, but I felt everyone around the table relax for real, even Hiroto, Nick's father.

Yumi walked back to her place at the table, next to Nick, and sat down.

Picking up her napkin, she laid it back in her lap.

Then she motioned to the platter of roast beef.

"Could you pass that along, Elvis?" she said politely to Cowboy.

Cowboy picked up the platter, smiling at her. "Yes, ma'am."

He handed the platter to Hiroto, who put it down on the other side of his plate, and began taking cuts of beef off with the serving forks. The asparagus began making the rounds after that, followed by mashed sweet potatoes, and rolls, and butter.

Once all the food got moving again, Yumi turned to Dalejem.

"How do you feel about children?" she asked him, stabbing her fork into an asparagus spear. "Do you like them?"

Angel spit out her mouthful of wine.

Bursting out in a laugh, she covered her mouth to try and stop it.

It was futile.

A few seconds later, all of us were cracking up.

Well... almost all of us.

Nick glowered around at everyone, but I could tell he wasn't really angry. Like Yumi said, he was halfway leaning against Jem even now, his expression softening, seemingly involuntarily, as the seer rubbed his shoulder, his eyes still overly bright.

I watched him look around at all of us sitting at his parents' table, his expression verging on incredulous as he seemed to take in every face.

I couldn't read Nick, now that he was a vampire.

I had no real idea what he was thinking at all.

At the same time, I found myself thinking I did know.

I knew exactly what he was thinking.

Nick had finally come home.

17

SAYING EVERYTHING WRONG

J ax looked at Kiko where she stared out the window of the
private plane.

She had barely touched the meal in front of her.

Jax knew she was worried.

She was already worried.

Look, Yarli murmured in his ear. *You don't have to tell her now.
But someone should. Really, the doc should have, as soon as you all got to
London... but that didn't happen, so it's up to you, Jax, if you want her to
know before she gets back here.*

Where are they now? Jax kept his thoughts neutral. *The boss and
the doc... are they around? Could they be the ones to tell her, at least? I
think it would mean more, coming from Black. She views him like a
blood relative... like her family.*

There was a silence.

Hello? Jax said. *Do you know where they are, sister? Or are you
looking for them?*

Yarli sighed. *You wouldn't believe me if I told you.*

Jax frowned.

What does that mean? he sent.

It means they're all having dinner at Nick's parents' house, Yarli
said, sighing. *Jem, Cowboy, Angel, Miri... and Black, if you can believe*

it... are currently eating with Nick and his human parents. And before you say anything... I know. All I can tell you is, the boss brought a gun loaded with those vampire bullets that rip the shit out of their heads and/or hearts. He also wore a sword on his back, under his jacket. One of the short ones. So there's a chance all of this will be a moot point by the time you and Kiko land.

Jax's frown deepened.

Then he exhaled, his eyes still on Kiko.

But you don't think so, he thought next. *You don't think he'll kill Nick.*

Yarli sighed, the sound audible even in the mind connection between them.

No, she admitted. *I don't.*

After another short silence, she sighed again.

I can't even say they're wrong, she admitted. *I've talked to him, Jax. And to brother Dalejem. Nick is... weirdly... Nick again. It was hard to remember he'd ever been that other thing, at least while I was actually talking to him. And I don't think he'd go near Kiko if you paid him. From what Jem said, the doc more or less forced the issue, or he wouldn't have gone near her, either. But the doc's known him a hell of a lot longer, and I think for her, it was more like seeing him rise from the dead. To her, that other thing wasn't Nick at all... and really, from what I've observed, her take is likely the more accurate one.*

Jax frowned, still watching Kiko.

I don't think it will be good for Kiko to see him. Not right away.

No one does, Yarli agreed. *Literally no one. Like I said, I doubt that will be an issue. I'm more worried about how she'll feel, knowing we're all talking to him, and working with him, and that he's a part of Black's team, even on the periphery. I don't want her to feel cut out. But I also don't want her to feel like we're going behind her back. I don't want her to feel betrayed... by Black, by the doc, by any of us. I don't want her to be hurt by Dalejem's being with Nick. I want her to feel heard... and seen. And important. To all of us, not just Black.*

Jax frowned again, thinking about that.

I might feel that way, he admitted. *Betrayed. If it was me.*

Still thinking, he added,

I might feel like everyone chose Nick over me. I might feel like my position on the team wasn't what I thought. He rubbed his chest, grimacing. *Honestly, it makes me feel sick, just thinking about it. It makes me want to hurt Nick... even if he is not the same.*

I would feel betrayed, too, Yarli admitted. *Mañuel says the same. So does Holo. We all feel sick about it, but we aren't sure how to tell her without bringing those feelings up in her. Really, there are only two choices, brother. Lie to her a while longer. Or tell her the truth. You are closer to her. I will let you decide.*

Jax nodded to himself.

He agreed.

Okay, he told the female seer. *I've got to go.*

Just be gentle, brother.

Jax nodded to that, too, but didn't really answer.

Really, there was nothing to say.

H e brought her ice cream.

He knew it was feeble.

It perhaps even verged on insulting.

Still, it was as good of a segue as any. He knew she would pick up on something, and she did. She immediately knew something was up.

"What is this about?" She quirked an eyebrow at him. "You're not standing in the corner? Smoking *hiri?* Watching me and looking worried?" she teased. "Should I be even more worried that you've decided to come and talk to me like a normal damned person, Jax?"

Jax didn't smile.

Some part of him wanted to, wanted to let her coax him into talking about something else, anything else.

Instead, he handed her the bowl of ice cream.

"Nick is alive," he said, even as she took it from his fingers.

The timing wasn't great.

She dropped the bowl.

It slipped out of her fingers, and he only just caught it, sliding his hand under just in time to cup his palm underneath.

"Sorry," he said, flushing.

She stared at him, even as he set the bowl down in front of her on the small table between the leather seats.

Jax sat across from her, setting down a bowl for himself.

"Do you want chocolate?" he said, glancing at the service area. "I think I saw syrup. And maybe some sprinkles... or peanuts..." Still thinking, he took a bite of ice cream, adding, "Also chocolate candies. Little round ones."

Kiko continued to stare at him.

She'd gone pale, but her jaw had hardened.

"Where is he?" she said.

Jax frowned.

"Nick," she snapped. "Where is Nick *right now,* Jax? Is that where Miri went?"

"No." He gestured a hard negative with his hand, seer-fashion, even as he shook his head, human-fashion. "No. She went because of the other dragon."

"The other dragon?"

"Yes. That is unrelated to Nick... but I can update you on that, too."

There was another silence.

Now Jax could feel mostly confusion coming off Kiko... and anger.

He could tell his random—in her mind, "bizarre"—manner of revealing this information to her hadn't helped her to absorb any of it, or even to pinpoint which parts to follow up on.

"I am sorry," he said, feeling a flush of embarrassment. "I said all of that badly. I just wanted you to be warned. Nick is back. It is complicated, but he is past the newborn stage of being a vampire. He is no longer dangerous."

There was a longer silence.

Kiko frowned, like she wasn't sure if he'd even spoken English.

"No. Longer. Dangerous," she said, pausing on each word.

"Yes." Jax felt his face warm more.

"What does that mean?"

He could feel the fear spiraling off her.

It was difficult not to touch her, but he managed it, mostly by scooping up and eating another spoonful of ice cream.

He noticed the ice cream in front of her hadn't been touched.

"I am sorry—" he began again.

"Jem?" She stared at him, and now her eyes were brighter.

She blinked it away, without looking away from Jax's face.

"...Did they find him?"

She said it like she expected Jax to tell her he was dead.

Thinking about that, feeling her grief, her certainty, he shook his head.

Then, realizing she would misunderstand that, given what she'd asked, he spoke out loud, again doing everything both too slow and too hastily.

"Jem's fine. He came back with Nick. They are together now."

Kiko blinked, her jaw loosening.

She stared at him, then blinked again.

Confusion and pain reached her expression, right before she looked away.

Watching her face, Jax grew worried for real.

"I am sorry," he said. "I didn't know how to tell you. There didn't seem a good way. But I am told the vampire who attacked you... the one Nick *was* for those weeks and months... he is gone now. Jem did something to help him through it, and now Nick is like he was before."

Pausing, Jax added, hoping it would reassure her,

"Miri is okay with him now. They are friends again."

Jax felt his worry turn into fear as he watched Kiko's face.

She was so pale now, he was afraid she would faint.

Reaching over the table, he caught hold of both of her arms, gently.

She looked at him and his heart hurt, so badly he felt tears come to his eyes.

"I am sorry," he repeated. "Kiko... I am so sorry."

At a loss, he considered trying to soothe her with his light, but he didn't want to violate her space. He could feel her indecision, the part of her that wanted to wrest free of his hands, but she didn't move, and didn't try to evade him.

She didn't meet his gaze, either.

Both of them sat there for what felt like a long time.

Jax didn't speak. He didn't move... not until he saw her breath hitching.

He saw her struggle to breathe, even as her face turned bright red.

Realizing she was fighting not to cry, he got up, and slid around the table in spite of himself. He wrapped his arms around her, doing it without thought. Pain slid through him as a memory flickered through his mind.

He remembered being trapped in a building in New York... a different New York, on a different world, a different dimension.

He remembered being in that elevator shaft...

It was a long time ago now.

Mostly, Jax tried not to think about those years.

It pained him, though. Even now, it pained him.

Back then, on that world, they just thought he'd cracked.

They chalked it up to what used to be called "battle fatigue" or "shell shock," and now usually got labeled as "post-traumatic stress disorder" or "PTSD." No one on his team back then understood why it affected him so much. He felt it on his friends, even Holo, who'd known him longer than anyone. They didn't understand.

It scared them.

He'd wanted to reassure them, but he couldn't.

He couldn't talk to them. He couldn't explain it. One of the seers on his team tried to help him find the source of the problem in his light, but he hadn't been able to tell her anything, either, or help her to unravel what happened to him.

Miri helped him.

Not entirely, but Miri helped him more than anyone.

But there'd been only so much she could do, too.

He was still too locked down.

Looking at Kiko now, he felt on her some of what he'd felt on himself. Something there resonated, that feeling of being alone, of having no one around her who understood. There was even that element of not fully remembering what happened to her. She didn't remember it really, which made it worse in some ways. The full extent of her violation was a mystery to her, something she dreamed about, something her imagination tortured her with.

Jax had that, too.

The blurry, blackout crimes against his person happened when he'd still been a child, in the black-market slave camps of that other world.

Those blackout memories somehow got triggered in an elevator shaft during a military op in a now-dead world. However they'd been triggered, they hadn't left him in the time since. Jax *still* couldn't remember exactly what had happened to him, but the darkness lingered in his light, making it so he had to talk himself into staying alive a lot of days.

On that other world, Wreg had helped him.

The Sword helped him.

Jon, Holo, the Bridge, Maygar, Balidor, Yumi... Chandre.

He'd had friends there.

Real friends.

He'd lost most of them, coming here.

But then he'd made new ones.

Here, on this world, the doc helped him. Black, Dalejem, Holo, Yarli, Mika... they'd all tried to help him, in different ways.

Kiko had helped.

He didn't even know how she'd helped, but she *had* helped him.

More than the doc, even.

Thinking about that, Jax felt the pain in his throat and chest worsen.

He wrapped his arms around her more tightly, almost roughly, with a kind of fierce gratitude and desire to help her he couldn't put into words.

Maybe for the same reason, he didn't try to talk.

He didn't try to voice any of it.

She didn't push him away.

Honestly, he half-expected her to, once he had his arms around her. He waited, holding his breath, ready to release her the instant he felt any kind of discomfort or resistance... but it never came.

He felt relief on her instead.

He felt a near-surrender.

She was the toughest human he'd ever met.

She was one of the best fighters, too.

Maybe because of those things, he sometimes forgot how physically small she was. Now, as she curled up in his lap, wrapping a small hand around his ribs, Jax couldn't help but notice.

She let him pull her against his chest.

Kiko didn't wrap her arms around him, like he did her.

She *merged* into him instead, as if huddling inside his warmth.

Once she'd gotten comfortable in his lap, she rested her cheek against his chest, curling up on his thighs, wrapping the one hand more tightly around his ribs, slinging her leg around his. She let him tug her the rest of the way against him, and relaxed more when he began to rub her back, and the back of her neck.

He let out a low purr as he did it.

He infused the purr with his living light, warming her chest and belly, doing anything he could think of to comfort her, to let her know she was safe.

She didn't push him away that time, either.

Instead, she began to cry.

Rocking her gently, he just kept rubbing her, pooling his light in her limbs, stroking her back, her arms, the back of her neck, her fingers...

She put her hand on his cock.

Jax tensed.

It wasn't a "no" tense, but she stopped, her hand still on him.

She looked up, studying his eyes.

"Is this all right?" she said.

He hesitated.

He nodded, then he hesitated again, even as her expression relaxed.

"Is this... a good time for this?" he said, watching her brown eyes.

"You like me, right?"

Jax shivered, nodding. "I like you. I like you a lot."

"I like you, too, Jax."

She massaged him slowly, and his eyes closed, opening again after a long-feeling second.

"I didn't mean it for me," he clarified, still watching every nuance of her expression. "I meant for you. Is this a good time for you?"

"I honestly don't know what that means," she said, her voice flat. "I just know I haven't been with anyone since then. Before that, there was Jem."

She paused, as if turning this over in her mind. Her hand continued to massage him sensually, causing him to bite the inside of his cheek.

"I suppose Jem had a thing for Nick, even then," she said after a pause. "I think I even knew that, somehow. Jem wanted Nick. Nick wanted Miri. Then Nick got turned... everything changed. Right?"

Watching her eyes, Jax nodded slowly.

"Right."

He felt his worry about their timing resurface.

He hesitated, fighting back the pain in his light.

He grew more sure about the timing being wrong when he saw the grief in her face.

"It is too soon," he said softly, laying his hand on top of hers. "It is too soon, yes?"

She frowned a little, looking down at his hand on hers.

Her eyes shifted back up.

"Have you ever known that to matter?" she said. "In something like this?"

She fell silent, watching his eyes, maybe looking for a real answer.

"I don't know," he said truthfully. I have not been with many people, Kiko."

She nodded, biting her lip.

Her dark eyes continued to study his.

"I haven't," she said. "...Known it to matter. If someone is sad and they want to be sad with someone else. Whether that ends up being sex or not-sex, or whatever else... the fact that there's sadness there doesn't make it not real." She paused, thinking. "I just know I don't want you to be anyone else. It doesn't feel like you want me to be anyone else, either. To me, that feels good. To me, that's enough. Do you understand?"

Jax waited to make sure she was finished.

Then he nodded, still turning over her words.

"Yes," he said. "If that is what you meant, then I agree."

He felt her relax slightly even as she leaned against his chest.

For a moment they just sat there together.

Jax thought of something else.

"What about Dex?" he said.

Kiko frowned, but the frown was more amused and puzzled than annoyed.

"Dexter? You think I want Dexter?"

Embarrassed, Jax shrugged.

He managed to hold her gaze.

"I know you have a choice," he said carefully. "If you want that choice, it is there. I was not sure how you felt about him. But I know you could have him... if you wanted. He cares very much about you. He also wants you. Like I want you."

She gave him another puzzled smile.

"Dex is like my brother. We've been friends for years. We've been fighting side by side for years. I think if Dex was interested in me at all, or saw me like that in any way, I would have picked up on it by now—"

"He is," Jax blurted. "He *is* interested. Maybe he wasn't before, but things change. People change. You *do* have that choice. If you want it."

There was another silence.

That time, Jax felt a flicker of hurt on her.

It was different from the hurt of finding out Nick was alive.

It was different from the hurt of Nick being accepted back onto Black's team. It was different from the hurt of finding out Nick was with Dalejem.

"Are you trying to push Dex on me?" she said. "Really?"

"No." Jax shook his head, vehement. "No, I am absolutely *not* wanting that. I would be very upset if you chose him over me. But I wanted you to know."

Swallowing, feeling his face warm, he met her gaze.

"I wanted to make sure *you* knew you had that choice. In case you would rather choose differently. In case it would feel like a missed opportunity..."

He trailed, feeling somehow at a loss.

It occurred to him that he'd blown this. She'd offered herself to him. She'd actively tried to seduce him, and he'd blown it. Worse, he'd made her feel rejected.

There was another silence.

Realizing he should be focused on comforting her, that this

was about what Nick had done to her, not whether Jax himself got to court her, he felt his face warm.

"I'm sorry," he began. "This is not the time. I wanted to speak to you, but not today. This is my fault—"

"No." She shook her head. "No, Jax. It's not. And you say that way too much."

When he fell silent, she leaned her head against his chest, sighing through the thin material of his shirt. She still had her hand on him.

His hand still lay on top of hers.

When she looked up next, her eyes were serious.

"I'm going to kiss you now," she said. "Unless you don't want me to."

He felt a flicker of pain run through him, making him wince.

He held her gaze.

"I want you to," he said. "But I will probably feel at least slightly guilty for wanting this right now."

She laughed.

Hearing that sound, hearing the realness behind it, brought an intense bloom of heat to his chest. It caught him off guard... threw him completely off-balance. He winced at his own reaction, even as his hand wrapped around her thigh.

He was still studying her eyes carefully when she sat up.

That time, she wrapped her arms around his neck, studying his eyes just as carefully back.

He watched every increment of motion, every tiny expression on her face, every flicker of feeling that glanced over her irises.

Then her mouth was on his.

She kissed him cautiously.

It was almost a question.

His arms coiled around her, and again, he was struck by how small she was.

His fingers wrapped into her thick black hair, and he leaned up, returning her kiss, then kissing her harder, parting her lips with his tongue, feeling her chest clench, then let out a low gasp when he yanked her deeper into his lap.

He didn't know when, exactly, he'd started to view her differently.

He knew he lied to himself about it, when he got jealous of Jem... when he got jealous to the point of being openly resentful of the handsome seer.

He hadn't really noticed the crush Jem had on Nick, not at first.

He'd been annoyed when Holo told him, annoyed by Holo laughing about it, annoyed at Jem for being a dick, annoyed that Jem appeared to be using Kiko, strangely relieved Jem had no real interest in her, coupled with an indignation that he didn't.

None of it made any sense.

Jax chalked it up to the sessions with Miri.

He'd been confused.

He'd been working on himself with Miri then, and he got confused... first by transferring his feelings onto her, then by doing the same with Kiko... or that's what he told himself.

He'd been alone for so long.

Holo was there, but somehow, it didn't help.

Kiko put her hand on him, and it jerked him out of his mind.

A wave of heat rose in his chest, and he let out a groan.

He felt desire ripple off her from the sound.

She was unfastening his pants then, and Jax remembered abruptly where they were.

They were still on the plane.

The rest of the plane's occupants had left them alone, back in the executive cabin, the one Black and Miri usually occupied when they were on board.

Black told Kiko to use it. Really, he told all of them to use it, to get some sleep if they could, but the others let Kiko have it.

The bottom line was, they weren't alone... not really.

Someone could walk through those curtains at any minute.

Even if the construct wasn't completely open, now that they were protecting themselves from seers again...

He pulled away from Kiko with an effort, glancing at the doorway.

Peering over the back of his seat, he saw seers and humans in the other compartment past the blue curtains. Most of them pretended not to notice his stare, but he caught the eye of Mika, who was sitting in one of the seat areas with Ace, Jorji, and Alex Holmes.

Mika quirked an eyebrow at him, amusement playing at her lips.

Ace, who sat across from her, noticed the direction of her stare and turned around, craning his neck and head. Seeing Jax there, he burst out in a grin. They could obviously see enough of Kiko to have some idea of where she was sitting.

When Jax looked back at Kiko, she lifted her own eyebrow.

"Do I want to know?" she said.

Jax exhaled, pursing his lips.

"I'm not sure." His voice came out apologetic when he added, "It is not... private. I could close the door, but that won't be particularly private, either. The seers, all of us... we have less privacy right now. Since you are with me, that is less privacy for you."

Her mouth pursed.

Then her expression cleared.

"Ah. Those construct things, right?" She motioned above her head, as if the construct was a physical net sitting over all of them. "They changed something with that? Because of this new seer tracking down Black and Miri?"

Jax nodded, relaxing slightly.

He'd forgotten.

Kiko was highly intelligent; he hadn't forgotten that.

It was the other thing.

Black mentioned it to all the new seers here, not long after they arrived.

The humans here were different than the humans on Old Earth, maybe because they didn't have their own, indigenous race of seers. Whatever the reason, the humans here had evolved with more of a quasi-seer interface with the world.

They definitely *weren't* seers. But they also weren't as blind as the humans Jax had grown up with on Old Earth.

Kiko was one of the more sensitive ones.

She understood and felt a lot, and not only with her mind.

She had a certain intuitiveness he'd seen in only a few other humans, at least to the same degree. Angel was one. Manny was another. Cowboy was probably the *most* like this, of any human Jax had ever met, on either world.

None of the humans where he'd been born were like Cowboy.

Then again, none were like Kiko, either.

Black mentioned he thought this ability in them could be trained, just like it could be with seers. Black claimed Cowboy had already received some training when he encountered him. Black had bolstered that training in the time since.

Kiko smiled. "Are you going to answer me?" she teased. "Are you under the impression that the state of the construct is some kind of 'seers-only' secret? Because I hate to pull rank on you, but I *do* outrank you in this particular army, Jax."

"No," he said, shaking his head.

Then, remembering her first question, he shook his head again.

"I mean yes. It is the construct... they changed it. I meant no, it is not a secret. I just forgot how intuitive the humans are here."

Thinking about that, he met her gaze seriously.

"I could train you. Or Black," he added, when her eyes widened in surprise. "It wouldn't have to be me. But if you're interested, we could arrange for this. I think Black forgot... but he meant to do that. Before everything got bad with Faustus and the vampires and Nick. He likely just had to put it aside, given everything."

She blinked.

She didn't look annoyed.

He was unwilling to read her to find out exactly *what* she was thinking.

Leaning closer, he kissed her lingeringly, instead.

"I'm not crazy about the audience," he admitted next. "I don't know how you feel about it, but I'd rather wait until we can be alone."

He kissed her again, feeling her light soften at his words.

"I want this," he added, kissing her again. "I really want this. More than I can say. I want to be alone for that part, too... for the talking part."

When he looked up that time, her eyes had softened with her light.

Then she smiled, and he felt a jump and flutter in his heart.

He hadn't seen her smile like that in a long time.

Leaning down from his lap, she kissed him.

Raising her head long enough to smile at him, she lowered it and kissed him again.

He fell into that one, and for another long-feeling, however-many minutes, he forgot all about Mika's smirk, and Ace's wink and laugh from the main cabin past that doorway.

He really didn't care about any of it.

18

RANK 10 SEER

Yarli nudged her human mate, smiling as she pretended she had to elbow him out of the way, even though four feet of space existed on either side of him.

When Manny didn't look up from the monitor he was staring at, didn't change his frowning stare, she lost her teasing smile and moved closer.

"What is it?" she said. "What're you looking at?"

"There's someone at the door," he muttered.

Yarli frowned back. She slid closer to him, staring down at the color, three-dimensional image in the inset screen.

"So?" she said, puzzled. "Isn't security down there?"

"Yes. They're with him now."

There was another silence.

Yarli looked at Manny's face, then back down at the screen, puzzled.

She hadn't felt anything unusual in the construct. She was about to aim her seer's sight more specifically on the man down on the ground floor, when Manny spoke up. His words remained a distracted mutter, but he glanced at her, his eyes worried.

"I mean, I'm not crazy, am I?" he said. "That's him, isn't it? Isn't that the guy?"

Yarli blinked.

Then she bent down, staring at the image.

Hitting a few keys, Manny zoomed up on the man's face, showing a clearer image of his features.

Once he had, Yarli felt her throat tighten.

Gaos. How had she not seen it?

His hair alone, which hung down to his shoulders... not to mention the color of his eyes... the two things were so obvious now, she wondered how her eyes had glanced past both. Those silvery-white streaks in his dark brown hair stood out, shockingly bright in the zoomed-up image.

The colors and contrasts of his hair strangely blended, clashed, and contrasted the pale gold eyes, not to mention the bizarre ordinariness of the clothing he wore.

She stared at his sculpture-like mouth, the tell-tale of a seer.

She recognized the exact curves and lines of his thick jaw and cheekbones.

He didn't look like an ordinary seer exactly; the features of most seers were smaller, more delineated, less coarse, more handsome. But he wore enough of the tell-tales—height, eye-color, mouth, high cheekbones—it was impossible to un-see his race.

He wore clothes now.

Maybe that's what threw her.

He wore a dark shirt, faded blue jeans, dark blue tennis shoes... even a gold watch.

He didn't wear a coat or jacket, which was unusual for San Francisco at night, even in the summer... sometimes especially in the summer.

Despite those unusual-for-a-human eyes, and the metallic silver in his hair, he looked strangely, disarmingly normal.

Yarli hit through an emergency sequence in her headset even as she slid her consciousness into the Barrier. She connected solidly with the military-grade construct they'd re-established over the building.

She tried scanning him while the connection went through.

She pulled back when she both felt and saw him flinch.

Then those pale, white-gold eyes were staring upward, directly into the camera.

That shapely but stern mouth tightened perceptibly.

Just then, Yarli made contact with the other beings she'd sought out in the construct.

Boss? She fought not to shout at him in the Barrier. *Doc? Can you hear me?*

She opened her light to both of them.

Black? she sent, a touch louder. *Dr. Fox? I need one or both of you to answer me immediately... or call in to me or Manny at the Raptor's Nest.*

Black's mind rose.

We're eating dinner, Yarli. You're going to get me in trouble with Yumi Tanaka. That woman doesn't miss a damned—

Yarli didn't let him finish.

He's here, she sent frantically. *The seer from Hollywood... the dragon. Silver and white-streaked hair. Gold eyes. Same face. He's here.*

There was a silence.

Miri's presence rose.

Where? the doc sent.

Yarli changed her focus without missing a beat.

On the premises. He's down in the lobby, boss. He just walked in through the front fucking door. Now he's talking to your security people. Feeling her jaw harden, Yarli added, *I didn't feel a damned thing. Manny saw him on the monitor and recognized him. He's just outside the private elevator...*

There was a silence.

In it, Yarli heard and felt nothing.

She didn't pick up so much as a whisper, despite the dense construct.

Then Black's mind rose.

Cold.

Stripped of emotion.

It wasn't even his military voice, but... something else.

Evacuate the building, he sent. *We're on our way.*

Y arli heard a faint ping go off in her ear.

She glanced at it, but just to note it in passing.

She scarcely ID'd the signal before she dismissed it.

One of the secondary security notifications, indicating that the elevator was in use.

Someone had recalled it to the penthouse floor.

It was probably Wu.

Black had Wu running things for the operational side of things, for the duration of the time Black and Miri were gone. They'd never transitioned back, so Wu was still in charge, although Manny helped him out a fair bit, especially when it came to building security. Yarli herself handled the infiltration team, and the constructs.

So the elevator was probably Wu.

Wu either brought it upstairs to keep anyone on the lobby floor from using it—which was smart; Yarli honestly wished she'd thought of that—or Black had him moving around some of the human military-security types, putting them on a few different floors to cover different areas of the building.

Knowing Black, he'd want redundancies built in, even if he planned on handling the guy on his own. He'd want to know there was a back-up plan, in the event he failed.

Black was good like that.

Sometimes, Black really reminded Yarli of his blood-cousin, the Sword.

In other respects, however, they could not be more different.

Really, that particular style of military mindset—a strategically cautious, verging on paranoid way of thinking—was the only thing Yarli could say with confidence the two men shared in common.

Black told her to evacuate the building, but Yarli wasn't the only one doling out orders, even here, inside the Raptor's Nest. Yarli hadn't paid a lot of attention to what the others were doing. She focused on the duties in front of her, namely, furthering the evacuations Black tasked her with.

She'd already gotten more than a third of the building's occupants out, starting with tech and high-security personnel, most of them stationed in the science wing, the computer center, or working in the company labs. Black had a lot of equipment housed here now, not to mention vast stores of data, so she'd been forced to sequence the teams carefully, leaving more time for those who had to upload sensitive data and/or cut the cords to cloud systems until it was safe to reinstate them.

Frowning at the thought, she shunted it aside.

She focused on the seer infiltrators, instead.

She now had seven of them on the line.

The main ones talking so far had been Mika, Jorji, Larisse, Holo, and Kiessa.

They'd been looking at the thing in the lobby—from the Barrier, that is.

"The Barrier" was seer shorthand for the inter-dimensional space from which they derived most of their seer abilities.

Since all of them were currently offsite, on private planes owned by Black Securities and Investigations, Yarli assigned them all of the surveillance, construct, and infiltration work. They couldn't exactly help her here, on the ground, and presumably, they were safe under the mobile constructs she'd set up around both planes.

Yarli tried to stay on the line with them while they worked, even as she got the team at the 'Nest organized, packed up, and relocated off-site, mostly via the helipad on the roof.

You're sure that's him, Jorj? Mika sent the words, her thoughts openly skeptical. *I mean, I agree... physically. It looks like the same guy. But he doesn't feel anything like him. Or look anything like him from the Barrier.*

Agreed, Holo jumped in.

There was a bare pause, then he switched to his headset.

"The Barrier signature is all off. I agree there is a physical resemblance—"

"How is that possible?"

Dalejem, that time.

The older seer's voice still made Yarli jump, after all those months of radio silence.

Some part of her was still shocked to remember he was alive.

"How is that possible?" Jem repeated, his voice harder. "I mean, *look* at him. Are we really going to try and convince ourselves that a being who looks *that* much like the thing that showed up in Hollywood somehow *isn't* the thing we saw in Hollywood?"

There was a silence.

Exhaling, Jem added, "Has anyone tried to talk to him? Anyone other than the security guards down there?"

Remembering the ping she'd heard, Yarli frowned.

Then she turned, looking for the correct monitor on the security screen in front of her.

"Where's Black?" Mika said. "He and Miri left where you are, right Jem?"

Yarli noticed Mika didn't mention where Dalejem was.

"Yes," Jem said stiffly. "They should be there in approximately ten minutes, unless they encounter some kind of problem en route."

"What about you, Jem?" Kiessa said. "Are you going to—"

"Black told us to stay here."

Again, Yarli noted the lack of specificity to the "us."

She also heard the faint note of aggression in Jem's tone when he cut Kiessa off.

Both things came through clearly enough that there was a silence.

"What about the human faction?" Jem said, his voice

subdued. "Where's Kiko's team? Or Dex? Are they on the ground yet? Either of them?"

"Dex went to New Mexico," Zairai said. "He's not with us. We're at the airport. We're on our way back in."

"I'm on the flight with Kiko," Mika added. "She's in the other compartment... Black's private quarters at the back of the plane." She paused. "With Jax."

She said that a little funny.

Yarli knew she wasn't the only one to hear it, but she dismissed that, too.

She glanced at the monitors again and noticed the helicopter was almost back.

Abruptly, she switched channels, muting the one with the infiltrators.

"Luric?" she said. "Your team's up. Are you all ready?"

The medical tech sounded flustered, annoyed, a little put out, but also relieved.

"We're here. We're just inside the door."

"Good."

"Any word on where we're going?" the male tech muttered.

Yarli shook her head, once, seer fashion. "Don't worry about that. Black has safehouses in a few points around the city. They'll take you to one of those—"

"You don't know which one?" Luric said.

For the first time, he sounded alarmed.

Yarli sighed, sending a pulse of reassurance to her friend.

"You're going to be fine, brother. Black wants us to keep everything need-to-know right now, including the safehouse locations... at least until we know what this is. That includes not voicing them over the comms, or in the Barrier, if we can help it."

"Oh."

"I need to get back," Yarli said. "Can you make sure Hamish is ready with the next group? He'll have maybe fifteen minutes."

"Got it." The noise in the background on Luric's end got a

lot louder. He must have reached the top of the stairs, and opened the door leading to the helipad; Yarli heard the heavy beat of rotors and a gusting wind. "They just got here. We're going out to the helicopter now. I'll ping you as soon as we're inside."

"All right. Signing off."

Yarli ended the communication.

As she did, her eyes glanced back over the row of monitors.

A voice in the back of her head nagged at her, telling her she was forgetting something. She confirmed with her eyes that Luric's team was now making their way across the rooftop, heading for the Blackhawk helicopter that just set down on the round circle of the helipad.

She clicked over to Lawless.

"Hey, make sure they have fueling on their schedule. Both pilots."

"Got it," the older vet said. "Two more trips for this one. The one coming in can fuel up when they land. I'll let Michelle know there might be a delay."

"Okay, great. Tell Hamish, too. Out."

Yarli's eyes flickered back over the three rows of screens, a nervous tic she barely noticed she was doing.

That time, something caught her eye.

She stopped dead.

Leaning towards the screens, she punched in to the elevator car's speakers.

"What the fuck are you doing?" she barked.

She would have expected her boyfriend to jump a foot in the air, with someone yelling at him through the speaker like that.

Instead, Manny didn't move at first.

When he finally turned, his neck and head craned slowly but deliberately towards the surveillance camera. His iron-gray hair hung down to his shoulders, recently cut out of its long braid, in part for the upcoming dual wedding.

Manny's mouth curled in a hard frown, in an expression she hadn't seen on him before.

He paused before he spoke, his shoulders tense above crossed arms.

He seemed to meet her gaze directly, right through the camera.

"I'm going down there." Manny's voice came out flat, totally unlike him. "He needs to talk to someone. Someone who knows things. The security guards aren't helpful, and the construct is too dense... too foreign to his light."

Pausing, his affect still flat, Manny added,

"You may listen. I will leave the channel open."

Yarli felt her gut go cold.

Whoever was talking to her, it wasn't her boyfriend.

"Let him go!" she snapped.

"I cannot."

"Why the fuck not?" Yarli fought a swell of panic. "Who are you? Why won't you just talk to me? Talk to me... right now! You don't need him down there for that."

"He wants to come. He is interested in me."

"No!" she snapped. "He isn't interested in you! Let him go! NOW!"

Her voice came out half-fear, half rage.

The feelings in her clashed and swirled, settling on full-blown terror.

"Please let him go. PLEASE PLEASE LET HIM GO. *Dugra a' kitre gaos...* we have done *nothing* to you. Black has done *nothing* to you. This is a friend of his. A personal, close friend of his. He'll flip the fuck out if you hurt him, if you scare him or harm him in any way. He won't be happy about this at all..."

Even as she talked to the thing inside her boyfriend, she had already split her consciousness, the instant she realized it wasn't really Manny.

She threw her mind at the construct in full-blown panic.

She didn't waste time trying to shield.

WOLDON? ALICI? Feeling them flinch, feeling them hear her, feeling their presences grow more tangible in her light, Yarli went on even louder. *TURN OFF THE ELEVATOR! TURN IT OFF! NOW! NOW! SHUT IT DOWN.*

The elevator? Woldon sounded bewildered. *Isn't it on the penthouse floor? I thought it was already switched off—*

Alici's thoughts came through calmer, more clear on what Yarli wanted.

We can't do it, boss, she sent. *Not until it reaches the bottom. It's locked in with a security code, and we can't stop it from the Barrier—*

The bottom is too late! Yarli snarled. *Do it manually. Do it from the security console—*

We don't have access. The humans run that side of things.

Then CALL them! Call Wu. Or Javier. Get one of them to do it. Tell them it's a goddamned emergency. Tell them I need it right—

WHAT THE FUCK IS GOING ON?

Black.

Black's mind, Black's light, trembling the construct like a hard wind.

Any other time, it might have made her wince.

Now, she felt nothing but relief.

IS SOMEONE GOING TO ANSWER ME? WHAT IS GOING ON?

Boss, Yarli sent. *I need someone to stop the elevator. To send it back upstairs. Now. Right now. How would I do that?*

Yarli? His voice came through in a hard growl. *Why are you screaming in my ear?*

It's Manny, she sent, hearing the panic vibrate higher in her thoughts. She tried to dial it back, couldn't. *That thing has Manny, Black! It's got control of him somehow. It's bringing him down to the lobby It wants to talk to him, read him... something...*

Black's light went from angry to alarmed.

BLACK! Yarli snapped at his silence. *STOP THE FUCKING ELEVATOR! OR BRING HIM BACK... GET HIM FREE!*

Are you kidding me right now? Black's mental voice grew furious. *You're his MATE. You're a goddamned rank-10 seer. ORDER MANNY BACK TO YOU, Yarli. Right now!*

Anger rose violently in her light. *Don't you think I would have done that already, if I could? I can't reach him! I can't!*

YOU HAVE TO.

Yarli bit her lip, so hard she tasted blood.

Somewhere in her back and forth with that thing and then Black, she'd started walking. She'd left the conference room, walked through and past the bullpen, walked past reception and the lobby, out the doors of Black Securities and Investigations.

Now she found herself standing in front of the elevator doors.

Her thumb was pressing the call-back button.

She had no idea how long, or how many times she'd pressed it.

She was about to yell at Black again, when—

Black's voice rose on the elevator car.

Yarli's eyes jerked back to her headset, to the image of the security footage being projected through the virtual display. She had no idea how Black accessed the security system so fast, but she saw Manny jerk his eyes around to the surveillance camera when Black's voice exploded through the speaker.

"*Mañuelito.* Come upstairs. NOW. Or I'll force the goddamned issue."

Manny stared up at the speaker.

His expression didn't move.

His handsome face, *her* face, didn't move.

"Just let me talk to him," the being said calmly. "I would like to talk to him before you arrive. So I am better equipped to speak to you."

"No," Black snarled. "Let him go. *NOW,* goddamn it!"

Manny... or whatever had Manny... didn't answer.

Just then, the elevator car shuddered to a stop.

The doors gave a cheerful ping.

19

HOSTAGES

B lack wanted to scream in frustration.

Then he wanted to scream at Yarli to do what she'd already told him she couldn't do, to stop Manny... push him or coerce him or wrestle him away from the being who had control over his mind.

He already knew she couldn't.

He could feel her desperation, her panic, even more sharply than he could feel his own.

He could feel her terror and powerlessness.

Both of them just watched, silent, as Manny walked through the opening between the elevator doors, casually entering the area of the main elevator banks in the building's ground floor lobby.

Black felt Yarli reach out with her light, trying to reach her mate.

He felt her screaming in some part of her *aleimi,* trying to reach him and failing.

He felt Miri's grief as she accelerated through another red light.

Black reached out with his own light, that time trying to help Yarli reach him, instead of just doing it on his own. He tried to boost the strength of her *aleimi,* to lend her his structure as she struggled to reach her boyfriend's mind.

Both of them hit a hot, dense, tangled wall of living light.

Not Manny's light.

Not the construct.

Someone else's.

BLACK! Yarli yelled his name into the Barrier. *STOP HIM! PLEASE! PLEASE GOD STOP HIM BEFORE—*

I can't get through.

Black growled it at her in the Barrier, but his anger seemed to drain out of him as he watched his friend approach the end of the bank of elevators.

The two security guards just stood there, watching him approach, and Black recognized the blank stare in their eyes, as well, and realized they hadn't been stalling this Hollywood dragon fuck, but had been captured by him.

Despite his dense shields, Black could almost see him now.

He saw the other dragon's glowing outline inside the Barrier.

He saw those pale, gold eyes, the strange *aleimic* light.

But his infiltrators were right, too.

He didn't look quite the same as what Black remembered from that studio backlot.

It was definitely him, though.

There was absolutely no doubt about that.

Black tried again to get through that dense shell of *aleimic* light.

He couldn't.

He was just as powerless as Yarli.

Yarli, who was probably the most gifted seer on his team, apart from maybe Dalejem.

At the thought, his jaw clenched.

JEM! He half-screamed the male seer's name. *ARE YOU THERE? ARE YOU WATCHING THIS?*

Jem's mind rose at once.

Yes, he sent grimly. *We all are. We're all trying to get through. All of us. Nick contacted Brick. He's hoping he might be closer. How much time before you get there?*

Black refocused his eyes enough to put more of his consciousness back into the road.

Miri drove the car.

He'd made her do it, so he could try to reach the guy in his building's lobby. He knew he'd probably crash, given how much light he'd need.

She sat next to him now, focused wholly on the road, her expression hard as she glanced briefly his way. He watched her blow through a red light approvingly. Still, he couldn't help but flinch as cars blared their horns, swerving to miss them in the low-riding McLaren.

He relaxed marginally once he realized Miri was pushing them in advance, getting the drivers to change directions, to brake, to begin moving out of their path... well before they actually saw the McLaren's nose with their human eyes.

Black caught a street sign as they flew past at maybe seventy or eighty miles per hour.

Checking the map inside his headset, he grimaced.

Maybe ten minutes, he sent to Jem, frustrated. *Miri's going as fast as either of us could possibly go. At least without seriously risking both of us ending up roadkill, or cracking up the car so badly we'd end up walking—*

Can you hear them talking? Jem sent.

Black tried to listen through the Barrier, couldn't.

Surveillance? He spat the word. *Yarli? Are you getting the feed from the elevator banks? I can see enough to know they're just past the end of them... not far from the fountain.*

He gripped the car door, hearing the squeal of tires in some more distant part of his mind as Miri navigated them through the city.

Realizing he needed his headset, he opened his eyes again.

Without bothering to look at the road, he felt over his coat, then yanked the small piece of semi-organic metal out of his inside pocket and fitted it into his ear.

He gave subvocal commands, getting it to the right channel as he kept most of his mind in the construct, listening for Yarli.

He's got them switched off, she sent, her voice half-incredulous. *Woldon is working on it now... I've got Alici trying to get through to the security guards.*

They're both human? Black sent. *It's just those two? No seers?*

Another too-long silence told him he'd been wrong about that, too.

Who? Black growled. *Who else is down there?*

There's a seer in the lobby with them, Yarli admitted. *I couldn't see him, either. Not even through the Barrier. Woldon told me. They got him on camera before the... whatever it is... knocked out the system. I'm assuming he was compelled, like Manny. Maybe he's too difficult to read, so the thing called on Manny, figuring a human would be easier—*

Who?

Another pause, then Dalejem answered.

It's Holo, he said.

Black cursed under his breath, even as he glanced briefly at his wife.

He wanted to yell at her to go faster, but he bit his tongue.

He knew she wouldn't get mad, not now. He knew she'd know he was just venting. But he didn't want to fuck with her concentration to that extent.

He didn't want to risk he might throw her off, even a tiny amount.

He focused back on Yarli.

We're coming, he told her simply.

It was all he could say.

❀

olo stood frozen, right by the lobby desk.

He honestly had no idea how he'd gotten here.

He had no memory of taking the elevator, much less rappelling down the glass walls of the building to reach the ground floor.

He couldn't move.

Well... he *could* move, in some ways.

He could breathe.

He could swallow.

But whenever he tried to speak, or move his foot, or his hand, to grab his sidearm, or his headset, or, hell... a grenade... he couldn't figure out how to do it. It's like the body he wore didn't belong to him anymore. It felt like he'd completely forgotten how to use any of the mechanics of it. It felt like he'd been body-switched and they forgot to give him the new operating instructions.

For the same reason, when Holo saw Manny emerge from the aisle between the two rows of elevator doors, he couldn't shout out a warning.

He couldn't tell the Navajo human to go back—to make a run for the elevator and take it back up to the penthouse floor before the thing saw him.

He could only stand there, watching.

His body still hurt.

It was one of the only ways Holo knew it was still his.

He'd somehow left his bed and the private apartment Black gave him, on the floor just below the penthouse floor. His body hadn't liked that. However Holo had gotten down here, his body likely wouldn't have cooperated if Holo had been steering it.

That thing had forced the issue.

For the same reason, Holo's chest hurt badly.

He felt bones grinding, his breath fighting in his lungs.

He watched Manny approach the creature standing just past the security guards.

He hadn't expected to be able to hear anything.

He'd assumed the creature would simply read Manny, plumbing the depths of his mind to take whatever he wanted.

Now, however, he heard the thing speak.

"I am Vaari," it said.

Holo watched Manny stop in front of it, his face uncharacteristically blank.

Then something seemed to click.

Expression bled back into his brown eyes.

Holo had always thought the human had pretty eyes. They were a light brown, decorated with darker flecks of color. They were almost a seer's eyes.

Holo totally got why Yarli had been so attracted to him. Truthfully, Holo considered trying to bed the human himself before he noticed the way Yarli looked at him.

"I am Vaari," the dragon repeated. "You are Mañuel, are you not?"

He spoke smoothly, in a low, cultured voice, strangely friendly, like how he'd been in Los Angeles. He sounded different now, though. He didn't sound as blank here. There was more of a person in the dragon's eyes than what Holo remembered from the drone footage while Black spoke to him inside the walls of that movie studio.

"I am," Manny said, frowning.

He looked down at his body, that frown growing more pronounced as he seemed to take a kind of inventory.

"I can't move my body—" he began.

"Yes," Vaari broke in. "I did that. I apologize. But I need information, and none of those I asked seemed to know anything. That one..." The dragon motioned towards Holo with a hand. "He knows more... but he did not seem to have a very personal relationship with the other one like me. Or with our mate."

Manny's frown went from tense to tense and puzzled.

"Mate?" he said. "And who might that be?"

"Our mate," the dragon said calmly, as if it were the most reasonable thing in the world. "All beings have only one mate. Even intermediaries. We are Dragon. She is our mate."

He looked around the lobby of Black's building, his mouth pursed.

"I felt her. I felt her on that other world... but she was gone. I went to look for her, and I could not find her. I found him, instead. The other one. He brought me here. He told me I would find her here. And I did. But then he took her away."

Manny didn't look away from the dragon's face as he spoke.

Holo didn't either.

His ribs were starting to hurt.

He could feel himself bleeding somewhere.

He could feel his chest compressing wrongly.

He fought not to think about his body.

He fought to listen to the being as it spoke to Mañuel.

"Where are they now?" the being asked. "I came... more presentably this time. I came to speak to the other who is like me."

Manny grimaced, shaking his head.

Apparently the dragon allowed him that.

"He's not going to share Miri with you," Manny warned. "It's best you go find your own mate, friend. Or it's just going to bring a whole lot of hurt down on everyone."

"That is not acceptable," the being said.

Holo saw it struggling now, though.

The dragon's facial expression contorted, like it was holding back some intense pain—like a migraine, or maybe a birthing cramp, or, more likely, a seer's separation pain. The dragon struggled to push it back, whatever it was. Vaari grimaced as he gripped the arm of the human security guard standing next to him, using the human for balance.

The dragon gasped then, groaning.

There was a silence.

Then the weirdest damned thing happened.

Holo got his body back.

He collapsed onto the lobby floor, gasping, groaning in pain.

Briefly, he couldn't see at all.

He couldn't remember the last time he'd been in so much physical pain.

He groaned louder, unable to make it stop. He fought to breathe. He fought to scream as it ran fire through his chest.

The pain grew so intense he closed his eyes.

Both things brought up a wave of nausea so acute, he let out a weak cry, his body wracking with a dry heave that made everything hurt so much he nearly screamed for real. He wanted to. He wanted to scream... but he couldn't make a sound.

Now, however, his silence was no longer about the dragon.

He couldn't breathe.

He couldn't do anything.

It was more pain than he knew how to process.

When Holo could finally see straight again, he had no idea how much time had passed. Everything still hurt, but he was crumpled on the floor, holding his chest with one hand and arm, contorted so he could stare up at Manny and the dragon. Some part of him had instinctively tried to focus on the two of them, even while he was fighting for consciousness.

He still struggled to breathe, everything still hurt, but his mind started to clear.

That's when Holo realized Manny stood over him, gripping one of his arms.

Holo felt the pressure of the human's surprisingly strong fingers.

He was also fully immersed in the human's light, so he felt his thoughts, even without reaching out. He felt Manny's uncertainty about what he should do—if he should risk trying to pick

him up and run with him to the elevator, or if he might hurt
Holo too badly.

Manny was deeply nervous about trying to move him
without a stretcher.

Holo felt Manny's refusal to just leave him there, and felt a
rush of affection for the human so intense it brought tears to his
eyes.

"You should go," he managed.

He felt more than saw Manny shake his head.

"No damned way, brother," the seventy-something human
said, gruff. "But I called Yarli. They're sending someone down."

That's when noise seemingly erupted all around them.

Elevators dinged from the main banks.

More sound erupted by the glass doors to the street.

After a bare pause, the door slammed open from the garage.

Holo could feel Yarli on her way down, along with others
who'd been on the penthouse floor. He felt Yarli's terror for
Manny, and wanted to reassure her that he was all right. He was
about to try when suddenly it felt like he was surrounded.

He felt worried lights, seer and human, cluster around him
and Manny in a protective circle. He felt their cold anger, mixed
with relief they were both alive.

He heard voices in the space, telling people to bring a
stretcher down from one of the floors accessible by the main
elevators.

Then Black spoke.

Holo had never heard his voice sound like that before.

Black wasn't angry.

He was fucking murderous.

"Turn around, you piece of shit. Now. Or I'll shoot you just to
watch your head explode…"

Holo looked up.

He saw Black standing over him, a gun in one hand, his other
hand gripping the hilt of a short, single-bladed sword. Black
aimed the gun at the head of the dragon, who still stood near the

fountain, only a few yards from the edge of the black and white tile.

Holo felt the protectiveness and fury coming off Black in a dense cloud.

Next to him stood Miri, looking equally furious.

"TURN AROUND!" Black snarled. "NOW."

Slowly, the dragon-seer calling itself "Vaari" turned to face Black and his wife, along with a handful of guards who'd come up from the parking garage, and a wall of glass windows behind them to California Street.

As Vaari turned, the creature held up its hands warily, glancing over his shoulder at the twin elevator doors before frowning up at Black.

Once Holo could see the creature's face, he frowned.

Behind Holo, still gripping his arm, the old man exuded puzzlement as well.

Manny felt utterly confused.

"That's not him," the older Navajo man said. "He was here... but he's gone again. That's someone else."

Black didn't look over, but Holo saw the boss's well-formed mouth harden.

"What the fuck does that mean, *Mañuelito?*"

"It means *look* at him, Quentin." Manny motioned towards the dragon seer. "Look at his face... his eyes. He's not the same."

Holo had to agree.

At the same time, he struggled to explain it to himself in coherent words.

The male he'd seen talking to Manny, just a few seconds ago, was gone.

Instead, he saw a strangely more likeable and relatable face.

A strangely more empathic and real-looking expression lived on that face.

Black stared at the dragon without lowering the aim of his gun.

His gold-flecked eyes clicked in and out of focus with a

machine-like precision, telling Holo that Black was reading the dragon once more... trying to, anyway.

Slowly, then, Black lowered the gun.

He glanced at Miri, still frowning, but something in the frown had changed.

Before either of them could speak, the dragon himself spoke.

It wasn't to defend himself. It wasn't to explain himself, either.

Instead, he looked between Miri and Black in angry confusion.

The expression on his face hardened, right before he blurted words.

"Who the *fuck* are any of you?" he growled.

His voice came out openly hostile, thick with an accent Holo fought to identify. The accent wasn't Old Earth seer. It wasn't any human accent he was familiar with, which pretty much included any he'd ever heard, since he had a seer's photographic memory.

Glaring around at all of them again, the dragon raised his voice.

"...And where *the hell* am I?"

20

MISSING TIME

B lack blinked.

Then he matched the other's angry scowl.

"This game isn't going to work," Black warned, his voice growing colder. "Do I need to pull out the gun again? Aim it at your dick this time?"

Holo suppressed a perverse, totally inappropriate urge to laugh.

Following that, he was gasping again, holding his chest in pain.

He knew he had to be in some kind of physical shock.

He could feel Manny's shock, too, his realization of the lost time, of Yarli freaking out at his being down here. Holo couldn't even feel relief yet, despite being surrounded by Black and his people; he was too fucking confused.

Instead he stared up at the dragon.

Strangely, Holo found he believed the male's confusion.

Well, he believed it as much as he could believe anything right then. His own mind remained too confused, his body too wracked with pain, for him to trust what he felt.

Still, he *did* almost believe it.

The dragon seer felt and looked too angry to be faking his confusion.

The strange seer glared at Black like he thought *Black* had been the one to bring him here, that *Black* fucked with his mind, kidnapped him, wiped his memory, then pulled a gun on him... possibly when he'd tried to escape.

The seer seemed to hold Black personally responsible for all of it.

In Holo's experience, most people, even seers, didn't lie that well.

They would act befuddled or vulnerable or afraid, not face off with the people they were lying to, snarling at them like they were ready to rip out their throats.

Of course, if Holo was right, that made the seer more dangerous, not less.

If this dragon seer was afraid, if he thought Black had done something to him, or that he'd been kidnapped... experimented on, brainwashed, whatever... he could transform into a dragon in here and kill all of them.

Holo knew he couldn't run if that happened, but some part of him couldn't take his eyes or light off the creature, anyway.

"Speak!" Black growled. "You want to know who *I* am? Why not start with telling us who the fuck *you* are? Given that you invaded my home. Threatened my wife. Fucked with my friends. Hurt my seer brother over there. Incidentally, the wife piece of that *alone* is enough to make my trigger finger itch..."

Black flipped the sword around in a tight loop, brandishing it, one-handed.

He glared at the strange seer, and Holo felt another pulse of Black's rage, vibrating off the boss's living light, trembling the Barrier around them.

"Talk!" Black growled. "I would do it quickly, if I were you. I would much rather cut you than listen to you at the moment, given what you just did to my friends. Which means I'm going to find any way I can to rationalize it, brother..."

Miri laid a hand on Black's arm, and he fell silent.

She must have done something else, not just to Black, but to the construct as a whole. She must have told them to stand down.

Whatever Miri did, the light around all of them changed.

It grew softer, calmer, less volatile.

Holo took a deep breath, feeling something in him relax, too.

Then Miri was staring at the new dragon.

Holo noticed she didn't leave Black's side, or take her hand off his arm.

Which was good, because Holo was pretty sure he would have flipped out on both of them if Miri approached that thing on her own.

Miri glanced at him briefly.

It was a bare look, but Holo saw the warmth in her eyes.

She sent him a pulse of affection even as he thought it. Holo felt the worry there, mixed with relief, mixed with fear for him, at the way he looked on the floor, even now. Holo felt her anger too—about him, about Manny, about this creature threatening their home.

Turning back to the dragon—the new dragon—Miri spoke.

She didn't sound as overtly threatening as Black, and her voice lacked some of the underlying violence, but a thread of steel lived inside her words.

It was her "doc voice," as Black jokingly called it.

This time, it contained an added bite, an added weight of authority.

"Who are you?" Miri demanded. "Where do you come from? My husband may not have voiced it very tactfully, but he is right. We deserve answers."

The seer focused on her.

For the first time, Holo realized the new dragon had relaxed marginally, too—presumably due to whatever Miri had done to the immediate Barrier environment.

"I am Vaari."

"You told us that," Miri said, her voice just as cold. "Your name means nothing to us, brother. Who *are* you? Where do you come from?"

"I have been in many worlds..." the being began.

Black emitted a low growl.

The strange seer glared at him, then looked back at Miri.

When he did, something in that threat in his eyes dimmed. It struck Holo again that the being seemed willing to talk to the doc, to give her real answers.

Talking to Black just seemed to make it murderous.

"That's not an acceptable answer," Miri said.

The dragon met Miri's gaze. The pale eyes grew even less hard.

"I don't know," the dragon admitted.

It made a motion with its hand, in a manner Holo also didn't recognize. The gesture was graceful, and struck Holo as more nuanced than it appeared on the surface.

The being held Miri's gaze, his voice gruff, serious.

Before she could ask him again, he resumed speaking.

"I did not answer you because I do not know where I'm 'from,' in the way that phrase is normally meant. I jump dimensions. I don't remember which was the first. I would not have a name for it, even if I did know."

His words caused a silence.

Miri didn't look at Black, but Holo could almost feel them communicating.

The new dragon looked between them, scowling.

"What?" he growled. "Are you going to pretend you didn't know that about me?"

The silence deepened.

Looking around, frowning, the being added coldly,

"I don't know how I got here."

Miri frowned. "What do you mean by 'here'? This dimension? San Francisco?"

"Either." The being aimed his pale eyes back at hers. "Both."

"Why did you come to this building? What do you want from us?"

The being scowled.

"I already told you that."

The strange seer scanned the faces of the infiltrators and soldiers standing around Black and Miri, taking in each seer and human with his eyes. When he looked at Holo, towards the end, Holo saw absolutely no recognition in those pale gold eyes.

He saw no recognition when the being stared at Manny, either.

Miri looked about to speak, to ask him another question.

The dragon cut her off.

"I have no idea how I got here," he said. "I have no fucking idea who any of you people are. I assumed *you* brought me here. Really, I assumed he brought me here." The dragon seer glared pointedly at Black. "I'm still not convinced he didn't."

Miri frowned, her hand still gripping Black's arm.

"Why him? In particular?" she said. "You claim you don't remember anything. Who we are. How you got here. Why would you think *he* did this to you?"

She motioned with her head and hand towards Black, not taking her eyes off the strange seer.

"I don't know," the seer said. "Just a feeling. You and he are the only two who look familiar to me at all... who *feel* familiar to me. With you, that is a good feeling. You feel like a friend. Like someone I can trust." He glared at Black. "With him... let's just say, it feels different. The opposite, really."

He continued to glare at Black.

His eyes shimmered with *aleimic* light.

Most of Black's team, and Black himself, exchanged skeptical, deeply cynical looks. None of them spoke, at least not aloud, but Holo could almost *hear* the back and forth between them in the Barrier space—even though he wasn't hooked into the same military construct as the rest of them, and shouldn't have heard a damned thing.

Miri never took her eyes off the stranger's face.

"Do you lose time often?" she asked him next.

There was a silence.

The being's lips hardened in a frown.

"Fairly often," it muttered. He looked at Miri then at Black. "Who are you?" he said. "Are you really not going to tell me where the fuck am I?"

Black and Miri exchanged another look.

Miri's mouth pursed as she looked over the dragon with the pale gold eyes.

Resting her hands on her hips, she looked at him like she had no idea how to answer his question.

☙❧

I slumped into a chair in the conference room, looking around at all the others.

I honestly had no idea what to say.

I felt exhausted... like I'd run a marathon.

Something nagged at me, too, like I was missing a huge piece of this, something important, something that I should be remembering... something I *had* to remember.

"What the fuck do we do with this guy?" Black muttered.

He slumped down in the leather chair next to mine, the one that sat at the exact head of the table. I watched him rub his jaw. His eyes didn't focus on the room for a long-feeling few seconds as a good chunk of his team took seats around the rectangular, metal table with the monitors built into the polished surface.

"We can't leave him here," Cowboy muttered.

The seers and humans who'd been with Black in Los Angeles got here a few minutes after we brought the dragon-seer, "Vaari," up to the penthouse floor. They'd been en route from the airport at the same time Black and I had been speeding across town, trying to get here before the creature killed Manny or Holo, or both of them.

Holo still looked like hell.

They'd needed a stretcher to get him back to the medical lab upstairs.

We still hadn't called any of the seers or humans Yarli evacuated back yet, either.

Exhaling, I combed my fingers through my hair, looking at Cowboy.

"No," I agreed, thinking about all of Charles' seers, who we still had locked up in the building's lower levels. "We absolutely *can't* leave him here. It would be an unmitigated disaster."

All it would take is this "Vaari" turning into a dragon long enough to collapse the building, and we had a whole new set of problems.

I had my doubts we'd ever be able to surprise Charles' people like that again.

"Suggestions?" I said, glancing at Black, quirking an eyebrow.

It occurred to me only then how strange it was, Black being so quiet.

He looked at me at the thought, his eyes and mouth still hard.

"We'll take him somewhere. Let the techs look him over first... then we'll talk to him. Maybe he'll be willing to just leave on his own."

I nodded, biting my lip.

I didn't want this Vaari guy in the building at all, honestly, but that horse had already left the barn.

Even apart from the danger of having Charles' seers imprisoned here, I hated that he'd taken Holo and Manny. Plus, we were still getting bomb threats and whatever else from the Purity terrorists. They likely knew Black's plane had returned to San Francisco by now, which meant we'd need added security at the front of the building, not to mention whatever fallout we'd have from the media after what happened in Los Angeles.

We were losing control over the narrative already.

I knew that would happen eventually, but nothing prepared me for losing control over all of it in less than twenty-four hours.

"Don't worry about that yet," Black said.

When I looked over, his eyes held a faint warning.

"I've asked Grant to fly to New Mexico in the next few days... to interview me there. He was open to it. I told him we'll even do that thing while he's there, if we can pull it together a few weeks early..."

"That thing?" Angel burst out in a humorless laugh. "You mean your *wedding*, Quentin?"

Cowboy muttered from next to her, folding his hands over his sternum.

"Not to mention *our* wedding, darlin'."

Black scowled at both of them.

"Miri and I are already married," he growled. "But yes. Our wedding. Your wedding. I'll fly all of your people out early, too, if you're okay with the new timeline. But you're welcome to wait or speed things up on your end, whatever you want."

Black glanced at me, firming his mouth. "As for us, we were already going to make it a media event. Now we'll just make it *more* of one. We'll let Grant bring his cameras along. It'll help normalize things a little."

"How much sooner are you thinking?" I folded my arms, huddled in the leather seat.

"Three days? Four?" Black gave me a faintly apologetic look. "I was thinking this weekend. If we can make it happen."

"What makes you think we could do that?" I frowned at him in disbelief. "You know you're talking guests, catering, flowers, clearing out the resort three weeks early—"

"I have people who can handle the logistics of it, Miri." He gave me a slightly more tense look. "Can we talk about that end of things later? I want to figure out what to do with this asshole. Preferably before he breaks my building."

Pausing, he glanced around the table.

"What are our working theories on this right now? Interdimensional traveler. Obviously some manifestation of that dragon thing Miri found scattered over multiple dimensions. But what is he doing *here?* Why now?"

I nodded, thinking.

My shoulders relaxed as I put my focus on the problem.

"I figured the blackouts are a different manifestation of what happens to you with Coreq," I said after another beat. I met Black's gaze. "You don't black out... but you said you can't control things when Coreq is in charge, either. You said you felt like a kind of 'passenger' when it first happened to you inside those Pentagon labs. Like Coreq even had his own agenda... something apart from you, that you weren't even fully privy to. He definitely has his own personality, and his own way of reacting to things. He even has his own *aleimic* fingerprint, and his own *aleimic* structures... or maybe just access to different ones of yours."

Black nodded slowly, the frown still playing at his lips.

"Yes," he said. "It was exactly like that. He hijacked parts of me. But I never lost time. I was there for all of it. I could even talk through it... at least when Coreq wasn't using me to talk. Same with my light. I could use the parts of it that Coreq wasn't actively using. I tried to tell Charles that. I tried to warn him I was two people... that I couldn't control the thing in my light controlling my body and *aleimi...*"

Remembering that, Black grunted.

"...He didn't believe me. I'm pretty sure he thought I'd cracked. He also tried to talk to Coreq as if it was me, and Coreq mostly ignored him."

Easton, the muscular, tattoo-covered New Mexican transplant, looked at Kiessa and Cowboy, then back at Black.

"Coreq?" he said, frowning. "What the fuck is a Coreq?"

I saw others around the table lean forward, too.

Truthfully, I was a little surprised when Easton decided to remain in San Francisco.

Most of the other New Mexicans had gone back to their home state.

They relocated out of the Raptor's Nest not long after we all got back from the Thai island of *Koh Mangaan*.

Frank Blackfoot—who Black met along with Easton in a federal prison in Louisiana—now ran the White Eagle Spa and Resort, Black's high-end hotel property in Santa Fe.

Frank hired Devin on the spot, bringing him on board as assistant manager.

Other New Mexican natives who'd come to live with us in San Francisco also returned to the Land of Enchantment. Magic, a teenager I'd been particularly fond of, and who was scary good with a longbow even *before* Dalejem started training her, got into the University of New Mexico and moved back to Albuquerque to study artificial intelligence.

Joseph, who was in his seventies, and his wife Geraldine, who was a few years older, moved back to a property they had with their kids on the Rez.

A few other younger kids went back to go to school.

I missed them, but truthfully, I was relieved when they went.

It didn't feel safe for them here.

I liked knowing they were moving on with their lives, without the constant threat of vampire attacks and now dragon seers from other dimensions.

I'd been so excited when Magic got into college that I cried.

Honestly, a tiny part of me was jealous.

Maybe not such a tiny part.

I realized I was daydreaming about sitting in the bubbling hot tub I remembered by the glorious outdoor swimming pool at the White Eagle Spa...

...when it occurred to me the meeting was wrapping up.

I heard people pushing back their chairs.

Glancing at Black, I flushed a little when he quirked his eyebrow at me humorously.

It was kind of nice to see him smile, though.

I hadn't seen a real smile on him since we'd gotten back from Hawaii.

You want to see me smile, doc? he sent softly. *Let me kill this dragon asshole... and you and me fly to that damned resort. We'll make Frank give us the honeymoon suite, get married inside that swimming pool, and fuck like rabbits for the next six months straight.*

Pain left him in a rippling cloud as he let himself think about that.

Gaos. I'm not even kidding. I got hard just joking about that. Painfully fucking hard, doc. I haven't been in this much separation pain since Koh Mangaan...

I felt my own gut clench.

Honestly, Black's plan didn't sound half-bad.

Except the killing-a-seer-we-knew-nothing-about part.

"Let's go talk to him," I said instead, speaking out loud. "Maybe we won't have to kill him. Maybe we can just ask him nicely to piss off and go home."

I fought back my own wave of separation pain as I thought about that.

I tried to think the rest of it quietly.

...but gaos gaos gaos, husband... I breathed inside my mind. *I'm so completely and totally onboard with the rest of it...*

When I caught him staring at me, I honestly couldn't tell if he'd heard that last prayer-wish of mine, or not.

THAT NAGGING VOICE

Something nagged at me. It nagged loudly, persistently, maddeningly from the back of my mind, but I couldn't make out any of the words.

I had no idea what it wanted.

I had no *friggin' idea* what the hell it wanted from me.

Whatever that voice was, it gradually grew louder.

Like a worm burrowing deeper inside my brain, it frustrated me and made me manic and distracted me, all without illuminating a damned thing. I couldn't think past it... not easily, or clearly... nor well enough to recognize what bothered me.

That distracting, vibrating warning told me not a damned thing about what I should feel warned about, not in the more conscious areas of my mind.

It was louder now.

Louder than it had been in the lobby, when I was too worried about Holo, and too angry about what that seer had done to him and Manny, to really be able to think clearly.

Now, things were quieter, and I still couldn't figure it out.

Something was wrong.

Something had tilted things, just the tiniest bit... but enough to throw everything out of whack, including my *aleimic* light, including everything I felt off our people and Black.

Something was wrong.

"Miri?" Black growled. "Will you talk to this asshole? He sure as fuck won't listen to me."

My eyes clicked back into focus.

I glanced over at where Black scowled, standing next to a doctor's padded exam table, the same table where the strange seer sat, now wearing a pair of light blue boxers and a white T-shirt. If it bothered him, sitting there in front of us, wearing only underwear, nothing showed on his high-cheekboned face.

"He won't wear a collar," Black growled. "He seems to think that my concerns he might suddenly decide to try and *murder* us all again, and abscond with my wife, aren't 'reasonable.'" Black grunted in annoyance. "Or not reasonable enough for him to wear the goddamned thing until we know more about what triggers these blackouts of his..."

I sighed.

Walking over to the seer, I folded my arms.

"What's the problem?" I said.

"It will prevent me from jumping," the male seer said at once.

He glared up at Black, then aimed a more subdued version at me.

"I must be able to jump. I will not tolerate making that impossible."

I frowned, studying his face.

I could see the fear there, the absolute, immovable insistence that he have access to that escape route should he need it. I suspected he came by that fear honestly, but that didn't change a damned thing from our perspective.

We might have to force the issue, Black murmured in my mind.

"I would not try it," the seer snapped, glaring at him. "How stupid do you think me? You would not get it halfway around my neck before I would jump!"

"I would if I knocked you out with horse tranquilizer first," Black muttered under his breath.

The being glared at him, his eyes and light furious.

I barely heard either of them. I frowned instead, staring at the tile floor, feeling that nagging thing jabbing at the back of my neck.

"Where did you come from?" I asked him again, refolding my arms. "What planet?"

"I told you." He shook his head. "I cannot answer that."

"I don't mean where you were born," I clarified. "I mean the last planet. The most recent one before this. Wherever you were before you jumped to *this* dimension."

There was a silence.

"I don't know what this is called, either..." he muttered.

He gave me a harder look.

"And I do not even know for certain it *was* the last place," he added darkly. "It is the last place I remember. I suppose it is relatively logical to assume that is where I was when I blacked out and began to make the journey here... but there is no guarantee of that. After all, how would I know? How would I have any idea of how long the blackout even lasted?"

Black folded his arms, scowling down at the seer.

I waited, too.

But the other seer didn't go on.

Exhaling, I fingered some of my hair out of my face, trying again.

"Can you describe it? Was it an Earth planet? Like this one? Was it the same basic planet... but a different timeline / dimension?"

"I don't know," he said. "I think so."

"You *think* so," Black muttered, annoyed.

I gave him a warning glance, then looked back at the strange seer.

"What level of technology?" I said. "Cities? Mostly agrarian?

Post-apocalyptic? Were there humans there? Seers? Vampires? Or some other dominant species?"

I saw the seer's brow clear.

"Humans," he said. "Agrarian. Definitely agrarian. They lived pretty simply. I don't remember any other seers..."

His eyes slid out of focus as he stared off, obviously trying to remember.

Something about the look on his face made me nervous.

Nervous enough that I spoke sharply, jerking him out of wherever he'd gone.

"Can you show us?" I said. "Via the Barrier?" Thinking then, I considered another possibility. "Maybe you could just take me there—"

"No," Black growled.

He stared at me after he cut me off.

I stared back, mostly surprised. Then, thinking about it, envisioning that scenario from Black's perspective, I found myself conceding his point.

I looked back at Vaari.

"I think he's right. If the same thing set you off as before, I wouldn't be safe." I gauged his eyes. "You get that, right? To you, you just black out... to us, you turn into a sociopathic monster who thinks I'm his mate."

Vaari flinched, his eyes widening.

From his expression, he really hadn't thought about it from that perspective.

Sighing, I looked at Black.

He didn't have to speak.

My eyes returned to the strange dragon-seer.

"You're going to have to wear the collar—" I began.

Out of nowhere, it hit me.

I knew suddenly, exactly what my light had been prodding me to realize.

I'd been to an agrarian world recently.

One without other seers. Without vampires.

Charles.

Goddamn it.

※

"Where is he?" I had to fight not to shout the words. "Where is the male seer you brought here with you? The one who told you where to find me?"

The seer stared at me, angry confusion back in his eyes.

I had an overwhelming desire to slap him, but I didn't.

Some part of me wanted to scream at him, now that I realized what had been bothering me, what I'd been feeling in my light ever since the dragon-seer showed up in the skies above Los Angeles.

Charles was here.

I knew, even before I *knew.*

That same dragon-seer now sat in front of me in boxer shorts, his mouth curled in an angry frown.

"I already told you. I don't remember anyone. I don't remember anything at all... not before your asshole mate waved a gun in my face, ranting at me about breaking into his damned building and doing something to his friends. I definitely don't remember meeting another seer."

But any sympathy I might have had for the strange seer had vanished.

Now his attitude about his own blackouts just angered me.

They struck me as cavalier.

They struck me as irresponsible.

Some part of me wanted to hit him again.

I'd already made him show me the world he last remembered.

I recognized it.

I'd made a point of recognizing it, so I could find Charles again if I ever needed to.

The part the seer, Vaari, showed me wasn't the same part where I'd left Charles, but every world, every dimension, had a kind of vibration, a signature my living light could recognize. I couldn't put those signatures into words, but my *aleimi* could; those vibrations acted like a unique fingerprint in my light... like a street address I could identify and find again.

It was definitely the same world.

Worse, I should have known that.

I should have known it from the beginning.

The coincidence of a creature so much like Black showing up here, so soon after I left Charles on that world... it couldn't really be a coincidence at all.

He must have felt you, Black muttered in my mind. *He must have felt you from his dragon form, and the dragon part of him must have tracked your light to Charles. Now this asshole conveniently forgot all of it.*

I scowled at Black, but his words felt right to me.

What are we going to do? I sent. *If he really can't remember, then how are we going to find him? We don't even know if he brought Charles back here with him. But if he did, you know by now Charles is holed up somewhere, hiding behind some kind of military-grade construct in one of his hideaways in Russia... plotting around how to bust all of his buddies free so he can start his "conquer the humans and kill all the vamps" thing all over again.*

Black grimaced.

I felt him thinking, even as the seer on the exam table in front of me cleared his throat.

I looked at him, and Black looked at him, and the seer scowled.

"I can hear you, you know," Vaari growled. "I can hear every damned word."

"With all seers?" I asked. "Or just us?"

Vaari grew silent briefly.

I wondered if the question had even occurred to him before I said it.

I decided it hadn't.

"Just you," he said, looking between us. His pale eyes grew wary once more. "I can only hear the two of you. Why is that?"

Black's darker, deeper gold eyes hardened.

I found myself staring at those eyes I loved, the irises flecked with glints of bright yellow, gold-white, gold-blacks and greens.

Black's eyes were gorgeous.

The longer I'd known him, the more I saw in them.

Vaari frowned at me, like he'd heard that, too.

The stare Black aimed at the strange dragon-seer turned cold.

"You should go," he told him. "You should go back to wherever the fuck you came from, brother, before we're forced to kill you. Can you do those... jumps... the interdimensional thing you do... in this form? Or do you have to turn back into the dragon, first?"

The seer swiveled his stare from my face to Black's.

Again, I saw the hostility there.

Even in this form, Vaari seemed a little too nice to me, a little too not-nice to Black.

I understood why Black wanted him gone.

When Black didn't react to his glare, Vaari exhaled in annoyance.

"I can do it in this form," he said. "I can jump like this."

"Then go," Black growled. "Now. Before you change back into an even bigger asshole."

There was a silence.

The dragon seer pushed off the padded medical table.

He landed on his bare feet, wincing a little as he shifted his weight on the cold tile.

Vaari looked at me for a few beats too long, then looked at Black, his lighter gold eyes shimmering with living light.

Without so much as a nod to either of us...

...he vanished.

The pale blue boxers and the white T-shirt fluttered to the floor.

Black and I just stood there for a few seconds, staring at the empty articles of clothing on the tile.

Then I turned to face Black.

"You know that probably won't help," I said, grimacing at the thought. "If he really *is* connected to Coreq...or to you... or to me... or to all three of us... he might have the same compulsion to return to us, as soon as he regains his dragon form. He could just jump right back here, the next time the dragon decides to take over his consciousness. He could show up *here* next time, Black. Right here, in this very room. We have no idea if he can remember things from the *non*-dragon side of himself, but we should assume he can."

Thinking about my own words, I frowned.

"If his powers work anything like mine, he'll remember how to get back. I don't have the dragon thing you have, but the specific resonance with this dimension should remain imprinted on his light. He'll know *exactly* where we are, Black... unless he somehow changes his *aleimic* body entirely, between the two states of consciousness."

I felt my jaw harden briefly.

"Worst case scenario, which we can't rule out... he remembers everything he knew in this form whenever he changes back to his dragon form. If that's the case, he'll likely come straight here... possibly in a matter of seconds, as soon as he flips back."

"Yes," Black said.

His long jaw hardened, but I strongly got the impression that same thing had already occurred to him.

"He'll know where Charles is, too, doc," he added, his voice hard.

There was a silence.

I couldn't help thinking about that.

Black wasn't wrong, but what he was proposing was dangerous as hell.

I could see Black thinking about it, too.

When he looked at me, however, eyes grim, he gave me a taut smile, the barest shadow of his killer grin.

"Well," he said. "Maybe we'll never see him again. Problem solved."

I nodded, forcing a smile of my own.

"Problem solved," I echoed.

I really wanted to believe that was a possible outcome of all this.

I wanted Black to believe it, too.

Sadly, it didn't feel remotely likely to either one of us.

WHAT SHE TOOK

F austus walked up a set of narrow metal stairs, leading to a rusted-out metal door that appeared to be locked by a heavy padlock.

The whole area, in the far reaches of northwestern Poland, in a small island and town known as Swinoujscie, appeared to be abandoned, and not only because it was currently the off-season for the small resort town situated on the Baltic Sea.

"No one would destroy it, you know why?" his Polish cab driver said in English with an overpoweringly thick accent. "No one destroy it here, our beautiful island, for the same reason anything was spared by those monsters..."

The taxi driver gave Charles a knowing, almost indulgent look as he let his pregnant pause fill the inside of the yellow taxi.

"Hitler liked it," the cabbie whispered conspiratorially. "He wanted to keep it as a vacation spot for upper members of the Reich..."

Faustus frowned, but only on the inside.

Truthfully, he had his doubts that was the real story.

But World War II stories somehow remained alive and well in this part of the world, just as the war itself did. It was the strangest thing to Charles—the way awareness of the second world war seemed to scar their collective psyche and linger in the air like a foul stench.

If he were being honest, Faustus thought it was a colossal waste of time, analyzing and picking at that same war, seventy-five years after it had finished.

But the taxi driver wanted to talk.

Even after he pulled up to the back of a rusted-out looking warehouse, covered in splashes of graffiti, most of it made up of various obscenities in Polish and Russian, the man wanted to talk. Even when Charles stood there, holding a newspaper in his hand, making it clear he wanted to go, the man wanted to talk.

In the end, Faustus had to push him to get him to leave.

Raising a fist, the seer pounded on the metal panel.

He listened, but heard nothing.

Faustus tried pounding again.

Finally, he walked over to the small keypad hidden in the shadows to the right of the door. He flipped open the protective metal cover, and punched through a series of symbols. A swell of rage hit him when nothing happened.

They must have changed the goddamned codes here, as well.

This was the third such facility he'd checked.

He backed away from the door.

Staring down at the paper in his hand, he frowned at the date.

He still couldn't believe so little time had passed here.

What had been months, more likely years on that shithole world where Miriam left him, had been only a few weeks on this version of Earth. He'd watched seasons change in that other place. He'd seen babies born. He'd gone through cold, heat, rain, mud, humidity, more rain, flowers, fruit, falling leaves.

Here, almost no time had passed at all.

He seemed to remember one of his infiltrators telling him that.

One of the people Charles had watching Black and Miri in

San Francisco... what felt like a million years ago now... they'd mentioned "different passage of time" regarding the worlds Miri visited on her jumps.

Charles hadn't thought about that, on that other world.

He hadn't factored that in, coming back here.

Even if he *had* considered it, he suspected it wouldn't have made much difference.

It would have been a shock to come back here regardless, only to find that so little had changed... even as absolutely everything had.

He was about to walk away, to try the back entrance, when the speaker crackled and whistled, letting out a hard tone of discordant static.

Faustus ducked in reflex, right before the speaker clicked on.

"Yes?" the voice said. "Who is there?"

Faustus fought between fury and relief.

"Let me in. Now."

The speaker crackled.

Charles listened to the silence on the other end.

Then he felt them.

He felt their light. He felt the first darting probe to his *aleimi*... then a second... then a third. He felt their disbelief when they ID'd him for real.

There was a buzzing sound, and Charles caught hold of the metal door handle, yanking it towards him.

That time, the door gave.

The padlock had been a mere prop; it didn't attach to anything. The door opened outward easily, taking the metal padlock with it.

Charles walked inside...

...and came to a dead stop.

The small chamber past the main door looked like a dead end: three walls of cement, covered with a film of black mold. Faded lines of paint remained visible on the other side of the mold, but as he looked around, he didn't see any features on the cement walls, or any doors.

"What the hell is this...?" he muttered.

He was about to try and contact them through the Barrier space, when there was a grinding, mechanical sound, like giant teeth gnashing.

It came from his right.

Charles turned sharply, just in time to see an opening appear in what had looked like unbroken, moldy cement, cracked and worn away by water damage.

Now, he could see that it had been mostly a mirage.

The cement broke in a straight line on three sides.

The camouflaged door pulled open in thirds, showing a large shipping elevator.

Charles waited until the door had opened entirely.

He looked inside, fighting a sudden wave of paranoia.

The speakers inside the elevator crackled to life.

"Come in, sir," a familiar voice said. "It's all right, sir. The wall's organic. It's just a precaution... we're all in the sub-basement level."

Charles stared up at the speaker.

He knew the person on the other end.

He *knew* them.

Somehow, that realization hit at him only then, convincing him for the first time he was back—that he'd really made it back to his home, to his people.

A pain stabbed at his heart.

His hand rose to his chest.

Briefly, he couldn't breathe, or really think.

Emotion overcame him.

He remembered the first morning he'd woken up in that other dimension, staring out over a river and a field, realizing she'd left him at the approximate location of the White House, on both of the Earths he'd embraced as his home.

He'd hated her for that. He'd hated her so much for that.

She'd left him at the location of his previous seat of power...
only without the power.

Without his people.

Without anything.

Gritting his teeth at the memory, he shoved it aside, along
with the maudlin emotions that wanted to rise with it.

Without another second of hesitation, Charles entered the
square elevator.

He reentered his domain.

As soon as he'd crossed the threshold, the elevator doors
closed soundlessly behind him.

"Brother." The East-Asian seer choked on the word.
He wiped his eyes as they broke from their clenched
embrace.

"Gaos. My brother, my heart... we thought you dead. We truly
believed all of you had to be dead by now... or lost to us forever,
in whatever hellhole she'd left you in. We had to be careful even
looking for you from the Barrier. I was told to protect what
resources remained by those fighting towards the end, in the
event anyone might return. I confess, we'd about given up
hope..."

He wiped his eyes.

A smile broke on his lips.

Charles saw the pain that lived within the male's obvious joy.

He wanted to tell his brother how much longer it had been
for him.

His chest clenched, however, making it difficult to force out
words.

Meanwhile, Chu continued to beam at him.

"Gaos," he said again. "You have no idea how much good it
does my heart, seeing you here with us again. Just to see you
alive and well, brother Faustus... it is like a miracle. It is like a

true miracle to all of us. We have mourned you. We have mourned all of you... but most of all *you,* brother. Our Father. Our leader. Our one, true hope."

Charles wiped his eyes, looking around at the space where they'd met him.

Unlike where the elevator doors lived on the ground floor, here they fed into a long metal and stone corridor, lined on either side by torch-like lights.

The tunnels shimmered with *aleimic* light, visible to him behind the Barrier. Even with his physical eyes, the sheer amount of living matter fused into the metal gave the walls a strange, otherworldly sheen that evoked the organics that lived inside.

He cleared his throat, looking back at Chu.

"It is safe, then?" His voice came out gruff. "Your work, brother Chu. Black and my niece have not taken it all from you?"

Chu's expression grew slightly more grim.

"I'm not going to lie, brother... we thought you were them. We've been more or less waiting for them to come for us, putting off that day and biding our time as long as we can hold out. We've done our best to hide, to stay one step ahead... to put off our capture to secure as much of your work for future generations as we can. Above all, we have prioritized keeping the organic technology safe... and out of enemy hands. We have attempted to take out the Usurper and his wife..."

He looked at Charles apologetically, as if afraid he might disapprove. "I know you had wanted them alive, before. But we took a vote and decided, with you and the others gone—"

"You did the right thing," Charles said, his voice cold. "I no longer have any concern over keeping my niece or her husband alive. For any reason."

There was a silence.

Charles felt Chu's approval.

He felt it from others in the Barrier, too.

"You have not managed to kill them, I take it?" Charles prodded.

"No, sir. Not yet." Gauging Charles' eyes yet again, Chu seemed to relax more at whatever he saw. "We have been careful, as I said. We deploy our assets only from sites that cannot be traced back here. We have self-destruct protocols for much of the weaponized tech and organics... and we've sent out only a few at a time, with the exception of one full-blown attack, where we deployed several dozen. We had quite a few malfunctions in that first round, but we learned much from this, and have since been able to improve our models significantly. Despite our failure to eliminate either target, it proved a highly useful exercise for us—"

"Good." Charles nodded. "Very good, brother. I am glad you have been thinking in the long term with this. I am so very very grateful that you have managed to keep our work safe, and have even built upon it, despite everything you faced."

Chu gave him a hard look.

"I will tell you, brother... it was very difficult not to throw everything we had at them, the hell with the consequences. Many wanted revenge. Many of us, myself included, I confess, wanted it badly enough that we had to be talked down. But in the end, we all agreed. None of us could bear the thought of the Usurper and his wife, or any of their *thugs* getting ahold of our work here. The thought of them destroying it, or worse, giving it to the human scum to use against our own people..."

Chu bit his lip, as if forcing himself not to finish that sentence.

He shook his head, grimacing.

"This thought keeps me up at night still," he confessed. "So does my anger, brother. That they would do this to *you,* most of all, after all you have done for our people... that keeps me up at night. Thankfully, it has also hardened my resolve."

Charles fought against another tightening in his throat.

As he looked at the other male, he felt an intense swell of affection.

Not only affection.

Love.

A fierce, uncompromising love... a love of war and blood.

He would die for his brothers and sisters here, those who remained loyal to the cause.

Yet, so much of his emotion remained grief.

All the work he had done.

All of it... *all of it*... years and years... decades of planning and positioning his people, of waiting, of stage-setting...

It had all been destroyed in a matter of days.

And not by one of *them*.

Humans had not done this.

Vampires had not done it, either.

No, Charles' work had been destroyed by members of his own race.

It had been destroyed by one of his own blood.

"You were not wrong to assume me dead," he said thickly. He still gripped the arms of the other male, and now he met his gaze. "Perhaps my physical death was not accomplished... at least not yet... but I thought myself dead to you, my dearest of brothers. I truly believed I would never be here again, on this world."

"Where were you?" Simon's pale blue eyes shone iridescent under the flickering lights. "Did you see any of the others where you were?"

Charles again felt his throat close.

He'd been so shocked when he landed in the world where Miri left him.

He'd never felt anything so desolate in his life.

For years, he had felt not a single seer on that world, apart from himself.

Then, coming back here, he'd been shocked all over again.

The construct he and his people spent years perfecting... gone.

Most of the seers he spoke to every day... also outside of his reach.

He could feel none of his inner circle, none of his friends.

His people all over Washington D.C. had vanished.

His people in Moscow, in London, in Switzerland...

It was like Miriam took an eraser and just rubbed out Charles' entire existence.

Where had she taken them? Where had they gone?

Had she killed them all?

Had he been spared to suffer alone in eternity?

Miri had to have done it on purpose. There was no possible way she had done any of it on accident. Yet he still could not comprehend why. *Why* had she done it?

Did she really hate him so much?

Did she hate her own kind?

The thought truly shocked him.

Charles never recovered from that shock, in all those years on that other world.

That his own niece could have dumped him, dumped *him,* who loved and protected her all those years, alone on a world with none of his kind... it hurt him deeper than he'd thought himself capable of being hurt. After decades of fighting vampires, he'd thought those bloodsucking parasites were the most sadistic creatures any god had ever imagined.

Yet no vampire had hurt him like Miri had.

That she deliberately could have left him without the comfort of living light, permanently separated from his brothers and sisters... it was inconceivable.

But now it seemed she had done it to every seer fighting for their kind.

That assumed she hadn't just killed the rest of them outright.

It was beyond betrayal, beyond injustice. It evoked something in him beyond anger, revenge, beyond even grief.

It made him sick.

"No," he said, after that too-long pause. He refocused on

Chu. "No. I saw no one, my brother. Not until a solitary, dimension-jumping being found me there... the one who brought me back. The other Dragon."

Simon's eyes widened.

"A *dragon*? Did you say a *dragon* brought you here?" Simon's eyes widened a touch more. "Were you the one who set him on Black? In Hollywood?"

Charles released his arms.

He stepped back.

He gauged what he saw in Chu's face.

"You have seen him." He didn't voice it as a question. "Where? Has the creature really attacked Black? I arrived back in this dimension only a few days ago..."

Chu nodded vigorously, seer-fashion.

A smile broke his round face. He looked oddly excited, like he'd just been given an amazing Christmas present.

He waved Charles deeper into the dim corridor, past the rows of flickering, greenish lights set in dark-green, clearly-organic wall fixtures. Once Charles began to follow, Chu began walking more rapidly, backwards at first, then in a straight line, once Charles sped his pace enough to pull up alongside him.

Chu led him towards a much brighter light, one that lived past a curve in the corridor maybe a hundred feet ahead.

The technician began speaking in an excited voice.

"Yes," he said. "Honestly, we were afraid to view this as a positive development, at least without knowing more. It only just happened today... during an interview in a movie studio in Hollywood, of all things. Black's wife appears to have rescued him in the end, jumping him out before he could be harmed... but they definitely did not kill the second Dragon. We managed to get image capture on the new being, both before and after the initial conflict. We have been working hard to identify him, both via Barrier imprints and scans on what we could feel of him in the time since... so obviously anything you could tell us that might help with that would be most welcome..."

Charles nodded, gazing around as they approached the curve in the tunnel.

Chu went on in a voice that now sounded more like an official report, like something he would have given Charles before he'd been taken.

The sheer familiarity of the seer's speech cadence, of his tone as he fell back into their normal dynamic, straightened Charles' spine, squaring his shoulders, bringing back the seer he had been before Miri left him to die on that world.

"...As you know, we initially had the organics programmed to take out vampires. We even had specific vamps ID'd to eliminate first. Miri's friend Nick Tanaka, their vampire 'king,' Brick... a number of high-ranked fighters in Brick's inner circle... his main henchman, the vampire known only as 'Dorian,' and so forth..."

Exhaling, Chu went on in the same voice.

"...We added most of Black's inner circle to the program later. We've also recently refined a scaled, multi-scenario prioritization of that list, to aid the assets in choosing targets. That was the mistake we made on Hawaii. We gave them a list of primary targets without prioritizing. It confused their systems when confronted with multiple targets on the list at the same time. We believe we've fixed that glitch—"

"Are there still vampires programmed for elimination?" Charles said.

"Yes, sir. Absolutely. They are factored in as part of the prioritization, just like the seers. Black seems to have continued his alliance with the bloodsuckers, even after they crushed our leadership."

Charles winced, but Chu didn't appear to notice.

"...We don't know if that is because of Nick Tanaka, with whom they seem to have reconciled... or if it has something to do with your other niece, the one the vampires turned not long after your brother was killed."

Chu gave him a faintly cautious look before adding,

"We try to stay as up to date on those developments as we

can, but our intelligence apparatus is much diminished, as you can probably imagine. We work with what we can get, and tweak the kill lists accordingly, where it seems relevant."

"Do we still have someone on the inside?"

Chu nodded. "Yes. So far, neither of our primary infiltrators appear to have been ID'd."

Charles got distracted briefly as they entered that light at the end of the dim corridor, and he found himself in a high-ceilinged, cave-like room. He looked up at the rock walls, realizing the elevator had taken him down further than he'd realized.

He gazed around at rows of machines, lab stations, watery containers filled with animals and parts of living beings, including heads, limbs and torsos of humans, seers, vampires...

Applause broke out.

Charles, flinched, looked down.

Then he saw them.

Every face he saw smiled at him, some beaming grins from across the room where they clapped their hands enthusiastically in his direction. The clapping grew louder, the longer he stood there. Charles saw tears in most of the eyes he met, and his own vision grew blurry again as he was moved to see and feel the real emotion there.

And light... living light.

It surrounded him again, the light of his people.

A few let out whoops, and that spread too, until the rock walls echoed back what sounded like an enormous crowd, rather than the twenty or so scientists who'd somehow evaded capture from Miri and Black and their fucking vampires.

For the first time in weeks... months... Charles felt hope.

He felt hope, and with that came resolve.

He wasn't out of the game yet.

The war wasn't yet called.

He could fix this.

Thinking about the dragon being finding him, and bringing him back... thinking about the odds of that happening, in all the worlds and beings the dragon seer could have traveled to... a smile teased at his perfectly-formed lips.

He *would* fix it.

He would make this right again, if it was the last thing he did.

He had, after all, always been Lucky.

23

THE MORNING OF

"Are we really going forward with this?" I muttered the words under my breath, more to myself than to anyone I sat beside on the private plane. "We have to be insane... all of us..."

Angel, who sat next to me, snorted.

"Probably," she said cheerfully.

I was about to say more, when Panther, my dog, sat up.

He'd been curled up on the seat on my other side. It was an aisle seat, so maybe not the best place for a dog, much less a long-limbed, gangly, half-grown, Irish wolfhound pup, but I figured he'd be okay there, since he'd made it his spot immediately, dragging up a blanket and then flopping down on top of it.

Now he jerked out of his doze, clearly smelling something in the plane's recycled air.

Staring down the center aisle of the plane, ears perked, he let out a joyous, happy bark.

He immediately began wagging his tail.

From that bark alone, I knew who it was.

I knew exactly who I'd see entering the plane, even before I turned my head, even though some part of me couldn't quite believe it. His ghostly white face appeared from between the two blue curtains separating us from the flight attendant area and the cockpit.

Several seers and humans on the plane audibly gasped.

I watched Nick walk warily down the aisle, his eyes darting around like those of a stalking cat. I couldn't help feeling nervous for him.

I also couldn't quite believe he was here.

My eyes shifted to his seer boyfriend—who still sported a black eye from my husband's over-zealous fist.

I waited until they'd both reached our cluster of seats.

"Are you suicidal?" I asked, incredulous.

"Maybe," Nick grunted.

I watched him throw himself into a leather seat across from Angel's, just like he would have done back when he was human. The difference was, thanks to his concrete-slab of a vampire body, the airplane seat groaned in pain, reacting poorly to the added pounds and general unwieldiness of his new physique.

"You're crashing my wedding?" I folded my arms, pretending to scowl at him.

He lifted an eyebrow, unfazed.

"Crashing?" He grunted. "I was invited."

"Seriously?" I folded my arms. "What idiot did that?"

"That would be you," Dalejem said from the aisle, quirking an eyebrow.

"Oh," I said, exhaling. "Right." Looking back at Nick, I frowned. "Seriously though... I meant it about wanting you there, but I never thought you'd come in a million years, Nick. You said no way, as I recall. You laughed in my face."

Nick scowled, but didn't really answer. Reaching for the sun shade on the oval window, he yanked it down, even though it was dark outside.

I couldn't help but be happy to see him, even if it was sheer madness for him to come.

Maybe it had been a mistake for me to invite him.

"It wasn't just you," Dalejem said, hearing me. "He knew you'd want him there."

That time, Jem didn't mean Nick.

Black. Black somehow talked Nick into coming.

Black was behind this.

Because of course he was.

Looking out one of the oval windows at the darkness, I frowned back at Nick. I still couldn't make up my mind how I felt about him risking his life just to see me get married. Particularly since the spectacle of this was primarily to get human media attention.

"How will you even watch the wedding, given it's happening in broad daylight?" I said, refolding my arms. "Doesn't the sun equal vampire barbecue? Aren't you supposed to burst into flames whenever it touches your delicate vampire skin?"

I saw Nick wince.

Thinking about my choice of words, I grimaced.

I'd forgotten the fire in Thailand that led to Nick being turned into a vampire in the first place. The fire *we* left him in.

Black and I.

After the wince, Nick gazed at me levelly, his face expressionless.

"You think I'd miss your ridiculously over-the-top fucking celebrity dream wedding in the New Mexican desert?" He looked at Angel. "Or Angel's, for that matter?" He grunted as if that was the stupidest thing he'd ever heard. "Dream on, Dr. Fox."

He still managed to look genuinely defensive.

I saw him look around surreptitiously, scoping out the length of the cabin, noting all the eyes on us. His arms remained folded, his broad shoulders tense. From his expression, he had his doubts he'd even make it to the wedding.

As I thought it, Nick looked back at me.

After a bare pause, he leaned forward, his hands clasped between his knees.

"Honestly, I agree with you," he said in a low voice. "This is probably suicide."

He glanced at Dalejem, who'd just finished stowing away their carry-on bags, and now set his backpack down on the cabin floor, right before he sank into the middle seat next to Nick. I saw Nick focus on Jem's black eye, and scowl, like just seeing it there still angered him.

He looked back at me, that frown still on his lips.

"Black said we *had* to come," he added, gruff. "He fucking insisted. He was kind of a dick about it, if you want the truth. He paid for Yumi and Hiroto to come, too."

Angel burst out in a laugh, but I saw her smiling at Nick fondly, shaking her head.

Nick gave her a bare glance.

I couldn't help noticing his crystal-colored vampire eyes relaxed when he looked at Angel. They grew more guarded again when he looked at me.

"He said you'd never forgive him if I didn't show," Nick added. "He said, 'even if she won't fucking admit it, she'll hold that crap over my head forever'... and that he wasn't 'shouldering that shit,' as he put it, during his damned honeymoon."

Angel chuckled again.

Nick paused, as if waiting for me to refute or agree.

"He really insisted you would want me there," Nick said, clearly not satisfied with my non-response. "He *insisted*, Miri. I tried to make excuses, but he wasn't having it. I told him we'd never get there in time, that we'd have to drive since I couldn't fly commercial... so he said we had to come *this* way... on his private plane with you and Angel... or he'd send his people to come 'get' me."

Dalejem grunted a laugh.

Angel chuckled, too.

Nick gave both of them faintly irritated looks, but his eyes never really left mine.

When I didn't answer him that time, either, he frowned, leaning back in his seat.

He moved his hands out of the way a few seconds later, when my dog, Panther, jumped off the aisle seat next to me and ran over to him. The rapidly-growing puppy leapt into his lap and promptly began licking his face.

I fought not to smile, keeping my expression stern.

Nick ruffled Panther's ears, scratching and rubbing his back and chest, all without looking away from me.

I could almost see the question in his eyes.

Thinking about that question, I shook my head.

"I didn't tell him to do that."

Nick looked somewhere between hurt and relieved. "Do you want me to leave? We should probably get off the plane now, if—"

I let out a laugh. "Nice try, Tanaka. But no. You're coming."

Nick looked at Angel, who was even more vehement than me.

"You are *definitely* coming," she informed him. "Don't even think about trying to get off this plane, Nicky. You'll wake up in a bathtub filled with garlic and holy water..."

Dalejem laughed louder at that.

Around the plane, heads turned, staring at us.

They looked away a second later.

Nick continued to scan seats as he stroked and scratched and petted Panther. His crystal eyes looked worried now, and more than a little nervous.

It hit me suddenly who he was looking for.

"Jax and Kiko are taking the other plane," I informed him, my voice low. "Dex is already in New Mexico. He flew commercial, straight from Los Angeles."

"Where's Black?" Nick muttered, still looking around. "You forget your husband, doc?"

Angel grunted, refolding her arms.

I answered Nick.

"Him and Cowboy took the other plane, too. You know... tradition."

Nick's expression cleared slightly, but he continued to look tense.

When he just sat there, petting the dog, Dalejem cleared his throat.

"And that Dragon thing is definitely gone?" Jem said, his voice less hushed than both of theirs had been. "It seems odd that it came and went so quickly—"

"It is," I said, giving him a warning stare. "Gone."

The last thing I wanted to do was jinx things on that front.

Power of positive thinking and all.

The jets began powering up.

We were getting ready to leave.

I glanced down the aisle, then back at a stewardess, who used hand-gestures to ask me silently if I wanted another triple-shot cappuccino. Glancing down at my empty cup, I looked back at her and nodded gratefully.

I wouldn't sleep on the four-hour flight, even if it was still only like two in the morning.

I never slept on planes.

I definitely wouldn't sleep on *this* plane.

Dalejem grunted.

When I looked over, he was smiling, and not in an unsympathetic way.

"Wedding jitters?" he said, motioning towards my coffee cup.

"Something like that," I admitted. I glanced at Angel. "Did you sleep at all?"

"Not a wink," she confirmed.

The engines keened louder and higher. The plane began rolling backwards, away from the jetway, and away from the mostly-glass terminal. I let my eyes glance back over the occupants of the plane's cabin as we continued to taxi, moving away from the private gate Black rented at SFO, specifically for the wedding party.

Most of the seats were full.

In fact, all of the seats I could see were full.

A lot of people stared back at me as I scanned faces.

Everyone on the plane had definitely noticed our group at the back of the main cabin.

I wondered if Ace, Javier, Alice, or one of the other humans close to Dex might be texting the Marine vet, even now. At this very moment, someone on our team might be sending photos and live video feed that showed Nick and Jem sitting on leather seats in Black's private jet, playing with my dog, joking around with the rest of us.

The thought made me grimace.

It also brought back another wave of gut-wrenching nerves.

Then again, those nerves hadn't really left.

For the past twenty-four hours, I'd been so freaked out, I thought I might throw up, pretty much any time I let myself stop long enough to think about it.

I couldn't remember the last time I'd felt like this.

The feeling was akin to terror.

I was genuinely worried I might throw up during the wedding itself.

"You won't," Jem assured me.

He smiled as he laid a hand on Nick's thigh. I watched him massage Nick's leg, right before he leaned most of his weight on Nick's shoulder and side.

Jem continued to study my face and light.

Still watching my face, Dalejem added,

"Black is going to talk to him, *na?* Before the ceremony?"

I nodded. "Yeah. He wanted to talk to Kiko, too, even though Jax already talked to her. He'll probably try to talk to both of them at the same time, probably en route." Smiling humorlessly, I shook my head. "I suspect he wants to gauge the Kiko and Jax thing, too. And put the fear of God into Jax not to hurt his buddy, or he'll do something terrible to him..."

Jem broke out in a grin. "Poor Jax."

My voice grew more serious. "Actually, I got the impression Black approves."

"He damn well should," another voice said.

I looked up, surprised to see Holo standing there.

I hadn't seen him board the plane.

Frankly, I couldn't believe he was standing under his own power.

He made a polite, questioning gesture in my direction, indicating the chair next to where I sat, the one Panther occupied before. When I nodded, pulling the blanket off the seat that Panther had been sleeping with, Holo maneuvered his way into our six-seat area, lowering himself carefully into the recliner my dog had vacated.

I saw him wince and grimace as he did.

He jammed his cane into the space under his seat.

Once situated, he hit the buttons on the chair's outside arm.

I heard the engine whirr as it reclined the leather padding back.

Holo closed his eyes.

I frowned around at the others, then back at Holo.

"Should you really be here?" I said. "I mean, we all *want* you here, of course, but you look like shit, brother."

Dalejem burst out in a laugh.

Holo opened one eye, looking at me, then over at Jem.

"I like weddings," he informed me haughtily. "Black said I could come. He promised to make it worthwhile. He also said he'd have a wheelchair waiting for me on both ends, and for the wedding itself... and that I'd get my own escort for the space-cakes portion of the evening."

"Space cakes?" I mouthed, looking around at the others.

Angel shrugged, obviously not in the know, either.

Dalejem looked a little too deliberately innocent for me to buy it.

Nick's mind was clearly somewhere else.

Panther barked then, and jumped off Nick's lap.

I thought maybe the wolfhound was indignant that I'd given away his chair, but he jumped up on Holo instead, making Holo go *"Oof!"* Undaunted, Panther wriggled his way into the seat, seemingly determined to share it with the injured seer.

I snorted, rolling my eyes at my dog.

Panther didn't care.

He barely looked at me as he made himself comfortable... until Holo had the ball of black fur half on his lap and half in the chair with him, and he had his arm slung around the dog's back. Panther licked his hand, then laid his fuzzy head on his paws and sighed.

Something about seeing the two of them together brought a pain to my chest, followed by another dense wave of emotion.

I reached over, gripping Holo's arm, fighting the tightening in my throat.

Remembering seeing Holo sprawled and deathly pale on the tile floor, looking half-dead in the lobby of the California Street building, I gripped his arm tighter, wiping my eyes with my fingers.

"We're going to make you the flower boy," I told him seriously. "That means a costume, brother. And a flowered hat. Since we don't have any little nieces or nephews or anything... it's all on you, Holo. The ceremony is in your hands."

The seer grunted, rolling his eyes.

Then he smiled at me, clasping my hand in his fingers.

I looked back at Nick.

"I'm honestly not sure which of you is more nuts. It seems I'm not allowed to have a wedding without fearing for the lives of at least a few of the guests."

Frowning at my own words, I realized I meant them.

"Honestly, I *am* worried about you." I looked back at Holo. "...About both of you. Are either of you sure this is a good idea? Can't you just stay at the resort, watch the wedding together as a simulcast? Get hammered on margaritas together while you soak in the indoor jacuzzi?"

Instead of either of them, Jem answered me.

"Black assures us Nick will be fine." He looked at Holo. "I'm a little worried about brother Holo, too, but if he's in a wheelchair, and we find a place where he can relax and nap during the reception, he should be good."

"Absolutely not," Holo said, louder, his eyes still closed. "Space. Cakes. I will not be deprived."

Angel burst out in a laugh.

Holo went on in the same relaxed tone.

"Jax says Kiko is accepting it. Last time we spoke, Jax said Kiko believes the doc and Black that Nick is back to normal... more or less. Jax thinks Kiko will be fine. And he would know. He had her light all over him."

He opened one eye again, glancing around at them.

"He said she took it pretty well, all in all. He was surprised at how well she took it, frankly. Both of them were a lot more worried about Dex. Not just in terms of Nick, but in terms of the two of them." Holo gave Nick a warning look. "Either way, I wouldn't get too close to her, vampire. Not where Dex can see it... or any of her friends. Which means everyone."

Nick grunted, rolling his eyes a little, but didn't speak.

I watched his vampire eyes—those oddly stunning, crystal-colored irises and jet-black pupils—shift towards one of the oval view ports, his vampire-perfect mouth hardening as he grimaced out at the view.

He was a vampire now.

I still had to remind myself sometimes, but I'd mostly accepted it.

I was even getting better at translating his emotions from his vampire demeanor.

Like, for example, right now.

He was a vampire, not human, but if he'd still been human, I suspected his face would be some shade of green from Holo's comments about Kiko. Even as a vampire, he still managed to look like he felt sick to his stomach.

He wouldn't go near Kiko... not even at gunpoint, I suspected.

Not unless Kiko herself held the gun.

Panther barked.

From the direction of the dog's stare, he barked at Nick.

Dalejem reached up, massaging his boyfriend's shoulder with one hand.

Panther barked again. It sounded almost like a question.

Like, *Hey, friend! What's wrong with you? Do you need me to go over there? Lick you a bunch of times? 'Cause I will!*

That's when I realized Nick was crying.

He wiped his face while I watched, and while Jem continued to rub his back.

I didn't think; I blurted words.

"Vampires cry?"

There was a silence.

Nick gave me a look.

"Sorry." I felt myself flush. "I'm sorry. It's just..." I looked around at the others. "I didn't actually think they *could* cry. Not like a human."

Dalejem gave me an odd look. "You didn't think he could cry?"

"I mean, if pressed, I might have guessed they'd cry blood or something."

"Cry *blood?*" Holo opened his eyes. He looked at me, horrified, his face pulling into a delicate grimace. "That's disgusting, boss. Why the fuck would someone cry *blood?*"

Still frowning, he closed his eyes.

His arm tightened, hugging my dog in his lap.

"...Now I'm going to have that image in my head the rest of the day," he grumbled.

From my other side, Angel burst out in a laugh.

When Nick and I looked over, she covered her mouth with a hand, waving us off, her ears turning noticeably red.

Nick frowned at her.

Jem continued to rub his back, and Angel and I watched.

Holo closed his eyes where he lay back on his seat, but I strongly got the impression he watched too, likely from the Barrier construct, which still hooked into all of us.

It hit me then, feeling that construct.

It wasn't just me, Holo, and Jem.

All of them watched Nick.

Every seer on the plane watched Nick cry, while Dalejem comforted him.

Seers who weren't on the plane also watched Nick; since we remained connected to all of them via the military-grade construct, every seer on our team could see him.

As they all looked at my oldest and dearest friend, I felt something in the consciousness of the group shift. It was subtle, but feeling it loosened the knot that had formed in my chest— the one that appeared the instant I saw Nick emerge into the plane's cabin from behind those blue curtains.

Nick wouldn't have felt it, of course.

Nick was a vampire.

Like the humans, he wasn't in the construct. Unlike the humans, Nick's mental state was unlikely to be affected by the construct, either, even indirectly.

But I felt Holo notice, and Yarli, who sat in the cluster of seats just forward of ours.

I felt Jem notice, too, right before he met my gaze.

The senior infiltrator's pale green eyes brightened, contrasting even more with those stunning violet rings. I looked at the sheer happiness in him as he stared at me.

It wasn't just happiness that Nick was safe. It didn't stem *only* from fewer of Black's team actively wanting to kill his boyfriend.

The happiness came from Nick himself.

They were in love.

I'd known that, if only because Angel had been saying so for months.

But I could *see* it now, reflected in Jem's eyes, in the fierce protectiveness I felt on him where he massaged the back of Nick's neck, trying to reassure him.

Jem was still studying my gaze when he broke out in a smile.

Something in his smile made me almost envious.

I wanted to feel the way he did. I wanted to feel that relief. More than that, I wanted to feel that sense of a new day, of a new world... of love conquering all. I wanted to feel things were really going to start to get better again, that Black and I could be together and everything would work out... everything would be okay.

Everything is *going to be okay, my beautiful sister,* Jem murmured softly in my mind. *You and Black* can *be together, and everything* will *work out... for all of us.*

I wanted to believe that.

I really, truly, absolutely, *one hundred percent* wanted to believe that.

But despite it being the morning of my wedding day, a day Black and I had planned off and on for several years, a day I still couldn't quite believe was finally happening...

Well, and that was it. That was the problem, really.

I still couldn't quite believe it.

Some part of me still didn't believe the wedding would happen at all.

I was bracing, even now, for something to crash into the side of the plane, for everyone's headsets to start pinging with an alarm about some horrible occurrence happening elsewhere in the world... something that would force us to cancel, yet again.

I was waiting for someone to tell me the wedding was off.

"Well, of course you're afraid of that," Holo murmured from next to me.

I looked over, but he didn't return my gaze.

Sighing heavily, he went on, his eyes still closed.

"How many fucking weddings is this, anyway?" the seer muttered. "Seven? Eight? Ten? Black told me and Jem he planned the very first one before we even got to this dimension... in New

York. Another splashy publicity media frenzy deal, but you got so pissed off at him for how he infiltrated the vampires, he ended up sleeping on the couch for a few months instead. He said you fucked off to Hawaii..."

Holo said it loudly enough, it wasn't only me and Angel who laughed.

I heard laughter from Yarli, from Manny sitting next to her, from Lawless in the seat across the aisle, from Luce, Dog, Ace.

Holo opened one eye, smiling at me.

Then he closed it, snuggling deeper in the chair.

I knew he was right.

Black hadn't even told me all the times he'd tried to plan a ceremony for the two of us.

Those plans changed to include different landscapes (beaches, deserts, Golden Gate Park, the Palace of Fine Arts, a church, a Buddhist temple), countries (the United States, Thailand, France, Indonesia, England)... not to mention states, cities, venues, times of day, guest lists... even dimensions, since Black raised it again when we stayed with his cousin.

Our plans had changed so many times I could scarcely remember what we'd first talked about doing, or why we'd settled on New Mexico this time.

"Have hope, my sister," Holo murmured.

Reaching over, he clasped my hand, squeezing it where I still gripped his arm.

"Have a little faith in us... in your family. Trust that we won't let that happen to you this time."

My eyes stung.

I only nodded, even as I turned over his words.

I felt hope, yes.

I loved my family.

I trusted them, too.

I also felt, in the deepest part of my bones, that this wasn't over.

I could put it aside for today.

I could let this day finally happen... a day Black and I had wanted for years, even if we told ourselves we didn't care, that we already *were* married, in our light and on paper, and screw the ceremony, and screw the rest.

I could marry Black, in front of my friends.

Once the honeymoon was over, we would have to face reality again.

But today, I wouldn't think about that.

Today, I would be with Black, and I would be with my friends.

This is reality too, sister, Jem reminded me softly. *At the end of the day, this is the only reality that matters. The only one that remains.*

Looking at him, I blinked.

Then, turning over his words, I finally smiled for real.

24

THE DAY OF

The doors opened on the resort, and I felt myself take... and exhale... my first deep breath in probably a month.

I looked at Angel, and she grinned, then burst out in a laugh.

Arms linked, we aimed our feet for the front desk, where I saw Dalejem and Nick already standing, clearly in the process of checking in.

Before we could get there, we got waylaid by three people, two of which we already knew. Magic threw her arms around me and squeezed, laughing as she jumped up and down, holding me around the neck and forcing me to jump with her.

I was laughing too as soon as we started, then I turned to hug Devin, who stood behind her, smiling bemusedly.

"Where's Frank?" I said. "Where's Joseph and Geraldine?"

"They're on their way," Devin said, giving me one of his shy smiles as he pulled out of our embrace. "Everyone's coming, Miri. Don't worry. They're probably trucking half the Rez down here... and a few of the neighboring ones, too."

I laughed.

I noticed the third person who'd joined us.

She looked familiar to me, but it took a few more seconds to place her. She stood there, waiting, grinning from ear to ear, wearing a white, clinging dress, turquoise and silver earrings, a turquoise squash necklace, and sandals.

Devin saw me looking at her and waved her forward, smiling at me.

"Hey, do you remember Crystal? She and Juana asked to help you out in terms of getting ready for the ceremony... all the spa things, like facials, a massage, salt scrubs. The stuff you can do before Johann gets here for all the wedding preparations. She says she helped you and Angel out before? When you came here to visit?"

I blinked, then turned, staring at her.

I'd totally forgotten that trip.

It seemed like a million years ago now, my being summoned here by Black because of odd, otherworldly vampires that appeared in the New Mexican desert.

I'd been in Hawaii when Black got to New Mexico.

Not speaking to him.

Well, that's how Black put it.

Of course, I *had* been speaking to him... on the phone, that is... because I never seemed able to *not* speak to Black, even when I wanted to murder him... but I'd needed serious space from him after New York. Serious enough, I hadn't always answered the phone when he called, even from a few thousand miles away.

Serious enough, I couldn't talk to him at all for the first few weeks.

"Of course I remember!" I smiled at Crystal's shy grin. "I honestly don't know how you remember *us,*" I added after a pause. "Given how many people must pass through here."

Angel enveloped Crystal in a hug, beaming in her face.

"Speak for yourself, doc," she said to me, giving me a mock frown. "I would be deeply offended if Crystal hadn't remembered *me.*"

She winked at Crystal, her voice turning dry.

"Miri was dumb and only stayed a few days," Angel said,

motioning with her head in my direction. "Cowboy and I came back here and stayed for *weeks*. When we weren't eating our weight in tacos, and he wasn't dragging me rock climbing, or horseback riding, or base-jumping... I was dragging him down here."

"So no sleeping then?" I said innocently. "No jumping in the pool? Or getting hammered on margaritas?"

She waved me off, her Louisiana twang growing more audible. "We found time for all that, too. Among... other things."

She waggled her eyebrows at me suggestively, and I laughed.

"You're a dork," I informed her.

"And time's a-wasting," Crystal informed us, her voice suddenly turning businesslike. She clapped her hands, then proceeded to motion with them, as if she were shooing two particularly stubborn cows into a barn, waving us in the direction of the spa.

"We're on a tight schedule today, ladies. Chop, chop. You're just going to have to be smart asses to one another while you're getting worked on..."

I laughed, shaking my head.

"And *of course* we remember you," Crystal added, her voice a teasing scold. "Jeez, you know you're like... super *famous,* right? Juana and I are *obsessed.* Between the two of us, we have seriously collected, like, *every single article* we could find about you and the boss since you left here last time. Like, seriously... every single one. That doesn't even get into all the photos and magazine spreads and online fan clubs and chat groups. We've been following *all* of y'all since the last time you were here... really, ever since Mr. Black bought the place. We were just looking at all the *gorgeous* photos of the two of you from Hawaii..."

I fought to keep the smile on my face, remembering how some of those headlines and articles must have read.

Terrorists. Murderers.

Aliens. Vampires.

She must have seen some of that on my face, because she laughed.

"Oh, don't you worry, hon. We know they printed *all kinds* of nonsense. But we liked to see where you were. So many glamourous places! And then there were all the crazy stories about what was happening in San Francisco, and how you had to help out the government..."

She trailed, glancing at Devin, who was gesturing with his hand under his chin, making the *shut up* gesture to try and get her to stop talking.

She blinked, flushed bright red, and turned back to me.

"Anyway, we have the whole first part of the morning mapped out for the two of you!" She beamed at me again. "We had so much fun planning it, I gotta say. The boss called us with suggestions and they sent both of your dresses this morning... with Mr. Black's fashion consultant sending us suggestions for your hair we could show both of you. Everyone else is kicked out of the spa today... your party basically has the run of the place. And no press!" she added firmly. "The boss has security crawling all over, and he was *real* clear he didn't want any of them vultures in here until the ceremony's about to start."

Her enthusiasm and sweetness were like a tonic.

I remembered her with much less of an accent.

She'd more or less hidden her accent entirely the last time we were here, but now I found myself thinking she probably grew up in Texas.

Wherever she came from, by the time she finished speaking, I had to fight not to hug her.

I hugged Angel's arm against my side instead.

"All of that sounds amazing," I told her, glancing at Juana when I realized she'd joined us at some point while Crystal was talking. She just stood there, grinning, like she was tickled to be there at all. "We should really dump off our stuff, first... then we're all yours..."

Angel laughed, tugging on my arm as she leaned towards my ear.

"I think the stuff-dumping has been accomplished without us," she whispered loudly, grinning at Crystal and Juana. "You really haven't gotten this being rich thing figured out yet, have you, doc? Or how hotels work."

I looked around at the red and black, Navajo-patterned carpet on top of the stone tiles, and realized Angel was right. Our luggage had been whisked away, and I'd been too much of a space cadet to even notice.

Angel was already tugging me towards the spa, and I followed willingly enough, even as some part of my light looked briefly for Black.

No cheating, he murmured softly. *Don't help me cheat. I'm already climbing the walls, doc.*

Black—

No. No cheating. I mean it.

He sent me a tiny pulse of warmth, then winked out of my light.

৩১৯

I wanted tacos.

I wanted chips and guacamole.

I wanted to sit in the hot tub, drinking margaritas on the rocks, staring up at the blue New Mexico sky. I wanted to do nothing for three to five... maybe twelve... hours.

Alas, this was not that day.

Not that I minded being pampered in other ways.

I knew the desire to hide in the resort's jacuzzi was mostly nerves.

Crystal and Juana did their best to calm me down.

The massage made me melt.

The sauna and shower that followed were lovely.

The facial, waxing, hair softening treatment, pedicure and

manicure, aromatherapy, acupuncture, and whatever else they did to me, all with me wrapped in a fuzzy bathrobe, sipping fizzy drinks and smoothies, chatting with Angel while they did all the same things to her... all of it was lovely, but weirdly exhausting by the end, too.

Then Johann and his team showed up.

The New York fashionista grinned at me like a predator when he saw me, looking like it was Christmas morning and I'd just offered him a tree's worth of presents.

He and his team took over the entire spa, complete with air kisses, jokes, murmurs of disapproval with this or that thing about what they'd done to me so far, and a millimeter by millimeter scrutiny over my skin, face, hair, lips, eyes, eyelashes, toes, back, and even the bathrobe they'd put me in.

Then Johann played with my hair and announced they would cut it.

He put me in a much sleeker robe, and made me twirl until I was dizzy so he could decide some final touches on how he wanted the dress to hang on my form, and what he wanted with my hair, and how I looked at different angles.

Then Johann had his people cover every single mirror in our area of the spa with white sheets, so that Angel and I couldn't look at ourselves while he got us ready.

Angel's eyebrows had risen so high by the end of their pre-game show, I thought she might tell them forget it, that she'd hide in her room and dress herself.

Thank God, she didn't do that.

Both of us were ushered to chairs and Johann's people got to work.

They shushed us when we tried to talk to one another.

Johann played soft music, brought us fruit spritzers and strawberries.

Then he told us to close our eyes... *and just let it all happen, darlings.*

I did as he said, and then Johann and his people were trimming and styling our hair, dressing us, doing our make-up, our hair, painting on nail and toenail polish, rubbing ointments on our shoulders, arms, hands, upper chests... pretty much putting together all of the aesthetic touches on both me and Angel for the ceremony itself, since Black paid Johann to design looks for both of us.

For Angel, that meant building a look around the dress she'd picked out.

For me, the mission was a lot more open-ended.

Black and I had been so slammed with work and killer cyborgs and traveling to other dimensions... I just asked Johann if he would mind picking out everything for me, from the dress to the shoes and everything in between.

I don't think I'd ever seen Johann look that happy.

Now I wondered if I'd been an idiot, leaving all of that to someone else.

Black assured me it would be fine, that Johann was an artist, but I'm not going to lie, I was nervous as hell. Not being able to see any part of myself in the mirror as he gradually put me together didn't exactly help.

By the time they got to the dress... the final touch-ups with the fitting... then my hair done up for how it would actually look for the ceremony... then stockings, garters, undergarments, backless bra, jewelry... then finally putting the dress on for real... then the make-up... then the shoes... then a few more touches to my hair and make-up and a few flowers woven in... and suddenly they were done.

They finally wanted both of us to look in the mirror.

I stood next to Angel, wishing I stood next to just about anyone else.

Angel looked like a supermodel.

She looked like she was about to walk a runway in Paris, or maybe onto center stage in a world class theater as a prima ballerina.

She seriously looked like a magazine spread, with her hair

coiled artistically around her head, done up in perfect, elaborate braids, woven through with tiny wildflowers and baby's breath, with a few sprinkles of yellow and pale pink buds.

She wore a full-blown Cinderella dress, shockingly white, that accented her tiny waist, strapless to show off toned shoulders and perfect skin, with lace gloves, white stockings, insanely high heels decorated with pearls, a plunging neckline.

Everything about her looked delicate and precise, even the deep white of her dress, which *exactly* matched her satin shoes and Parisian veil.

Watching Johann and his team put her together, even as they flitted between the two of us, I couldn't imagine how I could ever look even half as good as she did.

Angel always had a certain quality I envied—something Johann picked up on and accentuated with every item he chose for her—a regal, queen-like quality that made people instantly take notice of her.

Of course, I knew from Angel it could intimidate people at times, too.

She joked that it served her well as a homicide detective... if less well with boyfriends.

Cowboy wasn't most guys, though.

He'd absolutely lose his mind when he saw her.

Angel was staring at me, though, her eyes shining. She looked about to speak, but Johann raised a hand, his voice booming in the small space.

"ABSOLUTELY. NO. TALKING. SILENCE!"

Angel closed her mouth, fighting not to laugh.

Then Johann's two assistants were whipping off the white sheets, and my eyes left Angel and focused on my own reflection in the mirror.

I admit, it shocked me a little.

Maybe more than a little.

I barely recognized myself.

I mean, I'd seen bits and pieces of what he'd been putting on me, so it shouldn't have come as such a *total* surprise, but somehow, seeing it all together like this, it was.

He'd cut my hair more than I realized.

The dress looked different than I expected, too, even from looking down at it while they put it on me. From one perspective to the other, it was a completely different dress... with little similarity between my limited perspective, and how it looked in a full-length mirror. From my perspective above, I just saw the piles of light-looking material, falling in a way that made it look bunched up, giving it a kind of ruffled, flower-type texture.

Looking in the mirror, those piles of light-looking material I'd been pulling at and stroking with my fingers, now looked like thick bunches of bone-white roses, with barely discernible highlights of black and gold.

In the mirror, those highlights shimmered and gave the dress depth, making the fabric look like it had been sprinkled with gold dust.

The top was a laced, low-cut corset in the back, but the bust didn't plunge overly low in front, fitting me snugly in that pale, bone-white, just a bare shade darker than Angel's.

Rather than strapless, like Angel's, mine had light, off-shoulder sleeves attached to the more severe corset, made of the same material as the lower part of the dress, and glimmering with just the faintest hint of gold.

It looked like the bottom half of me was immersed in clouds of bone-colored feathers, contrasting the severe corset on top, and my black hair, which they'd mostly left down, the soft curls accented with gold and pale green flowers.

I looked so different, I honestly didn't know how to react.

"Can I speak yet, damn it?" Angel grumbled at Johann, her hands on her hips.

"No," Johann said haughtily.

He winked at me as he said it, then looked back at Angel.

"You are gorgeous. You know you look gorgeous, you are dismissed," he informed her, waving her away imperiously.

I burst out in a laugh, but Angel gave him an incredulous look.

"You are not to touch a single hair on that girl's head," she said, pointing at me. "Not. One. Hair. She looks *perfect.*"

"Go away you impossible girl... I must speak to this one, for her husband insisted I do so, once I had completed my side of things."

I frowned at that, but when Angel quirked an eyebrow in my direction, I gave her a perceptible nod, letting her know it was okay for her to go.

Once she'd walked out of the back room and into the one in front, which we were using as kind of an "antechamber" for the wedding ceremony itself, Johann turned to me.

He instantly went from haughty to concerned.

"You are very quiet, my darling," he said, that worry reaching his voice. "Your husband told me, very seriously, that whatever I did to get you ready for this, I was to make you *happy.* He said he would have very, VERY hard words for me, if I did anything at all to make you feel bad about yourself, or to show you in any kind of unflattering light."

Something about what he said...

...it hit me like a punch to the gut.

For like the third or fourth time since that morning, I was again fighting tears.

I didn't even know why at first.

I knew I missed Black.

I missed just hanging out with him.

I missed things like going running with him, and our morning workouts, and going surfing, and going out to dinner.

I couldn't remember the last time we'd just done normal things.

The kinds of things we used to do before *Koh Mangaan.*

The kinds of things we did before my uncle went off the damned deep end and decided to enslave most of the human world.

Thinking about Charles, I simultaneously felt grief that he wasn't here, and honestly wondered why I hadn't killed him.

I'd never in my life resented him as much as I did at that moment, for his stupid obsessions and fears and paranoias about humans, and how that more or less ruined things for *everyone*.

My uncle, for all of his intelligence, was an idiot.

He'd feared the future so much, he'd set out to create the worst one imaginable, just so it wouldn't broadside him. At the end of the day, Charles projected his fears over the whole world, making his nightmare into everyone else's reality.

I tried to shove it out of my mind.

Even so, some part of me mourned the normal life I'd once had, even with Black. Again, I was reminded how little of that "normal time" I'd had with Black of late.

I forgot sometimes, that he could be incredibly sweet.

I forgot we liked to do a lot of the same things.

I forgot we'd been talking about spending time in Santa Cruz, and going camping, and both of us learning to surf for real... and maybe going back to, you know, solving crimes again.

Black genuinely liked P.I. work.

I did, too... although I hadn't fully realized it until it was gone.

It was so easy to forget *that* version of me and Black.

"Oh, my love." Johann sounded genuinely mortified. "I *have* upset you! What is it? We can rip this whole dress off you, my darling. I have other things we can put on you instead—"

I was already shaking my head.

Clearing my throat, not wanting to touch my eyes in case I messed up the amazing make-up job Johann's artist had done, I shook my head again.

"Absolutely not," I said. "You, my good friend, are not touching a damned thing."

25

UNDER THE BLUE-WHITE SUN

Jax looked around the outdoor seating area, a little blown away.

Being hooked into the main security construct grounded him to a degree, but the sheer size of the crowd overwhelmed him, even with that.

This place was a security nightmare.

Even with Black's people scattered throughout the guests, and the snipers Jax knew protected the ceremony from above... it was flat-out nuts that they were doing this like this.

Jax had already been told this was only for the ceremony itself, and the formal reception following, meaning the one that included *all* of the wedding guests.

Afterwards, they'd do more of a seer-human-hybrid reception-slash-mini-ceremony, with the place more or less cleared out of anyone who wasn't a close friend, or part of the inner circle of either or both couples.

This part, though?

This part was sheer madness.

Jax saw a covered area to one side of the main aisle and stage, where the vampire guests sat out of the New Mexico sun. Press circulated freely with people like Nick Tanaka's parents, who apparently had been Miriam's quasi-foster family after her own parents and sister died, not to mention their close relationship to Angel, who grew up next door to Nick Tanaka.

Angel's own parents were there, who were divorced, and apparently fighting.

Angel had aunts, uncles and cousins from Louisiana.

Cowboy (real name: Elvis Dawson Graves, Jax found out today) had friends and relatives from Louisiana, as well, and some of them looked like they'd just come out of a swamp and were wearing the same suit they'd worn to every job interview, funeral, and wedding they'd ever attended, back since they were eighteen years old.

Somehow Black rustled up a few cousins of Miri's from Native American reservations on the Northwest Coast of the United States and Canada, as well.

Those were the weird wedding guests you'd find at any wedding, though.

The far weirder aspect of all this came from those people mixing with reporters from major fashion and Hollywood magazines, not to mention the major networks... and the movie stars, talk show hosts, and members of Black's billionaire club who clearly didn't know how to interact with normal people.

That list included Wall Street and tech industry pirates, several big-name musicians, at least one movie mogul, and a number of other faces Jax vaguely recognized from the human world but couldn't place.

At least five *bona fide* movie stars were in attendance.

Jax didn't really know who they were, but the Navajo kids had been losing their minds, squealing at the sight of at least one male star, who apparently had some native blood.

Jax saw the guy and he didn't get it, frankly; the man was handsome, but he looked like a bit of a goof.

It didn't help that he wore a bright blue tuxedo with red leather shoes and a bolo tie, his hair looking like he'd stuck his whole head in a blender to cut it.

Grant Steele, that talk show friend of Black's, was there.

A number of military types also circulated in the crowd. Not just the team who worked under the Colonel when he'd been alive (although they were there, too), but a few actual generals and admirals in full dress uniform.

Everyone walked around like they were in a zoo and the other wedding guests were the animals. The family members gawked at the movie stars, the generals and politicians gawked at the vampires and the seers who walked around carrying guns.

Most of Black and Miri's closest and dearest were either sitting in their respective sections, staring around at the chaos with stunned, deer-in-headlights looks on their faces, or they were doing like Jax himself was doing—milling around the party, pretending to be a guest while he wore a gun and a headset and looked out for any potential problems.

The communications back and forth across the construct were insane.

Jax had his lines of report, but even with everything strictly organized, it still overwhelmed him, the sheer number of people sending in snapshots (most of those positively ID'ing guests and making sure they were supposed to be there) and discussing possible vulnerabilities of the venue itself.

A voice rose over his headset, private channel.

"Stop worrying," she teased him softly.

"Who's worrying?" he murmured back.

"I can see your face from here. You look like you think you're surrounded by hostile forces disguised in flowered hats and carrying designer handbags."

"I'm pretty sure we are," Jax said, quirking an eyebrow in her direction.

Kiko laughed, and he felt a ripple of heat go through his light.

He hadn't really wanted her to come to this.

He understood how insanely unrealistic that was, given who she was, not only to Black, but to Miri, Angel, and Cowboy as well... but his feelings on the subject hadn't really changed. Knowing that Nick Tanaka slunk around somewhere in this crowd, probably hidden back with the other bloodsuckers, didn't help.

At all.

"Really," she said. "You need to chill out, Jax. The boss's got this covered... nothing is going to go wrong."

"Until the killer robots show up," Jax muttered. "Until they send a drone strike to take out the whole wedding party... or one of the vampires gets a little too thirsty... or that freaky dragon dude comes back..."

Kiko laughed again. "You're cute when you're being a little stress monkey."

Jax felt another flush of heat hit his light.

"Cute?" he said, feigning offense. "Little?"

"Well, I can't exactly tell you what I *really* think right now, can I? Not only am I at a wedding, but technically, both of us are working."

Another voice cut in, even as she said it.

"Hey, stop flirting, you two," Ace joked. "We can all see you looking at each other... and we can see the 'private channel' light on your comm feeds."

"Piss off," Kiko told him cheerfully.

"Tsk, tsk," Javier broke in. "Such language. And from such a foxy-looking woman in all your wedding finery..."

Jax felt a flicker of reaction at the other's words.

He knew he was being ridiculous.

At the same time, he could feel the eyes on Kiko.

He could tell himself rationally that the vast majority of those eyes belonged to her friends, who were deeply worried about her still, and checking her out to make sure she was okay. He could feel the relief on some of them, the humans especially, that she really *did* seem to be okay, that she wasn't losing it from Nick being there.

Jax had already gotten into it with some of them, though.

Well... one of them.

Dex had to be physically restrained once that day already.

Well... twice.

The military vet managed to be relatively intimidating, even though Jax was a seer and Dex was a forty-year-old human, if an especially large and *fit* forty-year-old human. Jax had been a bit shocked, frankly, when Dex lunged at him the first time.

They'd just gotten off the plane, and Jax had been holding Kiko's hand.

Apparently that enraged Dex to the point where he lost his head.

Later, when Kiko got out of the pool in a tiny, sky-blue bikini, Jax had been staring at her openly, and motioned her over to whisper things in her ear.

Dex tried to hit him again.

Both times, Kiko and Dex's friends among Black's team held him back, talking him down. Kiko chewed him out, too, especially the second time.

Jax hadn't been sure what to do or say, frankly.

He'd had an urge to tell the Marine he hadn't had intercourse with her yet, but he suspected that wouldn't go over well, either. It also struck him as somewhat disingenuous, given that Jax fully intended to ask her for intercourse soon... likely that night... and she'd asked *him* for intercourse at least three times already.

Jax only refused for reasons of timing and situation: the construct being open, her being vulnerable with him about what Nick had done to her, and not wanting to do it when he thought there was a good chance they would be interrupted or overheard.

All reasons for not having sex with her were growing less compelling, however, especially after he saw her in the pale gold bridesmaid's dress she wore for the ceremony.

They'd set up two rows for that, too, with women and men on Black and Miri's side wearing gold dresses and black tuxes, and the woman and men on Angel and Cowboy's side wearing pale green dresses and black tuxes.

They all stood up there now on a slanted ramp leading up to the main stage, and Jax had to admit, the symmetry fascinated him.

Weddings were far more circumscribed for humans than the chaotic seer weddings he'd grown up with back on Old Earth.

Then again, he hadn't gotten to see a lot of those, either.

Because of the enslavement of so much of his kind, full-blown big-bash seer weddings were kind of a rarity on that world.

For the same reason, he was looking forward to tonight's party, after all of the non-family members left.

The music started.

While Jax's mind had been elsewhere, people started taking their seats for real.

Jerking his mind off the past, and his eyes off Kiko in the gold dress long enough to scan the rest of the stage, he realized Black and Cowboy stood up there already, both of them wearing tuxedos and standing perfectly still.

Jax noted Kiko a last time on Black and Miri's side of the stage—noting she stood just in front of Cal, a human friend of Black's who owned a restaurant in the North Beach neighborhood of San Francisco.

Yarli and Manny stood together next to them, then Dex and Gina, one of Miri's old psychiatrist friends. Lawrence "Larry" Farraday, Black's lawyer, stood next to Kevin Lawless, one of Black's old Vietnam buddies; the two of them stood just above humans named Maya and Naomi, who were apparently two of Nick Tanaka's human sisters.

The third Tanaka sister stood on Angel and Cowboy's side, next to Dog from the Navajo Rez. Easton stood with a human woman named Lucy, who was a childhood friend and cousin of Cowboy's from Louisiana. Ace and Mika stood next to them, then Angel's sister, Lara, and an old friend of Cowboy's from... somewhere. Another cousin of Angel's stood with Cowboy's half-brother at the very end, making it five couples for each side.

Jax knew they'd left a few people out.

Frank Blackfoot asked to bow out, since he'd be busy managing the venue.

Same with Devin, who worked at the resort as well.

Jax himself asked to be kept in security, partly so Holo wouldn't feel left out after he'd been injured and couldn't participate easily.

The other big omissions of course, were Dalejem and Nick.

No one really had to talk about why they weren't in it.

Jax scanned faces in the wedding party, noting Ace and Mika poking each other and laughing, and that Kiko and Cal were talking quietly, too.

Cowboy and Black just stood there, unmoving.

In the center, between them, stood Alex Holmes, who would be performing the ceremony for both couples.

The music swelled louder, and everyone in the audience turned, craning their necks and heads to look back towards the other end of the long, flower-coated aisle.

Jax turned his head along with everyone else, swiveling his upper body in his seat.

Then he saw them, and smiled, in spite of himself.

⊗⟨⊗

They say your own wedding is always a blur.

As is often true with the ubiquitous "they," it turned out for me, "they" were right.

I only remember a few things, here and there.

I remember being scared out of my friggin' mind when I saw all those people staring at me—gawking at my face and body in the dress and hair and make-up Johann used to remake me in his imagination.

In retrospect, that fear strikes me as fairly ludicrous, given the past few years I'd had, or even the time I'd spent at war with

Nick, back when we were both so painfully young it felt like another lifetime ago.

Ludicrous or not, the fear nearly had me hyperventilating.

I thought I might have a panic attack, or pass out.

I went back to worrying I might just throw up in the middle of the aisle.

Somewhere in that, I began to walk.

I think someone must have cued me, or even poked me, or shoved at the small of my back. In any case, Angel had already started walking, and some autopilot part of me must have started to follow... again, very likely after I got prodded by Johann or one of the other stylists standing behind me.

I felt the cameras more than saw them.

I don't remember seeing much of anything, truthfully.

I walked on flower petals in the absurdly high heels, and saw a wash of faces, both strange and familiar, looking at me like they scarcely recognized me.

A few faces stood out.

Yumi and Hiroto stood near the front. Yumi had tears in her eyes.

Jax smiled at me as I passed, and Holo, from his wheelchair in the aisle. I saw Nick's pale, strangely perfect face out of the sun, in the second row of the vampire section. Dalejem sat beside him, holding his arm and hand. They had Panther with them, too, sitting on the grass beside Nick's chair... which might have cracked me up if I hadn't been so freaked out at the insanely large crowd of people.

Somehow, I made it up to where Black stood.

Then I was looking at Black.

I looked at Black, and everything else disappeared.

I barely heard anything as Alex Holmes began intoning words in his deep voice. Black told me Alex used to be a preacher, in some Baptist Church in Virginia where he lived. Neither Black nor I was Baptist, but that didn't matter. Alex told us he'd do a non-denominational ceremony, and I let Black handle that end of things, anyway.

Like a lot of the seers, Black seemed more excited for the seer side of things anyway, which were slotted to unfold later that evening, after the press and Hollywood people and other non-friends and family had been booted out the door.

They say you don't remember your wedding... that everything is just a blur.

But I'm a seer.

Technically, I remember all of it.

I have all of it stored in my mind somewhere, for as long as I remain alive.

In the moment, however, most of that whirled around me, insubstantial.

I remember a few things clearly.

I remember everything my husband said to me.

He spoke clearly, quietly, but everyone in the outdoor seating area hushed to near-silence, listening, straining, for every word.

He spoke in seer towards the end.

That part, they may not have understood, but I did.

"*Liliere, ilya,*" he murmured softly, holding my hands lightly, almost delicately in his. *Untielleres uka ak-te, ilya. Ilya nedri az'lenm, Miri. Uka mikra untielleres. Liliere kitrra, i'thir li'dare, y ulen aros y'lethe u agnate sol...*"

A collective sigh rose among the seers, even as the humans looked puzzled.

I felt my face warm, but I didn't look away from the intensity and softness of my husband's gaze. His gold eyes shone with *aleimic* light, even as they brightened.

I felt tears come to my own eyes, but I smiled at him.

I smiled so wide, it almost hurt my face.

I knew enough Prexci by then, that I understood every word he spoke.

"*I love you, my darling. You and I are one until the end of time. You are my soul's work, Miri. My everlasting love. I will love you after death, under the blue-white sun, and always know in my heart you are why I was called to this world..."*

I know I spoke back to him.

I know I said things I hoped would touch him, that would convey how I felt.

After Angel said her words to Cowboy, it was our turn again, and I said my vows to Black.

I had a thing I'd memorized in Prexci too, but I probably botched it.

If I did, he didn't mind.

Both of us were crying by the time I finished, then he was kissing my face, kissing my jaw and my neck bared by the dress, and Alex Holmes had to clear his throat a few times before he could get in the last word and end the thing.

When he finished saying those final words, addressing them to all four of us, making Black and I *finally married* in the conventional sense... meaning, in front of the world, in front of all of our family and friends... and, hilariously, in front of the mainstream and Hollywood media... Alex Holmes beamed at all four of us, and closed the book he held with a snap.

He said gently, "You may kiss the bride."

...And it was officially over, and everyone laughed, since Black hadn't stopped kissing me the whole time Alex spoke.

Then Black and I were kissing for real, and everyone whooped as I realized Cowboy and Angel were kissing too, and the ceremony was over, and, well...

...no bombs had gone off.

No one died.

Nothing terrible at all occurred.

For me, right then, that meant everything.

At the same time, it wasn't even the most important part.

The ceremony itself had gone more perfectly than I could have ever imagined. But it was more than just the bare bones of us surviving such an insane and overly-public, dangerously timed, and probably ill-advised human marriage ritual... it was perfect for me as just an ordinary woman, too.

For as much as I had told myself a ceremony didn't matter to me... that the dress and the rings and the music and the party and the wedding cake didn't matter to me, either...

It did matter.

It mattered a lot.

26

UNBELONGING

"I cannot believe how insanely *gorgeous* you look, Dr. Miriam!" the woman gushed, gazing openly over my dress, waving a ring-covered hand to embellish her words, the one that clutched a champagne flute with a strawberry at the bottom. "I am just *green with envy* that you had Johann *Rognarth* design your look... he really outdid himself!"

I smiled as politely as I could, thanking her as I tried to make it not-obvious that I was scanning the crowd for Black.

He'd been dragged off by a bunch of his Wall Street buddies, and he'd let them because, as he said, he wanted to "get this part out of the way" so we could all have fun tonight.

I could have pinged him, of course... found him that way.

I didn't want to bother him though—not for what was essentially just me wanting a quick touch-base to know where he was.

For some reason, I still felt a flicker of nerves around having all of these people here, even with the crazy layers of security, including a full-blown military construct around the entire resort. Maybe some of that was due to the last resort where I'd stayed with Black... the one we more or less burned to the ground when Black was forced to turn into a dragon while he was still inside our suite.

Whatever the reason, if it was just crowd-phobia, or post-wedding adrenaline, or something more concrete I was picking up around things going on in the world more generally, I had to fight not to get clingy with Black, and just let him do his thing.

As much as today meant to the two of us, it had been done this way—out in the open and under the watchful eyes of most of the world via journalists and livestreams—in part as a publicity stunt and a means of rehabilitating our image.

Not only me and Black's image.

Really, we wanted to rehabilitate the image of seers as a whole.

The reaction to the situation in Los Angeles had been mixed, to say the least.

People who'd been there—everyone in Grant Steele's crew, Grant Steele himself, the studio audience in the bleachers—had all known it wasn't Black who appeared out of a wormhole and dive-bombed L.A.

But Black's people erased that memory on all of them.

It wasn't a comfortable decision to make, and the truth still might come out, but it made sense for them to do it. So now, the world outside our bubble believed that dragon had been Black. All of the subsequent news articles and video footage explained the new dragon away by repeating that same information—that it had been Black, that he'd made a dramatic entrance for his first interview since he'd come out, that it had all been a publicity stunt.

That they'd erased memories to cover that up didn't sit easy with me.

I understood the logic of it, but I really didn't like the precedent it set.

We couldn't get in the habit of just *erasing* unpleasant truths that circumstance thrust upon us, whether by other seers, vampires, or whatever else.

In this particular case, however, I decided I was good with it.

Everything was way too new for us to toss a second, blackout-induced dragon into the mix. Most of the mainstream press already expressed a lot of skepticism that Black actually was who and what he claimed to be.

I needed to get through the preliminary talks with the human governments, first.

Also, we needed to figure out how to handle the Purity Movement fanatics. Who, incidentally, staged a protest with several hundred people in downtown Santa Fe today, after reading about my and Black's moved-up wedding.

Luckily, we had a veritable army between us and them.

I wasn't too worried about them breaching the gates, at least not in any numbers.

But we needed to deal with them.

The biggest fear for today, however, was that another of those robot-cyborg things would show up, and open fire on the crowd. We had drones, people on the roof and street, people at every entrance and exit to the driveway, the resort grounds, any of the buildings, making sure that didn't happen, but it was still by far the biggest danger.

I smiled politely at the woman, who I realized was still talking.

Then a commotion over by the pool caught my notice.

Half-grateful for the distraction, I murmured my apologies and took myself in that direction.

I'd already recognized at least one of the voices by the time I got there.

It hit me that alcohol had been flowing pretty freely most of the afternoon by then. I was beginning to think a chunk of the guests, especially from the Raptor's Nest, might have started in the morning, before the ceremony even began.

"I don't give a good goddamn if you *like* her or not, you fucking freak..."

Alarm shot through me when Dex's voice boomed in the acoustics between the main resort building and the pool.

By the time I got there, I wasn't the only one.

"Brother." Jax's patient voice. "Calm down. Please. There is nothing untoward happening—"

"I ain't your fuckin' *brother*... brother," Dex cut in angrily. "We aren't even the same damned species, *bro*..."

I felt my heart leap to my throat.

I was close enough now that I saw Dex jerk his arm away from someone else.

"No! Let go of me, Javie! You know what I'm saying here. You *know*. These fuckers are all sniffing around Kiko, around Alice and Michelle, and I've had it... I've fucking *had* it! They nearly kill her, and now—"

"Dex!" Kiko's voice rose angrily. "You're being ridiculous! Jax and I are *dating!* That's it! We're *dating*. Are you going to try to tell me who I can *date* now?"

"How do I know you even *chose* to date this asshole?" Dex shot back, staring at her. "How would I even *know*, Kiks? How would *you* know? You saw what they did to those people in L.A. You saw what Charles' people were doing, the whole time they were in power. What about when we see things that happen to be 'inconvenient'? You so sure Black and his super-seer posse wouldn't wipe your mind, too?"

I felt a pain in my chest.

I should have seen this coming.

I should have realized.

I'd known for a while that Dex was struggling.

I thought it was with what happened to Kiko, with losing Nick as one of his best male friends on our team, then losing Dalejem not long after... then Nick coming back as he did.

I'd known Dex was struggling.

I just hadn't had time to check in with him on it in a real way.

"Brother..." Jax began, holding up his hands. "...Dexter. I'm sorry. I'm *really sorry*. I should have come to talk to you before. I thought it wasn't my place, not before I knew how Kiko felt. I didn't want to go to her male friend behind her back..."

The anger only grew harder in Dex's voice. "Are you trying to *handle* me right now? Is this you using that seer bullshit on my mind?"

"No!" Jax said, frustrated. "I would *never* do that! Never!"

"Why the hell *wouldn't* you?"

"BECAUSE YOU ARE MY FRIEND!" Jax snapped. "I *never* would do this! Never! Do you think you are my first human friend? That I have never held these boundaries before?"

"Bullshit! Bullshit... to all of you... *bullshit!*"

Dex aimed his finger at Jax, at Jorje, at Holo in his wheelchair, at Mika, at Kiessa.

All of them stood there, silent, their odd-colored eyes shining in the light of the setting sun. Standing all together like they were, they looked suddenly, indisputably alien, not human, not from this world, even to me.

My alarm spiked more.

Jesus.

It was starting.

Even in our own team... it was already starting.

I was still trying to decide what to do, whether I should be the one to try to talk to Dex, when another voice rose. It cut through the quiet that had fallen on the small group, so intensely the vibration of his voice hit at me on almost a physical level.

"Is it bullshit with me, too, Dexter?" Black said.

Every eye in the group shifted.

They stared at Black, who stood there in his tuxedo, his gold eyes blazing in the end of day sun. Black didn't look at any of them; he looked only at Dex.

"Am I not your brother, either?" Black said, his voice gruff.

Looking at Black, I realized why his eyes were so bright.

He wasn't angry. That wasn't anger I was seeing in his eyes.

He was crying.

Dex seemed to realize the same.

He stared at Black like he was looking at a ghost.

I could almost feel the conflict there, his inability to not see Black as alien.

He wanted to, I think... but he couldn't.

There was no going back with Dex, I realized. Some kind of threshold had been passed. I didn't know if it was Kiko, or Black's transformation into an actual fucking *dragon,* or me disappearing into other dimensions... or finding out seers could control his mind, even as vampires fed off his body.

At some point, Dex crossed some kind of line.

He couldn't see Black the same.

He couldn't see any of us the same.

And there was no going back.

There was only going forward.

The only way through this for Dex now was to push past it, to move *forward,* and I had no idea what he would decide on the other side.

I felt Black realize the same.

I felt the intensity of his grief, and not only for all the years Dex had fought by his side.

I felt the memory of that other world, the one he'd escaped to come here.

I felt the loss of that, of the human innocence here.

I felt it, and I had no idea what I could do to make any of it better.

Maybe Dex didn't know what to do, either. Maybe he didn't know what to think, or how and if he wanted to get past it. Whatever the case, at some point, standing there, face to face with Black, became too much.

Dex turned around and walked away.

"DEX!" Kiko shouted. "DEXTER! Goddamn it! Come *back* here! Are you really going to do this on his *wedding* day?"

She walked after him, breaking into a jog when he didn't slow down.

I let her go, and Dexter, too. So did Black.

So did Jax.

"**B**rother, don't give it a second thought." Javier shook his head, sounding angry. "This isn't about you, man. It's about *Kiko*. He's been fucked in the head about her for *months*. We've all heard it..."

The other humans around him nodded, grimacing as they exchanged looks.

"The idiot waited until she was dating someone else to realize he's got feelings for her," A.J. added. "It ain't even *you*, man," the human added to Jax, giving the male seer a grim look. "It started when her and *Jem* started screwing. Then the Nick thing happened... and you. Now he's just mad at the world, and blaming all the wrong damned people."

Jax grimaced, but most of what I felt off him was sympathy.

Also a touch of guilt.

"I haven't helped," Jax muttered, his hands on his hips. "I've been jealous. I should have been more... diplomatic. I am bad at talking about feelings."

Wu shook his head, handing Jax a beer.

"It's really *not* about you. He's looking for some kind of explanation, when it's himself he should be pissed at. You'd never know it, but when it comes to women, Dex tends to shy away from the ones who are actually good for him. Ironically, Kiks is the one who's been talking about that for *years*..."

Jax took a drink of his beer, nodding.

I approached the mostly-male group cautiously, watching Black wipe his eyes as he nodded to Javier's words. I still wasn't sure if I should be there, or if this was something between Black and the human vets on his team, many of whom had worked for him for decades.

Ace spoke up even as I thought it.

"I mean, Christ... it's not like it's some news flash, that you're a total freak, boss," the big human joked, winking at me before he looked at Black. "We've only watched you, you know... *not age* for like thirty years. I mean, even in the Hollywood, rich guy sense of not-aging, you were a freak. You don't look even a tiny bit different, and it's been like thirty years since you and I first found ourselves in a trench together..."

Javier grunted.

"And it's not just the aging," Javier threw in. "We all knew you were some kind of spooky weirdo psychic... Naz thought you were a damned medium or something." Javier laughed with Ace. "Remember that? He thought Black here was moonlighting as some kind of paid psychic. At the very least, he was convinced he killed animals in some spooky psychic ritual shit. And that was loooong before you actually *admitted* it. We saw you playing the stock market and knew something had to be up."

Chase motioned around at all of them.

"We all talked about it, man. You couldn't hide that shit from us entirely. Hell, remember? The Colonel let it slip once they had files on Black stretching back to the *fifties.*"

Black didn't answer, but I could feel him wanting to believe what they said.

In the end, though, he couldn't unhear or un-feel what Dex's words forced him to realize.

"This is just the beginning," he said. "It's not Dex. It's just inevitable. It's why humans enslaved seers back where I am from. They couldn't get past the fear. They couldn't deal with the power imbalance. And there was no way to convince them seers could be trusted."

Black grunted, thinking about that.

"The funny thing is, the seers they found back then really *could* be trusted. They were all basically a bunch of fucking monks."

Black looked at me.

"At the end of the day... Dex is right. We don't belong here."

There was a silence.

Then another voice rose.

"Or maybe they're the ones who don't belong," the voice said.

His words rang out through the early evening air, causing people to look over.

"...Not anymore," he added, colder. "Maybe they aren't as entitled to this world as they seem to think. Maybe they've proven they aren't up to the responsibility..."

I turned, disbelief and horror warring in my chest as I saw a face I'd never thought I'd see again.

It was Charles.

It was my Uncle Charles.

He was here.

He'd found his way back.

27

ENEMY

I looked at Black, and he returned my gaze, his own deathly still.

Then he looked at Cowboy, who I only then noticed standing on my other side, having walked up with Angel when they heard the commotion. Black motioned with his head, a bare gesture, and Cowboy melted backwards, into the crowd, taking Angel with him.

I had no illusions that my uncle hadn't seen me there.

For the same reason, I stayed where I was, half-incredulous as an opening formed in the circle of our friends to let my uncle walk right up to us.

I didn't wait.

I walked right up to him, wedding dress and all.

I'd already geared into the structures in my *aleimi* that allowed me to jump dimensions. I focused on a different world this time, thinking it clearly wasn't going to be enough to just dump him somewhere and hope for the best... especially since the vast majority of worlds I traveled to had some aspect of the Dragon living there.

I would take him to another kind of place.

One that would be much more difficult for my uncle to navigate as a seer.

I'd been loathe to do that before.

I knew Charles wouldn't like where I'd left him; he'd always been a city and luxury kind of person, even back when I remembered him as a child. That predilection only grew more pronounced after we renewed our relationship in the previous few years.

Charles liked caviar and expensive clothes, top of the line hotels and luxury suites, the very best guns and flying first class. He wasn't someone who would enjoy living in a hut on a mostly-agrarian world, no matter how fresh the air, or how plentiful the food.

But I'd hoped he might *learn* to like it.

I'd really hoped he might grow into a better life there, and maybe even a better person, without the need to fight a forever-war against every species that scared him.

Charles might like technologically-advanced worlds, but they didn't seem to do him any favors, in terms of his state of mind.

I decided to go a different route next time.

I would take him to a world with cities, but a world where seers had a much slimmer chance of enslaving every human on the planet.

I'd come across a few that might work.

A few of those options were pretty brutal, but I could think of a few that might allow him to carve out a kind of life for himself—again, if not the life he might have wanted.

I was already resonating with one of those versions of Earth as I walked up to Charles, moving silently, keeping my light shielded so he might not notice my approach. My hand and arm tensed as I got closer, ready to reach out.

Hand, throat, face.

Possibly his chest where his collar lay open in front.

Four steps away from him.

Then three.

I raised my hand, angling my outstretched arm to reach his skin—

Something shoved me back.

It *threw* me back—violently.

The force behind it was so overwhelming, so utterly unexpected... it sucked the breath from my lungs. I couldn't scream. I realized I was flying through the air.

I felt myself hit into Ace, Mika, a few people I didn't know.

Then something... which scared me even more... slowed me down.

I felt that tangibly, too.

My velocity through the air noticeably *changed*. My body grew softer, lighter; it began traveling less fast, as if slowed by an invisible hand.

Terror hit me.

I wondered what in the hell was going on—

My back crashed into one of the deck chairs.

The impact stopped me cold. It also stopped my body before I would have slammed into the glass table behind it.

As it was, I let out a grunt of pain as my spine connected with the metal and plastic.

I also managed to crack the glass top, though I didn't smash through it, at least.

Then my knees gave out, and I fell straight down, halfway over the chair and table.

I landed on the pool deck on my hands and knees, gasping.

I was so stunned, so in shock, I couldn't even decide how to feel.

Not to mention the pain. There was a lot of pain. I couldn't get up at all, not at first. Hanging there, on my bloody hands, I panted, my arms shaking. I was genuinely worried I would pass out. But I couldn't pass out.

I could already feel it.

Black was freaking the fuck out.

When Black freaked out... bad things happened.

But maybe now was a time when we needed bad things.

๑๙๙

Fire rose inside Black.

With that fire came a quiet voice, one that had been quiet more or less since Hawaii.

The presence of that voice swirled around Black's mind, filling it with stars, with galaxies, with slow, pulling waves of celestial ocean...

Who is that? Coreq whispered.

Black blinked, startled by the silence.

Then his fury returned.

You know this one, Black growled back.

He spoke to that emptiness, to the thing that rode around inside him.

It put us away before. In the lab. Underground. Remember?

Black felt Coreq remember.

Coreq didn't like labs.

Coreq especially, really didn't like labs, more than Coreq didn't like any other thing.

What does it want? the being murmured.

You know that, too.

So why should we care? Coreq now sounded bored. *It is no different now. It is the same as it ever was. Since time immemorial. Why must we care about this now?*

Black felt Coreq's interest in the wedding.

Black felt Coreq's interest in Miri, specifically.

Coreq's interest lay in the wedding night... in fucking Miri.

Coreq didn't care about whatever this other thing was.

Black turned his head, looking at where Miri struggled to regain her feet. He showed her to Coreq, showed him the blood on her hands, the blood trickling down the side of her face, and rage pulsed in him, even as he turned to face Charles.

Coreq's mind grew cold as ice.

How? he said. *Why?*

Telekinesis, Black told Coreq. *As for why, presumably he didn't like being dumped on that other world... the one where Miri took him. He didn't like losing all that power. Or to have his friends shoved naked into cells under the building on California Street—*

"You are talking to it," Charles mused. "Are you not?"

Black's eyes clicked back into focus.

"I have seen this before," Charles added. "I have seen it with the other. You get this odd look on your faces... different from how normal seers look when they are communicating with one another. It is like the frequency is different somehow... or perhaps you listen with a different part of your light..."

Black didn't speak, not at first.

He listened to Charles instead, muscles tensing under the sixty-thousand-dollar tuxedo he wore, fighting to control his light, to keep his mind moving in straight lines.

"Yes," he said simply.

Charles smiled knowingly.

The ice in his eyes never grew any warmer.

"The other one... the other dragon," Charles explained, waving a hand vaguely. "He explained to me how this works. His blackouts. How they got triggered. He might not have thought through that last part, because he more or less told me how to summon the dragon in him whenever I wanted."

Pausing to let his words sink in, Charles added,

"Rather simple, really. All I had to do was make the dragon think his life was in danger, or otherwise throw him out of his regular state of consciousness."

Charles shrugged gracefully with one hand, seer-fashion.

"I've found LSD works quite well. So does crystal meth... but it takes longer."

Black let out a humorless grunt, in spite of himself.

"You're dosing your telekinetic dragon with LSD?" Black grunted again. "Well, that's fucking genius. I'm sure that's going to work out great for you, Charles."

Faustus acted like Black hadn't spoken.

"He handed himself to me, more or less from the beginning," Charles added. "I think the lack of control had become a problem for him."

Charles paused, gauging Black's face, a smile ghosting his lips.

"Oh, and I promised him he could have Miri," Charles added. "That motivated him quite nicely, Black. Apparently you dragons have quite the yen for my niece. I'm not going to pretend to understand it... especially now that I know the truly vile and duplicitous nature of that little cunt." Charles' eyes grew colder. "At this point, I'll enjoy watching him rape her. Frankly, I'm quite looking forward to it."

Black felt every muscle in his body tense.

That time, he didn't speak.

Everything inside him seemed to be telescoping inward.

He was going to have to kill Charles.

It was a thought he hadn't let himself entertain since before he'd met Miri.

Family was sacred. He couldn't kill his mate's family.

Charles shrugged, his eyes as flat and lifeless as a shark's.

"The dragon took me here of his own free will, Black. He merely asked me to show him Miri so he could track her across dimensions... and I complied. It was relatively clear he wasn't in a wholly rational state of mind at the time. He became his true self again, somewhere in the process of our traveling to this dimension together. So I took him out to breakfast. He and I... we got along famously."

Charles smiled, but his eyes remained dead.

The green-eyed seer added, "We had long talks about what he was, about what triggered the transformation. It was quite... educational."

Black didn't change expression.

Still, he heard every word, as well as every word left unspoken among Charles' words.

"You have yourself a pet dragon." Black grunted. "How nice for you."

He forced his eyes to travel casually back to his wife.

Gaos... she was moving now, at least. She still looked dazed. Her jaw hardened as he watched her try to crawl her way to the metal and glass table.

He reached out for her, unthinking.

He couldn't fully go there, not now... not without losing his goddamned mind... but he reached for her anyway, knowing only that he needed her safe.

Jump, he told her. *Go, Miri. Now. Take as many as you can with you... Yarli, Jem, Angel. Whoever you can get out. Go somewhere where you can be of help to the rest of us.*

She didn't answer.

He felt her anger.

That anger definitely wasn't aimed at him, but she struggled with what he'd asked of her.

He couldn't argue with her.

He didn't have time.

"So your dragon is telekinetic," Black said, shifting his attention back to Charles. He lifted an eyebrow as he folded his arms. "A telekinetic, dimension-hopping dragon. That's nice, Faustus. That's gotta be a real expensive, rare pet you've got there."

He paused, forcing a faint smile to his lips.

"Is this where you tell me your dragon is bigger than mine?"

"There is always a bigger dragon, Black," Charles said, smiling humorlessly. "You should have remembered that." He narrowed his gaze. "I should have known you could not *really* be a manifestation of the One True God. I don't entirely understand it yet, but you are but a copy, Quentin. A copy of a copy of a copy, perhaps... definitely not the real thing, but likely a genetic clone from the Old World. Something meant to be a weapon."

Still gauging Black's eyes, the older seer clicked at him softly.

"You know, I was told of another like you there. One that left that world, not long before the end. Apparently they used your cousin's DNA to create that one. Perhaps it is something in your family... some genetic tolerance for certain types of intermediary powers..."

Black had no interest in any of that.

In that way, he was like Coreq.

He cared about his wife.

He cared about his wife so much, it took every ounce of his willpower to wait, to not launch himself at this fucker and strangle him with his bare hands.

He cared about all the people here who could die, if things went truly ugly.

If he *did* care, though, everything Charles just said... it all sounded wrong to him.

None of that sounded remotely like how any of this worked.

It sounded too... *physiological.*

Too genetic.

Too materialistic.

From what that old witch doctor on his cousin's world told him, Dragon was more of an multidimensional collective than a single being. It was a sophisticated, multifaceted consciousness, one that formed the building blocks of the very creation.

If there was a single "Dragon," it was more like that entity split its consciousness into many worlds, many beings.

It wasn't either a "genetic anomaly," as Charles was implying, or a single "god" in the sense of being a unified entity.

Dragon was... something else.

Perhaps something beyond what a mere seer or human mind could comprehend.

Either way, Black didn't care.

He really didn't give a fuck.

Miri? Black clenched his jaw. He could no longer feel her light. *I hope like hell you got out of here. I hope you brought Jem, Yarli, Angel, and some of the others out of here with you—*

He knew that was somewhat manipulative.

He didn't care about that, either.

—You have to trust me, baby. Please. Please trust me.

He hoped fervently that the manipulation worked. He hoped if she wouldn't leave for herself, she might leave to save the people she loved.

"So?" Charles came to a stop, leaving only a few feet between them. "What will it be, Black? Will your dragon take over? Must I put more fear into you? I confess, I'm curious to see who would die in a match between the two of you."

The pale, leaf-green eyes grew more metallic.

"I am thinking it will be you," he said.

Black stared back at him.

He found himself remembering Lucky from Russia, way back in the day... and from Vietnam before that.

He'd almost forgotten *that* Lucky.

It was difficult to view him entirely the same once he found out Karlov "Lucky Lucifer" Vasiliev was the beloved "Uncle Charles" of the woman he was courting... and later, the woman he wanted as his mate.

Now he found himself remembering.

He found himself thinking he knew why he could once again tangibly *see* that murderous psychopath shining out of Faustus's eyes.

Black had changed categories in Charles' mind, too.

In Charles' mind, Black and he were no longer family.

Back when Black first knew "Lucky Lucifer" Vasiliev, the two men were enemies.

At the very least, Black was an adversary who stood in the way of Charles' plans, an asset who'd proven maddeningly difficult to either eliminate or recruit. Black doubted he was the first seer on this version of Earth to say no to Charles, but he might have been the one who said no the longest, if only because he managed to stay alive.

Black could see that look in Charles now.

He'd forgotten what it was like, being on the receiving end of the stare.

Black was the enemy again.

Worse, given what Charles had just done... given what he'd just *said*... Miri clearly fell into the enemy camp now, too.

Charles finally hit his limit with his favorite niece.

Leaving him on that empty version of Earth had been the last straw.

For the same reason, Black didn't even try to play that card now.

"Where is he?" he said. "Your dragon. Did you leave him parked in a handicapped space somewhere, Faustus? Really, I'm surprised you just didn't order him to wipe out the whole damned city. I mean... what's one human city, in the wider scheme of things?"

Black carefully kept his mind out of the Barrier.

He knew Charles would have people there, too.

Charles would have seers monitoring him, and they could be doing it from pretty much anywhere.

Just then, it came.

Black didn't even hear it.

He saw Charles' face flinch.

The seer put a hand to his throat, a confused, angry look rising to his eyes.

Then he collapsed.

28

BACKUP

"Collar that son of a bitch!" Black snapped, motioning for Dalejem and Javier.

Yarli, he growled in the space. *Start the evac. Now. Tell Frank.*

Got it, boss.

Black glanced at Nick, who'd stood in the wings, waiting.

"Get the prototypes I gave you," he growled. "Do it, Tanaka. Now! If he wakes up from that dart, uncollared, we're all going to be really fucking sorry..."

Jem was already moving, snapping out of his confusion even as Nick disappeared and reappeared in seconds, holding a bag that came from... gods knew where.

Black was just glad they'd done as he asked, and hidden all of that crap with the vampires during the ceremony itself.

Black figured there was no way Charles would have his people searching the vampire guests, not even for that. For all his paranoia, Charles would never allow that Black might trust one of their kind with holding onto that tech in the first place.

And to be fair, Black hadn't trusted "vampires" with that.

He'd trusted Jem and Nick.

Most of the vamps only stayed past the ceremony because Black asked Brick for backup, as part of their treaty.

He'd called in a lot of favors that day.

He'd also hired *real* backup.

But he'd deal with all of that in a minute.

Black threw more words at Jem, this time from the Barrier.

When you're done with that, help Yarli get all of these people out of here, he growled. *The non-family. Make sure you loop Frank and Devin in. They had something in place for that as well. And you can tell Brick his people can go, if they want... as soon as we get the site secured. In the meantime, if they can find any more of Charles' people, we would really appreciate it.*

Black didn't wait to see if Jem understood.

He pushed his way through the crowd gathering around Charles' body, and ran for where he'd last seen Miri, even as he called out to her in his mind.

MIRI! WHERE ARE YOU? CHARLES IS DOWN...

There was an endless-feeling pause.

In that pause, Black covered half the length of the pool deck.

It's okay, Black, she murmured in his mind.

Relief flooded him, along with exasperation.

Miri! Why didn't you leave?

I'm okay. Just a little dazed. My head hurts.

I'm so sorry, baby... I had no idea he would do that. I didn't think he'd hurt you like that, even now—

It's okay. Really, Black, it's fine. If I hadn't tried, he would have been suspicious immediately. He probably would have rained hellfire down on the whole place if that happened, or maybe had his dragon jump both of them out of here.

Black reached the area of the deck where she was.

You still should have jumped... he scolded her, changing direction to run to the table. *You should have grabbed some of the seers and jumped the fuck out of here. Hell, I would have been happy if you'd gone with just Nick and Jem.*

She didn't bother to answer.

Black stood over her now, only to find his wife still halfway on the ground where Charles' dragon had left her. Angel and

Cowboy were bent over her, with Angel holding one of her arms, Cowboy holding the other.

Ace and Mika were there, too.

They looked like they'd gotten there first, actually. Ace held Miri carefully around the waist; Black watched the big Texan ease her into the nearest deck chair almost daintily.

Black didn't know if he wanted to bark at the other man, or kiss him.

In the end, he did neither.

"MIRI!"

He threw himself down on the pool deck in front of her, wrapping his arms around her and immersing himself in the folds of that gorgeous, sexy fucking wedding dress.

Most of all, he flooded her with his light.

"Are you okay, honey?" Tears came to his eyes as he cupped her face gently, looking her over with his eyes and his light. Without waiting for her response, he looked up and back at the rest of them. "Where's Luric? Someone find Luric... NOW!"

Even as he said it, he pinged the medical tech seer with his light.

LURIC GET YOUR ASS OVER HERE. POOL DECK. NOW. MIRI'S HURT.

He used the construct, showing him exactly where Miri was.

Feeling Luric acknowledge him, Black clicked back out.

He saw Euston, Dog, and Magic run off, too, presumably looking for Luric in person.

Jax, Kiessa and Jorji stood there now, too.

"He's coming, boss," Jax said.

Black looked only at his wife. He felt over her body carefully through the dress, noting where she seemed to be in pain, the way she sat in the chair.

"Gaos," he growled. "That fucker. He could have broken your back!"

"He didn't though, Quentin," she said, caressing his face. "It's okay."

"The hell it is."

Kiko's voice rose, sounding flustered.

"Who brought him down?" she said, panting, obviously out of breath. "None of our people seem to know." She swallowed her voice growing tense. "The vampires? Is that why they were here?"

"No," Black cut in.

He never took his eyes off Miri's face.

She was clutching at his fingers now, smiling at him, but he could still tell she was in pain. He had to fight not to yell at Luric in the space, tell him to move his ass. Black could feel pain coming from her lower back, her tailbone, her spine, and her head. So far, he didn't think anything was broken, but his light swam over her frantically anyway, looking for injuries, especially in her head or back.

He barely glanced at Kiko.

"No," he repeated. "I mean... yes, they were partly here for protection. They did some of the coordinating, too, since I couldn't bring my team in on this. I knew Charles would be watching all of us." He grunted then, giving Kiko another look. "Also, it's a fucking wedding. If Charles didn't show, I didn't want all of you working."

Kiko let out an outraged sound.

Ace, clearly hearing him too, burst out in a disbelieving laugh.

Jax's eyes and voice remained serious.

"Who was it?" he said. "If not us—"

"I hired Archangel," Black cut in.

There was a silence.

"It was the doc's idea," Black added, kissing her face.

Miri shook her head, her voice rough as she looked up at the others.

"No. It *wasn't* my idea to hire that crazy cult of rogue assassins," she corrected. "I just said, hey, maybe we should find *some-*

one. Someone outside of our circle. Someone we'd never worked with before. Someone Charles wouldn't be watching..."

Black smiled at her, feeling tears coming to his eyes as he kissed her face.

"That didn't leave me a lot of options, love," he reminded her.

She grunted, but he could feel her mind clearing, the more he flooded his light into her.

He could feel some part of her drinking him in, leaning on him.

Then she met his gaze, her hazel eyes bright, even in the relative darkness.

Somewhere in all of that, the sun had gone down for real.

Firelight reflected in her eyes, most of it from the tiki torches surrounding the pool, but also from the several fire pits scattered around the pool deck.

Most of the "non-family" guests were being escorted out.

Black could feel it, with Frank Blackfoot and Devin coordinating a lot of it, aided by Yarli and Dalejem from the Barrier.

"Where is he?" she said. "Did they find him? The other dragon?"

At that, Black could only frown.

"I don't know," he admitted.

Just then, from directly overhead...

...there was an ear-shattering roar.

29

BLACK OF WING

B*LACK, NO... where are you going?*
I have to.

He sounded distracted in the space, only halfway with me.

I could see him running, aiming his steps for the desert on the other side of the resort wall. I watched in my mind as he vaulted over the adobe barrier, climbing up it nimbly and throwing himself over the other side.

Black, you absolutely DON'T have to do this. We can find another way—

Too late for that. And yes. I do have to, wife. I have to draw him away from the resort, if nothing else... and away from Santa Fe. No one else can do that. We don't even know if we can communicate with him like this.

Pausing, still running, he added, *Maybe I can find a way to reach him. He seemed mostly reasonable when he wasn't in blackout mode...*

NO! she snapped. *Black, he'll probably kill you before you say so much as "hi"...*

Oh, come on, wife. He's not THAT much bigger than me.

He's TELEKINETIC, for crying out loud!

I felt Black shrug, even running.

I almost saw it in my mind.

Don't get paranoid now, wife, he sent. *We only saw the one thing. We have no idea if he can do that in dragon form... or if that was him at all.*

For a second, I couldn't even answer that.

What? I sent. *Black, do you have any idea how insane that sounds? I have SOME idea,* he admitted.

He was barely listening to me, though.

I could feel Coreq there now, already sharing some part of his mind.

I could feel them both mutually decide when they felt they were far enough away from people, from the resort—

BLACK NO! I shouted at him.

But I could feel him changing, even as I threw it at him.

I could feel it... and knew it was already too late.

۞

An earth-trembling screech exploded in the night sky above where they stood.

Nick looked up first, ducking in reflex even as he gaped up at the enormous shadow that blotted out the stars. Claws, scales, and leathery wings all caught glints of light as they passed over the firelight around the swimming pool.

Nick's vampire eyes easily picked all of that out of the dark, even the gold eye of the black-scaled creature as it streaked through the air.

An answering scream rent the sky, seconds later, and he ducked again.

They were already moving away.

Black was doing what he said he'd do—drawing the other dragon away from the resort.

The sheer insanity of that, of two dragons dueling in the night skies of New Mexico, made Nick think, yet again, they had to be in some kind of twilight zone, end of times place, or possibly that he'd already died, and this was his messed-up afterlife.

"Are you seeing this?" a voice asked over his headset.

Brick spoke almost pleasantly, but Nick heard the edge there.

"I see it," Nick acknowledged. "Do you have people out in the desert? People who can see what's happening for real?"

Instead of answering him, Brick opening a virtual screen, sharing it on Nick's side of the communication. In it, an enormous, bone-white dragon slammed into a smaller black one, throwing it into a red-rock bluff that overlooked part of the city.

Nick winced, hoping there weren't any houses up there.

The black dragon screamed inside the video, and Nick heard it in stereo.

He looked up at the sound, realizing the dragons' screams were still audible where he stood by the swimming pool.

"Fuck," he muttered.

"Indeed," Brick remarked.

"Any sign of that big white one using the telekinesis on the Black one?"

"Not as of yet," Brick said.

The vampire king paused, then added,

"He did not hurt our dear Miriam, did he?"

Nick frowned, then shook his head. "He didn't *not* hurt her. But from what I can tell, it was nothing serious. Black was pretty freaked. I think he thought that other dragon wouldn't hurt her at all, since he supposedly came here looking for her."

Nick felt his sire think about this.

Before Brick could say any more, Nick broke into his thoughts.

"What about Archangel? Are they still here?"

"They are," Brick confirmed. "They are standing by. They will not leave without Black's explicit say-so. He is the paying client. I am merely an intermediary."

Nick wanted to roll his eyes, but he only nodded.

He remembered dealing with these fucks before, back when he'd been human.

They really were like some kind of cult, or secret society.

Damned effective, though.

They were even more effective after Black gave them tech that hid their Barrier light from seers. Nick strongly got the impression that's how Archangel had been paid, in organic tech. Even Nick couldn't help thinking Black was really opening a can of worms with that one.

In the end, their method of bringing down Charles had been simple, yet effective.

They'd hit Charles in the neck with a damned blow dart.

That was some next level weird ninja shit.

"Did they find any more of Charles' people on the ground?" Nick asked next.

"We have ten in custody," Brick affirmed. "Zoe also located three long-haul trucks parked at a truck stop down the road. All three were filled with those cybernetic creatures that attacked Quentin on the beaches of Hawaii. These look like more advanced models, though."

Pausing, Brick added dryly,

"Charles came with a lot of firepower. Clearly, he didn't intend to take any chances this time around. We're actually damned 'lucky' ourselves that we were able to shut down those cyborg creatures before they could be activated... but Zoe located the truck before Charles made his appearance at the resort. Apparently, he intended to use them *after* he'd brought down Miriam and Quentin. Quite probably to destroy any chance of a viable treaty between humans and seers... or humans and vampires, for that matter."

Nick grimaced, but Brick's words felt true.

Charles intended to put a stop to any illusions about building a multi-species world, at least one living in any kind of peace... or even semi-hostile mutual tolerance.

"He probably could have done that with the telekinetic dragon," Nick muttered. "But Charles seems to believe in overkill these days, so that doesn't surprise me."

"Indeed," Brick agreed. "But Charles has *always* believed in overkill, darling boy... and in making unnecessarily bloody statements to hammer home his points. You didn't know him before he decided to play 'Magnanimous Uncle Charlie' with the seer world. He was a monster, my child. An absolute and utter monster."

Nick grimaced, remembering "Lucky" from his military days.

He could have corrected Brick on his supposition that Nick hadn't been aware of him back then, but he didn't bother.

"Have they got any more of his cultists outside the gates?" Nick asked instead.

"There are some, yes," Brick said. "We have most of them rounded up now. Frank Blackfoot and his people have involved the local authorities on that end of things. It is likely they will be taken off to the human jail, most of them. A number were found carrying illegal weapons, as well as gear likely intended for use against Black's wedding guests. Plastic handcuffs, tasers, extendable batons, handguns, even smoke bombs and grenades..."

Nick grimaced again, but only nodded.

He liked the idea of involving the human authorities, though.

The more of this they could do aboveboard, at least as far as the human authorities and media were concerned, the better. The more they could frame Charles' radicals, not to mention Charles himself, as a threat to *all* of the species, the better.

It might not solve the PR issues, but it certainly couldn't hurt.

Especially right now.

Dragon screams filled the sky once more, mostly coming from the VR screen in his headset. Nick could no longer hear them outside the virtual feed, even with his vampire hearing.

That could only be a good thing, though.

It meant Black managed to draw the other dragon further out into the desert.

Focusing on the images in his headset, Nick watched the dragons claw at one another from the air, then slam into one another in the space.

The white one grabbed the black one's neck in thick jaws, flying it into yet another cliffside, sending boulders tumbling down to the desert floor.

The black one screamed in fury, beating at the other dragon with its wings.

Its claws ripped into the other one's chest, and the white dragon released it, beating its own wings, creating a cloud of red dust as it rose higher in the air, screaming again.

Fire erupted from the black one's jaws, lighting up the desert sky, lighting up the rock formations that broke the flatness of the desert floor.

Nick watched it, his shoulders tensing.

He wondered how long it would take for videos of *this* insanity to make it to social media.

The white dragon didn't shoot fire back at the black one, but the fire didn't seem to faze it, either. It dove at Black even as Black roared a continuous stream of flames; the white one's lower claws and legs extended, its talons turning red and white in the fire.

Seemingly impervious to the fire engulfing its lower body... it slammed into the black one's belly and side. Nick winced as the white one tore chunks of flesh and scales out of the smaller dragon, causing it to scream in agony, twisting in the air.

That time, it couldn't get away.

The white one slammed the black one into the desert floor.

That time, Nick heard the impact, deep down in the earth, almost like a bomb going off, or a seismic event of some kind.

He heard it even without the virtual feed.

The black one let loose with another stream of liquid fire.

He aimed it at the white one's chest and head, writhing to get free.

Nick watched one of the white dragon's huge white claws...

claws wielding four-foot talons... close around Black's dragon neck. The white dragon dug those razor sharp talons in, squeezing, and Black screamed, sending up another stream of blue-green fire.

Nick felt sick.

Even he could see where this was going.

The goddamned thing was going to kill him.

The white dragon was going to kill Black.

Nick was so busy staring at the images in his headset, he didn't see or feel the human approach. He didn't even hear him through the black dragon's agonized screams.

"I knew you were here," a voice said then.

Cold, filled with hate.

Almost completely unrecognizable.

But Nick did recognize it.

It was the voice of a man he'd once considered one of his closest friends.

When Nick dropped the virtual screen, focusing on where he was in real life, he found himself face to face with Dex.

He found himself facing the gun Dex held in his hand.

"Rot in hell," Dex told him.

Nick raised a hand in instinct, but he was already too late.

The gun went off.

Everything went dark.

☙❧

"Jesus H... are you seeing this?"

Luke glanced over from where he'd been breaking down his rifle, his jaw hardening as he checked out the view on his lieutenant's tablet.

He watched as the significantly larger, white and gray monster clenched its talon around the neck of the black one.

The one on top, which had the black one pinned, reminded Luke of a corpse, and not only for the gray and white color of most of its body. Veins of red darkened the areas around the mouth and nose, evoking dried blood on a dead body. A pale blue ridge ran along its back and tail that somehow evoked broken veins as well. The thing was grotesque, bulging, its teeth yellow and thick, its eyes set too far outside its head.

It looked like a zombie dinosaur.

The black one thrashed under it, screaming fire into the night—red, orange, pale blue and green—but it was obviously weakening.

"That one on the bottom is Black, isn't it?" Davis, his lieutenant, muttered. "Does this mean we're not getting paid?"

Luke grunted.

Gotta trust an Archangel to have that bleak sense of humor.

"We got paid, Digger," he assured the other man.

He nodded towards the screen.

"Where are his people now?"

Davis lowered the screen.

He exhaled, then his voice turned to the cadence of a formal report.

"They've got Vasiliev in custody. Four psychics guarding him, cuffed at the wrists, ankles, neck, biceps... they still seem shit-scared of that asshole. They've also got one of those psychic-blocking collars on him, one of the new ones."

Luke nodded, thinking.

"What about those Purity jokers?" he said. "They still there?"

Davis shook his head.

"Santa Fe P.D.'s got them mostly rounded up. At least forty-five taken into custody so far. We're hearing mostly weapons charges, but also some trespassing, assault against police, destruction of property, and at least a handful of possible terrorism and conspiracy to commit terrorism charges, when all's said and done."

Luke turned that over, too.

"Do his people still want us here?" he said finally. "Black's?"

Digger made a face. "I talked to their contact person. The

bloodsucker. He seemed to think we could go whenever we wanted. They really only needed us for Charles."

Grunting, looking over the dark valley, where the screams of the two dragons had grown louder once more, Davis added sourly,

"That bloodsucker didn't think we'd be much good against those things."

"Why not?" Luke said wryly. "We've got most of the nukes those assholes in Kiev and Moscow were hoarding... Uri and Alexei. Believe me, Black knows that."

Davis grunted in that dark humor, shaking his head.

"I don't think Black is in charge anymore," he said dryly.

He pointed across the valley, in the direction of the screams.

Luke nodded grimly.

Both of them looked back down at the tablet's screen, where the live drone feed continued to play. They watched the dragons rip and beat wings, and bite, and claw at one another apart in silence for a few seconds more.

Without looking up, Davis shrugged.

"Your call, boss," he said to Luke. "Do we see this out to the end?"

Luke frowned.

He watched the white dragon as it sank its razor-sharp teeth into the side of the dragon lying on its back. The black one bellowed, thrashing its body sideways in violent arcs, hitting at the other one with its powerful tail, trying to knock it off. The black one was getting weaker, though. It still fought hard, trying to roll out from under the white one, to break free of the other's weight, but its thrashing and clawing gradually slowed.

It blew out more fire, screaming into the night.

"Pack it up," Luke said, deciding as he said it. "Looks like Black's no longer a variable. We'll regroup and gather intel, bring our findings back to the Base." He gave Davis another look. "Tonight was paid work. We did our job. We go."

Looking back out over the valley, he added grimly,

"Tomorrow, we're no longer on the client clock. Tomorrow we're on Archangel time. I'll get us an audience with The Priests. We'll bring everything we've got to them. Let them decide. There's still the factor of the woman."

Davis nodded, snapping the tablet shut.

"Sounds right, boss," he said approvingly.

He rose to his feet, hiking his rifle strap back up on his shoulder.

The two of them stood there for a few seconds longer, listening to the screams of the giant animals as they echoed across the desert valley.

30

UNDER THE LIGHT OF
THE MOON

B*lack's in trouble.*
     I felt it so clearly, so intensely clearly, I sat bolt upright.
They'd put me in the resort's small clinic on the first floor.

They'd given me a shot, something to help me relax while they examined me.

When I sat up like that, instantly, like four pairs of hands tried to hold me down.

I barely saw any of them, barely looked at the faces around me to know if I recognized any of them. I heard them talking amongst themselves, both inside the Barrier and without, enough to know they were worried about me.

There was something else.

Something that wasn't about me, wasn't about Black.

Shot him right in the head, using one of those "vampire killer" bullets...

...don't know if he's going to make it. The doc's trying to dig the bullet out now.

Got him in custody next to Charles in that same room...

I didn't care about any of that.

Not then. I didn't care.

I felt Yarli then...

She knew.

She knew I was right.

She just didn't think there was anything I could do about it.

I didn't think.

I didn't even care that there were hands on me, or who they belonged to.

I geared into those structures in my light...

...and I jumped.

※

"JESUS JEHOSAPHAT CHRIST!"

Angel didn't even manage get out that much.

She didn't so much as squeak.

She stood there for a few seconds, panting, shaking, pretty sure she'd just pissed herself.

Her wedding dress was gone.

The fancy underwear she'd worn for her wedding night was gone, too.

Cowboy, who'd yelled out those words right next to her, the instant they winked back into existence, no longer wore his tux.

She looked at her husband... *her husband,* her mind still paused to note.

She focused blankly on his naked skin, his tattoos, his sinewy muscles. He stood directly to her right, stark naked, shaking with shock. She looked him over, assuring herself he was all right... then she looked out over the desert floor.

It was cold.

A wind rose, bringing goosebumps to her skin.

An insane number of stars shone overhead.

She looked to her left, hearing more breathing, and saw Jax standing there, shivering, his arms wrapped around his chest.

His violet eyes stood out on his darkish skin, reflecting starlight.

It struck her, seeing him naked, that Jax was a lot more

muscular than she'd realized. He and Holo were comparatively smaller than Black and Jem and most of Charles' seers, so she'd always thought of him as being on the slim side.

But now she saw the bulging muscles of his arms and shoulders over a lean torso and muscular legs, and found herself getting why Kiko had been gushing over how hot he was, the one time they'd talked about her new relationship over drinks.

Even beyond the fact of who Jax was, or how much Kiko obviously liked him, or what a good kisser she said he was, Kiko *also* made it clear she found him extremely physically attractive, too.

Angel got it now.

She saw what Kiko saw.

Jax really was kind of hot.

Pushing the thought aside, Angel looked around at where they were.

Then, realizing how they must have gotten here... she looked for Miri.

She found her friend almost at once.

Completely and utterly naked, just like the three of them, Miri walked in a straight line, her black hair still hanging down her back and woven through with tiny flowers. Her strides lengthened as she went. Her feet aimed for the center of the red-rock valley floor.

That's when Angel heard it.

She'd been hearing their breaths, their low groans, their struggles.

She hadn't fully *heard* them, though, not until now.

Part of it was, the dragons were no longer screaming.

The white one sat atop the black one, and both of them were panting.

Then the black one cried out, writhing weakly, thrashing its tail, and Angel looked over, feeling her heart drop into her gut when she saw how big they were.

Angel didn't know if the black-scaled one had seen or felt

Miri, but its cries sounded frantic, desperate. They sounded like what they were—painfully obvious pleas for help. The creature didn't scream even then; the sound it made came closer to a groan. It gasped when the claw around its neck tightened.

Angel watched the creature struggle, trying to pull in air, right before it moaned again.

The moan dropped into a weak growl, a pained, half-breathy gasp.

Angel could hear the pain in it.

More than that.

She could hear him dying.

"BLACK!" she screamed, stepping forward. "LET GO OF HIM YOU PIECE OF SHIT! YOU'RE KILLING HIM!"

She burst into tears.

She could see them almost clearly now, on the valley floor.

Her eyes gradually adjusted, and then everything grew brighter still when the nearly-full moon came out from behind a small cluster of high-flying clouds. Strangely symmetrical rock formations loomed blackly in the distance, cutting into a sky still shockingly full of stars, even now that the valley glowed with moonlight.

That moonlight illuminated the dragons' bodies, splashing over the red rock cliffs and jutting formations that dotted the plain.

Miri had almost reached them now.

Miri had broken into a run.

Angel didn't hear her friend yell out, or make any noise.

She hadn't yelled at the white dragon the way Angel had... but Angel saw the exact instant when the white dragon grew aware of her.

It turned its massive head, panting where it looked down at her.

Unlike the smaller dragon beneath its weight, it didn't make any other sound while it squeezed its claw around Black's neck.

Angel couldn't help herself.

She screamed at the thing again.

"STOP IT! STOP, YOU PIECE OF SHIT!"

The gray dragon turned its head around more, almost like it heard her.

Then it looked down at Miri, who stood directly below it, only a dozen yards away from Black's flapping wing.

For a long-feeling few seconds, the gray dragon didn't move.

Neither did Miri.

Angel, Jax, and Cowboy just stood there, oblivious to their nakedness now, holding their breaths as they watched Miri face off with the enormous creature.

Angel had no idea how long she stood there, watching them.

Long enough to be terrified Black was dead.

Long enough to be terrified Miri would get herself killed, too.

Then, seemingly out of nowhere...

...the white dragon began to change.

Angel watched in disbelief as its lumpy, gray-white skin began to bubble and morph, turning smoke-like, exuding light in flashes as it began to change back. She noticed for the first time that the larger dragon didn't have scales at all, not like Black did. Instead it had rough, almost elephant-like or rhino-like skin. Coarse and bumpy, it made it look more like a dinosaur, and less like whatever Black turned into.

Somehow, it made that dragon more terrifying, that it looked so misshapen and ridged, with that white and gray mottled skin.

Black's iridescent black scales were beautiful in comparison.

He looked strangely perfect in his dragon form, almost like some snakes... specifically like a black cobra Angel had seen once in the San Francisco zoo, which looked to her child's eyes to be carved out of black volcanic rock.

Angel watched as the white dragon continued to morph and flash, as light-filled smoke billowed around its form.

Then it was shrinking.

It was definitely shrinking.

Angel saw the exact instant its massive claw released Black's throat, and then Black's dragon was gasping, fighting for breath, writhing from its back over to its stomach.

The gray-white dragon fell, sliding down Black's snake-like, gorgeous scales like they were a glass slide covered in water.

Angel watched in disbelief as the white dragon continued to fall... growing smaller... then smaller still... until it wasn't a dragon at all.

It was a man again.

Or, she told herself, it was *man-shaped* again.

Whatever the hell that thing was... it definitely wasn't a "man."

She stared at him, even as she felt herself starting to relax.

She was still panting, half in shock, but she told herself everything would be okay now.

Black was still alive.

Badly hurt, yes, but he was alive.

Miri could reason with that dragon thing, now... and with Charles in custody, they could send the dragon-man away. This time, it might even *stay* away. Angel knew all of that was probably a pipe dream. She stared at the strange, handsome, very naked man with the brown hair with the silver streak in it, and wondered if there would ever be an end to this shit.

They still hadn't even dealt with Charles' seers.

Those same seers were still locked up in the basement of the Raptor's Nest.

She wondered if Black would want to keep this thing collared and in custody with the rest of them, along with Charles and—

The black dragon lunged.

It lowered its head so swiftly, Angel's eyes barely caught the movement.

Before she could take a breath, those powerful jaws snapped.

They closed around the man who had been the white dragon so swiftly, he seemed to disappear.

There was a loud crunch.

Then the black dragon raised his head, opening his throat.

There was another crunch.

Then another.

Then another.

Angel stared up with Cowboy and Jax... fascinated, sickened... completely unable to look away. They watched Black crunch with seeming abandon through bones, flesh, muscle, sinew, skin, blood, hair.

Then the sound of a long throat moving in a satisfied swallow reached her...

...and for a long-feeling few seconds, the desert was quiet.

JUST A LITTLE LONGER

I heard the door open behind me.

I felt him come in, but I didn't turn around.

My eyes never left the man on the hospital bed in front of me.

Even so, I felt something in the core of my being relax when his warm hand fell on my shoulder, when he wrapped his other arm around my waist and squeezed me against his chest.

"How is he?" he murmured softly.

I finally looked away from Nick's face, glancing at my husband from only an inch or two away. "They think he's out of danger," I said softly, exhaling as I leaned into him. I looked at Nick, then out the window at the view of the Sandia Mountains in the distance.

Nick was in a hospital bed.

But of course we couldn't take a vampire to a hospital.

We were still at the resort, but we'd converted one of the rooms into a quasi-medical center.

Black hadn't needed it, funnily enough.

He almost died.

He told me he'd been more or less teetering on the verge of

unconsciousness and probable death, when he felt me jump out to that desert.

He joked that I pushed the dramatic save thing a bit far that time.

He teased me that it must be my love of the theatrical.

That I liked living dangerously.

That I clearly hadn't liked the wedding ceremony as much as he had.

Basically I was never going to hear the end of how I almost let him die.

He'd probably be complaining about it on his death bed.

"Probably," he murmured, kissing my temple.

Either way, Black made a full recovery from his own wounds.

Despite him almost dying, despite the white dragon clawing him up, biting him, ripping chunks out of his dragon skin and flesh... Black was completely fine, if utterly exhausted and borderline drunk-acting when he came back to his seer form.

Something in his dragon-y make up meant he was more or less healed when he transformed from the black-scaled dragon back to being Black again.

"So he's all right? He'll live?" Black said now, soft.

I sighed, looking at Nick.

Deathly pale, most of his face covered in bandages, he rested on top of a salmon-colored sheet, as still as a corpse.

I gestured a yes in seer. "It was damned touch and go, from what I heard... but he's supposed to be out of the woods."

Black nodded, kissing my neck.

Thinking, I pointed to my head.

Shouldn't we be talking this way? I asked, using my mind.

I motioned towards the chair positioned just to the left of the bed where Nick lay.

Another body sprawled there, next to Nick's.

"No," Black said, softer than before. "Believe it or not, that would wake him up faster. He's the reason I was speaking out loud."

I nodded.

Biting my lip, I began, "About Dex. What are you—"

"I'll deal with Dex, doc."

Black's voice came out as a soft warning.

I considered arguing, then nodded, reluctant.

He was right.

He and Dex went back decades.

I knew Black would do the right thing with him.

I knew Black loved him like family.

Still, I loved Dex, too.

"I won't hurt Dex, doc," Black said, softer still.

I heard the grief in his voice and shivered, gripping his arms where he held me. Nodding, I wiped my eyes when they stung, clearing my throat.

"What about the big bash?" I made my voice deliberately lighter. "Was a decision finally made on that?"

"It was a unanimous vote," Black whispered in my ear. "We're all staying here. If you have to meet with the London crew again... if they're really insistent that it can't wait... you can do it long-distance for now." Pausing, he added, "We're holding off on the seer wedding party until he can make it."

Black nodded towards Nick.

Pulling me tighter against him, he pressed into me from behind.

"Which sucks," he grumbled. "I'm putting off my wedding night for a goddamned vampire... again. But I guess I can wait a few weeks more."

"A few weeks?" I turned my head. I went on in a bare whisper. "So we're keeping to the no-sex thing until after the seer ceremony?"

Black winked at me, flashing one of his killer grins. "And the psychotic seer drug-party. Don't forget the psychotic seer drug party, doc."

I rolled my eyes. "Is it a good idea?" I murmured. "Us being out of commission that long? You know I can't be as effective long distance."

Black tilted his head sideways.

I felt him concede my point, without changing his mind.

"It might be good to let everything just breathe a bit, doc," he said finally. "Maybe we were rushing things before. Maybe we should be less directive. Less control-freakish. Let humans come to all this in their own time... at their own pace."

Pausing, he added more softly,

"Anyway, we've gotten rid of the serious threats... for now, anyway. It might be good to let everyone have a few weeks of peace. No headlines about seers. No headlines about dragons. I've asked Brick to tell his people to lay low, too... at least until the holidays are over."

I nodded, my mouth pursed.

Looking back at Nick, I felt myself give in.

Truthfully, I wanted to let things go for a while, too. I'd just been worried that was me wanting to hide from all this, that it was me avoiding responsibility.

"I really *would* like him at the seer thing," I admitted.

"Of course you would," Black said, kissing my cheek.

"I could tell he wanted to go," I added. "With Jem officiating part of the ceremony with Yarli now, he'll probably want to go even more. If you really think it's better to wait on the other stuff... meaning the world leaders and whatnot... then I'm okay with the rest of it. Even the no sex part. Assuming you're really okay with that..."

I let my words trail.

Black heard the implied question there, and hugged me tighter.

"Seems like we should," he said softly. "I mean, without the seer thing, we're only kind of half-married from the point of view of seer tradition. Besides, the other seers will be *ridiculously* disappointed if we don't do it after all this. Most of them have never been to a real seer wedding before... they're all geeked up about it now. Cowboy sounded pretty enthused, too. Even Kiko sounded intrigued."

Pausing, he smiled, shaking me a little.

"And we're going on a real honeymoon after that... right?"

Thinking about his words, I nodded.

I admit, the sex part was a serious bummer.

Black wasn't the only one in pain.

But I liked the idea of having something to look forward to.

"Anyway," Black whispered. "Jem's taken charge of the traditional cakes now, too, so we can't do that part without him. Yarli confessed she's not really comfortable doing it, even with Jem's help, since she's never officiated at a wedding ceremony before. She really wants him to take the lead on the whole thing. I guess imbuing food with different Barrier spaces is kind of a specialized skill. Jem trained under the Adhipan in the Pamir, so he knows all that stuff. Yarli, not so much."

Black snorted a low laugh.

"Oh, and turns out, he's supposed to be the one to do it, anyway. Apparently, Jem is *older* than Yarli, if you can believe that. He'd been holding out on his age with us a bit. According to Yarli, by all rights, Jem should be a bit of a gray-hair."

I grunted, rolling my eyes. "You weirdo seers and your non-aging."

He shook me a little. "Says the weirdo seer... with the best friend who's a vampire... the vampire who won't ever age at all."

I grunted again, but didn't argue.

Black looked at the seer we'd just been talking about, who was crashed out on the hospital chair next to Nick's bed. His eyes were closed. His fist propped up his jaw on one side, creating an indentation in his face.

"Should we go?" Black suggested softly. "So we don't wake him?"

I nodded, still looking at Jem.

I felt a pain come to my heart as I studied the seer's handsome face. Exhaustion, fear, and worry were written all over him.

He'd been half out of his mind, ever since he found Nick on the grounds of the resort, most of his face missing.

In fact, now that I thought about it, Jem probably hadn't woken up yet because this was probably the first time he'd slept in a week.

He'd been pacing this room and the outside corridors since they brought Nick in.

The other seers made him eat.

I saw Jax more or less force-feed him a tuna sandwich while Mika looked on approvingly.

It was touching and heartbreaking and adorable all at the same time.

When Black tugged at my hand, nudging me to leave the room with him, I gave both men a last look, feeling a sharp wave of love for both of them.

Then, smiling a little, I followed Black to the door.

I could wait a little longer.

It was worth the wait.

Space cakes, and all.

WANT TO READ MORE?
Check out the next book in the series!
NOW ON PREORDER!

BLACK IS MAGIC
(Quentin Black Mystery #15)

Link: http://bit.ly/QB-15

Brand new installment in the Quentin Black Mystery series by USA Today & Wall Street Journal Bestselling Author, JC Andrijeski!

The cat is out of the bag. Humans know about seers.

Whatever few still believed it was a giant hoax, a lie perpetuated by the powers that be, all of that got wiped away in the last, epic battle over Los Angeles.

Now the seer race is on trial, along with its two faces:

Charles "Lucky Lucifer" and his seer terrorists who want to wipe out the vampire race, enslave humans, and rule over all...

...and Black's hodge-podge band of seers and vampires, who wants the races to co-exist peacefully, who want the world to embrace a new way of existence.

Funnily enough, it turns out Black is the optimist.

Even among his own people, who witnessed how badly things can go wrong between seers and humans on another, now-destroyed world, Black's idealistic wish for a "live and let live" society generates more than a small amount of resistance. Even for those who want peace as badly as he does, Black's goals of a transparent, world-wide kumbaya strikes them as naïve in the extreme.

Even his own wife, Miri, worries that things won't go the way her husband hopes... even before Charles whips his followers into a murderous, fear-filled frenzy, plunging half the world into chaos and what might be the beginnings of its first real race war.

PREORDER NOW!

WHILE YOU'RE WAITING...

Want to learn more about what happens to Nick Tanaka? Check out the **VAMPIRE DETECTIVE MIDNIGHT** series:

VAMPIRE DETECTIVE MIDNIGHT
(Vampire Detective Midnight #1)

Link: http://bit.ly/VDM-1

Nick Midnight, homicide detective, had his heart ripped out, stomped on, destroyed. It nearly killed him.

He doesn't talk about that. Anyway, things will be different in New York. No complications. No kids needing his help. No relationships. None of that human-vampire-psychic crap that got him in trouble in the past, or turned him evil for nearly a century. He'd toe the line, keep his head down, and do his job for the NYPD, where he works as a Midnight, a vampire who helps humans hunt down murderers.

Then Wynter James shows up.

A gorgeous, sexy, disturbingly intuitive, seer-human hybrid, Wynter treats Nick like she already knows him, like they've known one another for years. Nick wants her, bad, but he knows it's an absolutely terrible idea, and not only because they're not even legally allowed to date.

Everything's already going sideways with his first, big case—dead hybrids, a seer kid who needs his help, graffiti that tells the future, and Wynter, a woman he's so drawn to, it makes him actually insane. Oh, and a possible conspiracy involving the richest humans in New York.

In other words, it's Nick's worst nightmare. It's everything he swore he'd never do again.

Now he's going rogue, likely to get himself killed for a woman he just met—or end up back on the run, in that dark place he thought he'd finally left behind.

VAMPIRE DETECTIVE MIDNIGHT is a gritty, romantic new series set in a futuristic, dystopian New York populated by vampires, humans and psychics trying to rebuild their world after a devastating race war nearly obliterates the previous one. Written by USA TODAY and WALL STREET JOURNAL bestselling author, JC Andrijeski, it features vampire homicide detective, Nick Tanaka, who works as a "Midnight," or vampire in the employ of the human police department. Perfect for fans of paranormal mystery and sexy urban fantasy!

See below for sample pages!

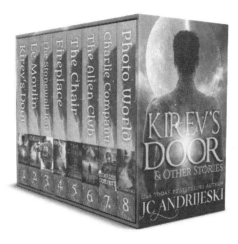

REVIEWS ARE AUTHOR HUGS

Now that you've finished reading my book,
PLEASE CONSIDER LEAVING A REVIEW!
A short review is fine and so very appreciated.
Word of mouth is truly essential for any author to succeed!

Leave a Review Here:
https://bit.ly/QB-14

SAMPLE PAGES

VAMPIRE DETECTIVE MIDNIGHT
(VAMPIRE DETECTIVE MIDNIGHT #1)

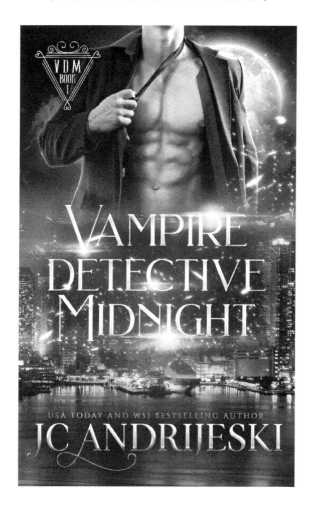

1 / SMELLS TOO GOOD

HE SMELLED THE BLOOD, even before he turned the corner into the alley.

He heard them talking about him only a few steps after that.

That was the problem with working with humans.

One problem, anyway.

They had shitty hearing, so they assumed everyone else did, too.

"Where's Midnight?" he heard the lead detective say.

Nick heard the man's clothing move as he looked around, maybe making sure a random vampire wasn't lurking next to him already, or that he didn't see Nick himself walking towards him in the dark.

"I thought he was coming to this?" the detective muttered, taking a sip of something—something hot from the quick, cut-off way he sipped it, likely artificial coffee given that Nick could make out the faint, bitter-tinged odor of that, too.

Of course, no one called it "artificial coffee" anymore.

They just called it coffee.

But Nick remembered real coffee, well enough to know the bilge they drank now wasn't it.

It was an insult to coffee.

The lead detective glanced around where he stood a second time. He checked his watch again.

"Where the hell is he?" he muttered. "We could use a blood-sniffer right now. Christ. Look at this mess."

The man standing next to him grunted. "Fucking bloodsuckers. He's probably paying a blood whore to jerk him off while he drains her dry in a dark alley somewhere..."

The man trailed, mid-thought, flushing as Nick rounded the corner of the building.

Nick stepped deliberately into the light, right as he entered the narrow alley where they were all crouched, standing over something he could smell but not yet see.

He'd been right about the artificial coffee.

The detective standing closest to the scene, closest to the female tech leaning over the nearest body, collecting samples and photographing it from all angles, took another sip of the watered-down crap, gripping one of those semi-organic, morphing cups in his left hand.

Damn, Nick missed real coffee.

He knew it wouldn't taste right to him anymore, not as a vampire, but he missed it anyway.

Only the truly rich could afford real coffee these days. The few plants still in existence were tended meticulously in greenhouses run by boutique farmers who catered exclusively to the super-rich—the same handful of people who basically ran everything.

"You're late," the lead detective, a tall, scarecrow-thin black man with gray hair named Morley, declared neutrally.

Nick ignored the dig, looking around the scene.

Six. He smelled six.

He only saw five bodies, three female and two male, but he smelled six different types of blood, six different DNA imprints. The sixth, another female, could be one of the killers, but it didn't smell like it.

She smelled dead.

"Check the dumpster," he said.

He motioned towards the bin shoved against the wall to the left and a few meters behind where the techs and detectives were focused.

"You've got six bodies," Nick added, hands still in his pockets.

He continued to walk the scene, his nose wrinkling as he got closer.

As he did, he was even more sure of the sixth body.

He was still looking around, smelling the air, when he felt his fangs start to extend.

In reflex, he clenched his jaw, repressing it. Even as he did, he glanced around surreptitiously, checking faces, although the likelihood one of the humans might have noticed was pretty much nil.

Fuck, had he come here hungry?

Why was his stomach getting weird on him all of a sudden?

Shoving the thought from his mind before it started to affect his eye color, or his overall demeanor, he focused his attention back on the scene.

From what he could tell, apart from the woman they'd thrown in the dumpster, the killers didn't get near enough to touch any of the other five bodies. They didn't leave much in the way of trace imprints as a result. They definitely hadn't gotten into any kind of physical fight with the victims, not enough to leave blood, or anything with DNA.

At best, the techs might find some fibers or a few stray hairs in the mix.

Nick had his doubts they would.

Whoever these assholes were, apart from the anomaly with the woman in the dumpster, they seemed to know what they were doing. Anyway, if there *was* hair here, he likely would have smelled that, too, despite the overpowering smell of blood.

Sniffing the air again, he frowned.

The blood in the alley was really damned pungent, even for

how much of it there was. It struck him as somehow more pungent than usual.

It bothered him, how pungent it was.

Shoving the thought from his mind, he focused back on whoever had done this.

He smelled four of them.

He smelled someone else, as well.

Someone more recent.

"The scene's been contaminated," he commented sourly.

Without waiting for an answer, he walked past the other detectives, aiming his feet for the dumpster he'd motioned towards earlier. He wasn't thrilled with rooting around a dumpster that smelled like dead blood, or even being this close to a bunch of dead bodies, but the sooner he got his part of the job out of the way, the sooner he could get the hell out of there.

Like most vampires, he hated being around dead things.

The irony didn't escape him, which is why he didn't bother to mention that fact to most humans.

Most of them would look at him like he was nuts.

Well, that, and, generally speaking, explaining to a human how differently their blood smelled to him alive, versus how their blood smelled to him dead, tended to make most humans more than a little uncomfortable.

Donning latex gloves of his own, he lifted the lid of the dumpster gingerly once he got close enough, and stared down at the contents.

A clump of black hair greeted him, long and tangled over a back wearing a faux-leather jacket with a brightly colored, virtual reality (VR)-enhanced cartoon dog on the back.

Someone had thrown her into the dumpster, face-down.

The cartoon dog bounced around her back in the dim light, oblivious to its owner's death. When Nick lifted the lid higher, it triggered the VR sensors a second time, and the cartoon dog started barking at him, wagging its butt and tail playfully.

It didn't make any sound.

Something about that silent, dancing cartoon dog and the crumpled corpse smelling too-pungently of blood and death made Nick grimace.

Holding his breath, he lifted the lid higher.

Definitely a woman, from the curve of her hip in the form-fitting, shiny pants she wore, and the high-heeled, VR-enhanced pink and purple boots.

She smelled relatively young.

Twenties. Possibly early thirties.

He sniffed again and frowned.

It wasn't fake leather. It was the real thing.

He glanced down the rest of her clothes, taking a second look at her metallic-sheen pants. They fit her perfectly. The pants also had a more subtle virtual enhancement, one that sent shimmers of sparkles down her long, toned-looking legs and curve of well-exercised butt.

Her knee-high boots looked expensive, and shimmered with virtual cartoon dogs that matched the one on her real-leather jacket. The boots might be real leather, too, under the VR panels. Her hair, where it wasn't matted with blood, was silky and expensively cut.

Whoever she was, she had money.

He glanced around the rest of the dim space of the dumpster.

It was empty.

No purse. No headset, or armband.

The only thing in there was the woman.

So why had they bothered trying to hide the body?

He squinted down at her, tilting his head to see her from the side, to try and get a better look at her profile.

"They destroyed her face," he announced after another minute. "Her teeth, too, it looks like. They might have even removed them. I don't see an ident-tat."

Frowning, he leaned closer, squinting down at one of her leather-clad arms. He stared down at the hand at the end of that arm.

"...They took her fingers, too," he added.

"Fantastic," Morley muttered from behind him.

Nick carefully lowered the lid to the dumpster, stepping back.

"Better photograph it," he said. "Whoever she was, she had money. Someone's probably looking for her."

Three police techs in white, semi-transparent decontamination suits were standing at a safe distance behind him, presumably waiting for him to move away before they started photographing and taking samples.

One of them cleared their throat, speaking up.

"Those too," she said, blanching when Nick turned.

She motioned towards the bodies on the floor of the alley.

"...They have money, too," she clarified. "Expensive clothes. Manicures. Some plastic surgery treatments. At least one pair of diamond earrings—"

"They left all that?" the younger detective said, puzzled. "Why?"

The tech looked at him, then back to Nick.

She didn't answer.

Realizing he stood between the techs and the woman in the dumpster even now, Nick backed off to give them room. From the looks on their faces, they weren't about to approach with him standing there, no matter how fuzzy and cute he tried to make himself.

Frowning up and down the alley, he looked for signs of tampering with the scene.

Who was the contaminant? Did a beat cop walk through here?

It didn't smell like a cop. He couldn't quite explain that to himself, not in so many words, but cops had a particular imprint, and he didn't get it off this person.

He didn't like the anomaly of the woman.

"It's likely she was the primary target," he muttered, mostly to himself as he continued to scan the scene. "The others may have been incidental."

"Cause of death?" Morley said, his voice pointed. "They all die by plasma rifle? Or did the one in the dumpster die by something else?"

Nick glanced at him, then frowned.

"Plasmas, yes. The woman in the dumpster, too. They hit her in the face." He motioned towards his own face in rote. "That doesn't strike me as an accident. They tried to use the rifle to hide it, but the superficial damage to hide her ID all looked post-mortem to me."

Still thinking, he added,

"At least one of the killers carried an old-school projectile. He shot the one in the dumpster at least once, possibly twice. At least once in the head. That shot didn't go all the way through."

At Morley's puzzled look, Nick jerked his chin towards the metal container.

"I can smell the metal slug," he explained. "Smells different than blood."

Morley grimaced.

Turning away, he muttered something in Russian, sipping at his coffee.

Nick pretended not to notice the grimace, or the Russian, or that both things were aimed at him.

Stepping back into the main part of the alley, he went back to walking the scene. Using his eyes now, as much as his nose, he carefully skirted the pools of blood and smaller chunks of flesh to keep it off his shoes.

He frowned down at the next body he encountered, a male, adding,

"I don't think you'll find much DNA from the killers, not even with them having screwed around with the one body."

He motioned behind him vaguely, in the direction of the dumpster.

"This looks to me like a professional hit. At the very least, these are smarter than average killers. They wore gloves—real ones, the kind we use. That, or they've had their fingerprints professionally removed. I don't smell hair or skin fragments. I don't see any shoeprints, so they must have known to wear flatteners. That, or they had someone come clean up, but I don't see any evidence of a blower."

Nick motioned towards the walls, where the blood-spatter remained intact.

"See that? That's natural blood spray," he said. "A blower would have pitted all of that with dirt, and fucked up the pattern. I don't see any of that here."

He saw Morley and the younger detective follow his pointing fingers.

The younger one scowled, as if annoyed he hadn't noticed that yet, or, more likely, annoyed a vampire noticed it before him.

Nick blew that off, too.

"No," he continued, frowning. "It's more likely they didn't leave tracks to begin with. I would bet on expensive, untraceable flatteners, possibly full-prosthetics and blood patches, professional level non-residue gloves, at least one antique gun... maybe an old school sniper rifle, or even a shotgun..."

Again, he motioned vaguely in the direction of the dumpster.

"...the plasmas all look like close-contact hits, maybe after they had them cornered in the alley, or maybe after they felled some of them long-distance, using the antique rifle. It's the only reason I can think of for someone to use one of those... it's why I wondered if it was a sniper. Unless they're just attached to that particular weapon for some reason."

Thinking about this, Nick shrugged.

"The slugs will tell you for sure," he added. "...In terms of the weapon. Whatever the exact scenario, I'd look for pros. Which means either some kind of militia—maybe a political one, given the wealth class of the victims—or someone hired them. I don't know of any amateurs who could do that to a body and not leave more physical traces of themselves."

Again, Nick motioned vaguely at the dumpster.

"Most amateurs are idiots," he added, unnecessarily, given who he was with. "They stick around, touch things, step in things, leave bits and pieces of themselves everywhere. I don't see any stupid here. Plus, what they did to the woman in the dumpster, it was thorough. Which means they knew how to disguise her ident, and came here *planning* to do it."

Nick exhaled, still thinking.

The exhale was more show than need, since he didn't have to breathe.

He'd learned a long time ago, the more he could imitate human mannerisms and body functions, the more humans tended to relax around him. They probably didn't even notice he was doing it, but some part of them reacted to it anyway, animal-to-animal.

Of course, he learned some of that back in the early days.

Back then, it was more of an aid in hunting.

Now he used it to reassure his human coworkers that he *wasn't* actively thinking about eating them. He did it to reassure them they had something in common, that he wasn't so different from them... that he *wasn't* about to eat them.

Exhaling again, he added,

"Given where it is, and the exposure risk, it was likely a fast job, in and out. They didn't make chit-chat with the victims prior to the kill, or—"

"But why?" the younger detective asked.

Nick recognized him from his first day on the job, two weeks back, when he'd been first introduced to his new precinct.

His remembered his name, even.

Damon Jordan.

Like Morley, he was dark-skinned, what used to be called black or "African-American." He was about thirty years younger than the senior detective, though. This was the first time Nick had dealt with him on an actual case.

They'd mostly farmed him out to smaller jobs these first few weeks, probably to check him out since he was new.

"Why?" Jordan asked again. "Any idea of motive? What was the point of this?"

Jordan had been the one talking about blood-whores before.

Nick gave him another glance, looking over the man's muscular, broad-shouldered form. He looked like a fighter, like he spent a fair bit of time in the ring. He was young for a Detective II. He must have a decent mind on him, even if he was a racist fuck.

"How would I know?" Nick said mildly. "I just got here. Right now, I can tell you what I'm telling you. No tracks. Four killers, three males, one female. Probably three plasmas, and at least one antique combustion weapon, firing ammunition that used to be considered armor-piercing... although it wouldn't do much to the organic shielding we have now."

Exhaling again, if only to try to put them more at ease, he added,

"I'd guess a semi-modified assault rifle, probably something late 21st Century. That, or a shotgun, like I said. Something with some kick. Definitely not a handgun. Six victims, as we can all now plainly see, four female, two male. And there was an eleventh person who was here, who stepped in the blood..."

He pointed at the track he'd seen.

"...Male. Young. Maybe early twenties... at most. I can smell him, but I don't think he was involved in the killing. He's the only signature out here that left traces of himself everywhere. My guess is, he stumbled on the scene afterwards, walked around in it, maybe in shock, then bolted. If an anonymous tip brought you here, it was probably him. You'll want to run him down, though. If only to eliminate his DNA and other trace evidence from the scene."

Jordan stared at him with dark brown eyes.

They shimmered at Nick while he watched, almost in an amphibious way. That shimmer briefly illuminated a ring around the edge of the iris, a narrow line of pale blue.

Enhanced eyes. How had he missed that?

Those couldn't have been cheap.

"You telling me how to do my job, Midnight?" Jordan said.

Nick held his stare.

He knew his vampire eyes would unnerve the other man.

It was their instinct to be afraid of him... just as it was his instinct to view them as food. He didn't usually pull dick moves around that fact, but this time, he used it without thought.

"I'm giving you suggestions," he said. "Midnights are consultants. I'm assuming you want my opinion, or I wouldn't fucking be here—"

"Yeah, yeah, okay." The other waved him off in annoyance, looking away from Nick's eyes even as he clenched his jaw. "Whatever, man. And you're sure this 'contaminant' wasn't with the killers?"

Nick shrugged. "Reasonably sure, yeah. He smells more recent. Not a *lot* more recent... but maybe a few hours after."

Thinking, Nick glanced up and down the narrow alley.

Something still bugged him about the smell of all that blood.

Worse, it was making him aggressive.

Even as he thought it, he scowled at Jordan.

"...Unless you had another cop in here," he said. "Did you have another cop in here, Jordan? Someone too stupid to know not to fuck with a multiple homicide scene?"

The detective scowled back at him, his enhanced eyes growing hard.

"You sure this asshole was human, Midnight?" Jordan retorted.

"I'm sure he wasn't vampire, *Damon,*" he said. "Want me to explain how our blood smells different than yours? I can tell you... yours smells a lot better."

Jordan's pale-blue ringed eyes grew cold as metal.

Nick didn't flinch, but continued to hold his gaze.

That time, however, he found himself regretting his words, at least a little.

He was too new here to be picking fights, especially given how he'd ended up in New York in the first place. They'd have every reason to distrust him here. He was an involuntary transfer, sent over by his superior officers in L.A., who essentially "sold" him—sold his government contract, at least—to get him out of their hair.

No doubt, all the detectives here knew his history.

They knew he was essentially booted for being a problem.

He wasn't doing himself any favors, acting like an arrogant prick. He wasn't doing himself any favors projecting their worst stereotype of a vampire, either.

He needed to feed.

It was putting him in a foul mood.

That, and all this fucking blood...

Nick frowned, staring around at the alley floor.

It hit him again.

There was something wrong with this blood.

It smelled too fucking good.

It smelled *way* too fucking good.

That couldn't all be Nick's hunger.

"Anyway, that's what I can tell you so far," he said, making his voice deliberately casual. "Without knowing who the victims are, or what brought them to this alley, it's pretty hard to speculate on motive, but..."

Nick hesitated then, realizing something.

Frowning, he stepped closer to the pools of blood.

Nose wrinkling, he crouched down so he could smell it from closer, even though the scent was overpowering, even from a lot further away. Taking a few full whiffs, he felt his fangs begin to extend in earnest.

That time, he couldn't pull it back.

A flush of heat hit his gut and chest, burning in his throat. It was intense enough, he almost got hard, but he'd gotten pretty good at squelching that reaction, too.

He stood up at once.

Really, he lurched back.

It happened so fast, that smell and his reaction to it, Nick forgot to modulate his body's natural reflexes to accommodate the people around him. He was up and moving in a heartbeat, darting back in pure instinct, without slowing his movements at all.

He moved fast enough to make the humans around him freeze.

Instantly, they turned into prey.

Ignoring them, and ignoring their deer-in-headlights reactions to how he'd just moved, Nick backed away from the pool of blood with a scowl.

He backed away from the human detectives and tech team, too.

"They're hybrids," he said, emotion reaching his voice.

He turned around, staring at the humans sharing the alley with him.

The stared back at him, faces blank, eyes holding flickers of fear.

Frustrated, wanting to smash through that frozen prey look, Nick let his voice turn into a harder growl.

"Jesus fucking Christ," Nick said. "Did you hear me? They're all fucking *hybrids.*"

When they still didn't speak, he averted his gaze with a scowl. His eyes returned to the alley. Staring around at all of that blood, it sank in what it really represented.

Once it had, he couldn't help but feel sick.

2 / THE FIRST SIGN

NICK HAD INTENDED to leave, right after he gave his initial summary. He'd meant to give them the bare bones, then just leave.

Once he discerned the race of the victims, he found himself lingering, for reasons he couldn't fully explain to himself.

No one told him to leave.

Then again, no one asked him to stay, either.

Morley ended up being the first to break the silence after Nick told them what the victims were.

"Did you say hybrids?" The older detective blinked, then frowned, still staring at him. "The victims?"

Nick nodded without looking at him, grimacing as he stared at the lake of blood. He couldn't stop seeing it differently now that he knew what it contained.

He fought the reaction off his face. He knew he mostly failed.

"Yeah," he said, gruff. "I think all of them are. Were."

"*All* of them were hybrids?" Jordan said, speaking up from behind Morley. "All six? Are you sure?"

Nick turned, staring at the other male. "I'm pretty fucking sure, yeah."

Seeing something in his eyes, Jordan backed down. The anger in the human's eyes dissipated, shifting into something closer to fear.

Looking at him, it occurred to Nick that his irises had probably turned bright red—right around the time his fangs extended.

Right around the time he ID'd the hybrid blood.

Ignoring Jordan's reaction with an effort, Nick attempted to reassure Morley, who he more or less liked. As far as bosses went, and humans, Morley seemed to be okay.

But the older detective wasn't looking at him anymore.

Morley was staring down at the blood.

"Jesus." He whistled under his breath. "Six hybrids? And they just *happened* to be hanging out in this alley at the same time? That can't be a coincidence."

"No," Nick agreed. "It can't." Pausing, he added, "The woman in the dumpster. She had a human tat. The barcode was cut or burned off, but the 'H' sign was still there. Are any of the others wearing the marks? Have you scanned their ident-tats yet?"

Jordan shifted his attention off Nick. His face and neck remained flushed, either in embarrassment or fear or both, but he'd regained control over his expression.

He also seemed focused back on the job. He was staring at the blood with the rest of them, latex gloves on his hands, hands on his hips.

Now he shook his head to Nick's question.

"None of them had the mark for hybrid, I know that. They all had human tats. Pureblood. We're running the IDs now with Gertrude."

Gertrude was the artificial intelligence that ran most of the bureaucratic functions of the NYPD. Nick didn't know where the name came from. Probably someone's idea of a joke, unless it was named after the aunt of one of the AI's programmers.

Nick nodded to Jordan's words, but the frown remained on his face.

"Yeah," he said, when the silence stretched. "Well, I guess make sure the medical records weren't falsified under whatever Gertrude turns up. And yeah... make sure I'm right. About the hybrid thing. If they *were* all hybrids, and all of them are unreg'd, living under fake IDs, I'm guessing you have your motive. Part of one, anyway."

Jordan and Morley exchanged looks.

The female tech, who was still photographing the blood, stared only at Nick.

The three techs over by the dumpster stared at Nick, too.

Still fighting to get the cloying smell of hybrid out of his nose, Nick didn't look at any of them. He stared down at the blood, unable to remove the grimace from his face.

If these hybrids had human tats, that was more evidence they had money.

That, or someone sponsoring them had money.

Fake idents were no joke these days.

They took serious connections, people able and willing to pull strings, to procure fake documentation that would actually pass the verification process. To maintain a fake blood ident over time, they needed someone on the inside to alter the databases in the main registration banks, not to mention enough connections at a high enough level to get the street-level grunts to look the other way in random spot-checks.

That meant medical records, birth records, blood records, blood patches for random street and travel checks, fake finger-prints and usually fake X-rays.

The internal organs of hybrids rarely matched up closely enough to a full-blooded human's for them to pass through most check-points. Blood could be dealt with using fingertip patches, but only at the older checkpoints. The newer blood-draws were trickier to fool, but even so, generally-speaking, blood was the easy part.

Internal organs? Those were trickier.

Some of the newer checkpoint machines even had booths that scanned for organ placement, along with DNA strand checks on hair or skin. There were organic vests that could fool the machines, but those were damned expensive too, not to mention illegal to own, so only available on the darkest threads in the network.

Whoever these hybrids were, chances were, they didn't do a lot of traveling, at least not via commercial carriers.

What traveling they did, it was likely on private jets.

Nick was still staring at the ground when one of the techs by the dumpster spoke up.

"Hey! Could you come over here..." He looked at Nick, fumbling, maybe unwilling to use the moniker "Midnight," or maybe just uneasy about addressing him at all. "...Mr. Midnight," he finally settled on. "You should look at this, while you're here."

Glancing at Morley and Jordan, Nick began moving in the direction of the tech, careful to keep his footsteps slow and human-like.

He heard, felt, and smelled Jordan and Morley following him.

As soon as they got within a few feet of the tech, Nick saw where he was pointing.

Something had been painted there, on the wall.

It must have been exposed when they shifted the chrome dumpster. It didn't look like normal graffiti, even the more artistic varieties.

It looked like a painting.

Like a *real* painting.

Frowning, Nick stepped closer, studying the part he could see, which turned out to be a detailed depiction of a masked form, holding an antique-looking shotgun. It looked like an old Remington 870, like something Nick might have had in a black and white, years ago.

So... not a sniper rifle.

"What the fuck is that?" Morley said from behind him.

Nick shook his head, still staring at the painting.

"I don't know," he muttered.

"A confession?"

Nick turned and found Jordan standing just behind him, staring at the painting, his eyes narrowed. The younger detective didn't take his eyes off the wall.

"Some kind of signature?" he muttered.

Nick thought about that. "Could be," he admitted.

"Should we move the dumpster?" the first tech asked, the one who'd called Nick over.

He looked between Nick and Jordan, as if not sure who he should be addressing.

When no one else spoke, Nick did.

"This thing has wheels, right?" he said to the first tech. "Can these other two climb down and pull it away from the wall? Try rolling it sideways?"

The two techs working over the dead girl blinked at him.

Then they looked at Morley, as if for confirmation.

The older detective nodded, his mouth pursed.

"Do what he says," he said, taking another sip of the not-coffee.

The white-gloved techs with their white, raincoat-like lab suits exchanged looks, then, as if by silent agreement, climbed down carefully to the same side of the bright silver container. From there, with the first technician, the one who'd pointed out the painting in the first place, they each found clean parts of the dumpster to push with their gloved hands.

Slowly and carefully, and watching where they placed their bootie-covered feet, they rolled the metal dumpster sideways, exposing the wall behind it without running those wheels through any part of the nearby pools of blood.

Luckily, the dumpster wasn't heavy.

Even more luckily, those small wheels under the chrome dumpster still functioned.

Nick stopped thinking about any of that as the wall gradually became exposed.

The meticulously-drawn brush strokes, what he'd only glimpsed when the dumpster stood in the way, grew into a full, coherent image, unfolding into an elaborate painting that covered a few feet of the back wall.

Now, instead of the one masked face, Nick saw four masked figures, each of them holding guns. The other three carried plasma-rifles.

The figure holding the antique gun turned out to be shorter than the others, and drawn in such a way that Nick now wondered if his gunman was actually a gun-woman.

So, the female carried the shotgun.

A pretty weird choice in weapons.

A sniper rifle would have made more sense. Long-distance shooting was an unusual skill set nowadays, but still practical, even with the proliferation of drones.

The shotgun was just... idiosyncratic.

After the techs finished moving the dumpster, they walked back around to stare at the image along with the detectives and Nick.

For a long-feeling few moments, no one spoke, or moved.

The image was disconcertingly life-like.

Unlike most street art, it didn't appear to have been done either in that newer, metallic, VR paint, or even in old-school spray paint.

Instead, it looked like some more "classic" painting material —maybe acrylic, or even some kind of oil paint. Nick didn't know paint well enough to know for sure. It smelled pungent, which made him think it might be oil-based.

Whatever it was, the deep blacks and brighter colors stood out, giving it a strangely three-dimensional effect, even without the added dimension of virtual enhancement. That effect managed to add to the realism of the painting itself.

It showed the gunmen—with possibly one gun-woman—

aiming their weapons at five figures, two male and three female, who stood halfway down a narrow alley with a chrome dumpster. The dumpster stood against the metal-coated back wall of the alley, just like this one, only in the painting, the container was shiny and pristine, with no splashes of blood. The lid was open, and from the angle, which was slightly elevated, Nick could see black hair, along with the vague outline of a body crumpled inside the metal container.

If the image was right, the woman in the dumpster died first.

She may even have been killed somewhere else.

But why? Was she bait to get the others here?

And why destroy her face?

Nick's eyes flickered back to the killers.

He found himself examining the antique shotgun a second time.

It was such a strange choice, for this time period. Since the seer wars, guns like that had more or less disappeared. Ironically, it was probably worth a lot of money, as a bona fide antique, and if the painting was accurate, it was in good shape.

Still, it was strange to think of the weapon that way too, when such things had been a part of his everyday life, once upon a time.

From next to him, Jordan muttered under his breath again.

"What's the point?" he said. "I mean, fuck. Why go to all the trouble? Is it a warning? Some kind of taunt?"

Next to him, Morley grunted.

"Maybe we'll have a better idea once we ID the one in the dumpster," he said, his voice diplomatic. "DNA should give us a hit. Face or no face."

Nick didn't bother to point out the obvious fact that if she was really a hybrid, and unreg'd, all of her DNA and medical records would be bullshit, and might not tell them a damned thing about who she'd been before this.

Jordan glanced at Morley, his enhanced eyes openly skeptical.

From the look there, the same thing had already occurred to the younger detective.

Of course, they had other ways to track her down—including through the other victims—but if everything *legal* about her had been falsified, it might not be all that easy to ID her. The fact that she clearly came from money could either help them or hurt them, depending on who was behind this, and who wanted it covered up.

That wasn't what had Nick's attention right then, anyway.

The attempt to hide the woman's identity, while unusual, made sense.

What made a lot *less* sense, and was a hell of a lot more disturbing, was the reality of the painting itself—and what it meant once he'd glanced over the physical details more closely.

Blood spatter covered part of the image.

Parts of the painting had been worn away and discolored by dirt.

Other parts had been pitted and scratched, likely by street cleaners, or maybe by the prongs of the garbage truck as it emptied the chrome dumpster on its weekly rounds.

The painting wasn't done by a witness to the crime.

It had been here before the murders happened.

It looked like it predated the murders by at least a few days.

Possibly longer.

Staring at the painting, Nick felt a vague sickness grow in his gut.

He couldn't have said why, exactly.

The painting should have piqued his interest, like it clearly had the interest of the two human detectives. Nick should have seen it as a clue, perhaps even as proof of premeditation. At the very least, he should have been curious, the way he could feel a buzz of curiosity growing among the humans staring at the image alongside him.

He couldn't get onboard with any of that, though.

Truthfully, he just wanted to get the fuck out of there.

Maybe spend an hour or two inhaling bleach.

Anything to get the smell of that seer-infused blood out of his head.

Anything to wash the view of that painting from where it wanted to burn itself into the dark spaces behind his eyes.

3 / MIDNIGHT

"IDENTIFICATION, PLEASE."

The female-sounding voice droned the words from the other side of transparent, semi-organic shielding. It didn't sound like a question.

It really wasn't a question.

"Naoko Tanaka Midnight." Nick unholstered his sidearm, laying it on the round, greenish-silver plate in front of the speaker. "Homicide division. Ident tag 9381T-112."

"Year of change?"

"197 B.D."

The woman behind the organic nodded, once.

Nick honestly couldn't tell if she was an image implanted in his mind through his semi-organic headset, a hologram, or a robot.

He guessed a robot.

Maybe he just liked the idea of a robot best, of the three options.

"Stand for retinal and ident scan," the voice droned.

Nick froze in place in front of the scanner's multiple eyes, unblinking as the organic arm emerged from the wall by the transparent cubicle, its blue light flickering over his face, temporarily blinding his sensitive vampire eyes before sliding over the rest of him.

He held his inner arm out and flat, so the tattoo showed up easily, and the implant would be readable without multiple passes.

The bar code on his arm stood out on his pale skin, next to a dark red "V" about two inches long and painted with organic metal to counteract his skin's natural healing abilities.

For the same reason, his "tattoos" were really more like another form of implant.

Like his deeper implant, they were designed via organic tech to fool his vampire body into thinking they belonged there.

Both scanners flickered over every inch of his skin, then clicked off.

"You may enter," the voice said.

Nick grunted, watching his sidearm disappear into the morphing, full-organic metal of the round plate outside the registration cubicle.

Even now, after more than ten years of this gig, he never expected to get that gun back.

Hell, he never *fully* expected to be allowed to leave the building, not once he'd walked through one of those outer security doors.

He did it anyway.

He didn't have a lot of choice.

Well, he didn't have a lot of *good* choices.

The door buzzed then clicked, just like doors had back in the time when he'd been a human cop, in San Francisco, what felt like a million years ago now. Grabbing the unlocked handle, he jerked open the heavy, bulletproof, semi-organic panel after the buzz, and stepped inside before the sensor started beeping at him again.

Immediately, the sounds of the police station washed over him.

Those sounds were eerily timeless.

Letting the door fall shut behind him, Nick made his way down the featureless corridor towards the origin of those sounds.

His vampire senses of smell and hearing kicked in, telling him most of what he needed to know before he entered the main bullpen beyond the corridor.

He heard them talking about him again.

He was still the new guy.

This time, he got to hear about how the "new blood-sniffer" who'd recently transferred here from "fuckin' L.A." got in a few lucky hits out at that mess in the Bronx.

Some just called him "the new Midnight," which, honestly, Nick preferred.

In this new world, vampires got assigned government-issued surnames to make them more easily distinguishable from their human counterparts who worked roughly the same jobs.

Nick supposed it reassured humans, to make vamps as easily identifiable as possible.

There seemed to be some fear that random vampires could slip past them otherwise, maybe by wearing contact lenses over their crystal-colored irises, or long sleeves to cover the telltale "V" ident-tats and barcodes—as if vampires weren't segregated, regulated, tested, blood-checked and surveilled in every other fucking way, as a condition of being allowed to roam free.

As if vampires might start dating their cousin, or fucking their wife, and no one in the global or local interspecies enforcement bodies would notice.

The thought was laughable.

For the same reason, Nick strongly suspected a fair-few of these rules, including the name-tagging system, served more political functions than anything. Enforcement bodies did it to normalize the whole set-up, and render it more "polite."

Whatever the exact logic of the Human Racial Authority, or H.R.A., in coming up with the name-coding, vamps who worked for the police—at least those in homicide and interspecies relations, which was most of them—all got tagged with the surname "Midnight."

It was a better name than a lot of vamps got stuck with.

Then again, the H.R.A. had to pick surnames not in common use by humans.

Vamps working in medicine got tagged with the surname "Serpent," presumably in honor of the Rod of Asclepius and/or the Caduceus, both symbols of medicine and healing and both containing serpents.

Engineers were all "Machine."

Research and development got the moniker "Galileo," unless they worked in weapons, then they got "Supernova." Career military vamps, the only other option offered to Nick by the H.R.A. when they were assigning employment, were all "Centurion."

Teachers and professors got "Library."

Those pulled into think-tanks and strategy got "Chessboard."

Those in full-time sex and blood work were "Incubus," or "Succubus," the only surnames that depended on the claimed sex of the individual vampire.

Nick had most of the list memorized.

Then again, so did most people, human and vamp.

The Inter-Species Friendship Council, or "I.S.F.," as most humans called it—or "I.S. Fucked," as most vampires called it—was technically responsible for vampire code enforcement on United States soil. While the I.S.F. fell under the authority of the H.R.A., at least on paper, they also designed and rolled out policy, whether official or not, and far more quickly than the H.R.A., which tended to move at the speed of your average glacier.

Often, the H.R.A. adopted changes *after* I.S. Fucked already enforcing those changes on U.S. soil. By the time the rule change was legally in the books, other countries were often already following the United States' lead.

Most of the vampire code surnames were country-specific, so

the I.S.F. likely had a hand in designing the specific names now in use in the States.

Supposedly, all of this worked out to make the system easier on everyone.

Nick didn't see a lot of "easy" in the system, though.

Well, not for vampires.

He couldn't exactly blame humans for taking the steps they did to ensure their safety. Despite their vastly superior numbers, humans were still, after all, *food,* to Nick and his people. That simple fact pretty much annihilated any basis for trust that may have existed between the two species. But the realities of the system meant to keep humans safe still kept vampires a semi-enslaved class.

At the very least, they were something significantly less than full citizens.

Of course, like most things, that relationship was complicated.

Organized crime and the black market were riddled with vamps.

A lot of those outfits were led by ex-military, too—with some of those vamps being shockingly well-connected, and closer to terrorists than simply crime lords. Some of those militias grew right out of the seer wars.

Even the whole hunter-prey dynamic got pretty fuzzy these days.

Plenty of humans *liked* being bit by vampires.

Enough of them liked it, in fact, that vampires could make a full-time living charging for the privilege, especially if they mixed bloodletting with sex.

And that was just pureblood humans.

Hybrids, back when more of those existed, got full-blown addicted to vampire venom.

They got addicted to the point where the I.S.F.—followed by the H.R.A.—were eventually forced to pass regulations forbidding hybrids from offering vampires their blood, or for soliciting vampires for sex, which was more or less the same thing.

Vampires were also explicitly forbidden from feeding on hybrids. The difference being, of course, that hybrids, if caught, would get hit with a fine and maybe do a stint in human jail.

Vampires, on the other hand, would be thrown in a government lab somewhere for what was politely termed "reprogramming." Or, if they were considered "incurable," they would have their hearts removed from their bodies with these claw-like, retractable tools the government created expressly for the purpose, called "alligators."

Nick had seen those things in action a few times, while he was still in L.A.

A few times, as it turned out, was more than enough.

It was gross as hell.

It still didn't entirely discourage vamps from biting, fucking and even dating hybrids, of course. It still happened. Meaning, hybrid and vampire sex and feeding still happened.

Even now, it still happened.

Hybrids were rare as hell, but they were still around, as the killing in the Bronx clearly demonstrated. But it was nothing like the early years, before the I.S.F. started passing regulations against hybrids and vampires more generally.

Seers, the other race that briefly shared a history with this world, had been even more vulnerable to the effects of vampire venom than their hybrid offspring.

Seers, well...

Seers lost their damned minds, when it came to vampires.

If a vampire wasn't too scrupulous, they could turn a seer into a literal slave.

A venom-addicted seer would do pretty much anything a vampire wanted—a difficult temptation to fight given how fucking amazing seer blood tasted to your average vampire, not to mention how incredible sex could be with one of their kind.

A seer's blood was Grade-A prime rib.

It was steak dinner, a fine wine... real coffee and chocolate rolled into one.

Compared to that, human blood was more like a defrosted tofu burger on soggy bread, covered in fake ketchup, with artificial coffee to wash it down.

Luckily, most vampires these days didn't know that.

Unfortunately for Nick, he did.

Shoving the thought from his mind with an effort, he didn't manage it successfully before a pair of pale green eyes rose briefly to the spaces behind his eyes. With that image of stunning, violet-ringed green eyes, came a flood of unwelcome memory, along with something that was nearly pain to his chest and gut.

By the time he forced the memory out for real, he was already in a foul mood.

He was also hungry.

Because of both things, his face was set in a hard scowl when he reached the end of the featureless corridor and the space opened up, revealing the main offices of the 17th Precinct of the New York Police Department.

He didn't want to be here at all, but he had no choice.

This was where the inter-species offices were located for Manhattan, and where Nick had to check in every night he was on duty. It was also one of only two precincts in the city that Midnight detectives were cleared to work out of, as of about six years ago.

They liked to keep everything pretty tightly controlled, when it came to vamps.

The wider jurisdiction for Midnights also gave them the freedom to assign him to cases in any part of the city, not just those that fell within a particular geographical area.

Very few vamps got cleared to work on the kinds of cases they gave Nick. For the same reason, he was under constant, intense scrutiny—too much scrutiny to let himself start thinking about food while he was on the job.

The very *last* thing he needed was some human cop getting jumpy because they happened to notice Nick's eyes were redder than usual, or his canines happened to be extended the slightest bit, just because his stomach was a little rumbly.

As for his food-obsession right then, Nick still blamed that damned alley hit, if only for putting the thought of hybrid and seer blood in his head.

Still, after what they found in that alley, he was interested enough that he couldn't help wondering if they'd gotten the lab results back on the victims yet.

Even more than the victims, he was damned interested in that painting.

He wondered if they'd managed to get anything on the artist.

Back at the crime scene in the Bronx, Nick stuck around the alley long enough to see the lab techs run spectrometer scans and take scrapings off the alley wall, hoping to pick up enough DNA or other trace evidence to ID whoever made the mural.

While he stood there, one of the techs told Nick that whoever it was, they'd spent hours on the damned thing. The tech pointed out the fineness of the lines and brush strokes, not to mention the detail in the faces and the reproduction of the alley itself.

Nick hadn't noticed on first glance, but the artist even included details of irregularities in the alley's cement floor, along with scrapes on the metallic paint of the walls, dirt smudges, steam coming off one of the pipes running the length of the right side of the alley. The level of detail made it look in parts more like a photograph than a painting.

The whole thing was bizarre, and not only because some whacko chose to paint the faces of professional killers and their hybrid murder victims as an act of vandalism.

Nick knew, from listening to them talk, that Morley and Jordan both thought the person who painted the image was connected somehow to whoever ordered the hit on the six hybrids.

They theorized the mural was some kind of message—either to the victims when they arrived in the alley and saw their likenesses there on the wall, or as a warning to someone else.

That, Jordan hazarded, or the painting might be a calling card of some kind, a message to someone else about who'd done the job.

Nick had his doubts.

About both theories.

He was still standing by the corridor entrance to the long, weirdly egg-shaped room, when someone called out his name.

Well, not *his* name exactly, but he knew they were talking to him.

"Midnight! Hey! Come over here. Check this out."

Gritting his teeth, Nick snapped out of his quiet little reverie, which hadn't exactly been pleasant but had the advantage of being... well, quiet.

Walking towards the small crowd he hadn't noticed clustered around Jordan's desk, he saw them all looking down at something that apparently lay in the middle of it.

Nick knew most of them by name already, despite only having been here a few weeks.

He'd always had a good memory for faces, even as a human.

Now, he remembered almost everything.

"Hey." The cop who'd called him over, a female homicide detective named Charlie, was hunched over what Nick now recognized as a liquid monitor on Jordan's desk. "You might want to take a look at this... since you were there with the others when they found it."

Charlie's full lips smiled at him as she said it, accentuating the curve of her cheekbones, and the almond slant of her eyes. Those eyes were a stunning, light-brown color, and looked almost too big for her face.

Charlie was some kind of Eurasian-black mix, and shockingly pretty.

Her round, muscular butt rested on the corner of Jordan's

desk, and as she glanced between Nick and that monitor, the smile on her face grew as she looked him over, appraising his physical appearance openly.

Nick couldn't help but see a second, more knowing quirk touch her full lips after she'd taken in the details of his body and face.

Christ. He hoped she wasn't another vampire groupie.

No way was he starting up something like that, not with someone he worked with; he didn't care how damned pretty she was. Being the vampire in the equation, if anything went sideways, as it eventually would, it would all come down on him.

Probably like a ton of bricks.

Unfortunately, the longer he watched her stare at him, the more he found himself thinking she had that look.

Something in those light-brown eyes just screamed, "I've never been bitten by a vampire before, but I bet it's really hot," and/or "I really want a vampire fuck-toy of my very own, and won't my friends be jealous if I brought him to dinner."

Not. Gonna. Happen. Lady.

"Well?" she said.

Charlie quirked an eyebrow at him, folding her arms.

It occurred to Nick that he'd come to a full stop, and was just standing there, staring at her.

"Do you want to look or not?" she finished, motioning towards the liquid monitor by her leg. "It's your case as much as Jordie and Morley's, right?"

Hesitating, he nodded, then stepped forward, wary.

Walking around her to get closer to the monitor from the other side, he craned his head and neck, doing his best to get a look at the curved screen without leaning too close to her.

He stared for a few minutes before something clicked, and he realized what he was looking at.

"That's security footage," he said, surprise reaching his voice. "You got the whole thing on surveillance? Is it a drone? Or stationary?"

Jordan looked up, frowning from where he sat just to the right of Charlie. Glancing at her, Jordan aimed his enhanced eyes back at Nick with a scowl.

Great, Nick thought.

Jordan wanted to get into Charlie's pants.

He now saw Nick as a sexual rival, on top of everything else.

If Nick was right about Charlie having a thing for vampires, that wasn't going to help his and Jordan's relationship any, either.

"Stationary," Jordan said, still scowling after that too-long pause. "It's owned by the warehouse on the right side of the alley, but subsidized, so it's also a government feed."

Nick nodded, not taking his eyes off the recording.

"They get the whole thing?"

"Not the murder," Jordan said. "Tapes were clean for that. The squad that performed the hit must have hacked in and disabled the cameras before they took out the hybrids."

Still frowning, he added sourly,

"But we got your Picasso. The system was still up and working when the painting was made, a few weeks earlier. We just got the footage from the Feds."

"A few *weeks?*" Nick stepped closer, interested in spite of himself. "Were you able to ID him? The artist?"

"Artist." Jordan grunted, giving him a disbelieving look. "No, Midnight. We weren't able to ID the 'artist.' Not yet."

Nick frowned, still staring down at the image.

He could only see the guy's back.

Whoever he was, he was big, with broad shoulders. He was also tall. He wore a threadbare, light-gray, sleeveless sweatshirt with the hood up, along with paint-splattered black pants, so Nick couldn't see his face.

"Did he have his barcode covered, or—"

"No barcode." Jordan pointed at the image on the screen. "See? You can see his left arm right there. You see any kind of barcode, Midnight?"

Nick frowned, refocusing on the man's arm.

Jordan was right.

The pale inside of his strangely muscular forearm was completely bare.

Jesus. That was completely unheard of.

Even weirder, the outside of that same arm, all the way up to his shoulder, was covered in brightly-colored tattoos. The arm on the right was completely unadorned as far as Nick could see. There wasn't a single design anywhere on it—or on his neck or face—official or not.

Nick wondered what lived on the parts of skin the sweatshirt and pants covered.

"Any chance it's prosthetics?" Nick said.

When Jordan didn't answer, Nick glanced at him.

"The arm. Could he have covered up the bar code?"

Jordan frowned a little, then shrugged. "It's possible, I suppose. I don't know why he wouldn't cover up all his ink, if that's the case. Or why he'd wear a sleeveless shirt unless he was signaling he had no reg number."

Nick thought about that, pursing his lips.

Then he nodded. He couldn't really disagree with Jordan's logic.

The clothes themselves were damned weird. Not only were they retro as fuck, but Jordan was right. Why bother with prosthetics when a long-sleeved shirt would have done the trick?

A shirt would have at least dealt with cameras, if not the scanner patrols.

And conversely, why would someone with no reg barcode wear a sleeveless anything? The guy hadn't even waited until it was dark out. He'd done it in broad daylight, while committing vandalism on private property. If he'd been anywhere in the world in the past twenty or so years, he must have known he was likely being recorded.

The whole world was under surveillance these days.

In a city as dense as New York, where there was still a fair bit of money and enough vamps to make people nervous, it was more or less a given.

"Were you able to follow him?" Nick said. "When he left? Were you able to see where he went?"

Jordan looked up at him, his mouth hard.

"We're working on it, Midnight," he said, his voice cold.

Making a show of checking his watch, he looked up at Nick's face.

"Aren't you out of here?" he said, his voice pointed. "Sun's coming up, Midnight. Don't you turn to stone or something, once it's daylight? I thought that's why they only had your kind working at night."

Nick frowned, then glanced at the clock on the wall of the bullpen in spite of himself.

He'd forgotten to check the time.

He'd had three crime scenes to walk before the one in the alley, starting at around 7 p.m.

It was almost 6 a.m. now.

Again, Jordan wasn't wrong.

Rather than waste time with words, Nick gave them all a brief bow of his head—without really thinking about where the mannerism came from, or even what he meant by it, exactly—and stepped back from the desk. He kept his eyes on Jordan, who watched him back away, until he was a good six feet from where they all huddled.

Turning on his heel only then, Nick headed for the elevator that would take him to the lower floors of the building.

Despite the time, he couldn't leave yet.

He was required to check in at the station every night, give a verbal report, then submit to a physical to make sure he hadn't been feeding while he'd been out on the job.

He was a Midnight, after all.

❦

WANT TO READ MORE?
Continue the rest of the novel here:
VAMPIRE DETECTIVE MIDNIGHT
(Vampire Detective Midnight #1)

Link: http://bit.ly/VDM-1

Recommended Reading Order:
QUENTIN BLACK MYSTERY SERIES

JC Andrijeski is a *USA Today* and *Wall Street Journal* bestselling author of urban fantasy, paranormal romance, mysteries, and apocalyptic science fiction, often with a sexy and metaphysical bent.

JC has a background in journalism, history and politics, and has a tendency to traipse around the globe, eat odd foods, and read whatever she can get her hands on. She grew up in the Bay Area of California, but has lived abroad in Europe, Australia and Asia, and from coast to coast in the continental United States.

She currently lives and writes full time in Los Angeles.

For more information, go to: https://jcandrijeski.com

facebook.com/JCAndrijeski
twitter.com/jcandrijeski
instagram.com/jcandrijeski
bookbub.com/authors/jc-andrijeski
amazon.com/JC-Andrijeski/e/B004MFTAP0